DECEPTION DAYS

DECEPTION DAYS

I. VRONSKY

WITH RHYNIE GREEFF

WORLDBIN BOOKS

Published in Great Britain by WorldBIN Limited 2015

Copyright © I. Vronsky and Rhynie Greeff 2015
Print Edition
ISBN: 978-0-9932115-0-8

Written by I. Vronsky with Rhynie Greeff
Cover Design by Kocojelly – www.kocojelly.com
Cover photograph of I. Vronsky courtesy of George Popov
eBook Conversion by My eBook – www.myebook.co.za

WorldBIN Limited Reg. No. 04764898
Exceed, Bank House, 81 St Judes Road
Englefield Green, Surrey, Great Britain
TW20 0DF

Contact information for WorldBIN can be found at:
www.worldbin.com

For Hasleen

An Accidental Historian

Some rise by sin, and some by virtue fall

—Shakespeare, *Measure for Measure* II.1

THERE MUST HAVE BEEN EVIL spirits sharing the midday shade of the tree with me.

I was driving off when a bakkie – the South African term for an open-deck light delivery vehicle – hurtled around the bend in the dirt road. It was going at such a speed it slipped and collided sideways with me, and with such a mighty bang that I thought for a moment I had been shot. In a daze I saw the world twirling around me as my vehicle rolled. You cannot imagine the dust inside a vehicle during an accident. Like a wet dog shaking off water, an accident loosens built-up dust inside a car. Upside down through the dust I saw the culprit driving off.

Perhaps, if I had been a teetotaller then, as I am now, I could have avoided the accident – but that is all vodka under the bridge.

So there I was, hanging upside down like a fat bat, struggling to free myself from my seat belt. Damn difficult. In those happy juice days my body was more massive marshmallow than man and I found it difficult to strap myself into a seat belt even in an upright position, never mind trying to get out of doing something with a seat belt hanging upside down at the side of the road.

In that awkward position I heard running footsteps and knew at that moment that my British counterpart from MI6 must have heard the noise of the collision. You see, we were just outside his rented house when this all happened.

And then his face appeared at my open window. 'Good God, it's you!'

'Ah British Intelligence. Always there when you need them.'

I am still proud of that riposte.

Let me explain how this all happened.

I once served in South Africa as a foreign intelligence operative. It is not important which country I worked for but you will deduce that a Vronsky would not have conformed to the ideals of John Major, the first George Bush or Bill Clinton.

By the time I lived in South Africa the Berlin Wall had fallen, the Iron Curtain had rusted away, and my people had to contend with a more competitively open world. That was why we more than ever needed to keep an eye on the world. And that was my job. More public eye than private eye. Actually more like an actor playing the role of public relations man and entrepreneur with press links.

Intelligence is an invigorating career. No. It's more than that. It is like vodka. Intoxicating. Of course it can have its dreary moments but, ultimately, it is a game. So much so that I sometimes even shared the fun with my competitors. My accident that day led to exactly that.

In the hour before my accident I had monitored a discreet weekend meeting between four members of the ANC and my British counterpart whom I had encountered at stiff diplomatic cocktail parties. With FW de Klerk's white regime still in power, that meeting was held in a farmhouse the MI6 man had rented not far from the Union Buildings.

I sat in my vehicle in the shade of a tree until I knew exactly who all had arrived. Interestingly, in later years after the change to a fully democratic government, three of the attendees became cabinet ministers.

Having finished my job and the liquid refreshment I had taken along, I was quite satisfied and decided to drive off. Straight into a collision.

And that is how I came to find myself upside down in my car telling him how fascinating it was that British Intelligence was always there when you needed them.

I, unfortunately, cannot tell you in detail what transpired after the local Brit helped to free me but, to coin an African phrase I once heard from another ANC friend of the time, we are not Rhinos, we are human. Even opposing intelligence operatives can be decent to one another. My accident broke the intelligence mould that day because the four ANC guests knew me. From the house they saw that I had dropped in unexpectedly and my British counterpart, ever the gentleman, invited me to join them in the house so that we could call the police. We ended up chitchatting. After the ANC men had left, the Brit drove me home. That was when I learned that friendships are never planned. You just fall into them.

That accident was quite important to me because it led to a co-operative opening of a Pandora's Box. You see, the two of us became really good friends and eventually my British counterpart actually worked with me, not against me, when I started uncovering the skeletons you will read about in the rest of this book. It made sense for us to co-operate. Both in finding the facts and in burying most of them. As we say in my country: God marks the crook.

My MI6 friend knew some of the people involved and helped me to understand what they did and, more importantly, how they must have felt.

Those truths we uncovered have never before been made public. They remained jailed in the filing systems of our two countries. I believe that some of the facts are known in South African intelligence but I gather in that environment the facts are strewn about like badly tossed spaghetti. But then again, the dish was designed to be just that.

In this narrative there are quite a few people who regarded themselves as tonnes of gold when really they were only an ounce of brass each.

To avoid problems with those individuals I changed the names of people and companies in this book. I regard myself as a decent human being and not a Rhino. I also took the route of changing names to avoid legal problems. I have no interest in court action or becoming a stateless martyr in some international airport with no nationality and no future. I do not believe in jumping over my own head. Jailed intelligence information within and between countries can be sacrosanct.

Of course there are some people who are named directly in this book. People like Hitler, Bauch, Dassy, and certain South African politicians.

There are also historical incidents here that cannot be papered over fictionally, such as the hotel incident in Brussels on Hitler's birthday, the origin of the old Boer ruins in the Fôret de Soignes in Brussels, the air attack on the Gestapo in Brussels, and the activities of Erleigh and Milne.

Other than that, though, I am giving you the facts in a fictional style.

I tried to write the story from an Igor Sikorsky perspective. Like Sikorsky, who was born in my hometown, I tried to hover above it all, finding the facts and placing them in the minds and voices of those involved. In a way this also helped me to protect people drawn in collaterally.

Here and there I could not resist adding my own brief author's notes to highlight some background, but I did not want to intrude too much with my own voice. Even though my author's notes might be viewed as small intrusions, you will see that, wherever I became directly involved with some of the people and their activities, I removed myself into becoming just an additional third person. Truth should be victorious. I have always loved the words of the founder of PanAmSat, Rene Anselmo, who, in his fight against government-ruled Intelsat, added a huge cartoon of a dog called Spot and his company motto on his rockets into space: *Truth and Technology Will Triumph Over Bullshit and Bureaucracy.* In a sense, that is what I want.

Of course, I could not fictionalise everything. With a little effort the reader can verify the actual truth behind everything from the air attack on the Avenue Louise to the events in New Orleans and Barberton. Just do not try to find too much on the Internet. These events I describe took place right around the birth of the Internet when things were not immediately digitised into search engines like today.

I am very grateful for the help of my project manager, an ex-diplomat and businessman, Rhynie Greeff, who sat down with me for hours in London, took my scribbled notes from the past, prompted my memory, assimilated my views and helped me to write down what happened in a coherent 'factional' manner. In addition, he managed to seamlessly integrate the MI6 man's items and information. As Rhynie said to me: 'For evil to triumph, just distort the truth.'

In our search for truth, which was the common bond in our friendship, my MI6 counterpart and I discovered a piece of history that had not been documented. We were like Rodin's sculpture The Secret where two right hands are holding an unknown object, separating the palms even though the fingertips are touching each other. We held history in our hands. It needed to be freed. Whatever your political persuasion, whether East or West, in our profession, deception is acceptable for patriotic purposes, but despicable if done with personal injustice or false patriotism in mind.

It has been said for many centuries that winners write history. I disagree. I believe winners can only temporarily paint over history until cracks appear and the truth escapes.

And often, when the truth escapes, it reveals a lesson in ethics as well as love.

To understand that we have to start in Brussels under Nazi occupation in 1944.

CHAPTER 1

A water drop cuts through stone

—Russian proverb

20 April 1944, Brussels

THE FÜHRER HATED SMOKING AND would have disapproved of one of his officers sucking fumes in the uniform of the Wehrmacht Verkehrsdirektion. With smoke swirling around his nostrils, this officer of the German armed forces movement control watched the guests milling around in a non-military manner.

For the German officers this was a night in martial heaven, a night to honour the one who had given them their Third Reich. A night to forget about Arbeit Macht Frei – Work Sets You Free. To have some fun. Spass.

It was also a night for local power, the aphrodisiac to draw female collaborators.

For the Belgian girls who fluttered through the hall this was a way of escaping their ugly reality by feeding off high-ranking officers of the Wehrmacht, the Schutzstaffel, the Gestapo, the Feldpolizei and the Luftwaffe.

Sex has two sides.

At the edge of the dance floor, an SS officer grabbed two glasses of Moët et Chandon from a passing waiter. He clicked his heels and presented a flute of champagne to a young woman in an exquisite evening gown. Their fingers touched.

'Merci.' A smile on her lips. Pewter sadness in her eyes.

'Bitte.' His thin lips creased in a grin of superiority.

Keeping his jackbooted legs straight, he bowed his head, stared at her with piercing, steel-blue eyes and clinked his glass with hers. He also touched her breast with the back of his hand. Almost accidentally.

Sex is not only two-sided. It is also non-verbal.

Formal attire was a requisite. Elsewhere in the crowd, in contrast with the young woman's expensive evening gown, a clutch of Blitzmädchen tried unsuccessfully to look attractive in their drab grey women's auxiliary uniforms.

The orchestra started up with a rousing waltz.

The blonde officer and his female companion put down their glasses and took to the floor. The uniformed members of the orchestra played with the vacant impassivity of normal wartime routine tasks. After all, repetitive music was preferable to being drafted into the Reichsarbeitsdienst where those who did not find themselves in the armed force were commanded to work where they were told.

Brussels. April 20.

Just another weekday.

And yet, a special day – the Führer's birthday.

A few hours earlier, rumour on the eighth floor on the Avenue Louise had it that Reichsmarschall Göring might personally attend the celebrations to commemorate the Führer's birthday. This year SS-Obersturmbannführer Bauch of the Gestapo had decided to opt for the smaller hotel on the Boulevard Anspach instead of any of the larger international establishments like the Metropole or the Palace for this celebration.

Bauch and Giscard Dassy, the maître d'hôtel, stood side by side, surveying the crowd.

Despite his hatred for the Boche, Dassy was proud tonight. Bauch had decided to hold the reception here, not only because of the large banqueting hall and excellent catering facilities, but also because Dassy was renowned for his superior service. And Dassy knew that Bauch regarded his slight command of German, although tainted with a Walloon accent, as a bonus.

'Zauberei, Herr Dassy,' Bauch said through eisbein lips.

Magic it was, indeed.

'Danke schön, Herr Oberst.'

Dassy's words trailed into a void, as Obersturmbannführer Bauch swung his fat stomach, a chunk of beer-cultivated flesh, to an officer on his left and jabbered away in rapid German. At their first meeting it had amazed Dassy how apt Bauch's surname was; the German for Bauch translated into paunch or belly.

Still, Bauch's comment had massaged Dassy's ego. He agreed. This was sheer Zauberei. Magic. With a little help from a few black marketeers, of course. One could always rely on the black market for the best food and drinks, and fortunately people like Bauch turned a convenient blind eye to that.

Tonight they had ample Russian caviar, pate de foie gras from Strasbourg and pate de la champagne from the Ardennes, smoked salmon, fish in aspic, the best of German wurst, and cold cuts lying in the no-man's land between hills of sliced pumpernickel and a rocky area of various types of freshly baked bread. It was the smell of luxury.

The chef was at his post behind a huge baron of beef, carving knife in hand. A parade of cheeses lined the tables and there were wines from the Moselle, the Rhine, Burgundy and Bordeaux. The Moët et Chandon from Epernay had a red stamp over the label proclaiming that the champagne had been especially reserved for the Wehrmacht.

Tonight Dassy was bringing joy to almost three hundred guests. The only pity in his mind was that this gourmet evening had been set up in celebration of the despicable Adolf Hitler's birthday.

'Monsieur Dassy, how did you manage to put together such a wonderful spread?' one of the Belgian girls asked in French.

'Mademoiselle, it was a challenge but well rewarded.'

'Well done, monsieur.'

'Yes, I had to add a few waiters to my normal staff. Just too many guests here tonight. That's why I drew in an additional seven temporaries from the street.'

'You are kind, monsieur. Work is so scarce in these times.'

'True, mademoiselle.'

Very true. Dassy had received a flood of applicants in response to the sign he had put up at the hotel's front door a few days before. He was satisfied he had selected seven experienced professionals. They had come as a team. He had spent three hours that morning ensuring that the newcomers would know exactly what would be required of them. He had shown them around the banqueting hall, the kitchen, the wine cellar and the front vestiaire.

Now, watching the men in their black-and-whites moving efficiently between tables, he knew his orientation session had been successful. The temporaries were courteous to the point of anonymity, floating among the guests, serving from trays loaded with filled glasses and clearing tables between servings. Excellent work, Dassy thought.

At nine o'clock a high-ranking officer, whom Dassy had not noticed before, proposed a general toast and the crowd turned to a framed portrait of the Führer, set up between two huge red-and-white swastika flags.

'Heil Hitler!'

'Heil Hitler!' the crowd echoed.

Except for one voice, which rang out with 'Grüss Gott!'

It had been a split-second after the crowd, but it had unmistakably been 'Grüss Gott!' – a widely used general form of greeting in German, similar to hello, but which literally translated as 'Greet God'.

Dumbstruck, Dassy turned to face one of his temporary waiters, smiling benignly at him.

Everyone stood at attention as the orchestra struck up the German national anthem.

The last notes of the anthem had barely subsided when a young lieutenant turned on his heels and grabbed the offending waiter by the lapels.

'Ich hörte 'Grüss Gott', kein 'Heil Hitler'. Was sagen sie?' the officer fumed at the waiter, who stared blankly at the German.

'Are you mad to insult the Führer?' Dassy intervened in French. 'If you think this is funny, I can tell you it's the wrong moment.'

The temporary waiter's body was ramrod upright. His catlike eyes twinkled.

'Please tell the officer that Hitler is like a god to me, and that I greeted my god in the only words of his language that I know.' The waiter spoke French with a Flemish accent, his broad moustache lifting in a smile.

Dassy translated the waiter's words.

The officer frowned for a few seconds and then broke into laughter, slapped the waiter on the shoulder and walked away.

The waiter winked at Dassy.

A smattering of clapping accompanied the first bars of a medley of marches, eliciting a bored nod from the leader of the military orchestra.

A German Blitzmädchen ran her fingers surreptitiously along the buttocks of a wiry officer. Her fingers travelled up the officer's back and down again towards the empty holster clip on his belt. None of the officers carried a weapon. The accepted code of military etiquette for social functions with ladies in attendance required that officers had to remove their side arms, holsters and belts and leave them in a secure place for retrieval upon departure.

Earlier that day, on Bauch's instructions, Dassy had provided a long table at the end of the hall near the pantry and the kitchen. Each arriving officer had been guided by a waiter to the table where the officer would add his belt and loaded holster to the pile of side arms left by the others. The table had by now been covered with a steel tablecloth of small arms.

It was well past eleven when the music suddenly stopped. Abruptly in the middle of another routine piece.

The young officer and the woman with the elegant gown unclasped themselves from each other on the dance floor. Others did the same. All eyes turned to the orchestra stand.

'Ruhe, bitte!' A harsh command for silence from Bauch.

From the bandstand Bauch surveyed the guests with clenched lips.

'Meine Damen und Herren,' he began, almost growling the words, 'it is with great regret that I have to request you all to remain where you are. It seems that a few pistols are missing. Could the ladies please be seated? Officers, you are immediately to check your holsters on the table. Report to me if any of your side arms are missing. Our guards have sealed off the entrances and exits. Until further orders, nobody may leave.'

The crowd murmured.

Dassy bolted into action. The sight of the ladies sitting down and the officers jostling at the pile of side arms spurred him to order the waiters to serve the guests fresh trays of drinks.

Every now and then an officer walked back for a few words with Bauch, who remained granite-faced on the bandstand. After a few minutes it was clear: fourteen handguns were missing.

Behind his back, Dassy heard strong words between two men. He turned around. The same officer with the steel-blue eyes who had had an altercation with the impudent 'Grüss Gott' man was in deep discussion with a baby-faced officer who had left his briefcase on the spot closest to the kitchen door. After a while, they walked over towards Bauch, whose fat cheeks and sloping forehead now bore the sheen of sweat.

A small contingent of grim-faced officers left the hall as Bauch ordered a search of the hotel rooms. The orchestra softly played Beethoven's *Für Elise*.

Ten minutes later everyone had strutted back. No clue anywhere.

At this stage, huddled in conference with his group of officers, the thought finally occurred to Bauch to summon the maître d'hôtel.

'Herr Dassy,' Bauch boomed at Dassy, 'are your employees trustworthy?'

'Of course, Herr Oberst.'

'How many do you have here tonight?'

'Why, my usual twelve full-time workers, for whom I can vouch fully, and seven temporary waiters.' Dassy's voice had trailed into a whisper.

Bauch motioned to the band to stop playing.

Silence.

'Seven what?' Bauch demanded.

'Temporary workers for the evening.'

'You took in extra staff?'

Bauch leaned towards Dassy, his head tilted in such a way that he seemed to impale Dassy with his left eye.

'Yes,' Dassy said and then stuttered, 'I have my regular nine kitchen and serving staff, but normally I have only three full-time waiters. For so many people, I had to get extra help. Of course, of all the applicants, I hired only those with the most outstanding references, Herr Oberst.'

'I want to see them all. Bring them here!'

Shaking, Dassy rounded up his staff but he knew immediately that there was trouble.

One by one, they lined up in front of the bandstand, concerned about their own sudden predicament. They all knew that, following a fit of rage, they could very well end up being interrogated in the building on the upper end of the Avenue Louise. And everyone in Brussels knew what happened there. It was a place to avoid.

Bauch counted the group of men, his index finger flicking like a conductor to the rhythm of a march. And then his porcine face screwed up in anger.

'Herr Dassy, you told me you have nineteen men in all, of which twelve are full-time and seven temporary. I find only twelve. Where are the other seven?'

'I'll go and look for them, Herr Oberst.'

Dassy ran back to the kitchen but he knew already. Not a soul. His patent leather shoes clattered downstairs to the wine cellar. Nobody there either. He ran back to the vestiaire in the foyer where the two duty guards told him they had been at the door the whole evening and none of the staff had left through that entrance. Dejected and afraid of the possible consequences, he returned to the hall, spreading his arms in a gesture of despair.

'Dassy, you obviously know who's not here!'

'Yes, Herr Oberst, the seven temporary men are absent.'

'Scheisse!'

'But, Herr Oberst, I took their names, addresses and identity detail.'

'Dassy, this is outrageous.'

'I apologise, Herr Oberst. Their credentials were good.'

Dassy hoped the young lieutenant with the woman at his side would not notice that the 'Grüss Gott' man was among the missing.

Bauch removed his glasses, rubbed his closed eyes in thought and then rested a stern gaze on Dassy. 'We have to accept that these seven men have gone.'

'I, I am so sorry, I—'

'Shut up. I want to know how they got out of here. Nobody saw them leaving via the front or the back doors. Dassy, is there another exit from the hotel?'

Dassy thought for a moment. 'There is only one possibility, Herr Oberst: They could have left through the wine cellar door, but it has been padlocked now for many years.'

'Bitte! You show the way!'

A military retinue led by Bauch followed the nervous maître d'.

At first sight, the cellar door seemed in order. It was closed, but Dassy immediately noticed the few dull, limp strands where a mass of spider webs had once sparkled in the light of the single electric lamp. The links between the lintel and the door had been torn. The padlock was broken. Bauch opened the door to face a dark, deserted, cobble-stoned alley.

Returning upstairs, Bauch knew two truths. They had been raided by the Resistance and, for his own good, he had to save appearances.

'Meine Damen und Herren, it is now almost midnight. We apologise for having kept you so late. We have found valuable information and we now know who were responsible for this incident tonight. We also know where they are. I can assure you they will be caught and punished. Let us rather end this evening in the manner in which we started it – in a spirit of celebration. I bid you good night.'

Bauch lifted a glass and raised his hand in salute.

'Meine Damen und Herren, Heil Hitler!'

'Heil Hitler!'

A resounding chorus and a wave of raised hands ended the reception.

ALAIN STUBBED OUT A HAND-ROLLED cigarette. He smoothed his moustache. Madness. Unquestionably.

There were eight of them out there in the forest before daybreak, seven ex-waiters from the reception plus one. Four of them on this side of the winding Avenue de Tervuren and four somewhere in the darkness behind the trees on the other side. The war had depersonalised them. None of them used their real names any more. They all used French noms de guerre, including Alain, who was Flemish and more at ease in Dutch than French. Seven of them were Belgian. The eighth man, whose nom de guerre was Pierre, was different. He was a serving German officer, working for the Allied cause. Or, probably more truthfully, for himself.

While studying the documents from Paris, they had fortified themselves with a few bottles of wine they had taken from the cellar earlier that night.

Alain smiled.

Their raid on Hitler's birthday party had been a success. Of course the Resistance could do with a few extra handguns, but the object of the foray had been far removed from that. Nobody at the reception had realised that the theft of a few Lugers and Walther PPK's had merely been a distraction. Except for one man. Their operation had been entirely aimed at getting hold of the contents of the courier's briefcase and it had been almost too easy.

Their secret lay in a ninth man.

As planned, the ninth man in their team, Pierre's friend, an officer from Paris, had left his briefcase at the edge on the table right next to the kitchen door in a position where it could easily be taken unseen.

Alain was the one who had grabbed the briefcase on their way out.

As in all their other operations so far, they had worked on a need-to-know basis – each man knowing only as much as he needed to be an effective maquisard. Limiting individual knowledge was a way of saving the group. If one or more of them were to end up in the basement of the Gestapo's interrogation centre on the Avenue Louise the Germans would not be able to extract too much information. They all knew that even the strongest among them could break under torture. The less they knew, the less likely the chances of the others being caught.

As they lay in wait, Alain contemplated that only three people truly knew the underlying plan: he, Pierre, and the officer from Paris who had left the briefcase at the reception.

Earlier they had studied the contents of the briefcase in a basement near the Cinqentenaire arch. All the detailed information on the convoy had been there, down to the names of the officers in charge. At two that morning Pierre had arrived in time to accompany them to this spot in the Fôret de Soignes, the forest where the Avenue de Tervuren snaked out of town.

'I am a little sad that I had to take a slightly inactive role at the event tonight,' Pierre whispered in German-accented French, 'but your 'Grüss Gott' remark was excellent.'

'That poor man Dassy had great difficulty handling the situation.'

'Very original, Alain. Very funny. I had difficulty not to laugh until it was right for me to laugh. It was brazen.'

'I was just following the scriptures according to the gospel of Saint

Adolf.'

'I suppose there is a thin line between the two chants, Heil Hitler and Grüss Gott.'

'Thanks for letting me off. You handled yourself well.'

'I am an officer and an officer always handles himself with decorum.'

'Except for your Bauch. Nasty piece. I think he's a dangerous idiot.'

'He was clever enough to know that he had to play everything down at the end. He would not want this incident to spread too far. Bauch likes the quiet life in Brussels. If he is shown up as a failure he could be sent to the front somewhere.'

Alain felt the crinkling of the document under his leather jacket.

The information from Pierre's officer friend from Paris was that they could expect an advance group of four motor cyclists with armed men in their side-cars, followed by a covered truck filled with guards, then five trucks laden with crates, another guard truck and a further two motor cyclists bringing up the rear. The convoy was to move through Brussels without stopping. The plans called for a change of drivers and guards in Liège at the break of day.

They had made their plans and they were ready.

Their stolen Horch staff car blocked the road and was filled with explosives linked to a detonator in Alain's control.

Each man knew exactly what to do. Alain would operate the plunger that would take out most of the advance motorcyclists. Two men lay in wait at different angles, each with a loaded Lewis light machine-gun – ready to spray nine rounds per second into the two guard trucks. Alain's instruction was clear: no one should come out alive.

Alain reflected on the variety of weapons that would shortly explode into sound. They had two Lewis LMGs, two Thompson guns and a few captured German Karabiner 98 Kurz, the German infantryman's standard weapon, each with its hole in the stock for joint padlocking on to a long rod in the barracks. One of them had insisted on bringing his hunting rifle along – a rifle that the German authorities had been unable to trace since it dated from before 1933 to a time when Belgians had not needed licences to purchase guns. They had the pistols they had taken earlier that night but their main assault weapons were ten Panzerwurfminen, shaped-charge armour-piercing stick-grenades that they had stolen from the German barracks at Etterbeek.

Alain traced the painted letters PWM(1) on the round head of the grenade, cold against his thumb. The tail of the grenade consisted of canvas, held in place by a tail-cap. The moment the grenades were thrown, the canvas would open up into four fins at the back, guiding the grenade head first to its target where it would explode on impact. An ideal weapon against a truckload of soldiers.

Alain knew they had only a few minutes in which to attack.

The noise was sure to raise a response from the city. As they lay there in waiting, the Fôret de Soignes was deathly quiet. Around them the lime-green spring leaves on the trees hung motionless in the dark.

A faint whistle sounded from the darkness at the bend in the Avenue de Tervuren. Action time.

Almost as faint as the whistle, they heard the distant rumble of the approaching convoy. The headlights of the leading motorcyclists zigzagged like fireflies towards them against the outline of trees and branches. Behind the motorcyclists trundled the trucks. The order of approach was exactly as the document in Alain's possession had stated: the motorcyclists in front, followed by a guard truck and then the rest.

Alain waited for the motorcyclists to throb their machines up towards the booby-trapped Horch car. The convoy stopped, engines running, the air filled with the smell of fumes.

'Was ist los?' a motorcyclist said.

Against the light of the leading troop-carrying truck, two soldiers struggled out.

'Grüss Gott,' Alain whispered. He pushed in the plunger.

In an ear-splitting woof the stolen German staff car exploded, disintegrating the soldiers next to it and sending debris into those further back. The flash of the detonation drew the other maquisards into the fray.

The Lewis guns sprang into life, wiping out the German soldiers seated behind the canvas on the backs of the two troop trucks. The Panzerwurfminen hand grenades soared like kites into the wounded rear group of motorcyclists and under the troop-carrying trucks, churning up the air with flying shrapnel. Body parts flew through the air. The odour of burnt flesh mixed with the smell of smoke, hot metal and burning oil. Sniper shots eliminated the drivers of the other trucks, each behind his steering wheel.

A few surviving German soldiers fell out of the rear truck but were immediately mown down in cracks and pops.

The rear-guard truck must have carried additional explosives because a well-thrown hand grenade created a huge explosion. The impact shuddered through the bodies of the attackers. In the midst of the explosion a legless body plummeted into a tree at the side of the road close to Alain.

A smattering of Schmeissers, a crackling of Lewis guns, and it was all over.

Here and there in the firelight a few German soldiers moaned, writhed in pain, or attempted to crawl away. Alain and his men strode forward, their guns aimed at the carnage. One by one, without compunction, they executed the wounded. Alain noticed their undercover German friend, Pierre, putting his Luger to the head of a crouching soldier. A crack rang out and the soldier slumped forward.

Tonight they could not afford anyone any leniency. Not even from one German to another.

Expertly the maquisards stripped the dead soldiers down to their identity tags, until only the naked bodies of the dead dotted the road and each maquisard had a Wehrmacht uniform over his civilian clothes. In an opposite mirror-like action Pierre in turn took off his upper layer of civilian clothes, threw them into a burning guard truck and walked away in the German uniform he had worn at the reception. The other men bundled the spare uniforms together and threw them into the driver's cabin of one of the trucks. Others in the Resistance could use those uniforms. The two guard trucks had been destroyed, but Alain and his men had been careful to keep the remaining five trucks with their precious cargo intact, save for a few shots into the drivers' cabins. They knew each truck had one crate.

'Allons-y!' Alain ordered. Let's go!

Dressed in their newly-acquired Wehrmacht uniforms, they boarded the remaining trucks and drove away with wheels squashing dead bodies and crunching distorted metal strewn over the Avenue de Tervuren.

Alain, in the first truck, led the way. After a few minutes, he veered right on to a bumpy dirt track and led them into the depths of the forest, past a pond, until they came to a stop in a clearing where, once long ago, a stone building had stood. Now, only the outline of the foundations still remained ankle-high in the soil. In the centre of the ruins, a huge hole had already been dug the previous night.

'Hurry up!' Alain ordered, this time in Flemish, glancing at his wristwatch. They had limited time before daylight.

The men unloaded the five heavy crates from the backs of the trucks and, carefully, laid them next to each other in the hole. The dimensions of the hole had been dug correctly.

'What are these ruins?' the man who had come with his hunting rifle asked as he helped with a shovel.

'It used to be a Boer ammunition factory here in Brussels for the war in South Africa. That's why this part of Brussels is called Transvaal.'

'Interesting.'

'Yes, something to think about – later,' Alain said. 'Now hurry up.'

By the time they had covered up the hole to Alain's satisfaction with soil and an artistic layer of shrubs, ferns and leaves, daylight was upon them. The trucks were now camouflaged with netting and the dirt road swept with branches to wipe out the tracks. They all crawled in under the trucks to wait out the day – all, with the exception of Pierre who, in his German uniform, walked away into the forest to find his way home.

Alain had grown accustomed to Pierre's work with them but he still wondered what Pierre's hidden motive was for fighting against his own people, although Pierre had insisted he was part Belgian as well. Whatever the motive, Pierre did good work. Alain dozed off.

One would have had to walk right up to the hidden trucks to realise that there was indeed any machinery underneath the brown and green netting.

That following evening they still lay hidden. Hunger gnawed at them by now. The darkness and the time that had elapsed from the day before now gave them sufficient cover to leave. The camouflage came off and, one by one, the trucks sprang into life, each driven by someone in a German uniform.

It was well past midnight when Alain returned on foot through Auderghem into Brussels while the others drove the trucks through to Namur where, in the woods of the Ardennes, the Resistance had a depot for seized goods.

The ruins in the Soignes forest held buried a secret known only to nine men, although six of the men did not know of the existence of the ninth man.

But the real secret lay even more hidden.

Author's note: I find it a strange coincidence that the events happened at the site of that Boer ammunitions factory, the ankle-high ruins of which can be seen still today. This might just be conjecture but one or more of the men involved might already then have thought of a link to South Africa. No one will ever know. During the Second World War that part of Brussels was known as Transvaal because the old South African Republic of President Kruger was known as Transvaal, the homeland of the Boers who had produced ammunition there for the South African War of 1899-1902 against Britain. Today few people know that, even until the mid-1970s, there was a Brussels tram to Transvaal.

CHAPTER 2

When money talks truth falls silent.

August 1994, New Orleans

THIS RICKETY BALCONY SHOULD CARRY a health warning, he thought.

The thumping rock music from below vibrated through his chest and stomach. Keeping time with the bass tremors he tapped his right index finger on the rail and peered down the length of Bourbon Street, but he could not see her yet.

Where was she? In fact, where had she been earlier this afternoon?

He had called her on her new-fangled cell phone.

Please leave a message. Such a nice voice. Always.

'Hi, it's me, John. I've arrived. I'm calling from a public phone at the airport and I just wanted to touch base with you before tonight. Anyway, if I don't hear from you, I'll see you on the balcony as agreed.'

No answer. He now wished he'd remembered to bring his recently acquired cell phone. Bad executive decision, John. They could have spoken. These electronic things are the future, John. You should remember to have them with you.

He listened to the lyrics of the rock song downstairs.

'Baby you're a magician/ You're magic to my mind/ Oh-oh my mind leaps in confusion every time that I see you're playing a trick on me.'

Was she not playing a trick on him tonight?

'Looks like you got a dead man here.'

'What?' He could not make out the waitress's words against the loud rock music.

'I said it looks like you got a dead man here,' she said, leaning over so close he could feel her breath on his face.

'Dead man?'

'Yeah. Empty bottle. You want another beer?'

'Oh. Yes. It'll be great fun to witness the resurrection of a dead man right here in front of me.'

'I should've known a cute lookin' man like you would have cute words.'

'You probably say that to all the guys who are able to calculate a service charge.'

'See, I told you. You ain't no dope in the chat-up department. I guess with your mid-Atlantic accent you ain't from this here part of the world,' she said, taking away the empty Dixie beer bottle and sweeping his table top with a cloth. She smelled of citrus.

'Mid-Atlantic?'

'Sho'nuff. Horse sense really. You sound English but you got an American twist in ya. Kinda goes with your tan and your gold chain. Englishmen have bleach-white cotton skins. Yeah, mid-Atlantic. That's you,' she said, a broad ivory smile against an ebony face.

'Never thought of myself like that. Mid-Atlantic. Maybe that's why I'm sweating so much. We mid-Atlantics are not used to this humidity and heat.'

'I'll cool ya down even more with a good ol' frosted Dixie.' She left.

Damn it. He should have insisted on a meeting in an air-conditioned place. He picked up his cardboard beer coaster and dabbed at the sweat on his forehead. He took a deep breath but still felt sticky and irritated. He hated the waiting, even though he had long ago been trained to be patient. After all, Uncle Erick's maxim was that patience was the path to profit and he was Uncle Erick's creation in so many respects.

He gazed at the glittering glare of neon all the way down Bourbon Street. Still no sign of blonde hair among the bobbing heads below. Normally he would have enjoyed an evening out on this weird entertainment ribbon, this Main Street of the Deep South with its quaint drinking holes, but, despite his words to the waitress, tonight it was just a slightly irritating hothouse of t-shirt shops, prostitutes and protectors of the law, hawkers and gawkers. He liked women. Some would say too much. So on any other night he would have spent time in that topless bar with its mechanical plastic leg swinging out of an open window down the street, but tonight his mind was elsewhere.

He told himself to keep calm. He had landed knee-deep in shit this time but had to stay composed. Persevere. He had done it before. He could do it again. It was the only way he was going to unravel this tangled web he'd stumbled upon. Just get to the truth. Clear up the mess. To get to the end of all this he was going to have to be ruthless, maybe even brutal. Those two traits probably went with patience. Hey, maybe Uncle Erick might even adopt this as a variant on his maxim of profit through patience. When did the two of them have that dinner in DC the last time? Two years ago? Or was it the year before in 1991? And now they had an appointment with the old man in his house on the bayou. A key appointment.

Damn it's hot.

He would much rather have been in that line of people below shuffling towards air-conditioned bliss behind a doorway with a sign proclaiming the weathered building to be Preservation Hall.

'What's Preservation Hall?' he asked the waitress when she arrived with his beer.

'That's the headquarters of jazz, honey bunch. They got a midnight show. It's first-come-first-served down there.'

The balcony shook to the beat of driving rock drums and saxophones coming from the doorway of the Kool Klub below. Oddly, the screaming sound of trumpets reminded him of Bach's *Brandenburg Concerto* tinnily played thirty years before on a brand-new early Sixties

Pilot radiogram. Bach, on his mother's scratched vinyl record, a long time ago on a distant continent.

Yes, he'd come a long way from being six years old and lying on the floor in front of that radiogram on Twenty-second Avenue back in Africa. He knew how to climb that corporate ladder and he had a lot to show for it. Flashy cars, comfortable houses on two continents and a lavish lifestyle, far removed from his humble origins. Life's a dream, John, even when you hit crap times like these.

A horse trolley packed with noisy tourists rattled past. He put down his beer and glanced over the balcony railing. The trolley passed a policeman and policewoman who sat side by side on two horses under the corner lamplight.

A pedestrian lifted a hand and stroked the head of one of the horses.

She was late. Up in D.C. she had also been late before but then ten or fifteen minutes, not more than an hour like tonight. He picked up his beer, swirled it and sniffed its vapour. Good. He gazed at the human carpet below. Bad. Somehow something was wrong. It looked like she was not coming tonight.

How many beers had he had now? He brought a hand to his nose. Even his fingers smelled of beer. Well, Mister Businessman, you have to act like a banker and get rid of your excess liquidity. He smiled at his own joke. What had happened to him? Where were those student days when he could slug down a case of beer with no need for biological relief? Was it age? Was he being stalked by his prostate? Where was the men's room again?

He would have to ask the waitress.

SOMEONE ELSE WAS ALSO WAITING. Flat on his stomach.

Higher up, on the worn-out corrugated-iron roof overlooking the balcony, the man turned on his side, unzipped the front of his black jacket and clicked open a rigid wood holster concealed in the dampness of his armpit. He brought the holster with its leather flap up against his chin and studied the view. His target was diagonally across, ninety yards away.

The gunman squinted in trained concentration. His body ached. He had been lying on the hot roof for fifteen minutes now.

Heady Cajun aromas swirled around him. His stomach rumbled. He could do with some gumbo right now. But that was for later. Now concentrate, Bubba.

Although it was almost midnight the roof still radiated the sun's warmth. Soaked in sweat and lying face down with his head uncomfortably lower than his feet on the down slope, he slipped the walnut holster from underneath his chin and laid it out at eye level in front of him. You don't want this stuff to slide down the roof, Bubba.

He had bought the 1936 Browning walnut holster a long time ago from a contact in Arizona who had also helped him with the modification to his Colt. He flicked open the flap over the wider end of the holster, lifted the hinged lid and lay the two parts open in front of him. A Colt Government model 1911 A1 pistol nestled in the hollowed-out right-hand side. You beauty.

This guy was a friendly target, chatting up that waitress.

He took out the pistol and closed the lid. From his right pocket he took out a worn Maxim silencer and screwed it on. The six-inch barrel became a ten-inch barrel. It might be a cliché – his agent said it was – but for him there was always something erotic in this planned lengthening and strengthening of the barrel. Still – was it that Einstein guy who said this? – everything's relative. A shot with a silencer is not completely silent. It's just relatively silent. Tonight he had to plan the timing of his shot to coincide with other sounds as camouflage.

Still chatting, are you?

The wood holster had a spring-loaded latch that fitted into a dove-tail in the grip at the rear of the Colt. He clicked them into position. In one movement the pistol was transformed into a short-barrel rifle with the holster becoming the rifle stock.

He brought the butt-end of the rifle up against his shoulder. The silencer was secure, the telescope locked tightly. He aimed downwards.

He checked out his target.

The waitress pointed towards the washroom sign. The target struggled to get up. Space was at a premium. Tables and chairs were squeezed in so tightly that there was precious little room in which to pull back a chair. Blocked in between the tightly arranged furniture of the restaurant, his only way out was to climb over his chair. He balanced himself and stepped on the chair, his left hand gripping the railing.

The telescope now showed a clear view of the target's curly head of hair.

The gunman inhaled, held his breath and concentrated.

A twitch of a pale finger against the trigger led to a tongue of flame.

The target never knew what hit him as he flew in an arc over the balcony railing and fell downwards.

The jiving doorman of the Kool Klub froze in one of his poses and then screamed as the body hit him. Blood spattered against the neon sign over the doorway.

The gunman breathed out. Now he could get his gumbo.

Author's note: I visited the scene of John's death many years later. It is still there. Well-planned by the assassin. I am not sure how the gunman got onto the tin roof and, more importantly, off the roof in seconds. But he did. I tried to find the house on the bayou, but Hurricane Katrina had just passed through and wiped it out.

CHAPTER 3

The life of the dead is placed in the memory of the living.

–Marcus Tullius Cicero

RICK LAND CRADLED THE STURDY workhorse of his profession, his .375 Holland and Holland Magnum rifle, in his lap. The bush had left its thorny fingerprints on the stock and barrel.

He loved this harsh continent, particularly in winter when there was no rain to wash away the smell of dust in the day. If heaven had a smell, this would be it, he often told his clients – the aroma of dust and hardwood fires at night.

Winter days in the bush can often be warm. Today was no exception. Sweat trickled down his Adam's apple. His skin was still moist from the climb but a slight breeze tugged at his shirt. His clothing and his skin morphed with the brown boulder on which he sat. His throat was dry.

It had not rained since autumn. He expected the first showers of the new season would probably only arrive by late spring in October. Winter was a time of drought when he could show clients where warthogs were burrowing in the dry riverbeds until water seeped through. It was a time when antelopes also used their hoofs to tread the dried-out pans for seepage water. He never allowed hunting at a waterhole. It would be wrong. Winter mornings and afternoons were times of convergence at the waterholes, times for sightseeing with his clients. There is no skill involved if you shoot an unsuspecting animal at a waterhole.

He loved his perch at the top of the haphazard heap of boulders crowning the hill. He knew the spot well. It was his natural balcony overlooking the expanse of the African bush. He regularly climbed up to this specific spot. Here he always felt closest to both life and death.

Under the top boulder, directly underneath him, was a crevice inside of which a thick layer of milk-white bones stretched out into the darkness. Some would probably find the crevice ominous. Rick saw beauty in it. On his climb to the top, he would always peer in, hoping to see the resident leopard – not that he wanted to kill the cat. That would destroy his ritual pilgrimage to the rock. Sometimes the lair smelled of decomposing death when the cat had caught an animal and stored it to eat over the course of a few days. That smell of death would be off-putting to some, but Rick thought of it as the smell of new life because that's what it all amounted to: carnivores, scavengers, insects and microscopic organisms living off death, creating new life from decay.

Up there on top of the leopard's lair with the feline's view of the world, life and death were simple threads, interwoven to make up the fabric of nature.

Below the hill, the arid bush was broken by a dry riverbed, lined with lush green foliage where high trees drew their sustenance from the depths. The green line snaked through the otherwise-brown environment towards a mountain range on the distant horizon.

The sound of untold numbers of cicada beetles pierced the air in a single, high-pitched, unceasing choir. They were celebrating the sun, as they had been doing since the beginning of time.

Rick lay back on the rock. He rested his rifle next to him. He drew his hat with the Zebra-skin puggaree over his eyes and revelled in the warmth of the late-morning sun. It was as if the blistering sun melted him into the rock.

Earlier that day, in the dark before sunrise, he had left camp with Themba, his Zulu tracker.

But Themba Twala was more than a tracker. He was a friend of nineteen years, a confidant and wise adviser who, on cue, would leave his kraal, his wives and children to follow Rick on his hunts. Themba's name in Zulu translated as trust, hope or faith. It was symbolic of the man. In addition to having the eyes of a falcon, the keen ears of an impala and the soft tread of a leopard, he had the heart of a friend. He noticed animals where others saw only grass and trees. He saw tracks where others saw only soil and stone.

As they had driven out before sunrise, their faces illuminated by the weak dashboard lights of the Land Rover cabin, Themba had talked about his wives and children. One child, he noted, was studying to be a teacher. Africa needed more teachers and fewer hunters, he had said. When Rick had reminded him that he, Themba, had actually taught Rick a lot about hunting, and was therefore also a teacher, Themba had laughed.

Rick had steered the four-wheel drive out to the area where Lauterbach had wounded the kudu bull the day before. Overseas hunters often made a mess of their first attempts at hunting in Africa and Dieter Lauterbach had been no exception. Maybe Lauterbach had been too tired after their long afternoon walk through the rough terrain. He was an overweight, unfit metals trader from Frankfurt, with the gait of an elephant and an undesirable penchant for too many Davidoff cigars. The day before had been very messy and they had lost the kudu for the night.

Twigs, leaves, grass and loose stones make it difficult even for experienced African hunters to move quietly. In winter it's like walking on crackling cornflakes. Noisy. Animals react and flee. The day before, upon their approach, Rick had been surprised the kudu had not darted away, as it had been within earshot of Lauterbach's laborious snap-crackle footsteps and within smelling distance of the sour odour of Lauterbach's cigar.

He had coached Lauterbach in the same manner he had always done with new clients: practise walking stooped forward from the waist with your hands at the back and crawl on all fours, even getting right down on your stomach, if necessary. Unfortunately, at the time of the attempted shot, Lauterbach had been totally out of breath, puffing like a steam locomotive. In fairness, it had also been a relatively difficult shot to execute.

They had, at first, seen only the majestic twirl of horns as the kudu had been quite far away in tall grass and partly camouflaged behind thick thorn bush. In the fading light of dusk, Rick had had his doubts as to whether Lauterbach should have attempted the shot at all, but Lauterbach was quite dictatorial in his outlook on life and insistent on having his own way – valuable for survival in the metals business but a waste in the bush. The German client had approached the kudu like any other speculative business deal. And he had failed. Yet it was no shame to miss, Rick had told him afterwards. A miss was merely a second-best shot. The moment Lauterbach's shot had rung out, Rick had deduced from the way the kudu had reacted that the shot had been high.

They walked over to the spot where the kudu had been standing and, after a brief search, found miniscule traces of blood, which he and Themba had shown to Lauterbach. In hunting tradition, this had meant the kudu had become Lauterbach's.

They followed the spoor immediately, but it had quickly become difficult because the kudu had not been losing as much blood as Rick would have thought. Even for experienced men like Rick and Themba, tracking had by that time of the day become difficult. In winter, darkness descends abruptly. It comes down like a sweeping curtain over the bush and, as a result of the fading light, they had to return to camp. Rick explained to Lauterbach that the kudu would lie down for the night, that its muscles would stiffen, and that tracking would be quick and easy the following morning. A satisfied Lauterbach insisted on sharing a celebratory bottle of red wine with Rick around the campfire that night.

Earlier that morning, at the first light of day, Lauterbach complained that the previous night's red wine had given him gout and he would prefer to stay put in the camp. Rick suspected the real reason had more to do with Lauterbach's bulk, and a reluctance to walk for hours in the hot sun. Lauterbach had the prerogative of the self-centred client and now it had become Rick's responsibility, as the professional hunter, to track down the wounded animal, looking for those tell-tale signs of hoof prints, broken twigs, resting spots and minutely small spots of blood on the tops of grass stems.

Now, lying on his back on the rocky hilltop, Rick remembered how he and Themba had retraced the spoor that morning and how they had had to use all their skill to spot the tiniest blood stains on the blades of grass. He remembered Themba's words when they had come upon the animal.

'Ingwe!' Themba had called in his smoky voice.

At their first encounter, many years before, Rick's feline eyes had earned him the Zulu name Ingwe, meaning Leopard.

'Ingwe! There. This one is a chief among chiefs.'

'You're right, Themba.'

Rick focused his binoculars on the kudu bull. They always look so dignified, even when wounded, he thought. The animal stood in an opening between a few camel-thorn trees under a yellow fever tree, its trophy-sized, curved horns at an angle. He could clearly see that Lauterbach's shot had only grazed the magnificent animal's shoulder – a slight wound that would heal easily.

At that moment Rick had faced a difficult decision because he could see the kudu would survive easily. Nature's healing hand would quickly have cured the superficial injury. But, unfortunately, he had had no choice in the matter any more. The kudu had been taken and Lauterbach's contract had to be fulfilled without pity. The kudu was Lauterbach's. That's the law of the bush.

Rick sat upright, adjusted his hat and gazed at the riverbed where the dead kudu now lay in the shade of a yellow fever tree, the tree trunk standing out like a bright yellow marking-pen in the bush.

He recollected cocking the .375 Holland and Holland. He remembered looking at the kudu through the telescopic viewfinder – taking in the beauty of its high, spiralling horns, its innocent eyes, the silky mane hanging from its neck and the blue-brown-grey tones of its striped hide. Although his heart had gone out at that moment to the grey ghost of Africa in his sight, he had forced himself to smother his own conscience.

'Tolo,' Rick whispered the kudu's African name, 'I'm sorry, but you've already been taken.'

The kudu had fallen where he stood – shot through the heart.

Rick had taken off his hat. He always honoured the dead. Themba covered the kudu with a few dead thorn tree branches, hooking his own tattered cap on one of the thorns to keep away scavengers.

'It was his time, Ingwe.'

'It was, Themba.'

'It is the way things are.'

'There is sadness about this death. I have the sadness of guilt.'

'Must I fetch Umkhaba?' Themba had given Lauterbach the Zulu name, meaning beer-belly.

'Yes, please take the Landie. I'll wait here.'

Themba had left and, with one last look at the antelope, Rick had turned away and walked towards the hill.

Now he sat there, overlooking the bush at a height normally reserved for hawks and eagles. The rest had brought him peace of mind.

He opened the leather flap covering the face of his watch, a flap to safeguard against any reflection of sunlight that could reveal the presence of a hunter to his prey. It was well past eleven. Far away, he heard the purring sound of the approaching vehicle. He stood up.

With his rifle slung over his left shoulder, he clambered down the rocky outcrop and started back to the kudu. A grey lourie, the scourge of every hunter from cat to man, shrieked at Rick from a treetop. Its nasal cry rang in his ears. 'Go-away! Go-away!'

Lauterbach opened the Land Rover door with a can of cold Castle

Lager in his hand, dressed in his hunting clothes – a pair of green knickerbockers, a green hunting jacket with leather patches on the elbows and shoulders, and a green Tyrolean hat.

'Your kudu, Dieter,' Rick said and he pointed at the animal under the branches.

'Ausgezeichnet! Excellent!'

Lauterbach walked up to the dead animal and whistled. Themba smiled as he drew the branches off the kudu.

'The horns are superb,' Rick added.

'Hervorragend – splendid. I am very happy, ja.'

'What tree is this, Rick?'

'Mopani.'

Following the tradition Rick had seen with other European hunters, Lauterbach picked a few leaves from the mopani tree and a sickle bush, doffed his Tyrolean hat, knelt in front of the kudu, and placed the green leaves over the two wounds. He then stood up and bowed to the animal, after which he turned around to face Rick. 'Weidmann's dank!' A hunter's gratitude were his words, and he shook hands with Rick and Themba. The man was decent after all, Rick thought.

Whilst Lauterbach prepared his camera, Rick and Themba cleared the ground in front of the kudu, rolled the animal upright, tucked its legs in under its body and turned the head.

Rick took several photographs of the hunter and his trophy. They then loaded the animal on to the trailer Themba had hitched to the Land Rover and left for camp with Themba and two assistants on the back. Many hands had been needed to handle the heavy animal.

'The horns are really good, not so?' Lauterbach asked as they set off down the dirt road.

'Dieter, I think they might even qualify for an entry in the Rowland Ward book of records.'

'Ja?'

Rick could see Lauterbach was impressed with himself.

They drove for a few minutes before Lauterbach remembered

something.

'Before I forget, a messenger brought you this,' and he handed Rick an envelope.

Rick recognised the handwriting of Piet Steen, the tough farmer in control of Rick's hunting concession area. The envelope was wrinkled and dirty. For a moment, Rick imagined a sweating Shangaan runner jogging through the bush with the message in his hand.

'Thanks. We'll open it at the camp.'

While Themba and his assistants unloaded the kudu and hooked it on to the pulley at the cold room, Rick opened the envelope.

It was an unsettling, but short, message.

A family matter?

He had divorced Melinda so long ago there could be no 'family matter' there anymore. As far as he was concerned, she had disappeared from his life and had entered a tunnel of oblivion, with her gynaecologist in tow, probably feeling like the satisfied owner of an expensive sports car employing a full-time mechanic for her exclusive use. The word 'faithful' had meant something different to Melinda, particularly during Rick's long hunting trips with clients.

Why would Melinda want to contact him?

Author's note: The events in the preceding and following chapters were sketched to me in detail by my MI6 counterpart who knew several of the people quite intimately – one of them probably too intimately. But then whoever said spying is not a people's job?

CHAPTER 4

Reason has always existed, but not always in a reasonable form.

–Karl Marx

THE RED BRICK BUILDING COULD have been any police station anywhere in the bush. Its blue exterior light was draped in dust. Its bare interior consisted of not much more than a scratched counter, a safe in the corner, and a wobbly desk and chair between the counter and the safe. The only adornment on the walls was an aged placard displaying photographs of AK47s, limpet mines, land mines and plastic explosives – a reminder of the recent low-level apartheid era war.

The charge office smelled of old wax polish on government furniture intertwined with stale pipe tobacco. A policeman in a blue, short-sleeved shirt with three pips on each of his epaulets stood behind the counter.

'Captain Sethole?'

The policeman nodded with a vacant expression.

'Rick Land. I received a message.'

'Ah yes, Mr Land, the professional hunter. Eish, I wish I had your job.'

'Out in the sun all day?'

'Yes, I've got too much routine. It really gets to you some days. I grew up on a farm close by. I don't like being chained to a desk. I would also rather be in the bush like you with all those nicely scrubbed foreigners with their lavender under-arm deodorants.'

'It can be tiresome.'

'Not as tiresome as settling squabbles in the farming community or in the villages around here. The white farmers? They are still difficult people. Some of them think they are going to get back to the old days of white rule.'

'I know what you mean.'

Rick understood the situation very well. The democratic election had brought peace and a changed face to the country but also new tensions. A new affirmative action policy in favour of black people was beginning to change the police force to reflect the composition of the population more accurately. Whites were retiring voluntarily, taking packages and lump-sum payments, so that people of a different colour could take over their positions. Rick felt this silent revolution would save the country but he knew a large number of conservative farmers hated it.

'We still have some way to go, Captain Sethole, but we're making progress.'

'Eish, true. President Mandela, he is in charge in Pretoria. Me? I'm in charge here in Waterpoort but, hey, most of the local white farmers here? No no, they don't think so.'

'They will change.'

'Ay, ay. These old trees amongst the whites are stiff. Like rusted metal. Maybe their young trees will bend and change more easily. Eish, a black man in charge of policing them? They don't like it. It's difficult but I do my job.'

'I received a message from Piet Steen to see you.'

'Yes.'

'Something about a family matter with Mrs Barton. She is not really family anymore because we are divorced. What's it all about?'

'Yes, Mr Land, I am afraid I have bad news.'

The policeman opened an incidents book. He moved his finger along a column.

'Bad news?'

'Mm. Bad news. I'm sorry to have to tell you this, but Johannesburg informed me that, unfortunately, your brother John has died . . .' Rick closed his eyes, scarcely hearing the policeman continuing '. . . and you have to call Mrs Melinda Barton at this number.'

The policeman wrote down a telephone number on a scrap of paper and handed it to Rick.

'When I spoke to Johannesburg on the telephone yesterday, they said Mrs Barton had all the details. You must talk to her.'

John was dead. The thought slowly started to sink in.

'What else did they say?'

'He died in America in . . . er . . . strange circumstances.'

'What does that mean?'

'I have been told that it was unnatural.'

'Come on! Unnatural?'

'Unnatural, yes.'

'What happened to him?'

Rick was impatient now, although he already feared the worst.

'He was murdered.'

'Murdered? Good God. How?'

'He was shot.'

'How did it happen?'

'I'm sorry. I don't know. That's all I know. I just got this message.'

'Could I please use your phone?'

'Mr Land, again I am sorry. According to the new regulations private telephone calls are not allowed from the charge office. Central decision. We are cutting costs. You know, the Force cannot allow everybody who's in trouble to use the station's telephone for free. Unfortunately I cannot make an exception. Of course, there is the tickey-box at the post office.'

The policeman walked out from behind the counter, took Rick by the elbow and led him to the door where he pointed a nicotine-stained finger at the telephone booth against the wall of the low building next door.

Rick stumbled out towards the post office. A kaleidoscope of images raced through his mind. He remembered a platinum sky, a shifting coastline and two little boys at their mother's side, clutching the wooden ship's railing at eye level. He remembered his lack of real comprehension and his expectations of a new life somewhere in Africa where, in his mind's eye, lions stalked their prey on city streets paved with gold.

Through the years Rick had seen life come and go. And now John was also gone.

Had he been wrong in his attitude towards John? Should he have been more accepting instead of rejecting him so strongly? After all, John had pleaded for understanding. Why had he been such an egotist that he could not have accepted his last remaining close family member? Maybe the murder would not have happened if he had had contact with John during the past few years. Had he not, through his own actions, possibly, been somehow responsible for John's death?

He bought a Telkom phone card at the post office and called from the phone booth. The instrument smelled of thousands of previous callers with bad breath. And of even staler tobacco.

The call rang for a long time before she picked up. 'Melinda Barton speaking.'

A voice he had once loved.

'Hello, Melinda.'

Hesitant silence for a moment before she replied. 'Rick.'

The same calculating, yet sensuous, voice. His stomach muscles involuntarily tightened. Their first words in how many years? He could not remember.

'How are you?'

The question was almost rhetorical. He did not really want to know.

'Fine. And you?' she mirrored him automatically.

'Fine, thanks.'

'What happened to John?'

Rick had no inclination to exchange any more pleasantries with Melinda.

'Someone shot him. It happened the day before yesterday in New Orleans. Really awful. Who would have expected that?'

'Why?'

'There seems to be no motive.'

'There's always a motive in a murder, even if someone is shot accidentally because then there's been a motive to kill someone else.'

'I mean there's no sign of a motive so far. They tell me there are no clues. It's all a mystery.'

'Was it a robbery, a mugging or some—'

'I don't know, Rick. All I know is he was shot in the head. Aucamp told me that. He says they got a call from the Washington office and they're pretty much in the dark over in D.C. . . . Where are you now?'

'Up in the north on a hunt.'

'You've got to get out of the wilderness and come home.'

'I'm shattered.'

'Come home. AfriBelgo organised for the body to be flown out from America. You need to see Aucamp, Coetzer and Partners as soon as possible to sort out the funeral arrangements.'

She spoke without any trace of real emotion for John or for him. Just like old times.

The rest of their conversation was one-sided. She rattled off that she was still happily married, satisfied with the love of her life (probably a lie), and planning a vacation in Europe. So there was a chance she might miss the funeral, wherever it would be, and goodbye.

There was no need to hurry. On his way back to the camp, his mind drifted. Life and death. Interwoven strands in the fabric of nature. Birth and decay. Animals and humans.

He remembered their mother's life and death.

The last time he had seen John was at their mother's funeral two years before. She had died in the way she had lived, with dignity. He thought of the dignified kudu for a split-second. And then he wondered what his father's life and death had been like.

The moistness in his eyes swirled him back to long-forgotten feelings.

Southampton

'RIKKI, JANNEMAN, BLIJFT aan mijn zijde, jongens!' (Stay at my side!)

In spite of her tone, his mother's words were soothing and reassuring. She had been the only person he and his younger brother had understood since they had disembarked from the ferry earlier that morning. Nobody spoke their language. He remembered asking her why these people could not speak Flemish, or even French, like some of the people back home, and he remembered her wry smile.

He had asked her that question earlier that day, after the accident. Coming down the gangplank, he had held a coin between his fingers, playing with it against his tongue. An old man with a weather-beaten face, who had been tying a rope to the gangplank, had caught his eye and had shouted at him, 'Good morning!'

It had sounded to Rick as if the man had shouted something in Flemish at him, which seemed like, 'You shouldn't!'

In fright Rick had swallowed the coin, but only partially, and had found himself battling to breathe. He had tugged at his mother's sleeve but in the rush of passengers coming down the gangplank she did not react. She had been too busy making sure that her younger son, still a toddler, would not fall off the walkway and into the cold water below.

Fortunately the old man had immediately noticed Rick's distended eyes and open mouth fighting for air. The old man had grabbed Rick and turned him upside-down.

And so it was that Rick had entered his first foreign country being held upside down with his head swinging at the old man's feet, one foot gripped by the old man, the other by his mother. The old man had thumped Rick on his back until the coin had dropped out on British soil.

'Thank you very much, sir.'

Out of the blue, his mother had spoken in that strange language called English.

'What's your name, young man?' the old man asked with a grin.

Rick could not understand the words but his mother interjected with, 'De heer vraagt je naam, mijn zoon.'

'Rikki. Rikki Land.' he had answered.

The man had just laughed, tugged at Rick's ear, said something incomprehensible again, and returned to the rope he had been knotting before the incident.

Now they were standing at the gangplank of yet another ship. This vessel was less rusty and much bigger than the one that had brought them from Ostende to this strange land with its fat frites and funny language, but in this new ship they were going to a much stranger place. They were going to sail to a land where everyone had a big house with a garden, where nobody lived in small apartments like theirs on the Avenue de Tervuren, and where every little boy kept a lion as a pet on his property. That was what Uncle Erick had told them when he had visited them a while earlier in Brussels.

They had never met Uncle Erick before, although their mother had told them he had been their father's best friend. Their father had had other good friends too, whom they sometimes saw. There had been Harry Ruys, Luc de Smet and Thom Thomas. What a strange name! Thomas. Just like Thomas in biblical times – the one with a burning finger against the wall, or so Rick had thought at the time. Rick had looked very closely at the fingers of this modern Thomas, but Thom Thomas of Belgium had only had black fingernails from working in the soil.

Of all of those friends, Uncle Erick had been such a good friend that Rick had been named after him. He could still remember the moment this best friend of the family had come visiting and walked through their front door in Brussels and how he and John had immediately liked Uncle Erick, mainly because his breath had smelled of the same aromatic pink sweets he had brought them all the way from Africa.

Rick had very little recollection of their own father – just a faint memory of tobacco smell, a moustache and big hands.

Uncle Erick lived on the other side of the Earth, in Africa. And that was a mystical place. There, the sun always shone and it never became grey like in Brussels. You could swim with whales there at Christmas and it never snowed because, in Africa, Christmas was in summer. Rick had had great difficulty understanding how it could be hot over Christmas. John was still too young to be bothered.

In Africa, Uncle Erick had said, there were no broken buildings from the war like in Brussels, and there were mountains of meat to eat every day of the week; not at all like Belgium where you had to eat waterzooi every day.

Sitting on the carpet, listening to Uncle Erick telling their mother about the wonders of a place where there were many Swarte Piets, Rick had been old enough to know that Sinterklaas, the Flemish Santa Claus, always arrived with many presents for all the little children. In Belgium Santa's gifts were always carried by his black assistant, Swarte Piet, Black Pete. John, at three, had also already known that Black Pete was good to children. When they had gone to bed that night, he and John had discussed Uncle Erick's stories about Africa and they had lain there in the darkness talking of this extraordinary place with so many Black Petes that you could not count them. Naturally, they had come to the conclusion that a place with so many Black Petes would be wonderful for two little boys from Belgium. That night Rick had dreamed of being showered with gifts from a circle of Black Petes standing around him.

'Kom, kom Janneman, Rikki,' and their mother guided them up the heaving gangplank, Rick first and then John.

Rick had already forgotten the experience with the coin in his throat. He now enjoyed the unsteady feeling of rising and descending on the gangplank. He stopped halfway, blocking everyone behind him, as he imagined himself on the back of a whale in the blue waters of Cape Town with Uncle Erick, smiling and clapping hands on the beach.

'Rikki!'

He continued upwards.

On the deck they turned around. John bumped his head against the railing. There were many people on the quayside below. Rick could see some people were crying and others laughing but all of them were waving good-bye. Deciding to laugh, because they were leaving these people with their strange and unintelligible language, he waved back at nobody in particular. John saw Rick's hand in the air and he too waved.

Their mother just stood there. Rick asked her why she did not also wave and she replied she knew nobody in the crowd below.

Rick felt he knew the world and the world knew him, because everyone in the world was waving him goodbye. But he stopped smiling and waving when he noticed the tears on his mother's cheeks and felt the trembling of her hand. Afterwards, in their cabin, when he asked her why she had been crying, she hugged both him and John and, in her soft voice, said, 'I would have laughed if your father were still alive.'

They sat in silence with the soft hum of the ship in their ears.

'At least,' she said and smiled at them, 'we are very lucky Uncle Erick will look after us. He's a very kind man and he has done so well in Africa that he is even more generous than before. Whenever I see him, I think of your father, which is good. Uncle Erick loves you both.' She gave John an extra hug.

Rick wondered what his father had been like. One photograph in his mother's valise showed a smiling man with a broad moustache and curly hair, lively eyes and a square chin. In another snapshot he stood next to his mother at their wedding. Then there was a photograph of him sitting, out of focus, on a tree stump in a forest and another torn sepia photograph of him leaning, with a pipe in his mouth, against a car. But Rick's favourite photo showed his father laughing with one hand on Uncle Erick's shoulder and a rifle in his other hand.

Every young boy has a hero. Rick had one – his father.

He had only the vague memory of the man who had died when John had not even been born, a few photographs and the sound of his father's name on his mother's lips. Albert. Albert Land.

According to his mother, Albert Land was named after another Albert, the man who had been the King of Belgium. Young Rikki was proud his father had had the name of a king because he knew of no other child whose father had the name of a king.

His mother had told them his father had been a famous hero during the war and that, when he had died, the *Le Soir* newspaper in Brussels had written about him. About his life in the war and his death in a tragic accident on the cliffs of Dinant. His mother had taken them to the rock face once and had told them how their father died, just like King Albert of Belgium, who died on the banks of the River Meuse at Marche-les-Dames, many years before, in a climbing accident.

Their father, Albert Land, had the King's name and died at Dinant in similar circumstances to the King. Dinant was not far away from Marche-les-Dames. In a small boy's mind, his father had lived and died a king. Nothing less. A lot more.

On a day when the mist clung mysteriously to the stone face, the three of them stood there at the river's edge in Dinant. John had been too young to understand, but Rick understood his mother's words as she explained how Albert Land had been on a rock-climbing outing with friends. Their father had loved the outdoors and enjoyed adventure. And just like the King, he had fallen to an untimely death.

For the rest of his life Rick would remember the sheer limestone cliff, rising forbiddingly from the River Meuse into the drizzling clouds. A hated sight, even if his father had been a hero there and in many other places.

'Uncle Erick always sent us a little money, especially at Christmas,' she had said on their second ship, bringing Rick back to reality, 'but he has done so well now that he has bought us a house in Africa. It's a house with a big garden. I do not see why we should cry. He will look after us, I am sure. The three of us are very, very lucky,' she said, wiping her tears away.

Rick did not enjoy the voyage. It was long. John contracted scarlet fever. At first, when John could not hold his food, his mother had thought it was nothing more serious than a bout of sea sickness, but when he developed flaming red cheeks, a raging fever, blistering sores around his mouth and spots over his body, the ship's doctor quarantined their cabin. The doctor ordered Rick to stay in the cabin too as he could also have been a carrier of the disease. For the sake of the other passengers, no chances would be taken.

Although Rick felt fine, he had to endure the cramped confines of their cabin for days on end. All he had was the sight of the outside world through a porthole. And most of the time it was a view of a boring expanse of water, although he did see a lot of flying fish near the Equator.

By the time they reached land in Cape Town, Rick was fed up with the sea, but they had to stay aboard when many passengers disembarked because they were sailing on to Durban, a few days north-east along the coast.

When the tugboats nudged the liner out of Cape Town harbour in the direction of the open sea, Rick and his toddler brother gripped the ship's rail at their mother's side. They watched the receding city, nestled in the arms of its mother, the majestic Table Mountain, rising even higher than the cliffs of Dinant that Rick remembered. The long, flat top of Table Mountain was covered in misty clouds, continuously rolling over the edge and disappearing into thin air.

Gazing at the beauty of the thick cloud band, slipping over the summit in the middle of an otherwise bright blue sky, their mother sighed and said, 'It really does look like a tablecloth.'

'Yes, it does,' a ship's officer, who stood behind them, interjected in Dutch. 'But I can tell you a secret. It is really a cloth of smoke.'

He crouched next to Rick, who could see that the smiling eyes of this man of the sea shone with knowledge – almost as if he had knowledge of the past and the future.

'You see, those clouds are really the devil, smoking his pipe.'

'The devil?'

The cragged mountain suddenly seemed evil to Rick.

'The devil himself. Do you see that peak?'

The officer pointed a finger at one of the two peaks flanking Table Mountain.

They all looked at the conical hill.

'It all happened on that peak, which is called Devil's Peak. Legend has it that, a long time ago, there was a Dutchman like you and me.' He laughed. 'This Dutchman's name was Van Hunks and he loved to drink beer in every tavern here in Cape Town. Unfortunately, he smoked a pipe, filled with the most evil-smelling tobacco you two boys could imagine.'

Tobacco did not smell evil at all to Rick. It was the good scent of his father. Tobacco was the smell of a man, not the sickly sweet smell of women with nothing better to do than to hug and smother the breath out of little boys.

'Van Hunks smoked such a foul pipe that the townsfolk objected to his habit. So they said, 'Van Hunks, please go and smoke far away from us. Just go away, go up the mountain and smoke your horrible pipe there.' This he agreed to do. He was a good man, you see. He used to sit on the saddle of Devil's Peak, that ridge there, and he would watch the ships come and go out here on the water where we are. One day, as he was sitting there puffing away at his pipe, a stranger, wearing a hat, challenged him to a smoking contest right there on Devil's Peak. Van Hunks took up the challenge. He knew he could smoke anyone under the table, if he wanted to. So he and this man with the hat smoked for hours and hours until, finally, the stranger collapsed. Guess what happened.' The ship's officer's voice turned ominous.

'What?' Rick and John asked in unison.

'When that stranger's hat rolled on to the ground, Van Hunks saw that the man was the Devil himself, because underneath his hat he had horns on his head. At that stage, Van Hunks and the Devil had smoked so much that a huge cloud of smoke had formed over the mountain. From that moment, every time the smoke on the mountain appears, a strong wind comes down Devil's Peak. It is then that Capetonians say Van Hunks is smoking with the Devil again.'

The story scared Rick.

He wondered whether his own father had not also, like Van Hunks, met the Devil when he had climbed the cliff at Dinant on the day he had died. With his own eyes Rick had seen that the forbidding rock face at Dinant also had a smoky cloud cover. Maybe his father had never had an accident. The memory of his father's tobacco scent had always been strengthened by the photograph of his father in his mother's album – the one in which his father had held a pipe in his hand. Could it not have been possible that, on the day of the accident, his father had been in a smoking contest with the Devil? Was it not possible for the Devil to have pushed his father over the cliff?

Looking at the mountain in front of him, Rick imagined a falling man, not screaming at all, because he was a hero. He was a man flying down the sheer cliffs of Table Mountain with a lit pipe in his hand, and a crowing Devil cackling through the eddying mists above.

Those thoughts revisited him when he watched water whirling around the tugboat in Durban as they docked a few days later. In contrast to Cape Town, which had been fresh and windy, Durban was hot and humid.

An acquaintance of Uncle Erick met them on their arrival and accompanied them through the streets of Durban to a door with a drab sign over it: Hotel Cecil.

Standing on the pavement in front of this nondescript, grey, two-storey building, Rick and John could see lapping waves on the beach, waves such as they had never seen before. A sweet smell filled the air, which they later discovered to be curry. The first time Rick tasted the hot sting of curry at lunch that day, Uncle Erick's friend explained that the dish had been introduced to Durban a long time ago by many

Indian labourers who had come to this country to work in the sugar-cane fields. The Indians had emigrated in the same manner as Rick, John and their mother were now doing. And the Indians had stayed, never wanting to go back again. Their mother replied that they too intended to stay and never go back.

The following day the Land family left by train for the Transvaal. His mother insisted that the window be kept locked to avoid soot, as they were in the carriage directly behind the steam locomotive. Spewing steam, and whistling now and then as if to please the two boys, the train chugged through the province of Natal. They now knew Natal had been named by a Portuguese explorer on Christmas Day in honour of the birth of Christ.

Images of the new world flashed by in rhythm with the clickety-clack of the wheels. They saw rolling hills, green valleys, quaint Zulu huts resembling Christmas puddings and Zulu women walking away from dams and rivers along narrow pathways with huge tins filled with water balanced on their heads. There were sugar cane fields littered with glistening black bodies in the hot sun and corrugated-iron roofs laden with white, withered, dried pumpkins to keep the loosely-laid roof sheets down. On a narrow tarred road which hugged the railroad in its ever-upward climb from the coast they saw big black cars and dusty donkey carts built from the chassis of discarded automobiles.

'Where are the lions and the streets of gold?' Rick asked towards the end of the day.

'Maybe further on, Rikki. Maybe tomorrow,' his mother said with a smile.

The next day the train rounded a hill to reveal a fair-sized city tucked away in a valley, decked out as if in a welcoming garland for them. The city was dressed up in the purple blossoms of jacaranda trees. They had arrived in Pretoria, the capital city of the Union of South Africa, their new home.

At the station, they met their benefactor. Against a backdrop of locomotive steam spewing onto the platform, Uncle Erick, who was in his late thirties, cut a strong figure as he approached them, dressed in a double-breasted grey suit with matching grey tie. He took off his hat, revealing a shock of blonde hair. He kissed their mother gently, hugged the two boys and led them and the porter, who laboured with their luggage, to his gleaming Chrysler at the station entrance in Paul Kruger Street.

It was the most magnificent car Rick had ever been in, with a foot-rest in the rear and a silver radio in the dashboard. The light brown interior smelled of new leather, and it was large enough inside for Uncle Erick to drive with his hat on. Where most of the other cars on the road were black, Uncle Erick's Chrysler Windsor had been finished in a wonderful maroon hue.

They drove down Paul Kruger Street, around Church Square.

'Why is Church Square a circle if it is called a square, Uncle Erick?' he asked.

'Search me, Rikki.'

They followed a purple tunnel of blossoms to their new house.

Rick and John scurried through the open garden gate into the property at the foot of Pierneef Ridge in Twenty-second Avenue in the quiet suburb of Villieria.

'My gift, Marie, to you and the boys. In memory of Albert,' Uncle Erick said in Flemish as he opened the front door.

Why they had expected a bare interior, they did not know. His mother cried again, this time with a smile. They looked in wonder.

They now owned a new couch, two armchairs, a coffee table and a blue carpet, on the wall a painting of a woman with a flower in her hand, and a drawing of the Grande Place in Brussels. Uncle Erick had even thought of installing a shiny, polished Pilot radiogram in the living room against the wall on the parquet floor. The windows were covered with strange, curled burglar proofing, painted white. The biggest surprise to the boys was that each had his own room with furry impala skins for carpets next to their beds.

In this square, three-bedroomed house, with its red corrugated-iron roof, on a rectangular fenced-in property with an avocado tree in the backyard and purple bougainvillea at the front, the Land family would live comfortably for years.

By the time the two boys were attending Hendrik Verwoerd High School, they had changed into strapping young men. Rikki had become Rick and Janneman had become John. Even their mother had by then followed the example of their school friends and called them John and Rick.

Author's note: By talking to one of Rick's high-school teachers, as well as a few school and university friends of the two boys, I was able to stitch together the detailed background to their move to South Africa and the house they lived in. No names can of course be mentioned. The property where they grew up is in a disgusting state these days. No large avocado tree, no purple bougainvillea, no real garden. Just a bare, dusty yard with two dogs when I went to look at it.

CHAPTER 5

Stille waters, diepe grond, onder draai die duiwel rond.
(Still waters, deep ground, down below the devil swims in circles.)

–Afrikaans saying

FOUR HOURS AFTER HAVING LEFT Lauterbach in the hands of Piet Steen, who was not just a farmer but also a licensed professional hunter, Rick drove through the streets of the Johannesburg suburb, Linden.

The sun had not yet risen. The streets were quiet. Lately, he had spent very little time at home. Absence makes a house grow impersonal.

In the solitude of his shower he had time to think. He had to meet Aucamp, Coetzer and Partners, but before that he wanted to see Karen Lee at Jana Safaris to pick up his correspondence and talk about the state of his business.

It was a relief to escape the smell of fishmoth pesticide at home when he reversed his BMW out of the driveway, leaving the Land Rover in his garage. He always felt more at home in the bush than in this lonely house.

Karen Lee, a senior travel consultant, handled Landtrackers Hunting as a joint venture with Jana Safaris. This woman was his most important link to his clients. She arranged their itineraries and catered to their every whim. More important for Rick, though, was that she took care of all his administration, leaving him to enjoy the operational side of his business. Never mind the pen being mightier than the sword, her pen was mightier than his rifle, he always said.

'Rick, I'm sorry. It's been all over the papers,' she said, holding his hand tightly.

'Thanks. I only heard yesterday.'

'I suppose you have a lot of arrangements to make now.'

'I'm seeing Aucamp today.'

'If you need any help, let me know.'

'I will. Thanks.'

'When is the funeral? And where?'

'I don't know yet. In fact, I know very little about the whole affair, but I suppose I'll find out during the course of the day.'

'Let me know if I can help. Here's your mail and a list of your telephone messages.'

A cursory glance at the messages showed Melinda's name. He picked up the message and, with raised eyebrows, turned it towards Karen.

'She called me to trace you in the bush with the news of John's death.'

He flicked through the other messages. A journalist from *The Star* wanted to talk to him. Uncle Erick had tried to contact him. His old friends Hannes and Tommy had called, as well as someone from Remembrance Monumental Gravestones.

'Ah, the amazing art of the alert salesman,' he said as he showed Karen the message.

He flipped through his pile of post. Junk mail containing never-to-be-repeated offers which could be thrown away. The Receiver of Revenue had sent him a reminder. He wished that could also have been chucked away. Rick noticed an envelope with only his name on it, obviously delivered by hand. He opened it and read the typed, unsigned message.

Rick Land, be warned. It would be in your interest to be careful.

A spider of the past ran up his spine.

He read the message again, lifted the paper to the window and noticed the watermark. Caxtons. Local paper.

'What do you think of this?' he asked and handed it to Karen.

She studied it. 'I think the elephant men are still mad at you.'

'Really?'

'Of course.'

'I would've thought it would have been a thing of the past by now.'

'It didn't happen that long ago. Rick, I was scared witless when I got that phone call at that time. You were an idiot to have your photograph taken and even crazier to have it splashed in *Time*. What do you expect?'

'I thought it was all settled.'

'Well, it's them for sure. It's in the same style as the threat they made then.'

The blue of her eyes seemed to have grown darker.

'Maybe.'

'Don't be an idiot. It's so similar you cannot mistake it.'

'I can see you're still upset but I don't think—'

'I don't believe this,' she said, shaking her head. 'Can it really be two months since that man called me? If you remember, Rick, his words were to the effect that I should tell you they would eventually catch up with you. I'm still scared, just thinking of it. One has to take care with something like that. 'Tell Land we will kill him!' That's what they said. Now that's damned serious!'

Could John's death possibly be related to that earlier threat or this curt message?

He clearly recalled that day in Mozambique close to South Africa's Kruger National Park when he and Themba had spearheaded the entrapment of Thys van Tonder, a game ranger who had colluded with a huge Asian ivory poaching syndicate. *Time* ran a story afterwards, accompanied by a photograph of Rick and Themba in front of a pile of ivory, stacked roof high, in a shabby storage shed, entitled: *Have You Heard a Dying Elephant Cry?* None of the real leaders of the syndicate were ever ever found. Could they be on a revenge path now? Still thinking of Van Tonder, Rick walked into the office of Hendrik Aucamp, partner in the firm of attorneys of Aucamp, Coetzer and Partners.

'Rick, please accept my condolences.'

Etched against the harsh light from his office window, Hendrik Aucamp measured his words in the manner he normally reserved for the courtroom.

'Thank you.'

'All of us here at the firm are very shocked. So deplorable.'

'Yes.'

'John was such a genuine guy. As you know, through our association with the AfriBelgo Group we worked closely with him on many things before his posting to the Washington office and we kept close contact afterwards too. Tragic. Very tragic. But even in trying times like these, when death touches one's shoulder, it's nothing more than a reminder that we, the living, have to carry on.' He spoke softly, his words muffled by his beard.

Aucamp's eulogy was a semi-hypnotic lullaby. Rick just nodded and gazed through the window behind the lawyer at the reflection of the sun on a yellow mine dump in the distance.

'You'll find John's last will and testament very straightforward, very clear. After all, we advised him,' Aucamp managed to pat himself on the shoulder. Glancing over the rim of his spectacles, he continued, 'He left everything to you, except for fifty thousand rand which he donated to the Abraham Kriel Orphanage in Langlaagte here in Johannesburg.'

Rick kept his eyes fixed on the gold mine dump in the distance, but Aucamp's next words wrenched his thoughts back to the present.

'There is, however, one proviso. Your brother specifically stated, in a codicil signed a few weeks ago, that you have to travel to Washington DC, personally, in the event of his death.'

'Why?'

'Search me, Rick. He gave no reason.'

'And it was a recent request?'

'Yes. The addendum just mentioned you should meet a legal firm called Sternson over there. Normally something like that has to do with finalising matters pertaining to possessions and effects.'

'May I see the will?'

'Of course. Although we advised John, we unfortunately do not yet have the original here, but Sternson faxed us a copy. The will is short and sweet. The codicil is longer – as you can see.' He handed Rick the fax.

In the event of my death, I, Johannes Land, hereby bequeath every-thing I own, excluding R50 000 from the sale of my AfriBelgo shares to my brother, Erick Land, to dispose of as he wishes, on the condition that he should visit the firm of Sternson in Washington DC to finalise the estate. The excluded amount of R50 000 is bequeathed to the Abraham Kriel Orphanage in Johannesburg.

'Everything has been arranged through AfriBelgo,' Aucamp said. 'The body has already been placed in a lead casket and is scheduled for a flight back in time for the funeral. In fact, I might be mistaken, but I think it's in the air as we sit here. Dr Martens personally gave the instructions.'

Four universities had bestowed honorary doctorates upon Erick Martens, Chairman of AfriBelgo Group, for his philanthropic endeavours and his contributions to the economy. Nonetheless, it remained a fact of life in Rick's mind that Uncle Erick had received his four honorary doctorates mainly as a result of his large endowments to those respective universities.

Rick reminded himself that he had to pay a courtesy visit to Uncle Erick before anything else.

CHAPTER 6

Put a value on something and it multiplies.

—Erick Martens

RICK DROVE DOWN STREETS LINED with high-rise concrete, steel and glass buildings towards AfriBelgo House, which towered thirty floors high on Marshall Street.

It was an architectural marvel. Creative drafting had knifed the building into its tapered gold bar form. Cloud movement reflected in the gold-tinted glass panes, accentuating the illusion that, at any moment, it could topple from its precarious balance into the financial heart of the Golden City.

AfriBelgo House was a symbol of the city's wealth.

Rick knew the place well from the time before Melinda and before his hunting. It dated from a time of impulsiveness, fast cars and fine clothes. It remained a memory bank of the passions of his youth.

After signing in at the security desk, he took the dimly lit elevator to the top floor, watching the numbers flash by, remembering his own office when the number for the twenty-third floor blinked momentarily.

The twenty-third floor. On that floor, as you came out of the elevator, the Fine Chemicals Department was to the left and the By-products Department to the right. He used to follow the same right-hand route every day, cooped up for two years in that office. Good money, great lifestyle, but terrible corporate infighting and the boring monotony of the job. Sulphuric acid, H_2SO_4 in chemical parlance. Thousands of tonnes of sulphuric acid. A corrosive, oily liquid. After a year, he could have sworn he had sulphuric acid coming out of his pores when playing squash after work.

That had been his little empire: the marketing of sulphuric acid by-product from the pyrites burning processes at AfriBelgo's gold mines. Dangerous liquids by the trainload, transported to file upon file of contractual and spot buyers all over the country – fertilizer manufacturers, explosives plants, paper factories, refineries, uranium plants, rayon producers and producers of dyestuffs and batteries.

How could any life be lived to the full by being absorbed in abstract figures all the time? And all those civilized scuffles with sly colleagues in budget meetings for allocations of money? There were no women in management, only men, and each man had been interested only in building non-concrete fences around his own little empire. And in breaking down other people's fences.

Rick had had no interest in the art of artificial fisticuffs.

After a particularly boring management meeting, he had realised he preferred concrete creativity to abstract arguments. It dawned on him that he wanted to return to the old values, build fences he could see, walk where he could hear his own footsteps and smell the wonders of nature. Still today, I would rather milk cows than milk budget allocations, he thought.

He had opted for controlled hunting, in such a way that he would form part of conservation and make game farming economically more viable.

'Why?' Uncle Erick had asked at the time.

To become a tool of game management, and to ensure that game numbers would remain at maximum sustainable, healthy levels, he had replied. Of course, in the end he had also become a hunter of people too – tracking down the indiscriminate mass slaughterers of Africa.

Oh yes, his life now was far more exciting than that of a sulphuric acid salesman. It had been the right decision. Leave those paper battles to the remaining swivel chair soldiers, he thought as he ascended.

On the top floor, Rick had to pass through another security hurdle. This time it was a thick, shatterproof glass enclosure, leading to an ornate reception area, decorated with laminated imbuia on the walls, Louis XVI furniture, Persian carpets and Zakkie Eloff paintings of life in the bush. Exquisite watercolours of soulful lions and darting impalas. The hunters and the hunted.

'Would you care to wait a moment, please? Dr Martens is still in a meeting.'

He sensed she disliked unannounced arrivals. That's another thing he did not miss from his corporate days, people who regarded themselves as human bricks in walls of protection.

'Take a seat, please,' she said and stared at Rick, a crease of curiosity between her heavily made-up eyes.

'Thanks.'

'Rick Land. Your name sounds familiar. Any relation to John Land?'

'Brother.'

'My sympathy, Mr Land.'

'Thanks.'

'Why have I not met you before?'

'I used to work here a few years ago.'

'That would've been before my time then, probably.'

'Probably.'

'You're still in the business?'

'Business?'

'Yes. Mining.'

'No.'

Rick laughed, wondering what she really thought of his appearance and how it added up with his past in the corporate world. Would she be trying to categorise him into one of the Chairman's regular visitors? He sensed his leathery complexion was neither that of an urban office dweller nor a mine official. Executives were always soaped and scrubbed like kitchen tops and mine officials were often men with translucent earthworm faces. Here he was sitting in a short-sleeved khaki shirt that probably carried a whiff of stale sweat.

'Excuse me, but what are those things?' she asked, pointing at his wrist bangles.

'Elephant hair bracelets.'

He removed one for her to inspect.

'Wow.'

'Yes, no ring on a finger for me. Just rings on my wrist.'

'Where did you buy them?'

'Mine came off a dead elephant.'

'So how does one get a bangle from a dead elephant?'

'You get it when you fail to protect the animal.'

'I don't understand.'

'I'm a professional hunter. I helped the Parks Board a while ago on an anti-poaching programme. This came from the last elephant the group of ivory poachers had been able to lay their hands on. I made these bracelets as a reminder.'

'Saving a life is noble.'

And failure to save is ignoble, particularly if it was your brother, Rick thought.

The telephone rang. She picked it up.

'Yes, Doctor. I'll come in.'

She stood up.

'I need to synch diaries with the Chairman and his guest.'

He glanced at the coffee table where the front page of a newspaper was dedicated to the first few months of President Nelson Mandela's new government.

She went into the Chairman's office.

There were also several copies of the AfriBelgo Group annual report for the previous financial year from 1993 to early 1994. He picked up one. The glossy cover was a spectacular night photograph of the headgear of Belgo Deep, the Group's flagship mine, with the Chairman's well-known business motto emblazoned in gold over the night sky: *PROFIT THROUGH PATIENCE, PROFIT IN PARTNERSHIP.*

This had been the credo of Dr Erick Martens since he had started out in the business. He had always said that there was no get-rich-quick formula in business. After having made his mark totally on his own, he had decided to follow a route on which AfriBelgo had expanded in partnership with other companies and other countries.

Rick smiled, knowing that Uncle Erick believed in co-ownership, but that he also believed in control. It was common knowledge that, in spite of all the grandiose words, Uncle Erick somehow always managed to retain control. He always contrived to hold shares with special voting rights, to retain supply contracts that could give him ultimate control, or to be in a position of nominating the majority of the directors on boards.

Leafing through the annual report, Rick read the historical section dedicated to how, in an amazing tour de force of business acumen, Erick Martens had built up one of the major mining houses in the world. He had not done it, as had so many others, by shuffling paper. No. In four decades, he had started virtually from scratch – from an insignificant mining option in the infant years to a mature mining giant with many other interests.

AfriBelgo Holdings was the parent company of this diversified business group with interests in gold mining, platinum mining, coal mining, mineral beneficiation, chemicals, manufacturing, distribution, food and property. The company's shares were listed on stock exchanges in Johannesburg, London, Paris, Frankfurt, and New York. Rick read that, in 1993, the year before, turnover had been more than four billion US dollars. Investors loved the companies in the group for their attractive earnings and dividends that multiplied Midas-like every year. A profile on the Chairman praised the foresight of Erick Martens, doctor *honoris causa* from various universities. Were they symbols of gratitude to a magnanimous donor or merely cash for honours?

No, because serial philanthropists deserve the adulation and givers also get, Rick decided.

In the early Fifties, Dr Martens, who had started out as an insignificant international trader in building materials, had had the vision to take up an option to buy a small, struggling gold mine, East Crown Gold. According to the blurb, East Crown Gold, nestling in the hills near Barberton, had experienced increasing losses due to a lack of productivity. Too little gold for too much work.

Rick knew the story off by heart.

Erick Martens had secured the East Crown Gold option and had linked his option to a management contract which had specified that he could pay for the shares through the profit he could generate. Miraculously, Erick Martens' management skills were such that he acquired new rights, moved production and brought in new techniques in new mining areas. This improved productivity almost overnight and brought soaring profits. Through executive genius, he had found the profits to pay for the East Crown Gold acquisition.

He had turned East Crown around, paid it off in the first year and, within three years, had taken control of two other mines to form the AfriBelgo Group. The first stock exchange listing had taken the market by storm. Take-over after take-over had followed. Through the years, investors had been fed a constant diet of healthy mergers and acquisitions, initiated by the brilliant Erick Martens. As the group had grown, the value of its shares had soared into the strata reserved for Blue Chip companies. At times Erick Martens had gone for asset stripping, somehow always managing to remember his other shareholders. At times he had targeted cash shells.

After a few years, he had diversified into related fields, becoming involved in platinum from the bushveld igneous complex, coal from beneath the bleak grasslands east of Johannesburg, zinc from the heart of the Kalahari, explosives, chemicals and manufacturing, leading to machinery, later consumer goods, agriculture, food, distribution and a major interest in a bank.

And AfriBelgo still accumulated assets daily.

The door to Uncle Erick's office opened again and the secretary appeared with the guest who was now leaving.

'Till next week then,' the guest said over his shoulder.

'Till next week,' Rick heard Uncle Erick say.

'Oh, Mr Land, let me introduce you to Mr Vronsky.'

'Sorry to hear about the death of your brother,' Vronsky said, his eastern European accent obvious to Rick.

'Very sudden. Very unexpected, Mr Vronsky.'

'In minerals we are all friends across borders. One friend's sadness is another friend's sadness. Be strong. Goodbye.'

The secretary beckoned Rick and he followed her trail of perfume along a thick-carpeted corridor. The large, rectangular office smelled of wealth. It had an aroma of leather and wood, and all the trappings of success: oriental carpets, antique furniture, polished wood, velvet curtains, a chandelier, bookcases, paintings, a desktop model of the AfriBelgo Falcon jet, a solitary Greek column and a small bronze statue of a horse.

'Rick, my dear boy!'

Uncle Erick's voice had grown tired with age, high-pitched and thin like an old woman's, yet retaining a slight Continental burr.

Dwarfed behind his desk and the large, tinted windowpane behind him, his smile was as bright as his gold-rimmed spectacles. He wore a dark suit, a blue pinstriped shirt, a red bowtie and gold AfriBelgo cuff links.

'Come on in.'

His hands quivered as he held open his arms in a welcoming spread.

'Good afternoon, Uncle Erick.'

'Ah, Rick. What a wonderful surprise! I thought of you this morning on my way in to town. I thought of John. Such a loss. Our loss. Such a shock. We need to talk about poor John, but it is still so good to see you again and, before we become too sombre, I want to know how you are.'

He proffered his hand in greeting, a slight trembling in the skeletal fingers the only remaining sign of the partial stroke he had suffered two years before.

For a moment Rick looked beyond the frailty of the old man. Again he recognised the strong young man who had welcomed a mother and two young boys at Pretoria station so many years ago. Uncle Erick was still as tall as then, but he had grown lean and stooped from the work burden he had placed on himself through the years. His penetrating eyes were still as blue as that day on the platform, but his eyelids had become baggy and his cheeks pale. The once thick crop of blonde hair had dwindled into a few snow-white strands on a shiny scalp with a freckled pate, but he still dressed well.

'How's my godson doing during this difficult time?'

He motioned Rick towards a hand-crafted chair near the window, placed next to the one remnant he had kept from his struggling days before he had entered mining – an imitation Greek column, poured in cement, with a small, bronze plaque stating: *Last Remaining Import Product from Belgo-Grec.*

Uncle Erick used to import the columns from Belgium and sell them into the construction industry through his first company, Belgo-Grec.

'Now come on, how are you, Rick?'

The old man seated himself opposite.

'Well, I suppose, under these circumstances …'

Rick noticed that Uncle Erick had started using a hearing aid in his left ear.

'Still chasing after defenceless animals then, are you, my boy?'

'Still part of conservation.'

'Many people say hunting has no role in conservation, Rick.' The old man's thin lips smiled, almost patronisingly.

It was an argument they had had before and Rick responded as always, 'The biggest threat to endangered species is not the hunter but the weight of human encroachment. Population growth. Farming.'

'Of course, of course. I'm only teasing. In 1960 we had barely three game farms and maybe a half-million game spread over game parks. Now we have a few thousand game farms and millions of head of game. Put a value on something and it multiplies.'

Although the old man smiled not a single laugh line cracked in the waxy skin around his eyes. That was another change, Rick realised. In the old days, when he and John had been children, Uncle Erick had enjoyed life, had laughed at the world. Lately he appeared sullen, unsociable and depressed.

'It's probably a mug's game, Uncle Erick, but I like hunting.'

In an unexpected, rare moment of jocularity, Uncle Erick stood up, leaned over, ruffled Rick's hair and said, 'I am as much a hunter as you are, my boy. I'm the urban hunter. You're the bush hunter. I might be a little frail but, let's face it, we both thrive on a good kill. In the business world, that's the only route to follow. Find value, young man.'

The old man picked up a pen and scribbled something on a piece of paper.

'We're all human and humans kill to survive,' he added, glancing sideways at Rick.

'I was up in the North, in the bush when I heard of John,' Rick said and Uncle Erick's smile disappeared.

'Rikki, they called me in the middle of the night from our American office. It broke my heart.'

Rick stood up and started pacing.

'On my way back, I had a few hours in the Land Rover to think about it. I just don't understand it.'

'John's death is a hell of a blow to me. I've always had a soft spot for him.'

Rick decided to be diplomatic and let the remark pass by without comment. It was old news; he had known well enough that John had been Uncle Erick's favourite all these years. John had been able to wangle anything he wanted from Uncle Erick – electronic equipment, sports cars, overseas trips, even the job in the USA. They had both been Uncle Erick's godsons, but John had always twisted their godfather around his little finger, often to Rick's detriment. Looking back on John's relationship with their 'uncle', nobody would have said that he, Rick, had been the one named after him.

'Well, John's dead and he'll never return,' was all Rick could think of saying.

'I missed you. I'm so glad you're here,' Uncle Erick said. He walked over and put an arm on Rick's shoulder. 'You know I've always looked upon you and John as my own sons. Now I've lost one son. Only one remains. You're all I have left.'

Rick saw a glistening in the old man's eyes.

'Uncle Erick, both John and I always looked upon—'

'We were three,' the old man interrupted him, 'we're down to two now, Rikki.'

Rick had to change the subject to get rid of the lump in his throat. He gently pressed the old man's hand for a second and then walked away to the imitation Greek column with the Belgo-Grec plaque. The cement was smooth, cool to his touch. It was almost as if he was stroking a dead body.

'I still remember how John and I used to play among these columns in the yard of your Belgo-Grec company. How you ever made money out of the importation of these columns I will never understand,' Rick said in an effort to talk about something less emotional than death.

'What do you say? Speak up, Rikki!'

Uncle Erick fidgeted with his hearing aid, moving towards Rick.

'I said I don't understand how you ever made money out of these imported Belgo-Grec columns.'

'Divine guidance, maybe?' Uncle Erick said with a wistful smile 'It was the one trading operation I was involved in that was a failure but I suppose I learned from it and turned around fast enough to move into something better.'

'Why did you keep this one column?'

'It's my own joke upon society, I suppose. No, wait' – he walked over and touched the column – 'I probably kept the column for the same reason you are wearing those horrible bangles on your wrist. You often keep the things that remind you of something in your past. In my case I originally tried to build my business on the hopes of those pillars, and so I kept the last column as a reminder of my true beginnings. I wanted a reminder of the pillar on which I built everything because that pillar was adversity. A failure. You see, I built everything on overcoming the adversity of Belgo-Grec and its columns.'

'The pillar's a lot like you, Uncle Erick.'

'You think so?'

'I definitely do. It's a symbol of how to overcome defeat. Proof of victory.'

'Belgo-Grec proved that, even in business, there can be life after death.' The old man said it with his hand over his mouth.

They fell silent.

Uncle Erick sat down behind his desk and Rick sat down across from him.

He had not changed his socks and, on Uncle Erick's Persian carpet, his boots smelled like ripe cheese.

Rick remembered the leathery new smell of the interior of the old Chrysler Windsor and he heard John's voice as they argued about who could sit in the middle of the back seat. He saw the parquet living-room floor in front of the Pilot radiogram on which he and John had often lain, side by side, listening to Bach's *Brandenburg Concerto*, Benjamino Gigli's *La Donna è Mobile* or just the morning programme for toddlers. The lump in his throat returned and he tried to get rid of it by concentrating on the view of the city behind the old man.

The Chairman's office was more eagle's eyrie than office.

'I saw Hendrik Aucamp earlier today and thought—' Rick broke the silence.

'I've asked him to organise everything. In a way, Rick, I'm relieved your mother isn't alive today.'

'She would have taken it badly.'

'Marie was a strong woman, but I know this would have broken her. She would've been devastated.' The old man stopped for a moment, closed his eyes and reclined on the couch.

'It is so senseless, Uncle Erick. Why would anybody want to kill John?'

'Who knows?'

'The strange thing is that I feel a little guilty over his death,' Rick confided.

'Why?'

'I lost touch with John. Maybe if I had kept contact then …'

'We all have to live with guilt from time to time,' Uncle Erick said.

'You know as well as Melinda and the others that I haven't been speaking to John for some time.'

'That woman was bad news.'

'She was bad news for me.'

'For everyone. Herself included. Do you still hear from her?'

'We spoke on the telephone. She knew of John's death. Aucamp used her to trace me up north.'

'Well, at least you're here. John's coffin is on a flight arriving to-morrow. He was an outstanding man. He did tremendous work for us in America. Truly destined for great things. You know, Rick, I would call him at four in the morning his time over in Washington DC, and he would get up and start working. He had an unbelievable reservoir of energy. Much more than you ever poured into your work with the company, I must say. I still don't understand why you didn't want to fully develop your career here with us. You were doing so well, Rikki. You should have had more will power, more energy. I'll never understand your motives.'

Uncle Erick's lips were thinner than before. The old man took off his glasses and, using a trembling index finger and thumb, rubbed his eyes, gathering his tears to the bridge of his nose.

'Uncle Erick, I was never cut out for the office. You know that. John was the born executive.'

'Bullshit!'

Uncle Erick's eyes were clear now and his hands steadier as he fitted his glasses back on the bridge of his nose.

'That is bullshit. Businessmen aren't born. They're bred. They are trained. Like race horses. Rats have no breeding and that's what you get in a rat race. In my business life I see Ascots, Derbies and Grand Nationals where the best bred and trained competitors always win.'

He leaned over and ran his bony fingers over the bronze statue of the horse on the coffee table.

'If you have a good bloodline,' the old man said, 'you have a better chance of beating the others, but I also know a lot of businessmen who overcame their own weaknesses. Although John was good, he had weaknesses – one of which was women. He could never keep his hands off an available skirt.'

'He sure loved to keep his women in the family,' Rick added, leaning against the windowpane. He could almost hear Melinda's voice.

Uncle Erick glanced at him over the rim of his glasses, irritation in his eyes.

'Enough sarcasm, Rick. It's not going to bring your brother back from the dead. Your grudge has now become irrelevant. For all we know John's wandering pecker might have been the root cause of his death. Many men, like you, don't take kindly to someone else's intimacy with a girlfriend or wife.'

Betraying no expression, Rick merely shrugged and gazed at the urban sprawl below. He did not want to show Uncle Erick how guilty he really felt – as if he had been directly instrumental in John's death.

'The horny bastard made a mess of my life.' Rick almost grunted as he said it. His brother was dead but there was still a rage that remained.

'Rikki. I can understand how you feel about John and maybe fate finally caught up with him. Do you know Marcia?'

Rick shook his head. No, he had never heard of her.

'She's in our Washington office. She believes that John had gone to New Orleans to meet a woman. I can believe that.'

Rick could believe it too.

They fell silent. Neither of them felt the necessity to talk any more. An old man in his seventies. A tanned man in his forties. The last vestiges of a once much stronger bond with no need for words.

Memories.

Author's note: I knew Erick Martens very well. South Africa and my country have strong mining sectors with co-operative capabilities, which gave me my cover. At that time I professed to be an analyst and company representative for my part of the world. I am not saying friends with similar interest could fix prices but let us just say we aligned sales volumes sometimes. I knew him so well I could smell his bad breath in a dark room. I have always been astounded that so many wealthy people would not spend money in curing their mouths from bacteria, bleeding gums or whatever creates halitosis.

CHAPTER 7

THE HEARSE BLOCKED THE DRIVEWAY leading to the church's main door, its back door wide open. The coffin was already inside the church. Parked vehicles overflowed from the Dutch Reformed Church's parking area, along the pavement and down the intersecting streets.

Their mother could never understand why John had converted from the ease of Catholicism to the austerity of Calvinism. But Rick understood. Both he and John had long ago lost their Belgian links and had become children of Africa. They had come to the continent as Flemish-speaking children and had settled in an area where people predominantly spoke Afrikaans, a linguistic mixture born of several languages with Dutch as the main ingredient. As young boys their Flemish language had been so close to Afrikaans that they had naturally drifted into Afrikaans society to become children of Africa – Afrikaners – themselves.

The soft notes of *Jesu, Joy of Man's Desiring* flowed from an organist's fingers. Back to Bach. In death.

Rick walked down the aisle towards the front row where, according to custom, family and close friends sat.

With a jolt, he recognised Melinda in the front row, her back to him, and the unmistakable lustre of her jet-black hair streaming from beneath a cream-coloured hat. She sat next to Uncle Erick.

'I thought you couldn't make it,' Rick whispered as he sat down next to her, breathing in the heady and inviting perfume she had always used.

'I didn't think it necessary for my husband to know I would be coming. We were with guests when you called.'

She spoke in a hushed tone, smiled and stroked his hand with manicured nails. Still the Melinda of old, playing mind-games.

She was also as beautiful as ever. Green eyes, inviting red lips against the white of her teeth, high cheekbones and a nose that twitched whenever she moved her lips. As the service commenced, she glanced sideways at Rick, and smiled. She brought his hand down on her lap and he looked down as she crossed her legs, displaying more thigh than the conservative dominee would approve. She knew in the old days Rick had loved to touch the soft, smooth area between her stocking and suspender and she allowed him now to take a good look, before letting go of his hand and smoothing down her skirt.

And in that moment, Rick remembered their first date, all those years ago in university. When they had arrived back at his digs, finding the house to themselves. He had it all planned of course. That's what friends were for. He thought back on his routine show, a presentation that would never fail.

'This is the lounge,' he had said, indicating with his eyes. 'This is the kitchen. This is the bedroom. This is the bed. This is a man,' he had whispered, smiling and stroking her cheek, 'and this is a wom-an ...'

Melinda had responded by laughing, taking a step backwards and standing in front of him, against the chaotic backdrop of his unmade bed, among the crumpled clothes he had worn the previous two days and left lying on the floor.

'This indeed is a woman,' she responded, running her hands over her full breasts. 'These are her buttons,' and she loosened one. 'This is a man's hand,' she said, stepping forward, taking hold of Rick's hand, guiding him to the valley between her breasts. 'And this is a man's work,' she said with a giggle.

Sitting in church he could almost feel the touch of her breath against his skin again, the pleasure of her hands, the softness of her lips, and the beautiful warmth of becoming one with her. And he felt the touch of sadness when they became two again.

He remembered the stillness, broken by Melinda's words.

'Rick Land, I love you.'

'I love you too, Melinda.'

Such a long time ago and so far from this moment at a funeral.

Now, the death of the one who had instigated their parting had brought them together again.

The preacher's sermon droned on.

And then Rick remembered how they had parted.

June 1976

THE HOMEWARD-BOUND TRAFFIC WAS EXCEPTIONALLY heavy. A never-ending stream of red backlights and white headlights dotted the route ahead. A thick, choking layer of smoke emanating from thousands of coal stoves in the township of Mamelodi covered the metropolitan sprawl like a dirty blanket in the crisp, wintry evening.

Rick felt drowsy.

He had difficulty keeping his eyes open and wound down the window to wake up. The rush of cold air revived him a little. The metallic taste of thick smog stung his tongue.

Before daybreak he had had coffee with his client and then set out on the hunt, which had been strenuous, but successful. Before lunch, his client had shot his buffalo. It had been a good, clean shot. Rick's work had been done. The client would rest for the night and Themba would take him to the airstrip the next day.

Rick had been away from home for two weeks. He felt in need of a good bath, his bed and the warmth of Melinda.

Forty minutes later, he stopped in the driveway of his house. A paved entrance to an average, middle-class brick and plaster cottage in an average, brick and plaster suburb.

Rick was surprised to see John's Mercedes Benz sports car blocking the entry to the garage. John did not regularly visit him. John had a luxury house with his own pool and tennis court in wealthy Saxonwold, all the accoutrements of a top executive, but Rick preferred his own lifestyle here with Melinda.

Rick turned the key in the front door and entered. The light was switched on in the corridor, from where he thought he heard muffled sounds.

Their bedroom door was ajar.

The image burst upon him. It was a nightmare. Worse, it was horrifying reality. He saw two people diagonally on the bed in front of him. Melinda giggled. Her long, black tresses hung over her face, partially covering her wildly moving naked breasts, glistening with sweat. She sat astride the man, upright with her hands on his bare shoulders. The man reached out, parted her hair and stroked her left breast. She writhed up and down, her legs spread over the arched thighs of the man below her.

Then she noticed Rick.

So did John.

For a moment she sat still, naked except for her watch. A moment impaled on John.

'God Almighty!' John said and threw her off to one side of the bed.

She flew from him with her legs still apart.

John covered his groin with a pillow and slithered down to grasp his trousers on the floor.

Melinda lay on her side for a moment, gazed at Rick in astonishment and then, without covering herself, rolled into a foetal position, her knees against her breasts.

'Sorry,' she said and put her hands over her face.

Silence followed.

The silence of deceit.

His beautiful wife. His brother.

'I apologise, Rick,' John stuttered, struggling to zip up his trousers, his eyes downcast. Then John noticed his underpants were still lying on the floor, which he quickly picked up and stuck in his trouser pocket.

'How could you … my brother … my wife … this …?'

'You were only expected tomorrow,' Melinda said, her words muffled by her hands and hair over her mouth.

Irrelevant words. No respect. No love for him. Just a statement in a marriage at war with itself. A war he had never realised existed.

'Rick, listen—' John said as he buttoned up his shirt.

John did not have time to finish his sentence.

Rick flew into him with clenched fists, hitting him in the face with all the pent-up fury of deceit and lost love. John doubled up, still tied up in the straitjacket of his shirt over his shoulders. Rick kicked him between the legs, sending him sprawling.

'Listen? To you! I trusted you. I trusted you both. My brother! My wife!'

John crawled on the floor, moaning, clutching his groin.

'How long this has been going on?' Rick screamed at them.

'Rick, it's not what you think.' She sat upright now with a bed sheet drawn to her chin, facing him, her unruly hair framing a frowning face.

'Not what I think? Well, what should I think? Are you telling me that, when I think I see my brother and my wife screwing the shit out of each other in my own bed, it is not what I think? There is nothing to think about.'

He could have killed in that moment. As a professional hunter he killed in a calculated, premeditated way. He had seen death in all the ways he had thought possible: glazed impala eyes, gaping kudu wounds, trickling warthog blood, broken bodies with their blood seeping in to the dried sand of the veldt.

Now he saw death in a crude manner he had never thought possible and it was a new death. The death of love.

At that moment, they both died, this wife he had loved and this man he had cared for. He looked at them. Melinda's face was as pale as the sheet covering her body. John's face was crimson with embarrassment.

As he walked away he heard Melinda sobbing.

'I'm sorry, Rick. It was really my fault, not Melinda's.'

He turned around.

'John, this is double deception.'

'AND NOW, BROTHERS AND SISTERS,' the reverend said in a seminary-trained voice, 'John's friend, Mark Aardt, will read the eulogy.'

Mark Aardt and John had been in the same class at university where they majored more in barrels of beer and social affairs than anything else. As John's best friend, Mark had little difficulty in finding a career at AfriBelgo where he had risen to his current position as Overseas Operations Director at Head Office.

'John Land was born as a son of Flanders,' he began. 'He was a descendant of one of the most famous Belgian resistance fighters of World War Two. Born in the small town, Aalst, just outside of Brussels, he unfortunately never saw his own father, who died tragically in an accident before John's birth. Dr Erick Martens, another hero of the Belgian resistance, brought John, his mother and his brother to South Africa after that. John grew up in Villieria, Pretoria, where he played rugby for the first team at both primary and high school level. He also made the Northern Transvaal Schools team and became Deputy Head Boy at high school. After his compulsory military training, he attended the University of Pretoria where he finished his Bachelor's degree in commerce. He worked on the university staff for a year and, during this period finished his Honour's in economics, after which he won a scholarship through the Martens Foundation to Oxford. Returning with a Master's degree in hand, he started at AfriBelgo where his outstanding qualities assured him of the highest accolades. Starting out as the personal assistant to the Chairman, he moved into management as an export executive.'

At this point in the eulogy Rick and Melinda glanced at each other.

'John Land was an extraordinarily gifted businessman,' Mark Aardt continued.

'But, the man, John Land, remained somewhat of an enigma to many. *Business Week* wrote of him as the Scarlet Pimpernel of Africa. The *London Financial Times* once referred to him as the African Factor. He was none of that.'

Yes. He was a pecker-crazy womaniser, Rick brooded.

'John Land was the personification of the leadership ideals of AfriBelgo and Chairman, Dr Martens.' Aardt's voice cracked slightly.

From the corner of his eye, Rick noticed Uncle Erick wiping away a tear.

'As we all know so well, Dr Martens built this firm on the principle of partnership. And John, in many ways, perfected this.'

Rick thought about Uncle Erick's famous profit-through-partnership edict.

Maybe John had approached Melinda as just another fifty-fifty business proposal. Fifty per cent Rick, fifty per cent John.

Whilst Mark Aardt droned on relating to John's personal life, Rick's mind drifted to the days he and John had climbed mulberry trees and targeted girls with their homemade pea shooters from behind the curtain in the school gymnasium, aiming in particular at the bra straps of those twelve-year-olds who had first started wearing them.

'So, brothers and sisters,' the preacher interrupted. 'Please switch on the head-lights of your cars, even though, praise the Lord, the sun is shining so gloriously today. Fall in line behind the hearse, which will lead our procession to West Park Cemetery. The traffic authorities will be present at all intersections to ensure a smooth flow of traffic.'

Next to him, Melinda played with the service programme, a folded paper with psalms printed inside and a lithographic cover depiction of doves of peace, rising in a blue sky with white clouds, broken by surrealist sunbeams. Rick had not concentrated much on the service. His mind had drifted into memories, brought back to reality only now and then by Melinda's noisy fidgeting with the programme – a diverting influence. Still, less diverting than her legs. Damn you, Melinda, he thought.

The gravesite was an anti-climax.

Two assistants, resembling scrawny vultures in dated suits, alighted from the hearse. One of their functions was to organise the pallbearers.

Rick and Mark Aardt carried at the front. Try as he did, Rick had very little feeling for the occasion. For a long, long time, he had shut out the past but, as he carried the coffin, he vividly saw two sweating, naked bodies entwined. It was difficult to pay the last respects to a brother who had committed adultery with your wife.

So, on a sunny August day, John was buried in the African soil. A few fluttering petals, some words of devotion, a handful of blood-red soil from a cleric's palm, Uncle Erick's jaw tightly clenched, and John disappeared into the earth.

Standing at the graveside, Melinda tugged at his sleeve.

'We've got to talk.'

'Why?'

She deserved abruptness. She had deceived him and, in the end, had probably deceived John with someone else.

Then he noticed she was crying.

'Darling, I need to talk to you – but not here.'

She had an irritating habit of calling everyone 'darling', which he had forgotten about until now.

'What is there to say, Melinda?'

She was quiet for a moment.

'Rick, I saw John recently in the States.'

'Really? What's new then.'

'Don't say that, and don't look at me like that!'

'Does Dr Whatsisname know about your recent sight of John?'

'Don't be nasty. Derick's an older man. He's a gentleman and a good husband.'

'The older they come, the easier to twist around your little finger, I guess.' For the first time ever, he realised she and John had the same manipulative abilities.

'Derick is mature in these things. We have an open marriage.'

'Open? Is that God's way to tell you you need another divorce?'

'Don't be frivolous, darling. I went to the US and met John by chance. That's all. Just listen to me, for once, I beg you.'

That damn 'darling' again.

The August breeze played with a wisp of hair in the corner of her mouth. What would it be like to unbutton her blouse again, to touch her and to feel her touch again? Come to think of it, when last did he unbutton any woman's blouse? He felt a stirring and, in self-defence, put his hands in his pockets.

'Don't just stare, Rick. We must talk. When I last saw John, he was different. Remote, as if he had lost all interest in his work ...'

Her voice trailed as her nose twitched in the captivating manner he remembered.

'Melinda, I don't want to discuss your relationship with John or your meetings with him, and I'm sure as hell not interested in your views on his moods. Maybe he was just tired of you.'

'You bastard! John died for a reason and you're not even mildly interested. I'm trying to help and the only thing you can think of is how your macho honour was once offended!'

'It has nothing to do with macho pride. It's got everything to do with the two people I loved and who—'

'Let me tell you one thing, Rick Land,' and she stabbed a finger into his shoulder. 'In a moment of weakness, John and I found each other attractive. We overstepped the line and we were caught, but you have forgotten that by then our marriage was a sham. You were in the bush for months on end. It was no wonder we grew apart. I couldn't stand the loneliness. I would have left you, in any case, in the end. Why don't you admit you were knocked out because I had the nerve to have sex with your brother? We all suffered the consequences. I know John suffered till the day he died. We've just buried him but you still want to rake up the past. I'm telling you to get off your soap box and to listen to me.'

'Why?' he heard himself asking, engrossed in her beauty, so close to him.

'Why? I'll tell you why, Mister Know-it-all. I think we can find out why he was killed.'

'All right. You saw John. So what?'

'Maybe I'm chasing ghosts, but John mentioned he'd discovered something only you could understand. Don't ask me what he meant. I don't know.'

'Did he give you any clues?'

In the back of his mind, Rick had a feeling a door was opening. His fingers tingled.

'Darling, he didn't give me any specific clues.'

'You have to think really hard, Melinda.'

'John told me something about a man in Washington DC, in some institute. I think it's a Jack Ferrara or somebody. I don't know what it means, but I have this feeling John's death was somehow related to the stuff he alluded to.'

'I don't understand. What did he say about this man Ferrara. Ferrari?'

'Ferrara. It was quite a long story about research they had done. We need some time for me to explain the whole thing. You've got to believe me. Maybe you'll understand it all. I don't know. Maybe this will be the key to the happiness you're looking for.'

'I am interested,' Rick heard himself say. 'Come over to my house and let's discuss it. People are not usually murdered for nothing. I suppose you still know where I live?'

She walked away from him, swinging her hips. For a moment, he felt no hate. He felt lust. He stood still, watching her, thinking back on how they had once loved.

'Well, are you coming?' she called from the other side of the service road.

Someone tapped him on the shoulder.

'Ah, Mr Vronsky.'

'My deepest sympathy, Mr Land, from me personally and my

group of companies. As I said, be strong.'

'Thanks.'

Melinda led the way in her convertible Alfa Spyder, her black mane fluttering in the wind.

Driving behind her, he idly entertained the thought of making love to her again. John was dead now. Maybe this was the way to heal the wounds of time. A little seduction could do wonders right now, he thought. And Derick's an old man. An old man in an open marriage. Maybe God's way of telling him that he and Melinda could have some shared fun.

She swung her Alfa into his driveway and walked to the front door. As he got out of his car, she struck a melodramatic pose. Enjoying her little joke, she lifted her skirt slightly and gave Rick a mock beauty-queen wave from the veranda.

'Mr Land!' she shouted. 'This is a garden and this is a house.'

She laughingly pointed at the lawn and then the house behind her.

'That's a man,' and she pointed a finger at him, 'and this is a woman.'

As she spoke the last words, she put her hands on her breasts and leaned back against the front door.

He thought he saw a spark of static electricity jump between her body and the door. As her back touched the door, a blinding flash of white light bolted him into dropping to the ground. An ear-splitting crack and a high-velocity wall of air whipped over him, followed by the heat of the flash.

Melinda never had a chance.

He saw her terrified, screaming face as she disintegrated with the force of the explosion, the heat and the shrapnel obliterating her.

In reflex he jumped to his feet as soon as the blast had passed. Stunned, he staggered forward. She had disappeared into the stench of the smoke-filled air. Flames licked through the hole where his front door used to be. A warped, bloodied, high-heeled shoe lay on the bonnet of his BMW in the driveway. A piece of singed flesh lay on the lawn, a grotesque offering to the demon who had devised this destruction.

He ran his fingers through his hair and noticed blood on his hands. He touched his face and inspected himself. He had blood on him but it was not his own; it was hers. She had exploded in his face.

Only then did he realise what had happened.

His body trembled and he fell to his knees, his head swimming. He saw her blood in the woodwork of the railing.

And for the first time in many years, he cried.

As a baby would.

Time and place did not exist for him. He drifted. He could not think. He could not see. He wiped the tears away. His nose was running. He heard someone cry. He recognised it was his own sobbing.

Then he became aware of a tangle of flashing lights, whining sirens, uniforms. He looked up. People were staring at him.

He watched his legs moving forward, as if they belonged to someone else. He felt arms supporting him. Someone spoke to him but, although he heard the voice, he did not understand. He was cold. He shivered.

A flashlight darted in his eyes. Shortly afterwards he entered a relieving darkness.

And then, from within the darkness, he woke up disoriented and ignorant of how long he had slept. He was cold as he opened his eyes.

The dark of night lay behind a window. A uniformed policeman sat on a chair.

'Mr Land. You're awake. Good evening.'

Rick noticed a name badge on the policeman's uniform: Israel Ndlovu. Zulu, probably. Like Themba.

Rick had difficulty saying anything. His body was a heavy, wet sponge, filled to capacity with a tiredness he was not accustomed to. Everything around him smelled of disinfectant. Somewhere behind the door the echoing sound of metal on metal clanged.

'You were in shock.' the constable said in clipped friendliness.

'They gave you an injection and you slept a few hours.'

'Hours?'

'Yes. It's night-time. How do you feel now?'

'Tired. No, okay, I suppose. Where am I?'

Rick sat upright but lay down again when something resembling a saw cutting through steel started up in his head.

'You're in General Hospital.'

'How come?'

'There was an accident at your house.'

Rick thought about it and then he remembered.

'It wasn't an accident,' he said more to himself than the constable.

He saw Melinda dying again and closed his eyes to shut out the vision.

'No accident. It was an explosion,' Rick said in Zulu.

'Yebo. You're right. Big explosion. You're lucky to be here.'

'My house is gone.'

'It's a wreck at the front but the back is still in reasonable condition. The fire brigade got there quickly.'

'So I should be grateful?'

'Yebo.'

'Which means I still have some things there,' Rick said, battling a blinding headache.

'We salvaged some clothing. The clothes you wore at the time of the explosion were torn and have been taken in as evidence.'

Rick looked down; he was dressed in a white hospital gown. He looked at his wrist – no watch or elephant bracelet.

'What happened to my watch?'

'Here, in your bedside cupboard.'

The policeman leaned forward and opened the door.

'We brought you some clothing from your house,' the constable said, pre-empting Rick's next question and handing him the contents from the cupboard. 'You'll find the wallet with your credit cards and the money you had on you inside the bag as well.'

Rick recognised his burgundy overnight bag, which the policeman lifted onto the bed. In amongst everything he found the elephant bracelets and his leather flip-top hunting watch.

'As soon as you are ready, maybe tomorrow, we will go downtown for a few formalities.'

'No. I've got to get out of here,' Rick murmured.

'You will have to check out in the morning. Doctor's orders.'

'I don't care. I have things to do. I need to go.'

'Mister Land, stay.'

'I am not in jail.'

Ignoring his persistent headache, he forced himself to get up. He rummaged in the bag for clothes.

'You are not ready, Mister Land.'

'Well, I'm not going to hang around in these medical pyjamas,' Rick stated.

After fifteen minutes of arguments between himself, the night nurse and the policeman, Rick and the policeman left through the front door of the hospital, got into a yellow police van and drove off.

The central police station in Johannesburg had once been known as John Vorster Square. With the change-over to a new democracy it had been renamed, but to Rick it remained an austere building, squatting next to the M1 double-storey highway in central Johannesburg, drably decorated with metal security slats over its windows.

Rick felt better by the time he sat propped up on a high-back chair opposite a chipped desk in an office with very much the same bland character as the police station in Waterpoort. Wire baskets overflowed with curled-up documents. The desk and other furniture were clearly marked with large white painted identification numbers to counter the theft of government assets. Who would steal from a police station? He stared at the regular placard on the wall depicting arms of terror. An officer breezed in, carrying a thin brown file. There had been a time when all police officers in South Africa had been white, but times had changed.

'Good evening. I'm Major Van Niekerk.'

Major Van Niekerk sat down behind the desk and spread the file out before him, revealing dark patches of sweat under the arms of his blue shirt.

'Evening.'

'You still look a bit pale.' The officer stroked his thin moustache as he looked up at Rick. 'You okay?'

'I'm fine, thanks.'

Rick's words were nothing more than an automatic courtesy because he had a pounding headache. He yawned. His eyes felt droopy.

'Let's see. You're Rick Land, professional hunter and owner of Landtrackers Hunting, aren't you?' Major Van Niekerk read from his file.

'Yes.'

'Your brother was murdered and you attended the funeral today. That's correct, isn't it?'

The officer made a note on the file.

'For God's sake, Major, you know all that!'

'Just doing my job. I see you have a number of firearms registered in your name.'

Major Van Niekerk pursed his lips and shifted compressed air from bulging cheek to bulging cheek, his moustache moving up and down like a seesaw.

'Yes, of course I've got firearms. I'm a professional hunter. They're the tools of my trade and they're all registered within the letter of the law.'

'Do you keep explosives, Mr Land?'

The policeman looked up from his file.

'What the hell are you driving at? I'm a hunter. Of course I don't stock explosives. You don't need four tonnes of TNT to kill a warthog.'

'Do you have any idea where the explosives yesterday at your house could have come from?'

'No. Look, I'm tired and I'd like it if you would get on with it.'

'Mr Land, we know a woman died in the explosion and we think we know who she was, but could you enlighten me from your side?'

'Her name was Melinda. Melinda Barton, married to Dr Derick Barton, a gynaecologist. She was my ex-wife.'

The officer jotted down something in the file.

'Did Dr Barton know you were seeing each other?' Major Van Niekerk asked impassively.

'No, he did not. Primarily because we did not see each other at all in the way you're suggesting.'

'Oh yes?'

'Today at the funeral, we met again for the first time in years and, on the spur of the moment, decided to go to my house.'

'Spur of the moment? Why?'

'You are insistent, aren't you? For a cup of tea.'

He felt guilty. Melinda had stood there, lovely, inviting and sensual. She had returned him the courtesy of his own show so many years before.

'Now, now, Mr Land don't get upset.'

'Major, I don't like your insinuations.'

'You've been through a tough day. It's understandable. Just remember, this is not an inquisition. We merely need to establish some facts.'

'Major, someone blew up my ex-wife and my house. No man will blow up his own house. Those are the facts!'

'The facts, Mr Land, are that your brother was murdered and, by the look of things, someone tried to murder you.'

'Me?'

'You, Mr Land. Someone probably wanted to get rid of you, not Mrs Melinda Barton. She was just in the way, seeing that the charge was set to catch you returning home.'

'Yes, it does make sense.'

'At the moment we have two violent deaths – all in the family, you might say. Your brother and your ex-wife. The question now is whether we can find a link between the two deaths. We're still trying to ascertain exactly what type of explosive device was used. First indications point to commercial explosives, but we need more information. Right now I would like to find the answers to two questions. Firstly, why would someone want to place a bomb at your front door and, secondly, who could that possibly be? Could you tell me?'

Rick thought about it.

Why would anyone wish to get rid of him? Yes he has been threatened and a few ivory manipulators might want to do that for revenge but, aside from them, he had no other real enemies he could think of. He lived a relatively sedate life, spending months on end in the bush. He held no grudge against anybody. Could it have had a link to the ivory issue? Or could it have been aimed at somebody else and been planted at his front door by mistake? He had been spending so little time at home that he did not even remember the surnames of his immediate neighbours, but he did remember that they appeared to be normal, well-balanced families – fathers with office jobs, mothers with school-going children. None of the neighbours looked like targets for terror, but then again, one never knew.

'Do you have any idea why anybody would wish to kill you?' Major Van Niekerk reiterated.

'I am sorry, Major. I am never in town, really. I only came back from the bush for the funeral.'

'Well, whoever planned the destruction knew you were not in the bush.'

Right, Rick thought.

Who could possibly know he would be in the city?

Unfortunately everybody, it seemed. A report, 'Deepening Mystery of the Land Murder', in which an interview with Rick had been included, had appeared in the *The Star* the day before the funeral. In the article Rick had stated he did not know who could have killed his brother; he had not seen him for several years; he had had no contact with the American authorities and he had no knowledge of any new developments. Yes, he told the reporter, he and John had had an excellent relationship and he would be missed by many, but no, he did not know why John had never married. In a play on words, Rick had been described as the 'Bush Land' and John as the 'Business Land'.

This was indeed a deepening mystery and he knew he had to expect that the newspaper would want to expand on its scoop. Somewhere a night editor was probably itching for the expected incoming story from a roving journalist. Somewhere the reporter who had interviewed him must be darting about town in search of a follow-up interview, not with Rick Land, brother of the murdered John Land, but with Rick Land, target of a killer. Rick had no desire to see the emaciated, bespectacled reporter again. At first sight, the man had resembled the male of the black widow spider, almost as if afraid of possibly being eaten alive by the object of his interest. But the moment the same man had started asking questions, he had gone for the jugular like a satisfied mongoose, and had throttled out his story from Rick.

'All right, Mr Land,' Major Van Niekerk spoke, 'if we need you again, I am sure you will co-operate. For now, maybe we should call it a night. Don't you think so?'

'Thank you,' Rick said with a sigh, 'but I could not possibly stay in my house tonight.'

'True. You've got a hell of a lot of damage and our men have been – probably still are – searching for clues in the rubble. Some of your stuff is still there in the back of the house. Of course, we do have someone on guard.'

'I suppose my car is still in the driveway?'

'We left everything untouched, Mr Land.'

'Does the guard have the keys to my car?'

'Probably.' The Major shrugged his shoulders.

'I'll take a few things from home and book into a hotel.'

At three in the morning the streets of Johannesburg resembled the funereal pathways in the cemetery he had been in a few hours before. The police car cut through the night with ease, its blue light blinking intermittently from the roof.

There was no lurking journalist at home, just another bleary-eyed man in uniform who handed Rick the keys to his BMW and helped him inside the house.

Torn planks, gnarled iron, broken bricks and shattered glass lay behind the cordon of yellow plastic thrown around the front of the house. The electricity had been cut off and the policeman showed the way through the back door, walking in front with his torchlight bouncing off the walls. A smell of pulverised cement mixed with cordite hung in the house. Rick sneezed.

The bedroom, being the furthest room from the front door, was perfectly intact. For a moment, still feeling the effects of the sedative, the idea of sleeping there slipped into his mind, but he swept the thought away, deciding he preferred to remove himself from the memory of Melinda's disintegration a few metres away.

With the help of the guard, he repacked his burgundy overnight bag, made sure he had his cheque book, wallet, passport and identity document with him, thanked the young policeman, got into his BMW, and drove off. It was a difficult trip, because he wanted to fall asleep on every straight stretch of road.

It was well past four when he woke up a surprised receptionist at the Sandton Sun. He signed the registration form with a shaky hand, took the bubble lift to the ninth level, stumbled into the room and, still under the influence of the injection he had received earlier on from the district surgeon, fell asleep in his clothes.

Author's note: My late MI6 friend had an affair with Melinda Barton during the time of her second marriage. Stupidity helps if you want to be adventurous. The day after her death he came to see me. He was devastated and wanted to get down to the bottom of matters. He believed there was a connection between the two deaths of John Land

and Melinda Barton, and he wanted to investigate John's AfriBe go situation and Rick Land's activities. He knew I was close to the company. That is how we started to open the lid. By unscrewing a fresh bottle of iced vodka.

CHAPTER 8

The only certainty is that nothing is certain.

—Gaius Plinius Secundus (Pliny the Elder)

STILL FULLY DRESSED, RICK WOKE up uncomfortably. His back ached. The sun was in his eyes. He smacked his tongue against a furry, morning-after dog-in-the-mouth palate.

He sat up in bed, inhaled deeply, yawned, and caught the strong odour of his own bad breath. Like a pit toilet in the bush. He rubbed the sleep from his eyes and scratched his overnight stubble. He needed the bathroom, not only to relieve his bladder, but to wash away his own stale sweat. After his ritual of lather, soap, shave, toothbrush and toothpaste, his stomach reminded him he had not eaten anything for a day.

He slipped on his wristwatch. It was a few minutes before the eight o'clock morning news. Just the effort of bending over and switching on the television in the room was a strain on his tired muscles. With his hands on the windowsill he stared out at the sunrise against the wintry smoke of Alexandra township. And then he quickly moved away from the window. If someone wants to kill you you don't stand around like a duck in a shooting gallery, idiot.

The main news item involved extremist right wing action by a radical group calling itself 'Witfront' – Afrikaans for 'White Front'. The previous day, the White Front had abducted Gertrude Amandla, the wife of the Minister of International Co-operation. Three men in balaclavas had held up her car and killed her driver. During the night her abductors had sent a badly filmed video of her in captivity to the television station.

Rick hated idiotic racists with a passion. He almost changed the channel but kept watching. Another news item followed.

Resembling a ventriloquist's doll, the newsreader spoke into the camera, his eyes shifting from left to right in the manner of Richard Nixon.

'Police are still investigating the explosion in Linden, Johannesburg, yesterday, in which Mrs Melinda Barton, wife of a prominent doctor, died.'

The screen filled with the destruction at Rick's house, showing the gap where the front door used to be. Splintered glass and debris covered the lawn.

'Mrs Barton attended the funeral of well-known international businessman, John Land, who had recently been murdered in America.' The camera moved to a scene at the grave, dissolving into a photograph of Melinda at her most beautiful. Rick could feel his heart pounding at the sight of her smiling face.

From shot to shot, the voice continued:

'Afterwards, she accompanied the late Mr John Land's brother, Rick, to his house. A police spokesman would not comment on speculation that the murder of Mr John Land could have had a bearing on the explosion, which occurred at the house of Mr Rick Land. Mr Rick Land is well known in wildlife circles. We spoke to an eyewitness, Mrs Van der Merwe.'

Rick recognised her as his next-door neighbour. She spoke in a rapid Afrikaans-English.

'Ja, I was there in the garden, watering my roses, you know, when I noticed the two cars coming into the driveway next door. Mr Land is away most of the time, you know. Ag, so I was just sommer interested seeing him again. I mean like, sies, a person should watch out these days. You know, we've had a lot of burglaries lately in our area. So, now where was I? Ag ja, I saw this very attractive woman – never seen her before, you know. But she was really larney and must have known Mr Land well because he was standing over there by his car and she was over there by the door and she lifted her skirt for him. Showed him a leg.'

'Showed him a leg?' the interviewer asked.

'Ja. Like a joke or something, you know? 'Course I was sort of minding my own business, watering the garden over here. It all happened just as I clicked in the nozzle of the garden hosepipe, because I was turning it, you know, to adjust the spray for my roses. Now, just at that very moment everything went boom. I caught such a fright!'

'Was it inside or outside the house?'

'Just there at the door. Ja, it was a terrible blast. I fell flat to the ground and, when I looked again, there was just smoke and stuff. My neighbour was on his knees, covered in blood. Ag shame, I tell you, that woman died just like that, you know', and she snapped her fingers.

The newsreader began speaking again.

'Mr Land was treated in hospital for shock and discharged. According to police, he was injured only slightly. And now, we turn to news from abroad ...'

Rick switched off the set.

In the solitude of a corner in the hotel's breakfast area, a multitude of thoughts rushed through his head.

Why would anyone want to kill John? Did the threatening note he'd found in his mail fit into this? Who had planted the bomb at his home and why? Melinda had had a feeling that someone in an institute in Washington DC knew more about John's death, that John's death was somehow related to something he had mentioned to her. What exactly had he told her?

Rick could not think of any reason why he should be the one to understand what John had told Melinda but that was what she had said – distinctly.

Why had John specified that he, Rick, had to go to the United States? Was there a hidden reason, or was it a question of just tying up loose ends? Could the threat from the poachers be one of those loose ends?

It seemed obvious now that both deaths were linked and, to make any sense of it, he had only one option. He had to track down those responsible for the deaths.

A sudden loud crash prompted him to jump up in fright from the breakfast table spilling coffee from his cup on his trousers. His heart raced. It was only a tray on the floor with someone's breakfast spattered everywhere. He sat down again. Calm down Rick, calm down.

From years in the bush, he knew he could track down anything that moved in the wilds. How many times in the past had he been confronted with tracks disappearing into water and reappearing on the other side? A spoor that ended at the edge of a river usually pointed to a trail on the other side. In this case, there were tracks to be followed on both sides of the Atlantic.

He would have to fall back on his own tracking senses. You had to start at the chronological beginning and follow through. The trail started with John's death in America and so far ended in Johannesburg. Experience in the bush had also taught him that, if you track an animal, you have to move as stealthily as the animal itself. If he and Themba had not moved as cunningly as the poachers themselves, they would never have been successful. Rick knew he had to follow that principle again in this case. The secret of hunting lay in the element of surprise. He had to retain that element. He had to move like a leopard, remain camouflaged, work on his own, tread softly, use the highest vantage point and take shelter in the lowest ground cover. He had to follow the scent, listen for sounds that could lead him to his prey. And, like the leopard, he had to work alone. He had to fall back on being Ingwe.

A man at a breakfast table opposite him was reading the back page of the morning edition of *The Star*. A large portion of the front page, held towards Rick, was covered with a colour photograph of the carnage at his house and a banner heading: 'Woman in Vicious Murder Circle'.

The journalist who had interviewed him a few hours before the funeral had been hard at work.

If he stayed in Johannesburg during the next few days, the press would certainly hound him. Melinda, married to someone else, had come to his house where an eyewitness had seen she acted suggestively towards him. He did not look forward to the idea of becoming the press's target for scandal and sensationalism. His every movement would be recorded and reported in the media, turning him into public property. It was clear he would have to leave for America as soon as possible, even if that meant he would not be able to attend Melinda's funeral.

After breakfast, Rick returned to his room and called Karen Lee for a flight reservation. He settled for that evening's British Airways flight to London, with a connection to Washington DC the next day.

'Is your passport still in order?' She was as efficient as always.

'Yes.'

He leafed through his passport, glad he had taken all his documentation with him the previous night.

'Of course you'll need a visa for the States. Do you have a valid one?'

'No.' He had forgotten about that.

'No problem. Just leave your passport at the hotel reception. I'll have it picked up and sent through to a contact at the consulate. We'll have it ready for you by the end of the day. You've got enough to worry about. Leave this to me.'

'You're lovely, Karen.'

'I wish you'd say that more often. Now, shall I book you into the Hilton in DC?'

'No, thanks. I suppose I could stay in John's house. If not, I'll make my own arrangements over there.'

'Okay, Rick. I'll issue the ticket, have your passport picked up, get the visa and arrange for your traveller's cheques.'

It was ten o'clock already. He had many things to do, including packing.

Driving around the corner in to Linden, Rick saw the journalist at the front gate to his house. The man's persistence was remarkable.

'Good morning, Mr Land. Remember me? Roy Neil from *The Star.*'

Rick had no desire to talk at length with this scrawny journalist somehow blocking his way.

'I would very much like to do a follow-up on our other article. Could we have a chat about all of this?' Roy Neil waved at the ruins.

A different police guard from the night before watched Rick and the journalist.

'Look, I don't understand what happened here, Mr Neil.'

'You don't? Well, the way I see it, your brother was shot and now your ex-wife has been blown up – please accept my condolences – and you are lucky to be alive. Now that's quite a strange coincidence, would you not say so?'

Rick ignored the journalist, instead nodding a greeting at the policeman as he entered the house.

'Mind if I join you?' Mr Neil, ever persistent.

Rick said nothing, retrieved his suitcase, and started packing.

'Going away?' the journalist asked.

'I'm going to stay in a hotel,' Rick said, thinking on his feet. 'It should be clear to you that I can't stay in these ruins.'

'Ja. Messy,' Neil agreed. 'Also too dusty by far. So, Mr Land, do you know that your ex-wife also had tea, drinks or maybe more with your brother in America a month ago. Do you know that?'

'Yes, but how do you?'

'It's part of my job,' Roy Neil said as he lay back on the bed and stared at the ceiling, his hands locked behind his head, his spectacles resting on the bridge of his beaky nose.

Rick tried to concentrate on counting socks and underpants. The Southern Hemisphere's winter is the Northern Hemisphere's summer and he had to pack accordingly. Roy Neil was a nuisance.

'What does the word 'Erfdeel' mean to you, Mr Land?' Neil asked, his nonchalance obviously calculated.

'Erfdeel? Never heard of it.'

'You sure?'

'Sure. Erfdeel is obviously an Afrikaans word; I would say Erfdeel probably means a portion of an inheritance.'

'I see. And do you know anybody called Peter Kraske?'

Rick turned around. He sensed something.

'Kraske? Nope. Who's he?'

Rick had now forgotten about packing. He stood watching Neil, still lying on his back on the bed, peering at the ceiling.

'I don't know either. That's why I'm asking you,' Neil said as he loosened his tie.

'So, where did this man crop up, Neil?'

Roy Neil just shrugged and kept his eyes fixed on the ceiling.

'Look, Neil, I've never heard of a Kraske. I'm not too sure what this Erfdeel remark has to do with anything, but you've tickled my curiosity and now I want to know.' Rick felt tension rising into his throat. 'I would very much like to know why you are asking me these obviously loaded questions. Who's Kraske? What is Erfdeel? What the hell are you getting at?'

'Nothing in particular.' Neil closed his eyes, reminding Rick of a satisfied anteater.

Rick had had enough. He lunged forward, grabbed Neil by the tie and pulled him up into a sitting position on the bed.

'You're strangling me!'

Rick drew Neil's reddened face closer. Their noses almost touched. Rick smelled whisky on the man's breath. This time of day?

'Neil,' Rick growled at him, 'people close to me have died. I'd like to know why. I think you know something, and now you're going to tell me unless you want the living journalistic shit beaten out of you.'

'Okay, okay! Take it easy! We can make a deal.'

By now Neil was gasping for air. Rick released him and he fell back on the bed.

'You, a reporter, somehow know that Melinda saw John in Washington. I would be surprised if even Major Van Niekerk knew that.'

Recovering his composure, Neil said, 'I would be surprised too. We journalists are sometimes quicker on the draw than the sheriffs.' He smirked.

'Let's get down to basics then.' Rick decided to change the flow of their discussion. 'If you tell me why you're asking these questions, it might make some sense to me. If it doesn't, I promise to come back to you the moment I find anything that fits in with your question. You have my word. What do you say?'

Rick thought he could almost hear the clicking of Roy Neil's mind as the man weighed the potential advantages and disadvantages of handing out information to Rick. Eventually, Neil turned on his side towards Rick, who leaned against the wardrobe door.

'I was at the newspaper yesterday when the story of the explosion broke. Minutes after the explosion, it was known that a Mrs Melinda Barton had died here at this very house. One of my colleagues was sent to cover this story. So, instead of coming over here, I immediately went to Mrs Barton's house. I was let in by her husband, Dr Barton. Of course he was stunned when I told him, the poor guy. I felt sorry for him, but he ignored me, rushed out, got into his car and left. He left me there in the house on my own.'

'And?'

'Mrs Barton's diary was next to the telephone. I had a quick peek at it. It was like stealing chocolates. She had been in America a month ago. It just so happened that, in the last few days, I followed the story of your brother's death and in the process I made quite a few telephone calls to AfriBelgo in Washington, so much so that I recognised that number in her diary. She had entered AfriBelgo's Washington DC number in her diary next to two flight numbers, departure and a final arrival time. Although she had not entered the name John Land in her diary it was clear she had called AfriBelgo and, as your ex, would have probably seen your brother over there.'

'How did you know she was my ex-wife?'

'Stupid question. I made a study of the murder in New Orleans and knew your family inside out. Anyway, so I checked the flight numbers in the diary and they were for DC. I took a flyer, tested it with you, and you confirmed my suspicion. She definitely saw him.' Roy Neil smiled – smugly.

'I should have guessed it.' Rick sighed. 'But what about this Erfdeel and the other character you mentioned. What was his name again?'

'Kraske. Peter Kraske. I don't know what it means but the telephone number and arrival time were written in blue and, underneath that, she had inscribed the word Erfdeel and the name Peter Kraske in red. I suppose your brother, John, Kraske and Erfdeel all have something in common. Your brother dies? Your ex-wife dies? A portion of an inheritance? What do you think?'

'John's will stipulates a donation to Langlaagte Orphanage here in Johannesburg. Maybe John felt threatened enough to ask Melinda to look after the bequest to the orphanage. That could explain the word, but I'm just guessing. Still, I promise to get back to you as soon as I know anything.'

'Do you think your brother was or felt threatened before his death?'

'Melinda told me that John had appeared to feel threatened in some way but she did not know why or how.'

'Did she also feel threatened?'

'I don't know. Maybe. Maybe not. This is as much as I know, which is very little.'

Rick had finished packing. He zipped up the suitcase and clicked the straps into place.

Outside, he shook the newspaperman's hand, got into the BMW

and drove off.

He now had to follow the trail.

Thirty minutes later he was having a cup of tea in the office of the Hostel Father at the Abraham Kriel Orphanage, a man as wide as his height, with puffy cheeks and bags under his eyes.

'No, we never had any previous contact with your brother, Mr Land, but we are grateful for the contribution,' he wheezed. 'This is a very old institution – I started life here myself – and many, many people bequeath money to us. Now and then someone who grew up here contributes money, but we often have donors with no physical link to us. They give because they believe in children. Maybe your brother was one of those. Whatever the reason, he must have been a good man. I always say we should give flowers to people during their lifetime rather than after they have passed on. But your brother's grave deserves a wreath from us because he has brought a bouquet to needy children now, when they need it the most.'

Rick had lost his concentration, deaf to the principal's views. Why would John leave money to this specific orphanage? Could Kraske have something to do with the orphanage?

'Do you have a Peter Kraske here or a Kraske somewhere related to the orphanage?'

'Kraske? No. Not that I am aware of. We could have had a Kraske here as an orphan, some time in the past. One would have to go through the records for that. You might want to call me a little later in the day for that information.'

Rick thanked the man and walked down the corridor to the exit. He had an uneasy feeling, as if he wore the building like a heavy mantle on his shoulders.

Only when he stepped outside did the mantle finally slip off. If something untoward had happened to their mother, he and John could easily have ended up as young children locked away in a similar institution. They had been lucky. Life had given them a second father. He steered the BMW towards the city centre. In the distance, on the

I. VRONSKY AND RHYNIE GREEFF

right-hand side, the skyline was dominated by the prominent gold bar shape of AfriBelgo House, which reflected the midday sun in a solid golden beam. In the core of that reflection sat the man he regarded as his own father – Dr Erick Martens.

HENDRIK AUCAMP WAS FREE FOR lunch.

Like a huge pigeon-house of glass, the Touch Down Restaurant clung to the southern stand of the Ellis Park sports stadium, home of the Transvaal Rugby Football Union.

Rick and Aucamp sat at a table next to the floor-to-ceiling window, overlooking the playing field. Sixty thousand empty seats, broken by advertising billboards, formed the panorama outside. At grass level, from the halfway line, a magnificent jet of white water spurted, covering the field in long sweeps of irrigation. The abundant water and green grass were far removed from the dry, thirsty bush. Rick wondered how Themba was doing.

During lunch, Rick used Aucamp's cellular telephone to make an appointment with Uncle Erick at four.

By the end of the lunch they had discussed all that was necessary. Aucamp would look after the insurance claims and repairs to Rick's house. He would also fax the legal firm, Sternson, in Washington, and arrange for Rick to stay in John's house. After all, the house had been willed to Rick. Aucamp promised someone from Sternson would meet Rick on his arrival in Washington.

By four o'clock Rick sat opposite Dr Erick Martens again.

'When I heard the news I was worried sick about you, Rikki.' There was sadness in Uncle Erick's normally piercing eyes. 'You cannot imagine how glad I was when I heard that you were safe.'

'Thank you, Uncle Erick.'

'What is the world coming to? First John. Now you. On top of that, I also had some trouble last night, which I reported to the police, of course.'

'What trouble?' Rick had not heard of anything.

'I was in my study, reading a feasibility study on the new phosphate development at Phalaborwa – maybe you saw the reports about it in the press – when someone fired a shot at me.'

'A shot? From where? Incredible. From inside?' Uncle Erick's property had walls high enough to block out the view of a curious giraffe.

'Yes, I was surprised. No, shocked. I have always believed my security arrangements are good. I didn't expect anything like that at all.'

'This is a step too far. You are not also going to be a target. That's my promise.'

'I heard a crack, like a single clap of hands, in the garden.'

'One sound?'

'Yes. The next thing I knew, the window shattered and there was a crater in the wall behind me. It ruined my Business Man of the Year Award.'

'Uncle Erick, how the hell can you sit here and be more concerned about a framed award? You could have been killed!'

First John, then himself, Melinda by accident, and now Uncle Erick ...

'Rikki, I could have been killed, yes, but like so many times before in my life, I was lucky. It reminded me of the war again. And now that you are sitting here with me, I am also reminded of your father, bless his soul.'

As he said it, it seemed to Rick as if the trembling fingers he held against his right temple were quivering even more.

'You say the shot came from the garden?'

'From inside the walls I am sure.'

Rick knew the property well, a select piece of real estate in the exclusive suburb of Houghton. Four acres of well-tended, landscaped garden, a tennis court with floodlights, an open-air heated swimming pool and a tranquil pond – all safely ensconced behind high, white walls. A huge Sardinian-style mansion was set in the middle of this private park. Round the clock, a security guard, in a little box building at the gate, kept watch over the single point of entry to the property.

An ornate brass plaque at the gate spelled out in huge letters: *Solitude.* Uncle Erick always pronounced the name of his house in French.

'How do you think someone could have scaled the wall?'

'I do not know, Rikki. It's a mystery. I called the police. They ran around the property with lights and dogs until the early hours of the morning. Kept me up all night, although that did not bother me too much. It seems that in my old age I sleep less and less. Some nights I lie there the whole night long with my eyes closed but wide awake.'

'And did they find anything?'

'Footprints in a flower bed which they thought were those of the gunman. They made moulds of the prints and left. That was all. Whoever it was got away.'

'Uncle Erick, you've got to be careful. You know as well as I that after your partial stroke, you're living on a thin edge. And take it from me, I don't think this kind of excitement could be good for you. Just look at your hands. You're shaking like a leaf.'

'I've lived a full life.' The old man closed his eyes, as if recalling his memories.

'Well, it looks like somewhere someone has declared a hunting season on our family.'

'It certainly does.' The old man's voice seemed to quiver as much as the hand over his mouth.

Rick stood up from the ornate chair and walked to the window. Down below, in Marshall Street, people scurried about their daily activities, shuffling goods around like dung-beetles from one place to the other. Suddenly, the disjointed bits and pieces in Rick's mind started to make sense.

'Uncle Erick, I think I might have an idea of what's happening.'

'What is it, Rikki?'

Rick had never liked the diminutive, but he had accepted it since childhood. Uncle Erick had always been like a father to him and had that paternal prerogative to talk to him as if he were still seven years old.

'I think it has everything to do with the poaching syndicate I broke up a while ago. Do you remember?'

'Of course. The Wildlife Society gave you and the other man each a medal for your work. Do I have to remind you, of all people, that I am the President of the Wildlife Society?'

'I know. That's the point.'

Rick explained his suspicion that the exposure he had had in the article in *Time* had been manna from heaven to the poachers. It had probably given them the lead to locate him in order to exact revenge. And then the two threatening letters he'd received. It was obvious the syndicate wanted to avenge their loss. Rick was convinced that somewhere in John's death either a man called Ted, from Atlantic City, or Ray Tsai, from Hong Kong, featured – or both. The men behind the poaching syndicate could be behind everything.

'But why would these people want to murder John?'

'Retribution, I guess. Maybe John and Melinda's deaths are warnings of things to come.'

'Warnings? Why would there be warnings?'

'I might be off-track, but the way I look at it, I did the cleaning up of the syndicate's operation. You, as the President of the Wildlife Society, handed me a medal. So you supported and rewarded the cleaning up and, if I remember correctly, that was also reported widely. They look at you and me, and what do they see? I'm the puppet; you pull the strings. Naturally, they will want to retaliate against both of us. But they also want us to suffer. So how do they do that? They decide, in cold blood, to kill John – my brother, your protégé – as a warning. Then they come for us on the same day, the day of John's funeral. Unfortunately, Melinda got in the way.'

'It does make sense … Frightening sense.'

It seemed to Rick as if the old man's blue eyes had suddenly become even more steely. And had his trembling hands stilled, almost as if the revelation of the threat had strengthened him?

'What is more frightening is that they could attack you or me at any time.'

'What do you suggest?' Uncle Erick asked, fidgeting with his hearing aid.

'I have to go to America.'

'Why?'

'Because that's where the track starts. Right there with John. I'm flying out tonight.'

'I don't know whether it is such a good idea for you to go, Rikki.'

'I have to. No choice.'

'Well, maybe it could also be a good break from the bush for you. Be careful.'

'Strange. That's what one of the threatening letters also said. 'Be careful'.'

The moment he said it, Rick regretted the remark.

'Rikki, I have always cared for you. And for John. Remember, your parents decided to name you after me. Sometimes, when I look at you, I see Albert in your face. You resemble your father so much I find it almost frightening. You are my godson, but, more than that, you are like my own son – my only remaining one, now that John is dead. I will pray for you.'

Rick could read the concern in Uncle Erick's countenance. Over the decades, Dr Erick Martens had been so involved in his love affair with AfriBelgo he had never had the time to become seriously involved with a woman. Rick knew that, infatuated with his expanding business, the old man prized the adulation that had come his way as a result of his growing power. Uncle Erick had once told him he never understood why people wanted to struggle with the complexities of physical intimacy. In Rick's view the old man's love life was cerebral; he revelled in the courtship of targets for take-overs and mergers, acting like the groom with the target as his bride, loving the act of wooing the managements of those targets, to seduce their shareholders into the willingness to get into bed with him. The Erick Martens Rick knew so well enjoyed the commercial coupling, the consummation of mergers and the procreative acts with so many different partners. Almost like a form of sex in business, a manner of reproduction.

Uncle Erick lived alone and, for a man with a wealth of business contacts, he had few friends. Like so many famous and wealthy people, he was a loner. Rick and John had been his surrogate sons. Now, only Rick was left.

'I promise to be careful. Thank you for everything you have done.'

Uncle Erick turned his face away.

'How will you get to the airport?'

'My travel agent will take me.'

'Oh. Will you have time to see Frank Faber?'

'Who?' Rick could not think who Faber was.

'Executive Director of the Wildlife Society. He might have some leads for you.'

'Sure. If it's possible, yes.'

'Good.' Uncle Erick walked out of his office. Rick heard him talking to his secretary.

He returned.

'Maxie is calling him now.'

As he said it, the telephone on the coffee table rang. He picked it up, listened, replaced the receiver and told Rick, 'Faber says he'll wait for you. You know where it is, don't you?'

'Yes. Delta Park.' Rick had been there before, but could not recall meeting Faber.

Their discussion drifted to other things. The old man felt that his company, particularly the less profitable mines, could benefit from the recent problems in Saudi Arabia which could boost the price of gold. Rick said he thought Mandela's first few months in power were also good for the future economy. The old man sighed and said the Zulus and Xhosas first needed to find peace between them for Mandela to succeed.

They talked of the early morning television news and of the White Front's abduction of the wife of the new Minister of International Co-operation.

But then the old man surprised Rick.

'Abduction is inexcusable under any circumstances, but even racist extremists sometimes have a point – not necessarily a good one, of course, but life isn't always perfectly black and white. Life can also be grey.'

'I'm not sure I follow you …'

'Don't be so taken aback, Rikki. I give money to everybody, from schools in the black community to cultural organisations in the white community, across the political spectrum. Like Getty, I also follow the maxim that money is like manure and the more you hoard it, the more it stinks, whereas the more you spread it around, the more it creates growth. The more it creates growth, the more money you make again. I like to spread it around, of course always with an eye on new opportunities, and so I am actively involved in every single group type you can think of – politics, sports, religion, culture, education, the whole caboodle. The one thing I learned a long time ago is that even the best people, in the best organisations, have negative characteristics, and the worst people in the worst organisations could have positive elements. Remember that. You should look at people with that in mind.'

By the time they had said their goodbyes, the sun was setting behind Brixton Tower. Their conversation had ended so strangely, Rick had forgotten to ask Uncle Erick whether Erfdeel and Peter Kraske had any meaning for him.

Rick bought the afternoon edition of *The Star* from a street vendor and quickly scanned the pages. During the course of the day, fresh news had pushed the story of Melinda's death off the front page. Now page three contained a short, insubstantial report on the blast, stating that clues were being investigated by the police.

Roy Neil was saving his ammunition for later.

Once he'd collected his travel documents from Karen, Rick drove to the offices of The Wildlife Society. The building reminded Rick of a

Second World War bunker. With a façade of unpainted concrete, it crouched low in a clump of oak trees. They followed the light to a door marked: Executive Director.

Frank Faber's face resembled that of a blue wildebeest, the African brindled gnu.

'I received a message from the office of Dr Martens, our president, to assist you in making contact with our conservation friends in America, particularly people who could help you in your specific search into the illegal ivory trade.'

If gnus had been able to talk, Rick thought, they would probably have produced Faber's nasal grunts.

'It's a pity we never met before, Mr Land. I missed the Carlton Hotel reception when you received your medal. I did a lot of preparatory work for the case against the poacher Van Tonder.

'How a man like Van Tonder can walk around free like that, with his bail paid for by a bunch of incognito crooks, I will never understand,' Faber continued. 'His case gets postponed continually. Absolutely disgusting!'

Rick nodded.

'And another thing,' Faber said, 'I can't see why the case is only against Van Tonder, when we all know where to look for the real thugs.'

Rick nodded again.

'Here you are.' Faber handed Rick a short hand-written list of names, addresses and telephone numbers.

'I wrote it all down for you. Randy Zellmer, at the Smithsonian, in particular, can help you a lot, but don't ignore a man like Alec Post, at *National Geographic*. They're specialists in anti-poaching measures.'

Rick had had an idea of starting with a few of his regular American clients who had often visited Africa, but Zellmer and Post could come in handy.

FLIGHT BA054 WAS READY FOR departure. The 747 taxied out into the wintry darkness, turned at the southern end of the runway and faced north.

'Holiday or business for you?'

'Family,' Rick answered the man in the seat next to him.

'Nice reason for a flight.'

'Mm,' Rick said. He thought of what he could have said. That a dead end with very high walls is an ideal place to turn back and fly out.

The hum of the engine noise slowly became louder. At first it was a mere hum. Then the humming sound gathered decibels until it became a crescendo of tumultuous thunder. Rick leaned back and closed his eyes in the controlled high-speed earthquake. The massive metal chamber tilted and, with a final convulsion, vaulted into the African sky.

As the shuddering passed, eerily lit roads and houses became smaller.

In the clear night, the Witwatersrand, the White Waters Ridge, running along the gold reef, lay stretched out in a shimmering sea of diamonds and sequins. Uncle Erick's El Dorado down there. Like an attractive woman out for a night on the town, the City of Gold was dressed for the occasion.

The aircraft banked and winged northwards to London and a connection to the USA.

Author's note: As a result of his closeness to Melinda Barton, my British friend got to know a lot about John and the younger Erick. Not to be outdone, I had a relationship with Maxie, secretary to Erick Martens. It happened in the course of the business of forging mining ties but I am grateful because, through that, I discovered many missing pieces in the puzzle. At this stage of events the Brit was also close to the journalist in his search for truth on his lost love. So the two of us were able to trade information and fill in holes where we lacked detail.

CHAPTER 9

The wind cannot be caught in a net.

–Russian proverb

RICK WOKE UP ON HIS connecting flight from London with the crumpled newspaper still on his lap. America lay in sunshine outside the porthole.

Through the window, steel and glass structures flitted by at eye level on the right. The aircraft bounded over a bridge, lined with bumper-to-bumper traffic, directly under the fuselage. It felt as if the landing gear dipped into the river as the McDonnell Douglas DC10 skipped over the water towards the safety of the runway.

On the other side of the administrative hurdles of immigration and customs control he saw a man holding up a sign with his name in thick black ink.

'Mr Land?'

'That's me.'

'Real neat to meet you. Jerry Cohen from Sternson.'

With Rick's baggage in the back, and Cohen behind the wheel, they glided out of the airport area and into America.

'You had a good flight, I trust?' Cohen asked the standard question, then added, 'I'm sorry about your brother.'

'Thanks.'

Only the air-conditioner whirred as Cohen's car crawled along in heavily congested traffic. After a while, the pace of the traffic increased.

Cohen had a bad habit of driving slowly in the fast lane, unconcerned with the hooting, flicking headlights and vulgar hand-signs around him.

'At this time of year Africa is dried out and brown,' Rick said in an effort to break the silence. 'It's a welcome contrast to see so much green here.'

'Yeah. We'll be cutting past the Arlington Cemetery, over there on the left, and along the Potomac River on the George Washington Memorial Parkway. Out on the Parkway is where you'll find the really green countryside. Kinda neat this time of year.'

Cohen lit a cigarette, slid open his window slightly and, as cigarette smoke curled around his nostrils, said, 'The house is out here in McLean, not far from the Parkway.'

Like all the other houses on Lynwood Hill Drive, John's house was set on a property without a fence, unlike the walled-in urban properties of Africa.

To Rick, accustomed to houses built of bricks and plaster, the house seemed to have been constructed of cardboard. The lawn needed mowing. On the roof, a cluster of knee-high weeds sprouted from the gutter.

Cohen parked in front of the double garage door, got out and walked ankle-deep in grass to the front door where he fumbled in his pockets.

'Can't find the damn code.'

Rick noticed the door had a strange box covering the key. 'What's that?'

'A lock box,' Cohen said as he tried the inside pocket of his jacket. 'It's a contraption that real estate sales people use. Ah, here. I've got the number.'

He held up the scrap of paper on which a few numbers were written.

'It's kinda neat. The box fits over the door handle and covers the keyhole, making it impossible for anyone just to enter through the front door. If you want to open the front door you got to crack the box first. Here, the box has a five-number code which allows you to open it.'

Cohen turned the numbers and opened the lid of the box, then unlocked the front door.

Rick picked up his suitcase and entered a dank interior, which smelled of metallic mildew. Unlike the draughty homes of Africa, houses in this part of the world were built to keep the heating of winter inside and the summer's heat outside. After John's death, the house had unquestionably been sealed off. It was as if he had entered a fruit jar.

Rick put down his suitcase in the hallway, walked into the spacious living room and opened the curtains and windows to let in air and light.

'I guess that's it then,' Cohen said and handed Rick the set of keys.

'I'll be on my way back to the office now. Of course, if you need anything, call me. You've got my number. If we don't hear from you, we'll pick you up tomorrow morning at nine, as arranged, for your meeting with Brian Sternson.'

After thanking Cohen, Rick waved goodbye from the front door, and turned around to explore the interior of John's house.

The living room displayed all the characteristics of an affluent bachelor. There were none of the usual framed photographs of smiling relatives on the rosewood side and coffee tables. No female hand had ever been allowed to add any frills. The curtains were heavy columns of cloth and not a single doily adorned the furniture. A reading lamp over an easy chair resembled a billiard saloon light shade. Three thick-piled Karachi carpets were of the colour found in the smoking rooms of men's clubs all over the world. A rosewood bookshelf was filled with collectors' books and a small bronze sculpture of a female torso. Ah, John's decorator touch. Rick had difficulty appreciating the two large abstract paintings that spattered the wall, although he appreciated the name on the canvas – Jackson Pollock. Those two pieces of art were probably more valuable than the house itself.

He opened a rosewood cocktail-cabinet, built into the wall, and poured himself a Jack Daniels neat, adding ice from a built-in ice machine.

Whiskey in hand, he went up the staircase leading from the marbled entrance.

There were four bedrooms, three of which looked like museum exhibitions where life had died long ago, but the fourth, the main bedroom, was roomy and light with a huge double brass bed, an easy chair with a reading-lamp, and another huge abstract painting on the wall – probably an abstract attempt at depicting a nude, Rick decided, although it could also just be a bunch of squiggles. He walked into the en-suite, bent over the basin and splashed cold water on his face.

Then he went downstairs again.

The kitchen was spacious and bright, a touch of insecticide in the air. He opened the refrigerator and gazed at another statement of bachelorhood; except for a six-pack of Budweiser and a piece of mouldy cheese, the refrigerator was empty.

The dining room was as cold as the refrigerator and as sparsely stocked, with a chrome-and-glass dining table and eight chairs. From the impersonal style of the dining room, Rick discovered the cosiness of John's study, furnished with a yew desk, a burgundy leather couch similar to the one in the living room, a television set and video tape recorder, and row upon row of books. He ran his finger along the shelf. John had accumulated a diverse range of investors' guides, financial annuals, novels, dictionaries, legal books, chemistry reference volumes, and books on photography, politics, finance, economics, golf and art. There was an encyclopaedia, a Bible and a book on childcare.

Why would he have wanted a childcare book?

On one shelf Rick found a photo album and leafed through it, stopping at a faded black-and-white photograph of John and himself, laughing on the beach, two skinny boys with the joy of new discoveries sparkling in their eyes, untroubled on their first day in Africa.

The photographs had been glued onto the pages in chronological order. There was one of John with his dog, Wolf, on the lawn of their house in Villieria. A picture of a children's party where John and Rick posed with John's friends around a cake with lit candles. Rick smiled at a team photograph of adolescent rugby players. This had been John's biggest triumph, when he had gained his provincial schools rugby colours. John was standing in the middle row with a self-satisfied grin, his forearms crossed proudly on his chest, his chin lifted, a short back-and-sides haircut, convict-style, and protruding ears. They had both loved sport, and the climate of Pretoria had been conducive to outdoor sports in all varieties.

Rick paged to a colour photograph of John, this time with longer hair cascading over his ears, and a giggling blonde at his side. A different form of sport. This had been John's true passion in life: women, in all shapes and sizes, through his years of bell-bottoms, jeans, golf trousers and business suits, until his death.

In the back of the album were a few loose press cuttings stuck in a plastic bag. Rick took them out. One was from the *Wall Street Journal* about the Cazco Chem takeover when AfriBelgo diversified into the United States. Rick was surprised to find the article from *Time* about the entrapment of the ivory poaching syndicate in Mozambique. He looked at the photograph of Themba and himself, standing in front of the pile of tusks. Another cutting, with no reference to its source, stated: 'Massive Barter Deal with Russia'. This had been one of John's greatest accomplishments when he had negotiated a three-point barter of Russian ammonia, American grain and Iranian oil. He paged through a few more cuttings about AfriBelgo's activities in the USA. The last one was a society photograph of John out on the town, at a reception with a sign stating Wiltshire Hotel.

He put the album down. He had to trace the activities of his brother. Did John keep a diary? He glanced around the room. There was a telephone on the desk, next to which he could see a telephone list.

In his private life, John had always been somewhat disorganised, but in his business affairs he had been methodical to the point of irritation. Names and telephone numbers had been entered alphabetically. Rick noticed that Melinda's number had been entered under M for Melinda as well as B for Barton. Remembering Roy Neil's discovery of the name Peter Kraske in Melinda's possession next to John's office number, Rick looked under K for Kraske and P for Peter but found no reference. He recognised some of the other names: AfriBelgo colleagues, among whom he saw the home telephone number of Marcia, old friends like Mark Aardt, Uncle Erick's home number, and his own home number in Linden which John had never dialled.

And then he remembered Melinda had mentioned someone's name at an institute. Who was it again? Ferris? Ferguson? Ferrara. He flipped to F and found it: Jack Ferrara, International Institute of Mining.

Rick dialled the number.

'Ferrara,' a voice answered.

'You don't know me but you knew my brother. I'm Rick Land, John's brother.'

'Yeah, I was really bummed when I heard the news. My commiserations to ya.' Ferrara spoke in a Southern drawl.

'I'm in DC to settle the estate and thought I'd call a few people at random, I mean, people who knew him. Just want to make sure there are no outstanding matters I don't know of. From what I've heard, you knew him well, so I thought I should call you.'

'AfriBelgo's an active member of the Institute of Mining out here, and due to that, yeah, I saw John quite often for business. Social-wise too. Did a few fun things together in our time. He was my buddy. Missing him.'

'Do you know of any debts or problems he might have had that I might have to sort out?'

'Nope. Not to my knowledge, and from many times of chewing the fat with him, I kinda think y'all shouldn't even be concerned about stuff like that.'

'Do you know of anything that might have bothered him?' Rick knew everything was probably still too foggy to start asking direct questions like that. But he had no choice. He had to take the chance.

'Bothered him? One thing bothered him definitely.'

Rick's heart jumped at Ferrara's words.

'Dames. He was one for the broads. That guy just loved a good wiggling ass. Full stop. That was my buddy.'

Closing his eyes, Rick heaved an inward sigh. He had to keep on trying.

'I know. That was probably his greatest flaw, Mr Ferrara.'

'Hey, he was a natural guy. Natural stuff has flaws; artificial stuff is produced to look flawless. Some of the greatest paintings in the world have flaws. He was like that. I would not call his love for skirt a flaw. An idiosyncrasy, maybe. On an on-going basis, he screwed his secretary silly, whilst alternating other babes, kinda in between. Never bragged about those kind of things, but it was always apparent. Like the last time I saw him.'

'When was that?'

'John and I had a round of golf out at Enterprise, a few Saturdays ago.'

'And?'

'Well, he talked about Marcia – that's his secretary. She often accompanied him to all kinds of social occasions.'

'Yes?'

'Well, we talked about many things. In the golf cart – I think it was on the way to the tenth tee – he talked about this new girl he had met. Said she was something special, but apparently keeping him at bay. He seemed kinda peeved and yet extremely interested in her. He told me he had a problem that night because he'd made a date to see this new girlfriend, but he'd forgotten that Marcia had invited him for dinner and, at the same time, an ex-girlfriend from Johannesburg had called him the day before and had wanted to stay over. That was his kinda life. Double-dating, even triple-dating chicks was run of mill for him.'

'Oh.' Rick could not think of anything to say.

'Of course I told him that kind of mix-up comes from crapping on your own doorstep.'

'And so what was the outcome?'

'The guy was up to his eyeballs in shit. He asked me, as a favour, to help him with an excuse for Marcia, to welcome the ex-girlfriend at the airport and take care of her for the evening. Must say, it was a pleasure. Beautiful woman. Took her out for dinner and felt real sad dropping her off at his house that night.'

'Who was she?'

'A girl called Melinda. Real nice.'

Melinda. Rick had difficulty speaking in a normal tone.

'I knew her once,' he heard himself say to Ferrara.

'Yeah, nice dame.'

He drained the last of the whiskey from the tumbler. He now knew he had to follow this up.

'Mr Ferrara, could I possibly meet you somewhere?'

'Hey sure. Say ten tomorrow, here at my office? Y'all have the address?'

'Yes,' Rick said, glancing at the address next to Ferrara's number in John's telephone list. 'I look forward to seeing you then. Thanks.'

'You're welcome. By the way, you'll probably also go to AfriBelgo's office tomorrow, won't you?'

'Probably. Why?'

'John asked me for some research material, which we put together for him. You might care to pick it up from me and take it over to AfriBelgo if you see them after me.'

With the telephone back on its cradle, Rick sat back and contemplated his next step. He had to set up the rest of his appointments with AfriBelgo and Sternson for the following day. He needed to arrange transport and didn't want a stranger driving him around. John had to have owned a car.

Sitting in the garage was a shiny red, convertible Ford Mustang.

Rick found the keys in the kitchen.

The interior of the car still smelled new. Moving in behind the steering wheel, into the seat that John had occupied, he had a strange sensation – as if John's body were taking over his. He looked at the mileage. Not even a hundred miles. It was a brand new 1994 model

With the top down, he drove off down Dolly Madison Boulevard. His winding route took him through a shaded, green tunnel of forest and undergrowth that ended at an arched bridge, spanning a rocky river-bed, which, Rick surmised, had to be the Potomac. Parallel to the river ran a canal on which a flat-bottomed boat drifted lazily. with a seated woman and a man wearing a straw hat. The traffic had come to a standstill and Rick had time to look at the couple on the water. In line with them, and at the edge of the road, Rick noticed a plant had sprouted from the bare cement through a crack at the top of a safety wall. Where no life could be expected, life was rooted in the most barren of places.

Referring to a map he had found in the car, he drove through Georgetown and found his way back to Dolly Madison Boulevard.

When he arrived back at the house, he noticed a white Oldsmobile Cutlass parked in the driveway. And then he spotted that the lock box was unlocked and off the front door.

Probably the real estate agent. He squeezed the Ford Mustang past the Oldsmobile, opened the garage door and drove in.

The automatic door rattled closed behind him and he walked through the inter-leading door into the house.

'Hello!' Rick listened for a response. 'Anybody here?' he tried again.

The silence was broken by a barely audible soft clicking sound. From the front door. It had to be the sound of the lock box closing outside. Someone had been in the house and had left through the front door. And had not responded to his calls.

He ran back through the inter-leading door into the garage and pressed the control button on the wall, waiting for the automatic garage door as it slowly rattled open.

The driveway was empty. No sign of the Oldsmobile.

He ran outside. From the driveway he could see the lock box was back in place on the front door. He waded through the long grass of the un-mowed lawn to the front door and tested the lock box, which was in place. The door was definitely locked again.

The person had entered with obvious knowledge of the lock box code and the person had fled.

According to Jerry Cohen, a certain realtor was the only person supposed to have the combination. He would have to trace that person through Cohen.

The moment he walked into the study towards the telephone to call Cohen, Rick knew a woman had been in the house. In the African bush his sense of smell had been honed through many years of tracking. The previous bland mustiness of the study now carried an almost-imperceptible trace of perfume. It hung tantalisingly in the air. Discreet. Inviting. An unseen track.

Jerry Cohen had been at the point of leaving for home when Rick reached him on the telephone.

'The realtor? Rita Shannon of Lucas and Love Realtors', and he gave Rick her details.

They also confirmed the following day's meeting at Sternson's office to discuss the winding-up of John's estate. He told Cohen he would find his own way to the office.

After some difficulty, Rick traced Rita Shannon in her car on one of the new cellular mobile telephones that had become a world craze of late. She was also on her way home but not too far away to take a detour and come and see him in a few minutes.

He had barely unpacked his luggage and made room for his clothes in John's wardrobe when the front doorbell rang. By the time he was downstairs, Rita Shannon had already opened the door and stood in the doorway with the lock box in her hand, waiting for him.

Rick offered her a seat on the burgundy leather couch. Well-dressed and well-manicured, she was somewhere in her early fifties, plump and friendly.

'I'm sorry to bother you,' he started.

'Not at all,' she said with a sales-lady smile. 'Mister Sternson himself told me you were coming and I hoped to meet you some time. On his recommendation, I have already started to test the market, but I have to know whether you indeed wish to sell the house.'

'At what price do you think the house will sell?' Don't rush her. Keep to the small talk, Rick.

'A house like this? You've got a nine-foot ceiling here at the entrance, crown mouldings, inlaid marble, good construction, this living room with a fire-place, the family room with a fire-place, a gourmet type kitchen and so on. I would say between seven and eight hundred thousand. Pity about your upstairs arrangement and the small garage. Otherwise you could get more.'

'I think I'll sell.'

Rick was impatient to get the business talk out of the way.

'All right then, sir. I'll run an ad in the *Washington Post* as well as the local *McLean Providence Journal*. If you're amenable to an open house, we can do that next Sunday. I'll send out some open house invitation cards. Of course the garden needs a little tending. If you want to, I could arrange that.' She made a note in her pocket diary.

'Do whatever needs to be done,' Rick instructed. 'I actually wanted to ask you something else. Were you here this afternoon?'

'No, I was doing an open house in Langley.'

'Oh.'

'Why do you ask?'

'Just that someone had the code to your lock box, opened it and entered the house.'

'Impossible!' Her vehemence surprised Rick. 'Mr Land, it's my personal lock box. I'm the only one with the code. I don't know whether you saw the box has a five-number code lock.'

'Maybe someone from your office could have had the code?'

'No. Impossible. We're very strict on security.'

'Someone was here.'

'Is anything missing from the house?'

'I haven't really looked yet.'

'I'm truly sorry, but at Lucas and Love we're very careful on these matters. You do understand, don't you? Of course I will change the lock box, even tonight still.'

'Don't bother. There's no rush. I just know there was a woman in here earlier today and that she had access to your code.'

Rita Shannon sat back on the couch, her eyes narrowed. 'A woman? Yes, it could have been her.' Her voice was distant.

'What do you mean?'

'Mr Land, this morning a woman came into our offices and asked to speak to me. She said she was interested in becoming a real estate associate herself. She told me she had seen our Lucas and Love 'For Sale' sign up on the front lawn here at your house. She wanted to know how she could become involved in selling a house like this one. I told her she had to be sponsored by a broker first, which we could arrange, that she would have to undergo the normal training programme and write the Northern Virginia Board exams. She asked me how long that would take. I told her my guess would be at least six weeks. I must tell you, this girl was very interested – she asked me a barrage of questions on licensing and dues and techniques and so on. Funny thing was, she asked me to take this house as an example – call it a case study, if you will – and run through the basic chronological order until the final sale and financing.'

'And you did that.'

'She had such an honest face. She had a strange accent but she looked honest.'

'What kind of accent?'

'I don't really know. Slight American tone with maybe a touch of Europe in it. I called up the computer program and we both worked through the factors relating to this house as they appeared on the screen. And now,' Rita Shannon seemed embarrassed, 'now I must confess, the code for the box was an element on the program. Naturally, I never pointed the code out to her, but the numbers were there when I showed her how a lock box works. She came across as a very friendly and intelligent woman. She could have easily memorised the numbers there and then.'

'Who was she?'

'Sir, to be honest, I'm not so sure anymore. She introduced herself as Lida somebody and said she would call me again, so I didn't bother to take down her details. She had such an open face. Attractive, blonde, and plainly highly educated.'

'Did she drive a white car?'

'I don't know. I only saw her in my office. I'm truly sorry for all of this.'

'Don't be concerned. Let's just keep this incident between the two of us. Nothing seems to have disappeared and there's no need to upset anybody.'

'Oh thank you, sir. To compensate, I will personally carry the cost of putting the house on our local homefinders' television channel.'

Jetlag and the time difference between Europe and America had taken a firm grip on Rick's body. His relief probably matched Rita Shannon's when she excused herself and left.

Author's note: I found it almost as strange as the link to the ruins of the erstwhile South African ammunitions factory that John lived in a house close to the CIA headquarters. Does subterfuge attract subterfuge? I was able to describe John's house in detail thanks to information from his office and a little brainwave when, during my own American stint, I took off some time to pose as a health inspector and walked through the house with the current owner. That is what we do in my business. We are actors. We just do not get Oscars. Not even the CIA's Tony Mendez got it for his role in what became the film *Argo*.

CHAPTER 10

Что напи́сано перо́м - не вы́рубить топоро́м.
(What was written by a pen cannot be erased by an axe.)

—Russian saying

IN A COLD SWEAT AND with a jerk of his neck, Rick woke up. In overwhelming darkness.

Disorientated, he searched for a spark of light, his eyes still heavy with sleep. Gradually his thoughts caught up with his body. Where am I? Ah, John's bed. The drawn bedroom blinds had pulled a vacuum of total darkness around him.

Lifting his head from the pillow, he fumbled in the pitch-blackness until he found the reassurance of the bedside lamp switch. He pushed the button and flooded the bedroom with light.

He blinked in the sudden brightness. A glance at his watch. Half past three in the morning. His body clock was set to daylight time on the other side of the Atlantic, which meant there was no way he could sleep anymore. His mind was already racing.

Coffee. He needed a good cup of coffee.

In John's bathrobe, he found his way around the kitchen. Well rested now, his mind was clear. A thought struck him. If John had felt threatened, as Melinda had said, he surely would have armed himself. Every Tom, Dick and Uncle Sam in the USA owns a gun. Somewhere in the house John might have kept a gun. But where? Logically, Rick reasoned John would have kept a weapon in the bedroom, within easy reach at night. Somewhere near the bedside light, possibly.

Steaming coffee mug in hand, Rick returned to the bedroom. He did not have to search too long. He found it lying in the top drawer of the wardrobe. His brother had been almost uncharacteristically careless in not bothering to put it in a safe.

A Smith and Wesson model 60 gleamed at him. How had John managed to acquire this police-type weapon? Snub-nosed, with a five-shot swing-out cylinder, it was a refined, modern revolver, suitable for concealed wear. Hardly an average gun.

Rick found a cardboard box with bullets and a holster. Without even touching the revolver, Rick closed the drawer. The discovery of the gun made his thoughts race further. Where would John have kept his personal correspondence? Again, logic dictated a search downstairs in the study.

But his search produced little of interest: stationery, a few old statements and invoices, a calculator, stamps, a few business cards and an empty waste-paper basket.

Reclining in the swivel chair, he surveyed the polished yew desk in front of him. There was not a loose scrap of paper to be seen. Everything had been arranged neatly, from the scribbling pad to the telephone and telephone list. Too neatly, he thought. There was even a slight smell of polish to the desktop. In fact, upon his arrival, in contrast with the untended garden, the whole house had been almost too clean, from the made-up bed to the kitchen and the study.

Of course! John had to have somebody to come in now and then to do the cleaning and possibly iron his clothes. Then Rick remembered the full refuse bags next to the car in the garage. Proof of a cleaner's work.

He brought in the two rancid-smelling bags and dumped them in the middle of the kitchen floor. Under the harsh glare of the neon light, he started a thorough search of their contents.

In the second bag he found bits and pieces that could have come from the waste paper basket in the study. He ironed out the crumpled bits of paper on the melamine kitchen top. John had been an obvious doodler, probably while talking on the telephone. Most scraps of paper had the signatures of a mind otherwise focused on scribblings, scratched drawings and patterns.

And then he found something. *New Orleans 8-8 Sonya/phone first.*

Cryptic words written on the back of a packet of Marlboro cigarettes. John had died on the eighth of August. The eighth day of the eighth month. It seemed someone called Sonya had something to do with the reason for his visit to New Orleans.

Who was Sonya?

Rick threw the empty cigarette box back into the refuse bag. He stared at the wall. And then he focused on a calendar in front of him displaying all the days of the year. He saw that the eighth day of August had been ringed in blue. A flight number had been written down on that day. He also noticed two similar rings on two other days in July. Had Sonya and John met a few times before?

He repacked everything into the smelly refuse bags, cleaned the floor as best he could and deposited the bags in the garage again.

Back inside, Rick grabbed the remote and switched on John's television.

Against the backdrop of orchestral music, Humphrey Bogart's voice filled the room as an old black-and-white film flickered onto the screen.

JACK FERRARA HAD FLARING, BLACK eyebrows that shot out over bourbon-drenched eyes. His face resembled that of a motorcyclist under the pressure of wind at high speed. In reality, Rick could see his face bore the ravages of years of exuberant partying.

'To be sure, as a golfer, your brother had his faults. Helluva hook. He darn well always struggled with it, but I can tell ya, in all other respects he was as hunky-dory straight as they come. That was John. I figure there's a little of that in most of us, the straight life with a hook here and a bent for the ladies there. Kinda makes us interestin'. To the gals.'

Ferrara grinned at the thought.

Rick smiled back, hoping they could now dispense with the pleasantries.

'Y'all play golf?'

'No. Never found the time or inclination, I suppose.'

Rick's negative answer seemed to leave Ferrara at a loss for words and Rick grasped the opportunity. 'But on another subject, I was quite interested to hear your account, yesterday, of John's problem with his clashing dates, and of how you helped out. That was just like him, wasn't it?'

'Man, he sure got into a heap of trouble with the broads every now and then. I was glad to be of assistance.' Ferrara laughed.

Rick decided to approach the issue circumspectly.

'You mentioned the names Marcia and Melinda yesterday. As I told you, I once knew Melinda and I heard Marcia's name mentioned by our chairman before I flew out, although I still have to meet her personally. So, aside from Melinda and Marcia, I was wondering whether I might not have known the third woman he talked to you about. Did he tell you who she was?'

'Yeah, he did, but I can't recall her name right now. Dunno. She could have been somebody called Sandy or such-like I think.'

'Sandy? Maybe Sonya?' Rick ventured, recalling the name on the back of a packet of cigarettes in a refuse bag.

'Oh yeah. Sho' nuff. That's it. Sonya. Y'all know her?'

'Very slightly.'

He had found his calendar girl; his heart began racing.

'Did John tell you what she looked like?'

'Hey, I kinda thought I heard y'all say ya know her. What's that all about then? Memory loss there?'

'Of course I know her,' Rick said quickly, covering his lie. His mind raced. 'It's just that I haven't seen her for a long time and wondered what she looked like these days. You know how women are.

They change the colour of their hair and their hairstyle on a whim.'

Ferrara nodded. Rick was not sure whether Ferrara believed him but he hoped he had passed the test.

'Nah. John didn't really tell me that much about her.'

They spoke for a while on the role of the Institute of Mining and 'John's input on the board', in Ferrara's words.

'The other thing I still wanted to tell y'all,' Ferrara said, 'was about the research stuff John asked us to do. Remember I mentioned it yesterday? Y'all said you'd pass it on to AfriBelgo for me.'

'Yes.'

Rick had forgotten about it. He had also forgotten to call for an appointment at AfriBelgo's office.

'Well, Rick, darn it, I can't seem to find it,' Ferrara said. 'It was here yesterday. Darn sure of that. I can only guess it must somehow have been mislaid. Tried my best to find it this morning but I found zilch. So thanks in any case for offering to be my courier but I'll pass it on tomorrow or so, as soon as I can trace it. Y'all know how it goes in an office like this sometimes: you work your sweet ass off just to get screwed by administrative slip-ups.'

'No problem. I even forgot to make my arrangements with AfriBelgo. Mind if I use your telephone to call them?'

Ferrara placed the call for Rick. Marcia answered and told him she had been waiting for his call the whole morning, knowing he had arrived the day before. Everything was fine and she looked forward to seeing him.

Ferrara walked with Rick to the office door.

'All the best with your work,' Rick said.

'Thanks. I just hope I can find this loused-up document on the Erfdeel matter.'

Ferrara had pronounced the word more like 'urfdeal'.

'Did you say Erfdeel?' Rick tried his best to conceal his interest.

'Why yeah. You pronounce it all funny like John did.'

Ferrara had a frown squeezed between his flaring eyebrows.

Rick could have kicked himself. How could he have forgotten the link that the journalist had found between Melinda, John, and the word Erfdeel? And how could he have forgotten that Melinda had told him Jack Ferrara had done certain research with John?

'I've heard about it, but what does Erfdeel mean?'

'It's a long story. I don't have all the details right now but, in a nutshell, it kinda concerns a mining scandal of many years ago. All back in Africa. John asked me for as much information as I could lay my hands on. We at the Institute have very skimpy information on the issue. Just brief references, footnotes, the likes. Nothing substantial, ya know. In the end, one of my people got the required information through the Library of Congress, up on the hill.'

'What kind of scandal was Erfdeel?'

Could Ferrara detect the thrill of discovery in his voice? Rick hoped he did not.

'A saltin' case. One of the classic ones in mining history.'

'Who was assaulted?'

'No man. It ain't got nothin' to do with assaultin'. It was all about saltin', like salt and pepper. In this case the saltin' of a borehole.'

Ferrara looked at Rick, seemingly surprised that Rick had no idea what he was talking of.

'Don't y'all know nothin' about saltin' of samples?'

'No ...' Rick confessed it a little self-consciously.

'Saltin's all about enhancing the values of mineral samples by adding extraneous stuff.'

This explanation still did not make much sense to Rick, who was at even more of a loss when Ferrara said, 'Erfdeel was a very famous court case in Africa. I still can't get my friggin' head around why John wanted us to beaver out the info. I mean, he coulda gone through his own channels.'

'It's a pity,' Rick said, 'I would love to learn more about Erfdeel.'

'I figure I could get ya a set of info.'

'I would appreciate that,' Rick said.

Ferrara walked back to his desk, picked up the telephone, spoke to someone and scribbled something on a piece of paper.

'This guy is quite knowledgeable in our field,' Ferrara said and handed Rick the paper.

Rick glanced at the note. Someone called Blackie Lawood at the Library of Congress knew more about Erfdeel.

Rick left the Institute, knowing he had finally found a broken twig. He was tracking in the right direction. Erfdeel had nothing to do with an inheritance, as he had thought originally. Erfdeel was a borehole scandal and it had bothered John. Erfdeel was most probably linked to John's death.

BRIAN STERNSON'S OFFICE SMELLED OF stale cigars, freshly renovated furniture and new money. His croaking voice suited his abrasive style.

'And sign here please.'

He slipped another document over the table for Rick's attention. Rick had been signing one document after another. He still could not see any reason for John's stipulation that he personally be in Washington to finalise matters. There was nothing special to any of the documents handed to him. In time, they could have been signed anywhere.

'This is the last one, Mr Land. It authorises you to collect your deceased brother's valuables, held in safe custody at Riggs.'

'Riggs?'

'Your brother's bank. If you want to, one of my people could accompany you there. Of course, we also need to take stock of those belongings. Maybe tomorrow?'

'Fine with me,' Rick agreed, thinking more of his need to go to the Library of Congress.

'I'll get Cohen to pick you up,' Sternson offered.

Rick had found it difficult to sign the papers related to John's assets, almost as if he had become an intruder. The only thing Rick enjoyed of his visit to Sternson was the welcome respite of the cool air-conditioning, despite the overwhelming cigar smell. He could not help feeling a little guilty, sitting across from Brian Sternson, accepting John's possessions, knowing he and John had been estranged for so long. Administrative affairs always bored Rick and his visit to Sternson had been uncomfortably administrative. So he was glad when he walked into the humidity at street level. He steered the Ford Mustang down K Street towards AfriBelgo's offices.

In this congested part of the city he noticed quite a number of cyclists on the streets, sweating through the traffic with special document pouches and mobile telephones strapped around their bodies. Dressed in light sports clothing with sleeveless T-shirts, they wove their bicycles through the lanes of cars, pedalling from one office to another, delivering documents faster than by any other mode of transport in the congested urban centre. The cyclists, with their protective headgear and pouches at their sides bulging with documents, reminded him of the messenger who had brought Piet Steen's note in the dust-dry African climate a few days before. Here, though, Piet Steen's messenger was far removed, lost in the past.

Subconsciously he must have built up an image of the normal actions of the cyclist couriers, pumping at their pedals with bulging leg muscles, sweating, weaving, rushing forward, then balancing like chameleons in a stationary position on two wheels, hanging low on the handlebars with bent backs and eyes glued to the road, waiting for the lights to change before they would pedal off again.

And so, it was his tracker's intuition that sensed an abnormal action outside the window on his left-hand side. Rick turned his head. Inches away, on the other side of the electric window, a gun's barrel was aimed at his head.

He absorbed the vision of the silencer, the finger on the trigger, the sweat on the hand holding the gun and behind that the grim expression in the face of the cyclist. And in that instant he knew he was facing a professional messenger of death.

His adrenaline welled up and erupted involuntarily.

He gripped the door handle, whipped open the door and, using the weight of his body to knock the door against the gunman, sent the man sprawling. He heard the puffing sound of the bullet, whizzing harmlessly from the silencer into the air over the Ford Mustang. He scrambled out towards the man who was now lying underneath his bicycle, struggling to get up.

Unlike the other fit-looking, lean and muscled cyclists, this cyclist was almost stout, with fleshy arms protruding from a too-tight sleeveless T-shirt. The other couriers were tanned from days of sunlit commuting; this man, although dressed similarly, was a sickly bleached-white colour.

Rick lunged for his attacker who, with one leg pinned underneath the bicycle, somehow managed to kick the bicycle from the road, the front wheel rammed into Rick's crotch. Rick fell back against the car door. His assailant got up. Half-stunned, Rick watched as the bulky killer aimed the gun at him again. Another bullet whiffed from the silencer, dangerously close past his head. Rick dropped to the ground and rolled over repeatedly, moving away as quickly as he could, feeling the sting of fractured stones and hot bits of tar blasting against his body as more shots kicked into the road around him.

He heard the screams of bystanders as he managed to roll away around the back of the car. Inches away from him tyres screeched to a stop. With the smell of burnt rubber in his nostrils he jumped up from behind the Ford Mustang in time to see the other man running towards a vehicle that had, a moment before, braked to a noisy standstill. Someone was holding open the rear door for the assailant. Without thinking, Rick ran after the car.

'Come on! Hurry up!' Rick heard from inside.

Rick's assailant was on the verge of diving into the car when, running at full tilt, Rick managed to get hold of the back of the man's sleeveless T-shirt. Another man on the back seat held the assailant by a wrist. Rick pulled at the T-shirt from behind, going down towards the tarred surface and the man went with him. As they fell to the road,

Rick noticed the man's handgun slipping and being caught by the man inside. Pinning the sweat-smeared slippery man down on the hot road, Rick heard the car accelerating away.

With the back of his head, the man butted Rick between the eyes. Dazed by the blow, Rick had a sickly sweet smell of creamy hair lotion in his nostrils and a vision of the man running away.

Rick got up and steadied himself. The man was about twenty yards away already, running down a service road parallel to K Street.

Still dizzy and with a painful numbness between his legs, Rick forced himself to pursue him. Rick's boots were heavy and slowed him down. For his bulk the man in front was fit and faster than Rick had anticipated. The man ran past shocked bystanders aiming for the imposing entrance of the Capital Hilton, where, under a starry daytime ceiling of lights, a cab driver was taking baggage out of the back of his vehicle. Rick saw the podgy figure jumping over a flower box, situated between the road and the entrance. He ran past the taxi driver into the hotel.

Rick followed, skipped over the flower box and pushed past two ladies coming out of the front door.

'What a rude man!' he heard behind him.

Inside the hotel a large number of men in dark suits milled around the foyer. Piped music and the murmur of many voices filled the lobby. Rick ran past a cluster of men, barely avoiding ripping into a large banner of the annual convention of the International Fertilizer Association.

He looked around. Pillars of blood-red polished wood swooped up from the floor to the ceiling, tapering off to the top to create an illusion of greater height. His assailant had disappeared into the crowd. Rick stood on his toes to look out over the ocean of heads.

The man had eluded him; there was no need to rush any more. He ambled around, searching through the clusters of men, peering around the columns, glancing to see if anybody stood behind the huge pot plants in the corners, avoiding the glass-topped coffee tables beside comfortable high-backed couches and stopping to inspect an open-bar area, filled to the brim with people in animated discussion. Not the kind of place for a man in a sleeveless T-shirt to hang around unnoticed.

At the back of the lobby, a corridor led to a hairdressing salon and the toilets. Rick scanned the length of the corridor where an old shoeshine man perched on his stool.

He walked towards the old man. 'Excuse me, I'm looking for somebody.'

'I'm also lookin' for somebody – someone who'd like to have his shoes done up like reflectors, man.' The old man's face cracked into a smile.

'You haven't seen a man in a white T-shirt, have you?' Rick tried again.

'Yeah, I seen a man lookin' like a trucker. Thought he was gonna do the fertilizer conference thing and crap in his pants, if ya get mah drift. Hee hee. Gotta tell you, man, this dude ran into the john like he was actin' in one o' them TV ads for a laxative.' He pointed towards the toilet door, giggling to himself again.

'Thanks.' Rick moved towards the door, his heart pounding.

'You're welcome,' he heard the old shoeshine man behind him.

He pushed open the door and caught the normal antiseptic smell. There was nobody at the urinals, divided by marble slabs. In the reflection of the wall mirror, he saw three cubicle doors, two of which were open. Only one cubicle door was shut, although the engaged sign was not on. He had found the man's hiding place.

Two facts were clear: firstly, the man was behind the closed door and, secondly, the man was – hopefully – now unarmed after having dropped his gun in the getaway car.

Rick slowly approached the closed door. He pushed at it. The door flew open.

Screaming, the man burst out, holding a large object between the crook of his elbow and his right hand. Rick saw the heavy lid of a toilet cistern coming down on him. He sidestepped the blow and the lid came crashing onto the washbasin slab behind him, chipping off at the edge. With surprising agility, the man snatched an object from the floor. Sneering at Rick, he now held the jagged piece of ceramic, broken into a knife-edge, in his hands.

'I'm gonna cut you down to size, Mister Africa,' he said, a slight lisp drifting from his curled lips. The sharp edge was aimed menacingly at Rick.

'Who the hell are you?' Rick's eyes swept the room for something to defend himself with but found nothing.

The man swung at him.

Rick had to swerve so much he slipped and fell to the floor. Now on the smooth marble floor, he anticipated the next action as the man thrust down towards him again. Rick kicked against the wall and slid on his back to the other side of the room. The ceramic broke on the marble where he had just been. He jumped up, his back to the entrance door now. The odds were more even now as they faced each other with only their bare hands. In the cold neon illumination the man glistened with sweat.

Rick feinted a kick towards the man's groin, to which his adversary reacted defensively. This allowed Rick the time and room for manoeuvre to aim a fist at the other man's face. Rick felt his knuckles kneading into the soft flesh of the other's cheek. The man staggered back, affording Rick the opportunity to grab him by his unevenly cut, flaxen-bleached hair. Rick pulled down the man's head, at the same time jerking up his knee into the sweaty face.

The man looked up at Rick, his smirk now replaced by a glassy look in his eyes. Rick now had the upper hand over his assailant. But then the door to the corridor opened behind him, pushing him off balance.

As Rick stumbled forward over the sprawling man, he heard an astonished voice from behind: 'Pardon me.'

The distraction gave his assailant just enough time to get up and launch a counter-attack. He rushed into Rick with a flurry of punches to the stomach, leaving Rick gasping for air. Rick saw the man's head coming towards the bridge of his nose. The man grunted in Rick's face as the blow fell.

THANK GOD YOU'RE ALL RIGHT. What happened to you?'

It was the same voice Rick had heard behind him when the door had opened and pushed him forward. He looked up into a white, plastic nametag dangling over his face and realised he was lying on the floor of the men's washroom in the Hilton.

'How are you doing? Should I call for medical attention?' the voice behind the plastic nametag tried again.

'No, thanks. I'm fine, I think,' Rick said. He sat upright. His mouth tasted as if he had swallowed a bag of salt. 'What happened to the other guy?'

'He pushed me up against the wall and ran out. Did he take your money?'

'Who?' Rick responded still feeling dizzy.

'The mugger.'

'Oh. No, I don't think so.'

Rick stood up and walked to the basin, gently touching the bruised area between his forehead and his nose. Blood trickled from the corner of his mouth. He ran cold water into the basin, rinsed his mouth, dabbed his face, and dried it with a clutch of paper tissues from the built-in receptacle.

'It's grossly unbelievable, I'd say, to think that you can be mugged here. What's the world coming to?'

'Yes, I guess so.'

Rick felt better now.

'Shouldn't we report it to the management?'

'If you want to, be my guest, but I'm not sure it'll serve any purpose really. I'm honestly okay, thank you for all your help.'

The man shrugged and walked away.

Alone, Rick again inspected his bruise in the mirror and noticed that his shirt had been torn. He combed his hair with his fingers.

Arriving back at his car a few minutes later, weary and sore, he was not surprised to see a policeman standing guard.

The bicycle was nowhere to be seen and the Ford Mustang had been moved out of the traffic into a parking space.

'Hi there!' a man standing next to the policeman called out. 'Officer, this is the driver,' the man continued, 'I saw the whole thing. The guy on the bike tried to get at him, but he put up a pretty good fight, you bet.'

'Are you the owner of this automobile, sir?' the policeman asked.

'No, but I'm driving around with approval,' Rick said, not interested in getting too involved in the details of John's death.

It turned out the bicycle had already been removed as evidence. Rick had to report for a briefing at a later stage.

Rick got into the car. Sweat dripped from the tip of his nose. He brushed away the moistness from his forehead and drew his fingers through his wet hair. The cool air from the air-conditioning soothed the bruise on his forehead but also served to increase his awareness of the throbbing headache he had developed. And his crotch did not feel too well either.

Who had tried to shoot him and why? His assailant knew exactly who he was and where to find him. Rick reasoned with himself that there could have been only two alternatives: either someone had followed him from John's house, or someone had known his movements beforehand, in which case they had to have been tipped off. But who would have tipped them off? The realtor? Ferrara? Someone from Sternson? He parked in front of AfriBelgo's office, walking briskly up the flight of stairs to the second floor. He could still feel the throbbing pain of the bruise on his forehead and a numb semi-paralysis between his legs.

The plainness of AfriBelgo's office surprised him. It had none of the luxury and extravagance of the Johannesburg head office with its gold bar building. The AfriBelgo office in Washington DC was functionally unpretentious, small and characterless. From the dry walling partition, a framed photograph of a much younger Erick Martens smiled down on the uncomfortable tubular chair on which Rick sat.

The moment he saw Marcia, he understood Jack Ferrara's view that her face compensated for her legs.

'I'm so glad to meet you, Rick.'

She smiled at him, her pouting lips moving enticingly.

'But what's wrong with you? You look like as if you've been run over by a bus.'

'Almost. On my way over here, a man tried to shoot me.'

'Come on, you're not serious. How did that happen?'

'Not important. These things happen everywhere in the world, Marcia. Forget about it. It was just a mugger,' he lied. There was no need to broadcast his problems too widely.

'Your brother was shot and your ex-wife died violently. No muggers there. What happened exactly?'

'Nothing. A guy on a bike aimed a gun at me and tried to take my money. Just a have-not wanting a have.'

'Why you?'

'Why me?'

'Oh Lord, you sound like Kris Kristoffersen. Yes, why you?'

'I don't know.'

'You go for a walk and some stranger shoots at you?'

'I was in John's car.'

'Now you've got me really concerned.'

'Forget it. I've already put it out of my mind.'

'Did you report it to the cops?'

'They were there.'

'At least you are in one piece. Come. We'll talk in John's office.'

She said it as if John were still alive, her breath borne on a wafting mixture of cigarettes and perfume.

'Coffee or tea?' she asked.

'If you could organise me a glass of water and one or two headache tablets I would appreciate it.'

'Have a seat in the meantime,' she said and waved him through an office door.

In contrast with the bland reception area, John's office had a warm atmosphere, built up by the effective combination of old-world wood panelling and bookcases, modern paintings, exquisite oriental carpeting and the rich look of leather. Rick eased his tired body into one of the two leather couches. For a moment he felt slightly dizzy. The last AfriBelgo Annual Report lay on the coffee table in front of him next to a miniature scale model in bronze of a gold-mine shaft's headgear.

'John often spoke of you,' Marcia said as she came in with two tablets in the outstretched palm of her hand and a glass of water topped with ice. That's America for you, Rick reflected, you even take your medicine on the rocks. He gulped down the tablets.

'John had great respect for you.'

'He did, did he?'

Rick realised he was responding like an idiot. He smothered his parrot-like response with a sip of water.

Marcia sat down on the other couch opposite him. She brought a slim-looking cigarette to her lips, took the scale model of a mine's headgear from the coffee table and flipped open its lid to produce a flickering flame.

Rick smothered a sigh. Did these people never stop sucking smoke?

From behind billowing puffs of smoke around the flame of the cigarette lighter she spoke joltingly.

'I can see,' she said, and stopped to inhale, 'that you're John's brother.'

She clicked the scale model closed and touched her nostril.

'There's a similarity here, around the eyes.' She played a painted fingernail around one of her eyes, squinting at him through wisps of smoke.

'I'm not sure, Marcia. I never thought we had much of a physical resemblance.'

'Mm. You definitely have. Also around the mouth. You even sound alike.'

She seemed pensive and Rick thought he detected a quivering sadness hidden behind her eyelids.

'You worked closely with him, didn't you?' Rick could have kicked himself. His words sounded hollow and stupid. Of course she'd worked closely with John. But he felt uncomfortable with Marcia – almost as if she were John's widow.

'Rick, I didn't just work for him and ... he wasn't just my boss. I loved him deeply in a way I will never ever love anyone again.'

She leaned back against the smooth leather of the couch, her head thrown back, her eyes closed.

'I really loved John Land, warts, faults and all. And I think he loved me, in his way.'

She leaned forward and put her head in her hands for while, then wiped her eyes and sat upright, red-faced with mascara smudges.

'He loved me.'

She said it as if to reassure herself.

'John was a good man,' she said and rubbed her nose.

He could not think of anything else to say. Somehow the dead always ended up good, even if they were not good before their death.

Rick leaned over and took her hand.

'Marcia, it's all over now and there's nothing we can do about it.'

She seemed not to have heard him. She tilted her head back against the couch once again, closed her eyes and drew at her cigarette.

'Rick, he told me about his affair with your wife. He told me everything about how he had been involved in the break-up of your marriage. I'm really sorry about her death.'

'It was shocking.'

'Head office faxed us the news cuttings. Somehow it didn't make sense and somehow it did,' she said and crossed her legs.

'What do you mean by that?'

'I mean, John's death was senseless and Melinda's too. But, on the other hand, John and Melinda had been involved with each other and she came out here the other day. He tried to keep her arrival a secret, but I found out. That's when he told me of how bad he felt at having torpedoed your marriage – sorry, torpedo sounds a little crude, war-like I suppose – but he felt like that and said that, since that day, he and Melinda had parted to become platonic friends. Even before her arrival I knew something was brewing. Maybe their deaths tie up.'

'What do you mean by that?'

'Well, he started acting very strangely a while ago.' She pushed out her jaw.

'How?'

'Out of the blue, he became aloof. We used to have a wonderful, warm relationship but, about three weeks before Melinda's arrival, John became distant. To me, that is. But I knew it was a woman from the way he acted. I thought my feeling was confirmed when Melinda called to discuss her plans. John was out and so she gave me the message.'

'What message?'

'Her flight details and arrival time to be picked up at the airport.'

'And so, at that moment, you thought he and Melinda still had something going?'

'I did until he told me emphatically that there was nothing romantic between them. He didn't expand on it. He just said I should believe him. Which I did. That's love for you. Unquestioning trust. She came out here and, to be honest, just by looking at how they reacted to each other, I could see that John had not been lying. The three of us even went out for dinner. On more than one occasion he told me of how conscience-stricken he felt about his role in your marriage break-up and that he could never again feel any passion for Melinda. Rick, the man felt extremely guilty and, although I think he never expected forgiveness, he had never meant to harm you.'

Rick pursed his lips and nodded his head. Living in John's house and driving his car had blunted the negative feelings of the past. All he now wanted to do was find out what had happened and why.

'Rick,' she interrupted his thoughts, 'he always had a very high regard for you, but he was also too proud, obstinate and free-spirited to set it straight with you. I wish you could understand that.'

'It's all over now and they are both gone. Let's rather try to find out who killed him or maybe both of them.'

'I hope it'll be possible to find the bastard or bastards. I'll help you where I can.' Her brown eyes seemed to twinkle with a strengthened determination.

Rick knew he was looking not just at a pitifully bereaved woman, but at the essence of calculated female fury. Maybe he had an ally in Marcia – someone to help him unravel the thread. For a moment he wanted to tell her of his intention to follow the trail to the end, but, examining her obvious bereavement, he curbed himself. If a stranger had the urge to gun him down on a sunlit street on his first day in DC, there was no need to draw her in too deeply. Melinda had been connected to both him and John and look what had happened to her. The less Marcia knew of his intentions, the better.

'I think you should be careful in helping me find the answers. Proximity to John and me seems to be dangerous. Well, it was for Melinda.'

She listened to him with closed eyes, resting her head on the back of the couch.

'Can you think of anything that could explain why anyone would have wanted to kill him?'

'I'm not sure. Maybe,' she answered through clenched teeth in exhaled bursts of cigarette smoke, her eyes still closed, the cigarette with its red, lipstick-smeared butt resting between manicured fingers next to her cheek. Then, with the other hand, she picked her nose.

'Did you know of any specific problems John might have had?'

She was quiet for a few seconds before she replied.

'Not really. He had the normal intricacies of business situations and things like that.'

'Why did Melinda come to Washington?' he asked in another effort to find the link between John and Melinda.

'She was on vacation and spent two nights in DC.'

'Marcia, Dr Martens told me that, in your opinion, a woman was connected to John's death in New Orleans. If there was no real romantic involvement between John and Melinda anymore, was there another woman in his life?'

She hesitated for a moment. 'I think so. As I said, before Melinda's arrival, he became secretive. There was something else, I believe. When he flew down to New Orleans, he told me he had a meeting planned for that afternoon. My deduction was that it had nothing to do with business. He stayed at the Holiday Inn on Royal Street in the French Quarter. The next morning I heard he had been shot a few blocks away.'

'Do you know anything about something called Erfdeel?'

'Erfdeel? No, why?'

As an American, she had been working with African business for such a long time she was able to let the word roll off her tongue in the correct pronunciation, even managing to roll the r.

'It sounds foreign, African maybe, to me. What is it?'

She killed her cigarette in the ashtray on the coffee table.

'I'm not sure myself.' Rick suddenly felt uncomfortable – for no apparent reason.

'I did all his filing I knew his filing system better than he did and I never saw anything like that,' she said, her eyes fixed on him.

'Marcia, do you know about the illicit ivory I tracked down a while ago?'

'Vaguely. John showed me an article once. In *Newsweek*, or was it *Time*?'

'It occurred to me that the poaching syndicate, whose network I had uncovered, could be connected with this. And if I think of the guy who attacked me in the street, someone who referred to me as a man from Africa, I am convinced there could be a link.'

Rick now regretted letting slip he had not merely been mugged; he had to remind himself not to draw innocent people into the vortex.

'I was only wondering whether there couldn't be a connection between the ivory poaching and John's death,' he said.

Marcia pushed her lower lip under her upper. With a smack of her lips she spoke.

'You know, now that you mention it,' and she touched her nostril again, 'I accompanied John to a cocktail reception hosted a while ago by the South African Ambassador to coincide with the annual conference of the Safari Club International hunting organisation. I think John went there to see if he could meet anybody who knew you and to maybe make contact indirectly with you. It was the normal do with lots of talk, drenched in bourbon and Cape wines. Many hunters in suits and ties talking of hunting wild boar in Mongolia and mountain goat in unpronounceable countries. I didn't find the conversation that interesting. Afterwards, when we drove away, I noticed John was unusually quiet. He seemed worried and when I asked him about it, he said he had heard something disturbing.'

Rick nodded for her to continue.

'Now that I think back on it, couldn't people in illicit ivory also be members of Safari Club International? It would be one way of keeping an eye on their business, sort of from a different angle.'

He had to agree with her reasoning and made a mental note that he still had to call Alec Post and Randy Zellmer. Why was he so absent minded? He could not even remember where he put the contact list Faber had given him at the Wildlife Society.

Anxious now to terminate the conversation and get to the Library of Congress, Rick opened the flap of his watch and glanced at the time.

'I should get going, Marcia. Thank you for everything.'

As she was walking him out, Rick, in an attempt to call his mind to order, asked, 'Who do you think will take over from John, here at

AfriBelgo?'

'Oh, haven't you heard?' Marcia stopped and looked at him. 'It's Mark Aardt. Two days after John's death, a fax came in with the appointment. I'm knee-deep in the arrangements for his posting here. He's on his way tomorrow.'

Author's note: I do not understand John's interest in his secretary. She might be curvaceous and have a lovely face but I do not like girls who pick their noses. She did, all the time I spoke to her. It is up there with halitosis.

CHAPTER 11

Die prys van vrede is vooruitbetaalbaar, dié van twis agterna.
(The price of peace is an advance payment,
the price of dispute is a deferred payment.)

–C.J. Langenhoven

RICK LOOKED AROUND HIM AT the elegant expanse of concentric oak reading-tables, each with its own reading light. He was standing in one of modern civilisation's grand temples of learning – the Main Reading Room of the Thomas Jefferson Building, the breath-taking heart of the Library of Congress, just beyond the south shoulder of the Capitol. Here and there people sat with bowed heads at reading tables, diminutive against the grandeur of the room. His eyes glided upwards, past the marble columns, galleries and statues to the sunlit windows. High above him, a huge dome capped this vault of ornate American Renaissance architecture. He flipped noisily through a pamphlet, lying on the reception desk, and whistled in amazement.

'Quiet!' the woman with the jowls hissed. 'This is a study area.'

'Sorry,' he whispered, 'it's just that this place is massive. I was just reading here that you've got a hundred million items stashed away on—'

'Yeah. Now shut up.'

Rick glanced at the figures in the brochure. There were five hundred and thirty-two miles of shelving, spread over sixty-five acres of office space.

'Wow.'

The woman glared at him for an instant and returned to her magazine.

A pencil tapped on the pamphlet and he looked up. It was the librarian he'd asked about Blackie Lawood.

'Mr Lawood's over at the African Section. It's in the John Adams Building, next door,' the prim-and-proper girl informed him, 'but you actually have to go back out into the street to enter that building It just so happens that I need to go over there myself and we have a direct connection. You may come with me. Just put on this dogtag first.'

She handed him a visitor's identification tag.

She strode out ahead of him and he had to stretch his legs to catch up with her.

'You a researcher?' she asked, glancing sideways at him.

'Yes, but probably not the most serious of researchers.'

'Well, you look pretty serious to me, unlike some of the less serious weirdoes we have to deal with at times.'

'Weirdoes?'

'Yeah,' she said and slowed down her stride. 'One guy hovered over a computer terminal for hours trying to contact China.'

'You're not serious.'

'Of course I am. You won't believe it but there was a woman a while ago who claimed to be the Official Tooth Fairy of the United States. Even a woman who called herself the Bride of Christ. She spent weeks going through the telephone books of various cities, writing down the names of people whose souls had been saved or had to be saved. Not sure what she intended to do with that.'

Walking beside her in the underground corridor to the John Adams Building, he wondered whether there was any real difference between himself and the strange people she had talked about. Was he not like the Tooth Fairy, attempting to give his brother a sweetener as compensation for the suffering of his untimely death? Were his attempts at finding the truth not as futile as trying to contact China on a library computer terminal? Trying to find whoever killed John was probably akin to locating a saved soul from a telephone.

'Is this your first visit to the Library of Congress?' she asked as they arrived at the African Section.

'Yes.'

'It's an empire where the sun never sets, or rises. We've got conveyor belts and roller tracks that ferry books from building to building, floor to floor, desk to desk, and person to person.'

'Difficult to imagine.'

'You know what they say about imagination, don't you? They say memory and imagination go together. How can you have an imagination if you don't have a memory?'

'That's true.'

'Well, this place is the world's largest memory bank and, for that matter, a wonderful source of imagination,' she said.

'A good place for the Official Tooth Fairy then.'

'You bet,' she said with a flickering smile.

Blackie Lawood was white, not black. But the palm cushion of his outstretched right hand had a red hue, a tell-tale sign of the liver complications often suffered by alcoholics. His office smelled of fresh peppermint and air freshener. His desk was tidy. Rick noticed a pile of papers held firmly in place by a Zimbabwe bird, carved in green soapstone. Posters of Morocco and Kilimanjaro adorned the walls.

'Kilimanjaro is such an experience,' Rick said as he sat down.

'Heck, I've never been to Africa but I sure as hell would like to go there one day.'

Lawood swivelled his chair to follow Rick's gaze.

'That mountain is a real beaut. And it is as if that herd of giraffe posed for the camera on purpose against the snow-capped backdrop. Amazing to think that, even though that mountain is almost on the equator, it's covered in snow at the peak.'

'Mister Lawood,' Rick thought aloud, 'back in Africa, we have a saying that the highest trees catch the coldest winds. Of course, it really has more to do with people in high places than …'

'No mister there, please. Just call me Blackie.'

'Okay, Blackie.'

'I knew from your accent you were from somewhere else. So you live out there in Africa. No wonder you were looking at Kilimanjaro. Is that what brings you to the African Section here at the salt mine?'

'I guess you could say salt mines in a way. Jack Ferrara referred me to you.'

'Oh yeah,' it dawned on Lawood. 'I helped those guys at the International Institute of Mining with a request a while ago. Now, what was it again?' He screwed up his face and seemed even ruddier than before.

'Maybe to do with Erfdeel?'

'Yeah, that's it. Not the kind of stuff drifting around in the Library's computerised catalogue. I finally got some helpful copies of old newspaper clippings from a correspondent.'

'Well, Blackie, the material you sent to them has been lost or mislaid, it seems. Did you make photocopies or keep the originals?'

'Yeah, the stuff should be on file.'

'May I have a look at it?'

Lawood got up, opened a drawer of a steel filing cabinet, retrieved a file and paged through it.

'Here.'

He handed Rick the open file. 'There are a number of pages in here with the full picture. I guess I'll leave you to it then, if that's okay. You may sit here and read. I'll be out for a few minutes.'

'Thank you.'

Disregarding the short covering letter from Blackie Lawood to the International Institute of Mining, Rick concentrated on the more interesting enclosures, which consisted of a few photocopies of pages from the Johannesburg newspaper *The Star*. Strange how that paper crops up all the time, he thought.

The Star Friday June 3 1949
EXTRAORDINARILY RICH GOLD STRIKE ANNOUNCED
IN FREE STATE

CHECKED ASSAY GIVES 56,105 INCH-DWT BOREHOLE
RESULT ON FARM BETWEEN HENNENMAN AND
WELKOM
EXCITED DEALINGS ON RAND AND IN LONDON

An extraordinarily rich borehole result is announced today in the
Free State on the farm Erfdeel, between Hennenman and Welkom
Townships.

Rick read that Joseph Milne, managing director of Union Free
State Mining and Finance, had described the laboratory assay as world
news. The geological sample was described as half an inch to one inch
gritty dark quartzite with stringers of pyrrhotite and pyrite, abundant
carbon and a speck of visible gold. Microscopic examination of the
crushed core showed abundant microscopically nuggety gold with
much carbon and pyrrhotite.

In another article on the same front page, the heading:

SHARE VALUES DOUBLE OVERNIGHT

The shares of Free State Gold Areas jumped from 8 shillings to 14
shillings and those of Union Free State Mining and Finance from
9s 7d to 18s 6d.

Rick flipped to the next page.

The Star Saturday June 4 1949
DRAMA OF GOLD STRIKE ON QUIET O.F.S. FARM

He scanned the articles on the page.

... sun was setting behind the rise west of the derrick above the
borehole ... world fame ... maize turns to gold ... 6000-foot

borehole sunk amid the thorn trees ... ERFDEEL OWNER TAKES NEWS CALMLY ... we will not lose our head ... carry on as usual.

NEIGBOURING RELATIVES GIVEN HOPE OF UN-DREAMT WEALTH

The neighbouring farms of Helder Water and Dankbaarheid also belong to members of the Van Rensburg family and are also under option to the gold mining company.

The Van Rensburgs are highly excited at the news brought to them yesterday. Drilling is being carried out on their farms and they hope that later results will enable them to share in the good fortune now overtaking this fringe of the existing goldfields of the Free State.

Rick could barely distinguish the photocopied photograph, but the caption was clearly legible.

Cheerful Mr G.T. Joubert holding up a portion of the core recovered from the borehole on the farm Erfdeel. Mr Joubert actually brought up the pieces of core, which assayed such sensational values. He is one of three drillers who have worked night and day in shifts of 10 hours each for more than 8 months at this borehole.

Rick turned the page.

The Star Monday June 6 1949
TELEPHONES GO DEAD IN THE CITY – SHARE BOOM BLAMED

The excitement of Gold Fever kept Johannesburg warm today in spite of a morning that began with frost ... tremendous excitement ... share values continue to soar.

Within three days the shares of Free State Gold Areas had soared from eight shillings to fifty-five shillings and those of Union Free State from nine shilling seven to an illegible figure that had not photocopied well.

He flipped to the following page.

The Star Monday September 20 1949

On June 3, 1949 a statement was handed to the Press for publication, in which it was claimed that the gold content of 3 samples of ore removed from a borehole known as E.D.5 on the farm Erfdeel 188 in the Orange Free State had been found to amount to the equivalent of 271 dwts per ton, 338.3 dwts per ton and 10,586 dwts per ton respectively.

The Government caused the facts mentioned in the said statement to be investigated, and although the investigation has not been completed yet, the Government deems it necessary in the interest of prospective investors, both in the Union and abroad, to disclose that it is satisfied that the gold content of each of the 3 ore samples mentioned above had been fraudulently increased before it was assayed, or, expressed in common parlance, that each sample had been 'salted'.

Rick scanned a few more pages.

That the Erfdeel cores might have been salted had been a calamity. Government had acted promptly and all further drilling and assaying had been put under police surveillance. One of the assayers in the laboratory had been under suspicion because of his share dealings and other questionable actions. Traps had been set by the police, including a 'dud' core. Rick was now engrossed in the story of an assayer who had performed certain suspicious actions with suspicious powder marks on his waistcoat, and of how the assayer under suspicion had been given enough scope to 'salt' the trap samples.

Extracts from a Supreme Court case, *Rex* vs. *Milne and Stevenson*, were also among the documents in the file.

A certain Joseph Milne and Norbert Stephen Erleigh had been the instigators of the fraud.

Rick had one more document on 'salting', in general, to read.

'Salting' is mining slang and is defined as: 'To make a mine appear to be a paying one by fraudulently introducing rich ore, for example, by sprinkling gold dust in it.'

Many ingenious devices have been employed in the past to 'salt' specific samples or mines. It is known that shotguns are sometimes used to spatter a rock face in a mine with particles of gold that have been loaded into the cartridges after removal of the lead shot. A hypodermic syringe, filled with gold chloride solution, has been found by swindlers to be a very useful tool to 'salt' samples even after they have been stored in sample bags, as these bags need not be opened and the needle can penetrate the bag without leaving any telltale marks. A method that has found favour with swindlers is the one whereby gold concentrates, bullion, or an extraneous fragment of rich gold ore are added to samples intended for assay.

A number of historical cases were mentioned in the document: The Drakenstein Mining Episode of 1740, The Roodedam Fizzle of 1898, The Madagascar Fiasco of 1905, The Doornhoek Debacle of 1934, The Bantjes Consolidated Mine Swindle of 1924-26 and the Erfdeel Inquiry of 1949.

Rick now finally knew what Erfdeel meant.

It was not just a word.

It was a place, a fraud a share scam lost in the distant past.

He had often driven over the dry soil of the flat and featureless Free State in the middle of South Africa, hot and dusty in summer when crops wilt under a pitiless sun, bitingly cold in winter when the chill of frost burns the land. And now in that place, somewhere in the past, cold-hearted men had burned the credulity of innocent investors.

So that was the answer to the mystery of Erfdeel, but there were still so many unanswered questions. The major issue was why would John have been interested in an account of men who had fraudulently loaded a laboratory borehole sample of rock with extraneous gold?

Could John have been involved in 'salting'? Could he have known of someone involved in the salting of borehole samples? Or of someone planning something similar to that? What had been so important about it that he had even confided in Melinda?

Rick sat back with his eyes fixed on the white top of Kilimanjaro, trying to make sense from the jumbled bits of information in his head.

Roy Neil had known of Erfdeel because he had traced it to Melinda. John had knowledge of Erfdeel and so, probably, did someone called Peter Kraske – whoever he was. Roy Neil worked for *The Star* and the newspaper clippings from 1949 were clippings from that paper. Somewhere there just had to be a link between Roy Neil, Melinda, John, Peter Kraske and Erfdeel.

John, being in the mining industry, must have had a reasonably good idea of what the Erfdeel scam had been all about. Why had he gone to Jack Ferrara with a request for information?

A stronger aroma of peppermint than before permeated the room as Blackie Lawood returned.

'Would you like to have the detail copied?'

'Yes, please, Blackie.'

Lawood, his eyes more watery than a few minutes before and his brow stippled in sweat, took the file from Rick and left the room.

HE WIGGLED HIS TOES, REVELLING in the cool freedom of being barefoot with a beer in his hand in front of the television in John's air-conditioned house. His forehead still felt tender from the blow, but his headache had cleared up. He felt better between his legs. And he realised he now felt more wary of his surroundings, even this house where he should be safe in a private space. He had to keep his eyes open.

He stretched out in the easy chair, pulled his arms behind his head and flexed his biceps. He yawned. He was in need of a bath – he reeked of stale sweat as he usually did after a few days on safari.

The telephone rang. It was Marcia. Would he like to join her as her partner to a cocktail reception at the South African Embassy? Her invitation was difficult to decline. Besides, she had known John well and it would give him the opportunity of priming her for more clues on the Erfdeel link.

She would pick him up and he needed to be in a suit and tie.

Author's note: The Erfdeel scandal, which Erleigh and Milne perpetrated, has all but been rubbed out from history. In May 1950 (*Rex* vs. *Milne and Erleigh*) they were both convicted, fined and sentenced to ten years in jail each. I believe they were released after five years. Some say the Nationalist government regarded them as Robin Hoods but it is an event that mining companies seem to try to ignore and it is difficult these days to find full archival details.

CHAPTER 12

Ukhala ngeso elilodwa. (He cries with one eye.)
—Zulu expression for someone who pretends he is sorry

RICK HATED THE IDLE COCKTAIL talk of the diplomats around him. He listened to the shrill female laughter against a bass underlay of male voices and ice cubes clinking against crystal, which mingled with a few twittering birds in the overhead foliage and the muffled movement of homeward-bound traffic in Massachusetts Avenue behind the grey building.

Marcia had dumped him in the centre of the crowd gathered in the garden. He felt uncomfortable in John's suit, shirt, tie and black shoes. Like a deer encircled by predators and scavengers.

He had always thought diplomats busied themselves with matters of substance. Never before having attended a diplomatic cocktail reception, his unexpected induction into the meaningless world of empty talk and sophisticated inanity came as a shock.

'You know, of course, what the world-wide abbreviation CD on a diplomatic car number-plate stands for,' a young man with tortoise-shell glasses standing next to him said.

'Mmm. Corps Diplomatique,' Rick answered absent-mindedly.

'That's what everybody thinks. No, CD actually stands for cheap drinks.'

'Cheap drinks?'

'Yep. CD. All tax-free. We diplomats are exempt from tax. You know, just look around you', and the young man, who had been introduced to Rick as a second secretary called Louis Malan, waved a gin-and-tonic at the assembly.

Rick smiled at the remark.

'Hey, you look like a unicorn.'

'What?'

'You've got a bump on your forehead. There.'

'I walked into a door.' He wasn't ready to tell just anyone about the attack earlier that day.

'You need to think faster on your feet than that. A hazardous door?'

Rick smiled again.

'Of course, diplomacy is a really hazardous career,' Louis continued.

'From the point of view of security?' Rick did his best to return the small talk.

'No. Security can be hazardous at times but the diplomat's biggest threat is – wait for it – alcoholism.'

'Are you complaining again?' Marcia saved Rick from Malan's vacuous grip. 'Louis has, in the past, won a few fights with his own department.'

Louis beamed – smugly.

'Come, I want to introduce you to the ambassador.' She led Rick away. 'Actually, most diplomats complain most of the time,' she whispered at his side. 'It's their pet subject at dinner parties, probably because they cannot always talk openly about their work like other people. The only thing they can discuss openly is their personal salary situation and they have elevated that to a kind of a diplomatic anthem – their theme song.'

Rick's nose twitched again. He had been sneezing ever since he had arrived at the outdoor reception in the embassy gardens. He whipped out a handkerchief, just in time to muzzle his sneeze.

'Hay fever,' she stated.

'Do you think so?' He wiped away the tears in his eyes.

'You're not used to the grass, the flowers, and the pollen here. You should buy some tablets or a spray from a drugstore,' Marcia said, leading him past perfumed ladies digging their high heels into the lawn, and suited men, each with a full glass in hand. They wove their way through the crowd to stop in front of a distinguished-looking, shiny-headed black man with tufts of greying peppercorn hair above his ears. Rick estimated him to be somewhere in his sixties.

'Marcia! So glad to see you.'

The man kissed her on both cheeks, as did all the other diplomatic types, Rick had noticed. The style, Rick observed, was not to touch the person's cheek with your lips, but to pucker up and kiss the air in the vicinity of them. Not like African lip-kissing.

'I am so sorry to have heard about John's untimely death. Such terrible circumstances too. Did your office receive our message of condolences?'

'Yes, Ambassador. Thank you. May I present Rick Land?' Marcia switched her gaze from one to the other. 'Rick, Ambassador Moholi.'

'Pleased to meet you, Mr Land. Are you in any way related to John Land?' Ambassador Moholi asked as they shook hands. His bony hand felt like canvas to Rick.

'I'm John's brother.'

'My condolences to you then, Mr Land.'

'Thank you, sir,' Rick said, finding the ambassador's hand once again shaking his.

'It was extremely shocking.' The older man's words were punctuated every now and then by a nervous twitch of his eyebrows. 'We sometimes encounter the death of our nationals on foreign shores but we fortunately don't have to deal too much with murders, particularly a murder of such a prominent national. I sent one of my men down to New Orleans to investigate and to assist with arrangements for the body to be flown back. All done now.'

'Thank you, sir. Did your man's investigations throw any light on the possible reason for the murder?'

'No. At this stage it remains a mystery.' The ambassador scratched his chin before continuing, 'I've been told the case is receiving top priority in New Orleans. Something about ballistics tests which are still awaited. It's out of our hands. We at the embassy have to wait for further information now.'

The inside of Rick's nose started to itch again and he reached for his handkerchief.

'You should get something for that, Mr Land. I get injections against hay fever every summer. Otherwise I would not make it through the pollen.' With that, Ambassador Moholi lifted his glass in acknowledgement to someone in the crowd. 'Excuse me for a moment, would you?' and, without even glancing sideways for a reply, the Ambassador diplomatically discarded Rick and walked away.

Rick wandered away through the crowd towards the edge of the garden, stopping at another white-coated waiter holding a plate of hors d'oeuvres. With a soggy piece of bread topped with caviar in one hand, and his glass of wine in the other, Rick leaned against the rough bark of a tree and surveyed the garden party.

A woman with a daring black dress, open to the lowest point possible on her back, was talking to a young man in a double-breasted suit. For a moment, Rick saw an image of Melinda in his mind. The ambassador was talking to a smiling young man and Rick could see from their body movements they were discussing golf swings or golf grips.

'Yes ja, and so howzit now?' Louis Malan spoke in his affected accent next to Rick. 'Are you bored with the party?'

'No. Interesting people and conversations,' Rick lied.

'Sometimes it's better to observe. In a manner of speaking, you know, we diplomats are political observers.'

'I find it difficult to break in when I'm an outsider and everybody knows everybody else,' Rick said.

'Is there somebody special you'd like to meet? I could introduce you.'

'I'm quite happy here on my own, but tell me a little about all these people. Who are they?'

'Right. Now let me see.' Louis scanned the crowd. 'Over there, that's, um, Senator Adrian Booth. And that's Dr Joe du Pisanie, our ambassador, you know, to the International Monetary Fund. Those people over there are embassy staff. Shit, they should mingle, not stand around and count each other's teeth.' He frowned. 'Bad manners.'

'So it's a congregation of senators, congressmen and ambassadors,' Rick remarked.

'We do have a few interspersed odds and sods like lesser diplomats, a few businessmen, journalists and lobbyists. Over there, for instance, are Don Cliffe and Peter Kraske and on that side—'

'Peter Kraske?' Rick interrupted.

'Ja. Kraske is a lobbyist. He knows everybody worth knowing in Washington. Friendly. Warm. Still a bit of a political contortionist, if you ask me.'

So that was Peter Kraske! The man he had heard of a few days before. A name in Melinda's diary and in a journalist's mind.

Kraske had the thinning hair and withered face of a man in his seventies but Rick could see his face was lit by lively, glacial blue eyes that showed an inner drive far belying his age. The skin on his forehead creased and ironed out in rhythm with his animated talk as he turned his hands in the form of a tulip in the air, engrossed in talk with a much younger man. He looked like a sprightly marionette, dressed in a dark suit, white shirt and bow-tie, cutting the air with expressive fingers.

'For whom does Kraske lobby?' he asked.

'He's a bit of an antique, in a way, you know,' Louis said as he fished out an insect from his tumbler of whiskey. 'He's semi-retired but still works for us and a few other countries. All lobbyists working for anybody, other than an American client, have to, you know, register as foreign agents. Kraske is registered as one of our embassy's lobbyists.

His links go right into the White House. It's said he's been a friend of all the presidents from Eisenhower till today, irrespective of whether they were Republican or Democrats.'

'Really?' So, a powerful Washington lobbyist was a possible link to John's death. 'I'd like to meet the man.'

'Sure.' Louis led the way through the crowd.

'Louis. Nice to see you.' Kraske's voice was as withered as his face.

'Peter, may I introduce Rick Land?' Louis held Rick by the arm as he spoke.

Kraske's handshake was firm. 'You must be John's brother.'

Rick nodded.

'I heard you were coming out here.'

'You have good information.'

'Yes, I have good information. Like all lobbyists, I'm an information peddler. Call me a glorified gossip columnist, if you want.' Peter Kraske's friendly smile, showing creased mouth corners and teeth well tended for his age, was the end product of decades of experience in public relations.

'So you knew John,' Rick stated the obvious.

'Yes, I did. Sad events around him indeed.' Kraske touched Rick's shoulder.

'Sad, Mr Kraske?'

'Peter. Yes, John and I met on many occasions. We even had the chance to break some bread over breakfast at The Jockey Club a few days before his death. He wanted me to go knocking on a few DC doors for AfriBelgo, which, of course, I did. He was a good guy. Always made sure my invoices and expense account were processed expeditiously. Nice. Sorry to say, however, he was a hothead and maybe a little strange at times. Do you know the guy used to pour maple syrup over sunny-side-up eggs? A little out of the ordinary!' Kraske said with a chuckle.

Kraske's remark reminded Rick of their dining table back in Villieria. He saw John's toddler fingers sprinkling a sausage with icing sugar and heard their mother's laugh. He remembered how John would eat an apple with its core, pips, stem and all. Kraske spoke, but Rick's mind was back in the past. Maybe that was the only way to live; you had to live life to the core, be different, and pour maple syrup over eggs, or mix scotch and milk.

'How long are you planning to stay in DC?' Kraske brought Rick back to the present.

'I'm not too sure. Probably only a few days until everything is sorted out.'

'Well, here's my card. Call me. Maybe we can do lunch some time before you return home.' Kraske gave Rick a beaming smile.

As he handed his business card to Rick, a woman grabbed Kraske by the arm and launched into a discussion on the wonders of vacationing in Florida. With that, another diplomatic curtain fell in front of Rick.

Pursing his lips, Rick turned around and accidentally bumped into someone behind him. 'Oh, I'm sorry,' he said in reflex.

'It was my fault.'

He heard her before he saw her. She had an appealing lilt to her voice and, as their eyes met, a captivating embarrassment in her smile. And her hand was wet with white wine spilt from her glass.

'Here, let me help you.' Rick took out his handkerchief from his pocket and dabbed at the wine in the slender valley between her thumb and manicured index finger.

'I can manage, thank you,' she said and walked away.

The incident and her departure happened so quickly he barely had time to study her face, but from one glance he could see she was lovely. There had been something vaguely familiar about her but he could not put his finger on it.

He looked at her as she walked up the stairs and on to the open patio towards the door, a lissom woman in high-heeled shoes. Although she wore a loose-fitting, white cocktail dress, he could see she was lithe and firm. Her honey-coloured hair, cut shoulder-length, swayed pertly as she moved through the crowd. A striking girl.

The attack of sneezing sprang upon him without warning.

'Bless you,' someone said behind him.

The attack now had Rick pushing at his itching nose with his handkerchief again and he smelled the girl's spilled wine on it. He knew he had to get out of the open air and ambled towards the building. Inside, the embassy was a chicken coop with a constant barrage of gobbledygook. Everybody seemed to talk at the same time and nobody seemed to listen. He had not seen Marcia outside for some time and looked around for her.

'Howzit again?'

He recognized Louis Malan's voice from behind.

'Have you seen Marcia, Louis?'

'Why? Are you thinking of leaving?' Louis said it in a manner that betrayed his own desire to depart.

'Yes.'

'Why don't you come to dinner with us? A few of us lesser mortals working in the embassy are going over to Georgetown for a bite.'

Rick had been looking forward to a good night's sleep, but he knew he was a captive because he had to stay with Marcia. 'I'll ask Marcia.'

'Sure. We just have to wait for the ambassador to leave first Protocol, you know,' Louis explained. 'We always have to arrive at a party before him and leave only after he has left. But I saw him outside at the start of his regular farewell routine. It won't be too long.'

A few minutes later the ambassador stuck his hand into Rick's, patted him on the shoulder and expressed his condolences again before leaving the reception. Peter Kraske followed close behind the ambassador but also made a point of saying goodbye to Rick.

'I heard there was a group going out for dinner,' Kraske said. 'I suggested to Louis that they include you and take you to J Paul's, which has a nice atmosphere. I've got contacts for your reservation there as well.'

Kraske left amid an avalanche of departing guests.

Marcia appeared upstream from the avalanche. 'Let's go, Rick. We'll meet Louis and the others at the restaurant.'

'I'm not sure whether I really want to—'

'Come on. The company will do you good.'

She dragged Rick away.

THE INTERIOR OF J PAUL'S Restaurant and Bar was as noisy as the assembly at the cocktail reception, with one major difference: this crowd was younger and dressed more casually.

'They're students mostly, from Georgetown University,' Marcia remarked.

Rick and Marcia sat at a long bar counter, resting their tired feet on a brass foot railing above floor level, waiting for Louis and the others to arrive. Behind the counter were four glossy, dark wooden columns with flaming wood grains built into a mirrored wall.

They were drinking Cape Cod cranberry juice, a light red, sweet and slightly wild tasting liquid.

The long bar counter had a partly sunken top in which the barman had placed a section of soft drinks, a section of glasses and, right in front of each section, glasses filled with drinking straws, like sergeant-majors at the front of the parade.

The military layout made Rick think of the Belgian Resistance and his father's role in the war. His father's war had been less regimented, less organised and less open. It had not been an overt war with soldiers in uniforms, laid out in strategy and backed up by discipline. His war had been one organised in secrecy, yet probably also disorganised as a result of a lack of regimented discipline. If only he could lay out all the facts relating to John's death in an orderly fashion, he would probably find the answers he was looking for, he thought.

'Howzit now?' Louis Malan broke Rick's reverie.

Inwardly, Rick sighed with relief. He felt safer with the arrival of Louis and the other diplomats. It was as if Louis's 'cheap drinks' squad were a shield to protect him from another attack at that moment.

'May I introduce you?' Theatrically, Louis Malan continued, 'You all know Marcia. This is Rick Land. And Rick, here you have Gerry from admin, his wife Bets. Daniel, Sonya and Francois.'

Sonya! He had found Sonya. He had dabbed at her hand with his handkerchief and not realised he had found her.

He looked her up and down but she hardly greeted him, avoiding eye contact. He might as well not have been there.

'We're waiting for a table. Have a seat at the bar counter,' Marcia invited the newcomers.

Rick hardly heard Marcia and did not even notice the others in the group with Louis. Then Sonya's eyes stared at him for an instant.

She was beautiful. It was clear why John would have been interested in her. She would be a magnet for any man with normal hormones. What was that scribbled message of John's again? Something about New Orleans, a date 8-8 and Sonya. And something about phoning first. Somehow John, New Orleans and Sonya were tied together.

He had found a link. A living link.

His eyes were glued on Sonya as she walked past him towards a barstool. Then it came to him and he suddenly knew what it was that had seemed so familiar about her at the reception. As she brushed past, ignoring him, he had smelled her perfume. It was the same discreet fragrance that had hung so tantalisingly in the air in John's house. She sat down on the furthest barstool from Rick. Louis sat down next to Rick.

'Louis?' Rick whispered as he turned to his right, 'does anyone in the group here drive an Oldsmobile Cutlass? A white one?'

'Yes, Son—'

A blaring jukebox had just started up and, in the noise, Rick could barely make out Louis's words, but he knew from Louis's eye indications that Sonya drove one.

Rick turned to his left, in time to see Sonya get up from her barstool. She came up to Louis, said something in his ear, smiled at everyone at the counter, studiously avoided eye contact with Rick, waved to the others and walked out.

'She says it's been a long day so she's going home,' Louis shouted in Rick's ear.

Rick watched her bobbing hair as she walked past the window that had been opened to the street. Just before she disappeared, she glanced back and their eyes met again for an instant.

At that moment he knew that she knew he had recognised her. He made up his mind to contact her the following day.

Mercifully, the noise from the jukebox died down.

'What does Sonya do for a living?' Rick asked Louis.

'She's a colleague. Consular work. Visas, passports, things like that, you know,' Louis said in between crunching peanuts.

'Has she been here long?'

'About three years.'

'In DC?'

'Not all of the time in DC. She spent the first two years or so in New Orleans until we closed our office there and shifted the whole caboodle to Houston.'

'So she's been a diplomat for some time.'

'Ja, that's true but I think both she and I will probably move on to different work at some time.'

'Why?'

'Affirmative action. A good thing, I suppose. She and I are white. We were appointed in the period before the new Mandela government. We expect that we need to stand back soon so that people of colour can represent South Africa.'

A waiter, wearing red trouser braces, asked them to follow him to a table where he seated them, stuck menus in their hands, told them his name was Skip and proceeded to rattle off the specials of the evening.

Rick stared at the narrow reddish-brown bricks in the wall behind Louis – bricks marked with tracks of erosion, like old leather, like veins.

Across the street, through J Paul's open window, Rick noticed a red-and-black brick building with three windows on its first floor and three on the second floor. All the windows in the building across the street were closed, except for the top middle one. In that open window, Rick could see a television set with bunny ears, perched precariously on the window sill, above the hurly-burly of Georgetown. In the darkness of the room, behind the television set, someone sat, not watching the world through his own window, but through an electronic window.

Around the table the talk turned to Rick's life as a professional hunter, his thoughts about John's death and about the events that had followed. He spoke about Uncle Erick and Melinda's death and about elephant poachers. The things he knew.

What he did not know was that his words were recorded at the table.

He was talking into an electronic window.

Author's note: In my career I had to endure diplomatic cocktail parties over several continents which I found to be incestuous duelling invitations between diplomatic missions in a city where you see and talk to the same people about the same thing all the time. Ultimately boring. Karl Marx wrote: 'Workers of the world unite; you have nothing to lose but your chains'. I would like to adapt that to: 'Small talkers of the world unite; you have nothing to lose but your sobriety'. Diplomats are exempt from taxes on tobacco and alcohol and, as a result, overindulge in these events where they walk around with fresh drinks and dull minds.

CHAPTER 13

Die Weisheit ist nur in der Wahrheit.
(Wisdom is found only in truth.)

–Goethe

THE TELEPHONE RANG. HE WOKE up, turned on his side and fumbled in the darkness for the lamp switch until he found the button. Light flooded his vision. He had difficulty adjusting his eyes to the sudden glare. What time was it? He drew the alarm clock closer. Just past seven. The telephone kept on ringing and he stretched for it, the muscles in his arm still stiff from sleep.

'Hello,' he croaked into the receiver and coughed.

'Rick Land?'

'Yes,' he cleared his throat as he answered.

'We need to share a few words.' The man spoke staccato-style.

'Who are you?'

Rick was wide awake now.

'That ain't none of your business. Main thing you gotta be concerned with is there's a guy who wants to share a few words with you. Be at the footbridge to Roosevelt Island in exactly two hours.'

The man's verbal bursts were somewhat incomprehensible and Rick was unsure of the meeting place. 'Where?'

'Roosevelt Island. It's on the Potomac. Be at the footbridge. We meet at nine.' It sounded as if the man was eating and talking at the same time.

'Who do I look for?'

'You ain't gonna look for nobody, man. We'll look you up. Hey, and don't try pulling no monkey business. No gun. Nobody else, you hear?'

'How can I trust you?'

'You can't. The only thing you can trust is that we could've turned you into salami from the moment you arrived, but we didn't.'

Silence.

'Just be there. Roosevelt Island. Two hours from now, at the foot-bridge.'

Click.

HE COULD HAVE KICKED HIMSELF for having forgotten to stop at a drugstore for anti-histamine tablets. The moment he got out of the Mustang at Theodore Roosevelt Island, he felt the build-up of hay fever again.

There were three more vehicles parked in the area near the foot-bridge. A couple walked hand-in-hand across the bridge from the island. A jogger trotted along the edge of the water.

Was this the right thing to do? Was he being ambushed? Whatever the outcome, he had no choice. He had to meet him.

Underneath an oak tree, an angler, wearing a baseball cap, cast his line into the Potomac, put the fishing-rod down, turned around and beckoned to Rick to approach.

'You packing any heat?' the man asked as Rick approached. 'Any gun on you? Are you clean?' the man continued when Rick did not respond immediately.

Rick realised he was looking at the person who had called him two hours before. 'I followed your instructions.'

Rick had indeed thought of taking John's Smith and Wesson along, but decided he would probably be searched in any case and he would not want to run the risk of losing the weapon.

The man disregarded Rick's assurance, walked up to him and ran his hands over Rick. He then retrieved a portable telephone from a yellow plastic box, which, under normal circumstances would probably have contained fishing tackle and bait, and punched in a set of numbers on the instrument.

'I've got a positive out here.' He spoke from the depths of his throat as if his vocal chords were locked in combat with one another. 'Yeah, our visitor has arrived. Naw, he's clean and coming over.'

A cigarette dangled from the man's lips as he relayed his message. While he was talking, the sound of a jet aircraft grew louder and louder. Rick looked up. Between overhanging oak branches, he saw a passenger aircraft coming in against the backdrop of metallic clouds, winging its way along the winding route of the Potomac River, on its descending approach to National Airport.

Forced to wait for the thundering noise of the aeroplane to pass, the man with the fishing rod and cellular telephone lifted his eyes upwards. In a deafening roar the aircraft glided a few hundred yards over Theodore Roosevelt Island.

The man touched Rick's elbow and brought his attention back to the spot where they were standing on the edge of the lapping water.

'This ain't a pleasure ride, bud. You gotta cross the bridge.'

The stocky middle-aged man squinted at Rick, paused and removed his Orioles cap, revealing a hairless patch on his head. 'On the other side, you gotta take a right, and go along the footpath until you hit a clearing where you'll find a statue. There's a guy out there waiting for you.'

Rick attempted to stifle the unexpected sneeze with his fist.

'Bless you.'

The man returned to his fishing rod and sat down to stare at the green waters of the Potomac.

Rick turned to his right and walked towards the arched footbridge. Again he sneezed. He really had to remember to get some medication.

From the footbridge he noticed that the man with the fishing rod held his portable telephone against his ear again.

Leaving the footbridge in to the island Rick entered a forest of oak, elm and maple trees. He followed the footpath through the cool darkness of the forest until he came to a clearing, in the middle of which a high shaft of sculptured granite overlooked an oval terrace.

Etched against the granite stood a huge bronze statue of President Theodore Roosevelt, his right arm raised in the air as if to greet Rick. Another aircraft roared past.

Next to the statue stood a man in a business suit and yellow tie. Except for the birds in the trees, the man was the only other living being Rick was aware of around him. Two people alone on an island in the centre of one of the world's major capitals.

Rick approached the man.

'Morning. Thank you for coming.'

The man wore dark glasses and spoke with a slight foreign accent. Almost a mixture of American and French maybe? With a touch of the Deep South? No real drawl there. He was clearly more cultivated than his fisherman friend.

'I thought it would be nice to meet here in the arms of nature, particularly as you earn your money in its embrace.'

The man leaned back against the pedestal of the statue, the convex lenses of his dark glasses giving him an impenetrable appearance. Rick saw his own reflection in the man's glasses. In spite of his strong facial features, the man's greying temples betrayed his age. He could be in his forties or early fifties. He did not resemble the type of person who could be involved with the rough, and obviously crooked, associate out in the parking area.

'I'm not quite sure why I'm here,' Rick said, wiping the sweat from his brow. Although it was still early in the day, his body already reacted to the rising heat and humidity.

'I love this place,' the man said, disregarding Rick's remark. 'When I was a small boy my friends and I used to come out here. We hunted squirrels, cottontails, chipmunks and even raccoons. Of course we were transgressing the law, but so what? I saw a red fox once out here. Over on that side is a swamp with birds a-plenty. I remember we used to climb up the Kuddu. Do you know what Kuddu is?'

'No,' Rick said, thinking of the grey ghost of Africa.

'It's a kind of vine on the trees.'

Definitely a touch of the French way of rolling his Rs, Rick decided.

'We used to climb the Kuddu to get to the birds' eggs. Ah, what a time we had. Come, let me show you.' He pointed upwards. 'Do you see that tree covered in English ivy? That's Kuddu.'

Rick noticed the clinging vine.

'Do you see that inscription over there?' The man gestured towards a tablet. 'It's Roosevelt's ideas on righteousness and decency.'

Rick read the inscription: *Ultimately no nation can be great unless its greatness is laid on foundations of righteousness and decency.*

'That's what we want to talk to you about. Those foundations of righteousness and decency,' the man continued. 'Don't for one moment think your brother was righteous or decent, and I'm not just talking about his womanising.'

'What do you mean?' Rick had his handkerchief out in time for his next sneeze.

'Your brother tried to gamble on some business deals with a few high rollers – and I mean real high rollers.' The man stressed 'real'. 'He was involved in the kind of deals that don't float in the open market but float in the veins of street people.'

'Drugs?' Rick sneezed violently. 'Do you want to tell me John was involved in drugs? Never.'

'It's as sure as the fact that the Pope also farts after peanuts, Chuck. I don't know all the people he got involved with and I might not know all the detail but I know because I'm the courier who's been told to give you the message.'

Rick stared at the man, wordlessly allowing him to continue.

'I've been told to tell you it's general knowledge that you once damaged the interests of certain individuals involved in the financing of ivory transactions. You really loused up some good business, Chuck. Those guys who suffered at your hands made contact with your brother in such a way he never realised he'd been put under surveillance. It was a kind of quid pro quo from the guys you hurt to get back at you while finding out more about you and your habits. Your brother and those guys became buddies. That's when the shit hit the fan, because without the knowledge of these individuals, your brother cut a deal with certain other people. In the process he moved in on the territory of one specific, very powerful man. This upset the very people who had been previously hurt by your actions. They got really jacked up, Chuck. According to what I've been told, a decision was then taken to deal with him. A contract was taken out on your brother and he acquired a lead suit for his trip home.'

The roar of another aircraft overhead drowned out their conversation and allowed Rick a chance to think. It also allowed him to sneeze.

It seemed almost impossible that John could have been involved in drugs because he had never shown any interest in them. Yet, Rick contemplated, John had also never taken an actual stand against drugs and had often been irresponsible to such an extreme that the idea could not be summarily discounted. And then Rick's thoughts turned to the threats against himself after the anti-poaching operation in Mozambique. How did those people know where to reach him? It had been common knowledge that the illegal ivory trade had been financed from a base in Atlantic City, halfway between Washington DC and New York. His doubts about John's involvement faded with the fading sound of jet engines.

'Damn noise!' The man adjusted his glasses, which had slipped down the bridge of his nose.

'Why are you telling me this?' Rick said, stifling another sneeze.

'It's my job. I'm the singer and the song is simple. You're partly responsible for your brother's death. My job is to tell you that you should look upon his untimely end as a penalty for your past actions, that the individuals involved have decided to regard the death of John

Land as a settlement of the account, and that the matter is closed. They'll keep an eye on you, however, until your departure. You're advised to be careful not to jeopardise their goodwill.'

Rick felt his face reddening with rage. 'If these people regard this as a closed case, then why did someone try to shoot me at point-blank range yesterday?'

'As I told you, these guys are in lines of business that do not normally feature on stock exchanges. Some of them are still very upset with you and would probably wish to overstep the informal joint position they have taken on you.' The man smiled at Rick like a used car salesman.

Rick suddenly felt very guilty. John had died because of him. That's it.

'Look, I gotta take a walk now,' the man said, still smiling, 'and remember I'm just the communications expert hired for the job of telling you to shove off quietly for your own good. There's a man who's less communicative, who's armed and watching you from the forest. I'll leave now. You may leave five minutes afterwards but walk slowly as you will be under surveillance until you get your wheels. Oh, and by the way, you really should get something for your hay fever. Salt water up your nostrils also helps. Better than some of the stuff John put up his.'

At that moment another jet roared into earshot. The man turned and walked away. Rick leaned against the granite, put his hands in his pockets and looked up at the aircraft rumbling overhead.

It all made sense.

After a few minutes he set off along the footpath back to the car. He had a strange, burning sensation in the small of his back and visualised the many times he had the crosshairs in the sight of his rifle trained on an animal in the bush, his finger on the trigger, a loaded bullet in place, inspecting his prey through the telescope before taking the final decision to pull the trigger. At the footbridge he noticed that the man with the fishing rod and portable telephone was gone.

Only when he had steered out of the parking lot and turned the red nose of the Ford Mustang on to the George Washington Memorial Parkway did he shake off the burning sensation in his back.

He had to team up with Cohen at Sternson, who would take him to Riggs Bank.

On his way to the offices of Sternson, he stopped at a drugstore, bought a packet of tablets to alleviate his hay fever and swallowed two, accompanied by a soft drink from a paper cup filled with crushed ice. Medication on the rocks again.

At Sternson, it took the receptionist a while to locate Cohen, who had not expected Rick so early in the morning.

Half an hour later a young man sat with Rick and Cohen in a cubicle at Riggs as they went through John's valuables, which had been left there in safe custody.

A few mint condition coins. Some jewellery. Why would John have had female jewellery? Maybe, Rick reflected, John had bought jewellery for one or more women who had returned it to him. Maybe he would stock up on gifts for rainy days. There were a number of documents, but nothing that could affect John's last will and testament. They waded through title deeds, purchase offers with acceptances, share certificates and bonds.

'Hey, this is far out.' The bank employee held up an old pipe, oily with age and chafed at the stem with teeth marks.

'It was our dad's. I'll take it.'

In the cold neon light inside the bank, the pipe in his hands felt warm. He could almost hear the creaking of the ship. He smelled the sea around them and felt his mother's hand on his shoulder and saw Table Mountain. It was as if the pipe brought back the cackle of satanic laughter as the devil stood at the top of the mountain with a lit pipe in his hand – as if he saw a man floating through the air, holding a cold pipe in his hand, disappearing into the swirling mists.

'Mr Land?' The sound of the young man's voice brought back his attention to the severe white lighting of the bank's interior. He realised his knuckles were bone-white from clenching the pipe in his fist.

'Yes?'

'What about this?'

The young man smirked as he handed Rick a VHS videocassette bearing a marking scribbled with a thick felt pen, *PERSONAL AND CONFIDENTIAL*, and underneath in ball-point writing, *J Land sex with Jackie, Laurie, Elaine, Carole.*

Rick took the videocassette.

Why would John have left this in a vault? Maybe not to have it fall in the hands of a housekeeper. He really was a bit strange. And not just with syrup over eggs.

'It's not the kind of thing we would wish to put on the list, although we should,' Cohen said carefully. 'It might be best if you could just take it and maybe destroy it.'

'Yeah, it's probably the best,' the young man said, with an expression that revealed the opposite. 'Who said there can't be sex after death?' he added a little wistfully.

'Hey, show some respect,' Cohen said.

'The safest course of action is that I take it with me, I suppose,' Rick said, realising the potential unpleasantness of the tape falling into the wrong hands.

How could John have done something like that? What did the man on Theodore Roosevelt Island say? John had no decency. 'I'll personally destroy it.'

After signing the release documents, Cohen drove Rick back to the Sternson offices. From there Rick drove back to the house in McLean. On his way back, he debated his course of action. What was he to do with the video?

As he waited for the roll-up door of the garage to open, he decided to first have a look at the video. There were so many unanswered questions that he had to follow up every possible clue, even if it meant having to watch whatever activities John had indulged in.

He stood in front of the video player for a moment, remorseful for his part in John's death, ashamed at his intention to watch the video.

The cassette entered the opening of the video player, in itself almost mechanically erotic.

Rick pushed the play button.

A few flickers on the television screen until clear images appeared. The camera had been placed in the living room, probably on a tripod, and had been aimed at the burgundy leather couch in the corner under the Jackson Pollock painting.

At first nothing happened.

Rick watched the still-life image of the couch, the lamp, the wall and the painting. Then there was laughter off-screen, followed by John and an attractive brunette in a low-cut dress coming into view.

John had an open champagne bottle in one hand and two glasses in the other. The girl giggled and winked at the camera as John poured them each a glass of champagne.

'Do you always do this after a formal dinner?' she asked as she undid his tie.

'No. I'm actually a virgin,' John said and winked at the camera.

'Well, I'm honoured,' she said in a slightly tipsy way, 'and this is my first appearance on TV.'

She turned towards the camera, slipped the thin straps of her dress from her shoulders and opened her dress to reveal two well-formed breasts. Looking straight into the lens, she cupped her bare breasts in her hands, pouted her lips and whispered, 'To all my fans out there, I love you.'

'To love!' John said and they clinked their glasses.

Love had nothing to do with all of this, Rick thought.

He watched as she leaned over and kissed John. Simultaneously they put down their glasses on the coffee table and held each other, John with his tie draped over his shoulder, she still topless. Within moments they were both naked and stretched out on the couch. She was underneath John, her milky skin contrasting with the burgundy leather, her legs rising in a clinch around his torso.

In the wink of an eye, the image disappeared and a new image filled the screen.

'Hello, Rick.'

What?

John spoke, sitting on the same couch he had an instant before been using for sexual acrobatics.

'What the hell!'

Rick was so surprised his mind did not even register his own exclamation.

'I am sorry to interrupt your viewing pleasure, but just as I transposed some of my fun moments of the past on to this tape, I'm transposing this little chat. I can assure you that all went very well that night and, after I have spoken to you, the video will return to more viewing pleasure,' John said and chuckled. 'Wasn't Jackie something, hey? She's a full-time dress designer and part-time nymphomaniac. A real pleasure to know.' He shook his head and sniggered. 'But, look, I have to talk to you. I'll be keeping this little tape in my bank safe, which means that if you ever watch this, I will be dead as a dodo. Do you remember the dodo, the one that became extinct?'

Involuntarily, Rick found himself nodding. Rick and Melinda had had a life-size replica of the bird as an ornament in their house at the time of the break-up of their marriage.

'The dodo,' John continued, 'a heavy-set bird, like me, I'm afraid.' He patted the bulge above his belt. 'Rick, I think there's a good chance I might also become extinct one of these days. That's why I went to my lawyers today and changed my will. I signed a codicil that, if I die, you have to come out here personally to see Sternson. The reason is that I want to talk to you through this medium. Very few people have the opportunity of life after death here on Earth. See, I planned that you would watch this video. I gave Sternson a private written instruction today that I have this personal adult cinematic work at the bank in safe custody and that, in the event of my death, nobody is to touch it except you. It is the only way I can think of in which I can speak to you and you alone.'

So Cohen had known of the tape! No wonder he had said it would be better not to have it itemised as part of the estate. Suddenly Rick felt more comfortable with Jerry Cohen. Good man.

'Before I go any further, there's one thing I wish to say, Rick. Look, I am truly sorry about all the grief I caused you that time with Melinda. I didn't mean to hurt you. I'm sorry.' John fell quiet and just stared at the camera with a clenched jaw. Rick could see genuine remorse. He felt the lump in his own throat.

'I know I cannot expect forgiveness,' John wiped at his left eye with the back of his hand, 'but I want you to know I've been walking around with this burden for many years now. I'm so sorry, Rick.' John sighed. 'I'll be seeing Melinda soon again when she comes out for a visit and I will tell her the same thing. But that is not all I want to say to you. Thing is, Rick, I received a threat against my life which, under normal circumstances, I would have ignored. But this one is serious. It started some time ago when I met a girl. Her name is Sonya Deine. She's a First Secretary at the South African Embassy – a gem amongst beauts, I can assure you. We got on well, although she kept her distance. I never could get her on a couch like Jackie, although I tried. Shit I did.' John cast his eyes downwards and patted the couch with regret.

'I could never understand why she wasn't interested in the least in me until one night when we were at the same dinner party. I was there with Marcia from the office. During dinner I tried to be nice to Sonya. Okay,' John rolled his eyes, 'I tried to impress her and I failed when she became absolutely vitriolic over the dinner table against AfriBelgo and Uncle Erick. I couldn't understand her at all. She absolutely hated Uncle Erick. Called him a 'robber baron'. Imagine that! Of course I defended the company and Uncle Erick, but our discussion became an embarrassment to the host and hostess and we stopped arguing after a while. The next day I went to see her in her office. She refused to talk there and we ended up having lunch. That was when she came out with the most incredible story. It was unbelievable and, at first, I took the whole thing with a pinch of salt. She told me she had been an only child, that her father had been a farmer and that he had become involved in some kind of joint venture with Uncle Erick in the early days near Barberton, in the Eastern Transvaal. During that time, for an unaccountable reason, her father had been shot and killed by an intruder one night. After his death, her mother had found that their farm and most of their possessions had been tied up as collateral at the bank for the joint venture, and that the bank would foreclose. According to her, Uncle Erick wangled it so that Sonya's mother was forced to accept a ten per cent compensation deal. Her mother walked away with only ten per cent of the bank's valuation of the farm and their other assets. Her mother had to move. Later on she then gave birth to Sonya. Shortly after that, the mother died of cancer and, being a destitute child with no relatives, Sonya ended up in the Abraham Kriel Orphanage at Langlaagte in Johannesburg. Very sad.'

John fell silent for a few seconds and stared at the camera. 'Before her death, and knowing death was imminent, Sonya's mother arranged for Sonya to be admitted to the orphanage and she wrote Sonya a letter, which was sealed, with an instruction to be opened on Sonya's sixteenth birthday. So, on her sixteenth birthday she received this letter in which her mother had written to her about the challenges of facing life as an adult and about her regrets that Sonya had to face the world as an orphan. It was a woman-to-woman letter. In a sense, that letter gave me the idea of doing this recording to talk to you, Rick. But, to get back to the letter, Sonya's mother wrote that, although she was not too sure about the exact situation, Sonya's dad and Uncle Erick had been involved in a mining venture, being financed by an American friend of Uncle Erick – a man called Peter Kraske. I have known the man for a while now. The day before Sonya's father was killed, her dad had apparently told her mother that he was going to end his association with the venture, and particularly with Peter Kraske, because it had become nothing more than another Erfdeel scandal. It took Sonya several years to find out that the Erfdeel scandal was something about salting and, even with that, she did not know much. At first, when Sonya told me, I didn't have the foggiest clue what Erfdeel meant. I wanted to follow up on what she told me and I faxed head office for information. I received an answer like lightning, directly from Uncle Erick's office. The reply was terse. Why was I interested? I faxed back that I had had an enquiry from a research student. I didn't want Sonya to be mixed up in the enquiry. Eventually I found references to the Erfdeel salting scam in books on the history of mining, but I'm still trying to get more detailed information. AfriBelgo is ignoring my request for information. What I do know is that it was an infamous salting incident when gold was added to a borehole sample. But to get back to Sonya, that's what she also knew. Sonya decided to find out who Peter Kraske was and, for that reason, she later joined the diplomatic service and went to great lengths to become an authority on the United States so that she could be posted here.'

John got up from the couch and walked up to the camera. The image disappeared but, a second later, reappeared as he walked back to the couch.

'Sorry. I had to go to the other john in the house, as they say in the US. Where was I? Oh, yes, she was successful in getting posted here, came out here and traced Kraske. He's a lobbyist on the Hill, a man I know quite well, as I said. He's a great friend of Uncle Erick and someone who prides himself on the fact that he helped form AfriBelgo by arranging finance and other assistance. The day after my request for information on Erfdeel from Head Office, who should walk into my office but Peter Kraske? He said he had been in the vicinity and had just come in for a chat. And we chatted. And I lied. Sometimes one has to. I asked him what he knew of Erfdeel because I had received a request from a student from Georgetown University. Kraske said he didn't have any idea what I was talking about and I left it at that, but two days later, I received a telephone call at the office from a girl who told me that the student requesting the information from me wasn't a student at all and that I should be careful because this so-called student was a journalist who had the intention of writing a negative story about AfriBelgo. Can you believe crap like that? I got a warning to be careful of someone who existed only in the imagination of my own lie to Kraske and head office. Then I received this anonymous note, stating that I was playing with death. That was it. 'You are playing with death'. Just like that. I told Sonya about my experiences and I told her that, luckily, nobody knew about her interest in Erfdeel. I look upon that note as a serious death threat, Rick.' John slit his hand over his throat as he said it.

'Sonya and I became friendlier, although up till this day she's remained a sexual fridge. She told me she knew much more than I could imagine, but it would be best if I could personally meet a certain person. She had met an old man in New Orleans, when she had been posted to the South at first, before being transferred to DC. This old man apparently was a mine of information and had known Kraske for many years. She had spoken to him in the past but she thought there would be things he could say which would make sense to me, whereas she would maybe not notice the importance of certain facts. I made arrangements to fly down to New Orleans, but, at the last minute, I had to stay behind because of a crisis at work. On a second occasion, I found my way down to New Orleans, met Sonya there and we went out to see the old man – a Cajun, living out in the swamps in a shack. If I say Cajun, he's probably more French. He came out from France just after the war. We sat there for hours but I couldn't really make out very much. The old guy's mind was slipping and he could only speak of being a small boy in some place called the Ardeche. He couldn't even remember Kraske. Sonya told me that, during her stint in New Orleans, she had found out that the old man and Kraske had been together in Paris during the war. Anyway, we decided to try him once more – something we'll do some time shortly. Maybe the eighth of next month. It's the only way to go.

'My own position now is that I know I am being watched. There's one specific idiot who's always in my vicinity, whether I am in town, driving out to the golf course or going to Tyson's Corner for my shopping on a Saturday or Sunday. I've been told by faceless people that I am playing with death. That's why I am now taking Sonya's mother's example of making sure of my message in the unlikely event that something should happen to me. My message to you is that if I die and it appears like an accident, I want you to investigate whether I could not have been murdered. In the event that anything happens to me, I want you to know that I do believe Sonya's father was murdered with this Erfdeel thing probably playing a part somewhere in that death. Also, I cannot discount the strong probability that something stinks at AfriBelgo. That's really all I wish to say. In reality, I can't think of anything more, and I am taking up valuable alternative viewing time.' John winked again with a broad smile.

'Once again, Rick, I am sorry for the pain I brought upon you. It's difficult for me to say it, so far away from you, but I've always looked up to you and I love you for being my only brother. We have come a long way from lying on the floor as kids and listening to music on that Pilot radiogramme, to you listening to me now on this video. That's all. If I am not around anymore, please go well.'

Through his tears, Rick watched John's last wistful smile being replaced by the image of a less well-endowed girl, wearing boots, a sheen of sweat, and nothing else, lying spread-eagled on her back on John's desk with John sitting bare-chested behind her, a pen in his hand.

'I always prefer a work of art to be autographed,' he said as he brought the pen to her navel.

Rick stopped the tape and rewound it. He turned it past the initial scene with Jackie and watched John's message again. He knew he now had to call Sonya. And he had to destroy the video. He had no interest in watching John's further sexual escapades.

He ejected the tape, ripped off the hinged tape flap, pulled out the magnetic tape, and turned it into an intertwined mass, which he gathered up and dumped into the rubbish bin in the kitchen.

He dialled the number for the embassy and asked to speak to Miss Deine.

'Sonya Deine speaking.' A lilting voice that drifted over the line.

'Sonya, I'm Rick. Rick Land.'

'Yes?' He sensed her reticence.

'I wish to speak to you, if you have a few minutes for me.'

'I'm very busy,' she answered brusquely.

'Look, I won't take up too much of your time. I just wish to talk to you about something.'

'As I said, I'm busy.'

'I need to talk to you about matters relating to my brother, John.'

'I know your brother is dead, Mr Land, and I sympathise with you, but as far as we at the embassy are concerned, everything has been finalised.'

'I merely want to—'

'The body has been flown out for burial. He is already buried. Our job is done. We have nothing more to do with the matter.'

'I know, Miss Deine, but I really need to talk to you personally.'

'I cannot see you, unfortunately, but if you leave me your number, I will get someone from the embassy to give you a call and set up an appointment.'

She was adamant. And so was he. 'I am going to see you personally.'

'Mr Land, how many times do I have to tell you I am not available? Now I am quite busy and I have to go. I will ask Louis Malan, whom you met yesterday, to call you. Thank you. Good-bye.' She put down the receiver.

Why was she being so abrupt? What had she been doing in the house when Rick had surprised her? She was not acting at all like the kind of person John had described in his video recording. She acted as if the matter of John's death had been closed. What did the man on Roosevelt Island say again? With John's death the account had been settled. Could she not have been involved with the very people who had killed John in the end? She had definitely entered the house by means of the coded lock-box with its secret numbers on the front door, and had been prying around in the house. When he had surprised her in the house, had she not possibly removed incriminating evidence?

Sonya could have used them or they could have used her to gather information on John, who could easily have been ensnared into believing her story. After all, she had remained immune to John's charm. Sonya had to be followed up, carefully.

He picked up the receiver, dialled the embassy again and asked to be transferred to Louis Malan. 'Louis? Rick Land here.'

'Howzit?'

'Fine, thanks. Tell me, at what time do you normally all go home? I still want to pop in there, if there is sufficient time available this afternoon.'

Author's note: Louis Malan later came out of the closet and is now living in a small town in the Orange Free State with his partner. I stayed in their Bed and Breakfast where Louis spoke quite candidly of the events in question. I can really recommend their guesthouse.

CHAPTER 14

The wages of sin is death but the gift of God is eternal life.

–Romans 6:23

HEAVY TRAFFIC FLASHED BY IN the one-way glass of the front door. Rick ascended the few stone steps from the driveway. He noticed the video camera just above the door, which automatically swung open.

The guard spoke with a heavy Spanish accent and motioned Rick through an electronic doorframe security scanner.

Behind a bulletproof glass window another man sat next to a flickering video monitor. He raised his eyebrows as a silent request for Rick to announce his business.

'I would like to see Miss Sonya Deine, please.'

The man picked up a telephone receiver and spoke inaudibly behind the glass shield for a few moments, after which he indicated that Rick should pass through a bulletproof glass door. Rick entered an enclosure containing a few chairs. The next door could only be opened from the interior of the embassy. He reflected that the security system must have been set up during apartheid days when South Africa used to be the polecat of the world, and the embassy a target for attack. Maybe now, since the ascent of President Mandela a few months ago, the security had become a little superfluous, he thought.

Feeling like a goldfish in a bowl, he sat down and waited. Every now and then, someone came through from the inside, but there was no sign of Sonya.

Finally, after more than half an hour, she arrived. 'I thought I told you I am not available.' She folded her arms and stood defiantly in front of him.

'I don't care what you told me,' Rick said, slightly irritated. 'All I know is that my brother and my ex-wife have been murdered and I am looking for answers. I think you can help me.'

'What makes you think so?'

'There was a trip to—'

The door behind Sonya opened with Louis Malan and another man, both carrying briefcases, emerging.

'I see you're not one for wasting any time.' Louis tugged at Rick's sleeve and winked at Sonya. 'We'll leave you two to your own devices. Bye.'

Rick waited for them to leave before he started speaking. 'This is not the right place for a discussion. I feel like a laboratory specimen in this glass enclosure. Why don't you let me buy you a drink?'

'I don't drink during office hours.'

'The noon jets have long ago come in to land over the Potomac. It's almost closing time. But we could have soft drinks.'

A short while later he followed her Oldsmobile Cutlass through the homebound traffic of central Washington until they both parked opposite a watering hole called Déjà vu. From the parking lot, Rick heard the beat of Déjà vu's music and the babble of the crowd.

Inside they had to cope with standing room only. Gingerly balancing her gin and tonic and his scotch and soda, he led Sonya to a less noisy spot, away from the blaring music.

'Okay,' she took a sip, 'tell me now what it is that you want from me.'

'Your perfume,' he started, 'that's how I know it was you.'

'Know what?' Her frown deepened.

'That's how I know you were in John's house the day before yesterday.'

'What?'

'I'm a professional hunter.'

'I know. So what does that have to do with an allegation of me in some place?'

'I'm a bush tracker. In Africa I have through the years gained quite a sense of smell. Higher than most people. You left quite quickly, but your perfume lingered.'

'You're making a mistake.'

'No, I'm not. Your car was parked outside the house. And another thing, I know you hoodwinked a real-estate company into letting you get hold of the code for the lock-box on the front door. If you still refuse to accept my logic, I could of course bring Rita from the real-estate company to the embassy tomorrow so that she could tell the ambassador how you pretended to be someone else. Not the normal thing to do for a diplomat, I'm sure you'll agree.'

'You drive a hard bargain. You should be in second-hand car sales.'

She looked at Rick with such a blue-grey strength in her gaze, he experienced a feeling of vertigo.

'Second-hand car salesmen can often read the truth in a customer's eyes,' he said, trying to cover his embarrassment. Sonya Deine was intoxicatingly beautiful at close range.

'I'm not your customer.'

He had a sudden impulse to caress her silky skin. She wore small platinum earrings set against glossy golden hair. A piquant nose gave her a sensual allure, highlighted by the chiselled strength of high cheekbones. And she had a mouth in which a man could lose himself.

'Sonya, you were there.'

'Okay, so I was in John's house,' she finally confessed and managed to cover her fluster by taking a sip from her gin and tonic.

'What were you looking for?'

'I'm not actually interested in talking to you or anybody involved with AfriBelgo about anything.'

'You seem to spit out the word AfriBelgo as if it were a curse.'

'It is. I had my reason, a good one, for being there and that's all I am prepared to say.' Her eyes were now fixed in a stare at the ceiling.

'You ... er ... have a problem with AfriBelgo.' His words came out as a statement.

'AfriBelgo is run by a despotic old man. If I have to be killed, like others, then so be it,' she said and closed her eyes.

'Despotic?'

'AfriBelgo is manipulated by a ruthless robber baron.'

'You're talking of an entrepreneurial giant in world mining. Erick Martens is a major philanthropist—'

'Philanthropist, my foot! He's a carrier of death! I saw the picture in the newspaper of you and that man at John's grave and I honestly shivered.'

'I didn't know Uncle Erick and I—'

'Oh, so, like John, you call him Uncle? Imagine that! Uncle bloody Erick,' she said with an ice cube in the corner of her mouth as if to cool her fury. 'Naturally I saw you.' She spat the ice cube back into her glass. 'We receive South African newspapers by diplomatic pouch. The last batch arrived yesterday and, lo and behold, there was a front-page photograph of that man with you at one side, and that poor woman at his other side. But, aside from that solemn picture, there were other photographs – terrifying pictures of the destruction after she had been slaughtered – with drawn-out journalistic sagas of how the blast had happened.'

'It was utter horror.' An image of Melinda's smile, disintegrating in a blinding flash of light, flicked through his mind.

'Look, I don't believe anyone or anything any more. I don't know what your angle on life really is, Rick Land, and I don't particularly care.'

'So what do you care about? Maybe that's a starting point, Sonya.'

From the corner of his eye he noticed that some of the other patrons were becoming increasingly interested in their heated discussion.

'Listen, I had an unexplained murder in my own family and there is a link here.'

'A murder in your family?'

'Yes. Don't try to go into detail on that with me. I had an unexplained death close to me. Your brother was murdered, your wife was murdered—'

'You're talking too loudly. People around us are too interested in this conversation. So, tone it down. And she was not my wife. She was my ex-wife.'

'Whatever. Okay, I'll speak a little softer. The point is, I know you hated your brother because he had an affair with your wife—'

'Ex-wife.'

'Whatever. I know you found John and your ex-wife in a compromising position because he told me. Understandably, you were mad at him and her. So the brothers never communicated again. But John felt penitent after the affair. He just wanted to get away from it all. That's why he arranged for a position here in DC. Did you know that? He told me that himself. You look surprised. Fine, so your brother came out here and what did you do? You remained a killer, going out into the wilds to shoot innocent animals for fun. And what happens to John? He, an innocent man, is shot and killed out here.'

'Do you insinuate that I had a hand in John's death as well as that of Melinda?' Rick had to control his shaking voice.

'I don't trust you, Rick Land,' she said, glaring at him, 'and I don't trust your Uncle bloody Erick either – particularly that creep of an old man.'

'I might understand your negativity if you gave me your reasons why I should think that way. Why are you so distrustful?'

'Because you are hand in glove with him. Your bloody uncle.'

From the resoluteness of her tone and the firmness of her lips, he could see she truly believed that he and Uncle Erick were evil. He had to force himself not to show his agitation.

'I don't appreciate your innuendo and I'm distressed that you regard me as a blanket killer.' He inhaled deeply in an effort to steady his anger before he continued.

'I'm not hand in glove with anyone, Sonya, and I don't kill for fun. Least of all, I would never touch a hair of anyone close to me, even if people disappointed me in the way John and Melinda did. On top of that, their infidelity happened many years ago. Why would I be 'hand in glove' with anyone to their detriment right now?'

From her uncompromising gaze he could read her contempt.

'You have to believe me, Sonya. I'm trying to find out why John and Melinda were murdered.'

'At one stage, I had a little hope that justice would be served, but now, with John's death, I've given up. I'm tired.'

'I'm sorry, I didn't want to put pressure on you.'

'I'm tired. So, buy me one more', and she proffered him her glass.

'Apologies.'

'I'll take my depression and go my own way. You can then tell your Uncle bloody Erick, or whoever else at AfriBelgo, that I have no interest anymore in anything. Take the glass, please, and tell the man at the counter I'll have less gin and more tonic.'

Rick walked over to the bar counter. Sonya obviously had a deep hate for Uncle Erick and it was clear that she believed that her father's death had a direct link to Uncle Erick. Now why would she also believe that he, Rick, was somehow involved in the deaths of John and Melinda? What did that man on Roosevelt Island say? He was partly to blame for John's death. He had been testing Sonya's feelings, but the time was now ripe to persuade her to co-operate with him.

Rick returned with two refills.

'Here you are.' He handed her the drink. 'Sonya, you think that I hated John and my ex-wife.'

'Yes.'

'Maybe I did, once. It's true that in later years we lost contact but what would you say if I told you John spoke to me about you and about Erfdeel?'

'Erfdeel?' He saw her genuine surprise.

'Yes, Erfdeel. He also told me about the joint venture between your father and Uncle Erick and that Kraske was somehow involved. Many things you mention are difficult for me to grasp. You must know that Uncle Erick has been like a father to both John and me. John told me of the death of your father, your years in—'

'How could he have told you that? You never had contact and he's dead!'

'He took a leaf from your mother's book. She wrote you a letter. He made me a video.'

She blinked at him.

'He told me that you believed your dad was murdered and he spoke of your time in the orphanage, your mother's letter, her reference to Erfdeel, and he even mentioned the old man in New Orleans. Do you know that John made a bequest to the orphanage?'

'No.' Once again she blinked.

'I also found out a few other things, such as that you went down with him to New Orleans on the day of his death.'

'How do you know that?' she asked, her eyes widening. 'You are now talking of events on the day of his murder. There is no way in which he could have made a video on the day he died. Nonsense.'

'No nonsense here. Just deduction. He left a scribbled date with your name linked to it. In his video he said you and he had already gone to see the old man in New Orleans—'

'Jacques.'

'In his video he said he couldn't make head or tail of the old man's ramblings. He also said that you were planning a date which fell away and that you and he were planning to go on the eighth of this month, which was the day of his murder. I think it would have been your third date for New Orleans but I'm probably mangling things. I'm sure you get the drift. That's why I think you know more about his death than you're prepared to admit.'

She ran her finger around the edge of the glass. 'Point is, I didn't fly out on the same plane with him that day. I arrived a day earlier.'

'Oh?'

'I got leave from the office telling them I wanted to go up to New York. I was supposed to meet John at a place on Bourbon Street. We were supposed to contact each other via our cell phones and I would have called him on his hand held. Problem was, when I left home I couldn't find my cell phone. Haven't found it since. I must have lost it. I didn't have his number on me there as I only had it on my own cell phone.'

'So you didn't connect?'

'Early that evening on the day of our intended get-together, the eighth, I received a note at my hotel. It stated that John's office had telephoned the hotel and left me a message that his flight had been delayed and he would only be arriving the following day.'

'Weird.'

'I never saw him after that. When I called his office from New Orleans the following day to ask about his arrival and they gave me the news of his death, I was so shocked I couldn't move from my hotel room.'

'Very strange. Why would there be a call from his office? I thought from his video it was a confidential trip.'

'It was so frightening I couldn't think of anything to do. Later I realised I was shivering. So I got into bed, covered myself and tried to sleep. I felt responsible for John's death. I still do.' Her voice faltered. 'If I hadn't come into his life, he would still be alive today.'

Unexpectedly, she burst into tears. Her body shook as she lowered her head and fumbled in her handbag for a tissue. A woman close to them stared at Rick with accusing eyes.

'Sonya,' Rick said and he touched her shoulder, 'it's not your fault. You cannot take the blame for John's death.'

'But he would have still been here – alive – if he hadn't met me!'

'He would have also lived if he hadn't moved to the USA to get away from me,' Rick said. 'If you blame yourself, then I must blame myself even more. It is just one of those psychological things that you want to incorrectly apportion blame for the death on yourself. I've seen it with other people. Don't do it.'

This seemed to have a calming effect on her. For a while they were both silent, but around them the cocktail generation chirped incessantly.

'Something bothers me,' Rick said, as he again stifled a sneeze by putting his hand to his nose. 'The person or people who killed John knew your movements.'

Rick took an antihistamine tablet from his pocket and gulped it down with his scotch and soda.

'You're right. I also thought of that. Whoever killed him must have had prior knowledge of his movements. And mine. How else could I have got a message in my hotel? Only John and I knew of our trip to New Orleans. Why would his office call me with a message? I still distrust you a little, but I suppose I'll feel better when I've seen John's tape.'

'I destroyed it.'

'What? And now you think I should believe you?'

'You have to.'

'Why would you destroy such an important piece of evidence?'

'There really was a tape,' Rick iterated.

'I don't think so. I think you are a liar, Mr Land.'

'Sonya, there was one. Very personal. I had to destroy it.'

'You lie, Rick Land. You're playing a game with me. I don't trust you or anybody.' She put down her glass on the counter and turned towards the door. 'Point is, Mr Rick Land, I wasn't too sure from the start about you. From my first sight of you with your pious face on the front page of the newspaper, to the whispered conversation you had at yesterday's cocktail party with that cultivated hypocrite, Kraske, I knew you were a lackey. Nothing more. Just a lackey for your dear uncle. Maybe you're more than that – you're a modern Cain! With your passion for killing you will probably not be much of a churchgoer, but you might know that Cain killed his brother, Abel, and for that he was banished to the wilderness by God. That's where you belong. Go back to the wilderness.'

Ignoring the stares around her, she stormed out of Déjà Vu.

He knew he had to follow her to set the record straight. He dug into his pockets, dropped a twenty-dollar note on the counter and ran after her. A few minutes later he was once again following her through the traffic. Her Oldsmobile tore through the busy streets, still filled with home-going motorists, and he had difficulty keeping up with her as she weaved from one lane to the other.

What a delightfully strange mixture she was, he thought. She had innocence and arrogance, confidence and uncertainty, trust in the familiar and doubts about the unknown, and all those opposites had combined to produce the fiery whirlwind she was, not at all the staid kind of person one would expect behind the steering wheel of a car with a diplomatic number plate.

She slipped through a set of traffic lights as they changed and forced Rick to jump the red lights in pursuit. A few blocks further, with the Oldsmobile Cutlass still ahead of him, he noticed a rundown church on the left-hand side. In the fading sunlight of the early evening, the neon sign in front of the church had already been switched on. The traffic had almost come to a standstill and they crawled past the sign that proclaimed: *The wages of sin are death but the gift of God is eternal life.*

And it turned his thoughts to Cain and Abel, and John.

Sonya had led him into a quiet, tree-lined street in an area he deduced from the roadside signs to be Bethesda. She turned into the driveway of an impressive apartment building, slung low in a lush park. Rick could not follow her, as there was a boom across the entrance. She disappeared into the undercover parking. He had to search outside in the street for parking, and then made his way to entrance.

It was easy to find her apartment from the boxes in the main lobby. There were only eight apartments in the building and the occupants were all listed by surname. He took the elevator.

Wondering whether she would open the door for him, he rang the doorbell. He had noticed from the way in which she had touched the rear-view mirror of the Oldsmobile that she had been fully conscious he was following her.

There was no immediate answer to the ring. He rang the doorbell again.

'Sonya! It's me. Could you open up, please,' he said, leaning with his hand against her front door.

'She's in the bath. You can't see her,' a man answered, his voice curt.

The voice seemed familiar. It had a very slight lisp. And Rick knew she was in danger.

He had to think quickly.

'I'm Dennis from next door,' Rick said, as timidly as possible.

'Yeah?' the gruff voice came back from the other side of the door. 'Didn't I tell you? She's in the bath. Go away.'

'My friend and I borrowed a bottle of Bourbon from her last night. I just want to give her the replacement I bought today,' Rick said. His reasoning was that, if he sounded harmless, he could get the man to open the door. 'Maybe you could just open the door a teensy bit and take the bottle. Tell her my friend Frankie and I think she's fabulous. Really fabulous. Best neighbour we ever had. Take the bottle and tell her Frankie and I send her a million kisses of thanks.'

Rick heard the latch on the other side of the door sliding away. The door opened slightly. Rick gripped the door handle, unsure of what to do next.

'Okay. Hand me the bottle,' the man said as he stretched out his hand through the opening.

'Here you are,' Rick said and, at that moment, throwing his body backwards while gripping the door handle, he yanked the door closed to catch the outstretched arm in a wire-cutting action between the door and the doorjamb.

The man screamed, his elbow and forearm protruding at an unnatural angle, fingers groping in the air.

In an automatic, recoiling action, still gripping the handle, Rick drove his body towards the door and swung his full weight sideways. Shoulder first, he rammed into the man's pincered elbow parallel to the wall. With his head against the arm, Rick heard the breaking of bone above the agonised scream behind the door. Rick clung to the now-limp arm, twisting and bashing it furiously against the doorjamb, against a howling cacophony from inside.

Keeping hold of the arm, Rick drove into the door and burst into the apartment. The man cushioned Rick's fall as they both went down, rolling over each other.

Rick saw a flashing glint in front of his face and instinctively grabbed the hand with the knife, pushing it away from him. This was no ordinary knife but a huge push knife – a six-inch blade protruding through the fingers of the man's clenched fist. Rick kept the hand with the push-knife away from himself; it helped that the man's other arm was useless. In one action he lifted himself and came down on the man, burying his knee in his soft groin.

With another roar of torture, the man's fist opened and the knife flew away, the point of it just missing Rick's shoulder.

Rick snatched up the knife and looked at it momentarily. It consisted of a T-shaped handle and a narrow piece of steel where the knife fitted through your fingers, with the long blade at the front. He clasped it in his fist and drew it forward, pointing the blade at the man who now slowly lifted his head.

When their eyes met, they were both astonished at finally recognising each other.

Rick looked into the beady eyes of the same sickly, flabby man who had tried to shoot him on the street – the man from the Hilton.

'Mister Africa. What a friggin' surprise,' the man lisped hoarsely through curled lips.

Then, he lunged head first towards Rick's face in a desperate head butt.

Rick jerked his head out of the way and parried the blow. The same sweet scent of creamy hair lotion whipped past his cheekbone but, as unexpectedly as the head butt had come, the man froze in mid-air, grunted as if he were picking up a heavy load, and fell forward on to Rick.

Lying on the floor with the man on top of him, Rick felt something like warm mud trickling over his hand. He looked down on the push knife in his right hand, now embedded in the man's chest. The man had accidentally knifed himself against the push-knife in Rick's hand.

Slowly, the man lifted his head and, lying face-to-face, their eyes met again. His eyes blazed and his nose almost touched Rick's. His breath smelled of stale beer as he weakly fought for air. A rush of new warm blood burst onto Rick's hand. The man rattled for air. His eyes still gazed in defiance at Rick.

Rick pushed him away, withdrew the knife and stood up. He couldn't see Sonya. On a table in the entrance lobby, within easy reach, was a vase holding a pot plant. Rick put down the knife on the table next to the vase.

He picked up the vase, heavy with well-watered soil, held it high over the head of the man who was now rolling over in a weak effort to get up. The vase crashed into the man's head and Rick knew there was no way in which he would get up again from that blow.

Rick retrieved the knife, wiped his bloodied hand and the blade clean against the man's shirt and turned around to search for Sonya, calling for her. He went from room to room. Not a sound. He should not have allowed her to storm out like that. In retrospect, he should have accompanied her. He could not bear the thought of possibly finding her dead. Not another death, please.

'Sonya!' She was sitting in the kitchen, bound and gagged on a chair in front of the oven. Her eyes were filled with tears.

With the knife he sliced away the gag.

'Rick! Thank God you're here!' Freeing her by cutting the bonds, she sobbed and managed to scream.

'Thank God you're alive. I took care of the man. You're safe now.'

'No, Rick. We have to get out! Now!'

'Stay calm, Sonya. The guy's dead and there's nobody else in your apartment.'

'You don't understand! He's put some kind of explosive device in the oven! He showed it to me!'

Rick peered in through the tinted glass of the oven door and saw a package inside, wrapped in brown paper. He knew very little about explosives but he imagined a ticking mechanism on its inexorable march to destruction.

'We have to get out! Come on!' She grabbed Rick by the arm.

'You go. Warn your neighbours! Everyone in the building! And get the police!'

She ran out past the sprawled body covered in potting soil.

Rick stared at the bomb, reasoning with himself. Why would the man have wanted to place Sonya directly in front of the oven? Could it have meant that the blast would be limited in action and be directed through the front of the oven only? Maybe he could localise the effect of the blast by putting something in front or on top of the door.

There was only one thing to do. He ran back, grabbed the man by his feet and dragged him into the kitchen to the stove. Rick swung open the oven door until it stopped, horizontal with the floor. The brown paper package lay open to view now. He lifted the limp figure from the floor. By using two kitchen stools, Rick managed to prop him up against the oven door so that his bulk now blocked the opening. The man sat there, his head slumped awkwardly to one side, his broken arm leaning on one kitchen stool, his shoulder propped up on the other, a huge bloody gash in his chest. Rick realised his own shirt was dripping with blood. He took it off and placed it on the oven door.

'Time to go,' Rick said to himself, dropped the push knife into the man's lap and turned to run.

He made sure to close the kitchen and front doors as a further –

probably futile – method to contain the potential effect of the expected blast, and then ran down the corridor.

In the early evening dusk, Sonya and a number of people, some in their pyjamas, milled around on the lawn.

'I think I've got hold of everyone in the building,' she said as he walked over to the group. 'I called everyone down on the intercom system from the front door.'

'Good, and the police?'

'Mrs Hobbs over there called them.'

'This all sounds like a load of bullshit,' a man in pyjamas said to Rick and Sonya, open irritation on his face. 'I'm not going to wait here for the cops to—'

A flash of light preceded the booming sound by a split-second.

The explosion cut through the twilight in a blinding roar. It vibrated through their bodies, throwing everyone instinctively onto the lawn. The detonation was trailed by the eerie tinkling of falling glass.

Then there was silence. And the smell of dust. Almost like the bushveld, Rick thought.

All the lights in the building were out. Flame-tinged smoke poured from Sonya's apartment, whirling through the broken windows into the night.

Rick took Sonya's hand and helped her on her feet. They stood there hand in hand, watching the fire in her apartment.

One by one, people got up from the lawn and stood transfixed.

Somewhere in the distance a voice called. The air now also smelled of hot metal and welding vapours. Far away, the faint sound of emergency vehicles grew louder and louder until a police car burst onto the lawn, followed by a red Plymouth Reliant with flashing red and white lights on its roof and a DC Fire Department sign in gold print on its side. Other emergency vehicles followed in quick succession.

'It's a nightmare,' Sonya said.

'Usually after a nightmare,' Rick said, 'one wakes up to reality.'

Rick noticed Mrs Hobbs pointing out Sonya to a policeman. 'Let's not make it too complicated, Sonya,' he whispered as he saw the policeman walking over. 'Just say you had a bomb threat a few days ago at the embassy and tell them the rest as it happened.'

'Rick, I'm sorry.'

'About what?'

'I distrusted you.'

'Sonya, You and I are in this together now. The man who tried to kill you tried to kill me.'

CHAPTER 15

Les nerfs des batailles sont les pecunes.
(The sinews of battles are money.)

–Voltaire

LOUIS MALAN'S FURNITURE WAS EXPENSIVE but impersonal, as was so often the case, Sonya informed Rick, in state-furnished diplomatic living quarters – living proof of the disparity in taste between different government purchasers in distant offices and different occupants over several years.

He had an ultra-modern lamp that could fit in a B-grade sci-fi film, two antique grey velvet couches more suited to the adult movie industry and what Rick considered a rustic fashion accident of steel chairs with seats made of worn woven leather thongs. A bad painting of Table Mountain hung against the wall and his white ashtrays were embossed with South Africa's coat of arms.

It was two in the morning.

Rick wore a clean shirt and a pair of trousers from Louis. His eyelids were lead. Then he sneezed the lead away. Having forgotten to take his tablets, hay fever had again taken hold of him. Louis's two Yorkshire terriers merrily yapped in echo with the sneeze.

'The ambassador wasn't too chuffed about being woken up in the middle of the night, but when I explained to him he understood, of course.'

'What did he say?' Sonya asked as she walked in with a tray of coffee.

'Ag man, he just of course asked whether you were hurt and he was relieved to hear you're fine and that you're staying over for the night,' Louis said, taking a cup. 'Then he wanted to know exactly how it had happened, who it could have been and why. He also said security should be stepped up in general for all of us. Oh yes, and he mentioned that if you wanted to come in late or if you preferred to rest tomorrow, he would understand.'

'Good idea that you should rest, Sonya,' Rick said.

'I couldn't rest tomorrow. One of my few remaining possessions is my credit card and I'll have to go shopping for clothes. Hopefully, tomorrow the office could put me up in a hotel.'

'You can stay here for as long as you like,' Louis offered with what seemed to Rick like a little too much interest in having Sonya around. He could not remember when last he had felt even a twinge of jealousy but he felt it now.

Down the corridor a door slammed. Sonya jumped and Rick grabbed the gun.

'Shame, you two are really on edge,' Louis said.

'We had quite a ride today,' Rick said.

'Well, as I said I've got room enough for both of us and you can stay for a while,' Louis said.

'Thanks, but no thanks,' Sonya said. 'We'll be here tonight and I am grateful but I prefer to do my own thing. Shopping for clothes will be part of it.'

Rick felt relieved. He yawned and dropped off to sleep.

STILL DRESSED IN LOUIS'S CLOTHES, Rick got up from his uncomfortable seated sleeping position. His head ached and he had a sore neck.

'Sorry, we should have woken you up and got you into bed.'

'Sonya, I can sleep on a washing line.'

'That's good then. Shopping time now.'

They left for Tyson's Corner.

When they had finished and got back into the car he said, 'I think it would be best if we go back to John's house now. You could take off the tags there and I'm sure there'll be a suitcase for you to pack your new clothes in.'

She smiled at him.

For the first time he noticed the small gap between her upper front teeth, just sufficient to make her mouth captivatingly different. She had a natural beauty, not doll-like or sculptured to perfection, but rather like nature itself where minor flaws highlight inherent beauty.

As they left the car park Rick noticed a cyclist from the corner of his eyes. Not another one! He slammed the car brakes. The screeching tyres frightened the cyclist so much that he fell off his bike.

'Sorry. Now that I have you with me I have a new responsibility and it freaks me out a little.' With an apologetic wave at the cyclist, they drove off.

'Sonya, why did you break into John's house?'

'I don't know.'

'You must have had a reason. Come on.'

'It's difficult to explain. I met him at a dinner party. In fact, I told you about that, come to think of it.'

'Yes.'

'He tried his Don Juan bit with me, but I've never in my life been anyone's fodder and I told him so. On top of that, he was from AfriBelgo and, well, you said yourself he told you of my dad, and so I got into an argument with him and—'

'Why don't you first tell me what you were looking for in the house and then tell me the whole story from the beginning?'

'As consular officer I helped with a good part of the arrangements to have the casket flown back home. I found out who had been instructed to sell the house and I knew Lucas and Love Realtors had the lock-box system. And so it is true that I spun the lady at Lucas and Love a story to get the combination for the lock-box. Point is, although John and I had a problem in the beginning, at that dinner I mentioned, we became friends in the end and I shared some of my deepest secrets and fears about AfriBelgo with him. And then suddenly he's murdered. Shot in the head. Just like my own father, like an animal in an abattoir.'

'Yes. Terrible.'

'Point is, Rick, he wasn't shot here in DC where he lived and worked. Oh, no. John was shot in New Orleans. As I told you at Déjà vu yesterday, it bothered me that I had received a note from the hotel receptionist in New Orleans saying that John's office had called me to say that his flight had been delayed. It bothered me even more when I found out he had actually arrived at the correct time. Someone in his office must have lied.'

'Or someone elsewhere?'

'Maybe, but that is why I went to the house. I just thought I might find some clues. And then there was the funeral and the death of your wife …'

'Ex-wife,' Rick reminded her.

'Sorry. But there was another factor.'

'Yes?'

'I was still in New Orleans when I heard John had been killed.'

'You told me.'

'Well, I was so confused I packed up and left without honouring the appointment we had made with Jacques Daniel at Bayou Biarritz. When I read about the death of your ex-wife, I tried to reach Jacques and, as incredible as it sounds, I was told he had drowned.'

'Another death?'

'Another one. Only thing is, he was not in a position to drown.'

'What do you mean?'

'He was an invalid in a wheelchair. Somehow this old guy who had lived safely right on the water for decades, in his wheelchair, had fallen into the water and drowned. I was told they had found him dead in his wheelchair, submerged in the water, next to his cabin. Fallen off his porch while fishing.'

'So you presume he was also murdered?'

'No presumption. I am convinced of that.'

'John told me that the two of you had gone down to see Jacques Daniel. He said that his mind had been drifting and that you had hoped to try again. What made this old man so interesting then?'

'Interesting?' She sighed, tapping at the window, watching the scenery float by.

'John told me in his video that Jacques had known Peter Kraske for many years.'

'Of course he and Kraske knew each other. He had been with Kraske in the war and, in lucid moments, he had some very interesting stories about Kraske. He was still very lucid when I was posted in New Orleans before my transfer to DC. I just wanted John to hear those stories. That's why it was so important to take John to Jacques once more in the hope he would be more compos mentis.'

'Also because you believe Kraske is linked to AfriBelgo?'

Sonya remained quiet for a while, still tapping her fingers against the windowpane, and then she spoke, slowly and deliberately. 'I know John told you about it, but let me tell you the story from my perspective, and stop me if I repeat things you know from John.'

'Right.'

'A man called Mauritz Deine once borrowed a lot of money from the bank and bought a farm. It was a good spread of land with good potential on the border of South Africa and Swaziland, where he farmed a strange mix of cattle and tropical fruit. He was still young and had been married for only a year when two men came to see him – Erick Martens, who was a trader in building materials, and Peter Kraske, an international financial broker. They told Mauritz Deine they were prepared to enter into a joint venture with him for the exploitation of the mineral rights on his farm, as they were sure there was a good chance of a gold strike. It just so happened that the farm was in the Barberton area, where already several gold mines operated. Mauritz knew little of business and within days became embroiled in a joint venture with Kraske and Martens. Sure enough they found gold and formed a small company which they called East Crown Gold Mining—'

Rick gripped the steering wheel tighter. 'Did you say East Crown Gold?'

'Yes.'

'So this was all part of the origins of AfriBelgo?'

'Precisely.'

Uncle Erick's credo of profit through partnership was built upon the infant years of AfriBelgo. Rick knew the story of those first years off by heart. It was a standard part of the AfriBelgo public relations machine. But Sonya's father and Peter Kraske had been written out of AfriBelgo's history.

'Please continue.'

'Okay, so Mauritz Deine was my father and soon East Crown Gold had all kinds of machinery on the farm and they started mining operations. And then one day my father returned from town and told my mother he had found out that Kraske and Martens were copying the Erfdeel scam. He explained to her what the scam was. But I must tell you, first of all, that I only found out recently what Erfdeel really meant.'

'Do you mean to say that AfriBelgo could have been built on a scam?'

'That's the point.'

'How?'

'I don't know. But my dad told my mom he had told Kraske earlier that day he would terminate the joint venture the very next day. That night, a hooded man walked into my parents' bedroom and shot my father at point-blank range where he lay next to my mother. He was sleeping. Thankfully, he probably never even knew what hit him, but my mother woke up to see the hooded man turn away and walk out with the gun in his hand. Unknown even to my father, and even my mother at that time, she was carrying a child – me. After my father's death it turned out that the bank owned the biggest part of the farm. On top of that, he had signed a contract with his partners which now gave them the option of the first right to purchase, which they did, dirt cheap.'

'You sure?'

'Of course. In effect, they just paid off the bank.'

'Well, well, well.'

'Then my mother received a death threat and was forced to move to the city. I was born eight months after my father's death.'

'What a terrible story.'

'My mother struggled for a while to make ends meet. Before I turned two she died of cancer and I ended up in an orphanage with no knowledge of anything that had happened. On my sixteenth birthday the orphanage handed me a letter from my mother, the one John mentioned to you. In that letter she told me about Kraske and I made a decision to trace him. In later years, I found out he was living in America. I then worked towards being accepted into the diplomatic corps and to being posted to the USA, in the process refusing several other postings.'

'And that was how you found your way to DC. But how were you able to trace Kraske to America in the first place?'

'I wrote to AfriBelgo,' she smiled, 'and told them I was a student in economics, which I was, that I was doing research on the history of the mining industry and that I wanted to know what had happened to Peter Kraske who had been one of the founders of AfriBelgo. The AfriBelgo public relations department gave me everything I needed.'

'Strange. I worked for the company and I never knew of Kraske's involvement in the founding of AfriBelgo. My first thought a few moments ago was that your dad and Kraske never featured in anything I saw in company publications.'

'I guess it was a case of the history according to Erick Martens,' she said.

'But the PR department guided you to Kraske.'

'Rick, you can avoid mentioning historical facts but they are like your bush tracks with one difference: You cannot erase them. They are in the archives.'

'Tell me everything you know of Kraske.'

'He was in the German Gestapo in the Second World War.'

'What!'

'SS. Intelligence.'

'You must be joking.'

'I'm serious.'

'You cannot expect me to believe that. This man is a top lobbyist. Every second journalist would surely have been on to such a story a long time ago. You yourself just said historical tracks remain.'

'They do remain. The AfriBelgo PR people had some historical reference that Kraske had been part of the origin and is still today here in the US a friend or associate or something of the company.'

'But then there should be a reference to Mauritz Deine, surely.'

'My dad's tracks stop before the origin according to your uncle. He was the farmer before the company started in the gospel according to St Erick Martens.'

'Amazing.'

'Rick, when I met Jacques Daniel the first time, he told me in the most graphic detail of how Peter Kraske had killed innocent people during the war. He spoke of people being bound and chained, their bodies hauled up on pulleys and dropped onto sharp-edged blocks of wood. He spoke of flesh torn with sharp pliers from screaming victims. But the ghastly reality was that old Jacques Daniel told me he himself had tortured people in Paris during the war and that Kraske had been his commanding officer in the Gestapo. Kraske must have had connections at the top because he was extremely young for an officer.'

'Sonya, surely in a city where investigative journalism uncovered something like Watergate, the name Kraske would have been uncovered in wartime records.'

'You don't want to believe it?'

'It sounds so far-fetched.'

'It's not. Kraske assumed his current name after the war. His real name was Franz. Jacques Daniel never wanted to mention his surname to me but spoke of him only as Franz, a Gestapo intelligence officer in Paris. After the war, Franz decided to co-operate with the Americans, handing them all the information they needed to tie up all kinds of loose ends. In return, the Americans showed their undying gratitude for his services by giving him a new identity. Under a new name, that of Peter Kraske, he ended up in South Africa for some years and then came to the States as an immigrant from the British Commonwealth to start a new life. Where do you think Kraske's initial political contacts came from?'

'I can now see why you're interested in Kraske and why John would have been interested in following it up.'

'I'm glad you see the light.'

Rick was silent for a moment. Then he nodded. 'It all makes sense now. Your father was murdered in the infancy of AfriBelgo after accusing Kraske of a scam. John obviously wanted to find out more because it affected the company and Uncle Erick, which is why he requested information on Erfdeel from AfriBelgo.'

'You've got it.'

'Being stonewalled, John turned to Ferrara for information. In his videotaped message John said his request had led to a visit from Kraske during which it had become clear that Kraske had known of the request. And then John was murdered trying to find out more about Kraske's past from an invalid who had been close to Kraske and who somehow then drowned in strange circumstances. Now I understand how I bumped into you at the cocktail reception. I was speaking to Kraske and you were eavesdropping.'

She smiled, crossed her legs, and distracted Rick's attention for a moment so that he almost missed the turnoff to John's house.

He had to keep himself in check. Neither he nor Sonya could afford to lose their concentration. He had seen it too often in the bush.

A client would go out into the wilds with him, using the best equipment available – a top-class rifle, the most sophisticated telescopic sight, expensive khaki clothes – and yet, when it came to the critical moment, the client would be distracted by something as insignificant as an ant or a dung-beetle.

'What are you thinking of?' she asked, tilting her head to look him in the eye, as they came to a stop in the driveway of John's house.

'I think it would be prudent if I went in first to make sure there's no unwanted visitor. If you had unwanted company at your apartment, I might have the same.'

He pressed the button to open the automatic garage doors.

'I'm right behind you,' she said. 'Buddy system.'

They went through the house and found nothing out of place. Hunger drove them to the kitchen where he lifted the rubbish bin lid and showed her the mangled remains of John's video exactly as he had discarded it.

'After the explosion I already believed you.'

'Maybe,' Rick mumbled with a piece of ham-and-cheese sandwich wedged in his mouth, 'maybe we have to corner Peter Kraske.'

Sitting opposite him in the breakfast nook, Sonya held the other half of the sandwich in her hand.

'Kraske has a place in town which he uses during the week,' she said, attempting to stop her sandwich from falling apart between her long, slender fingers.

'Do you play the piano?' he asked with a mouthful of food.

'No. Why?'

'You have the fingers of an artist. Sorry, you were talking of Kraske.'

'Yes, during the week he stays in the DC area in a place of his own but on weekends he goes out to Harper's Ferry.'

'Where's that?'

'West Virginia meeting the rest of the world. He apparently has quite a spread. His house featured in a recent write-up in a society magazine. They say it's a huge place, with a spectacular view from a hillside.'

'Could you find it?' he asked with the first inkling of a strategy forming in his mind.

'I've been to Harper's Ferry. I have an idea of the area.'

'Tomorrow is Saturday. Maybe we should go out there.'

Using one of John's suitcases, Sonya packed her new wardrobe while Rick showered, shaved and put on fresh clothing. Shortly afterwards they left for Sonya's apartment. Rick made sure to load John's five-shot snub-nosed Smith and Wesson and to store it under his car seat, together with the shoulder holster and a box of ammunition. He was not going to take chances with their safety anymore.

Scarred with black soot, Sonya's apartment resembled a wartime scene. The dark gaping hole stood out as an ugly cavity of destruction in an otherwise relatively untouched building. Surprisingly enough, the fire had been confined to her apartment. Rick had been right.

A policeman on duty informed them that, although the rest of the building had remained relatively unscathed, the structural damage was still being assessed and that nobody was, as yet, allowed to enter the building. As a result, all the vehicles in the basement were to remain there for the moment, including Sonya's.

Outside the property on the street a huge truck was parked under the trees, emblazoned on the side with the emblem and logo of the Metropolitan Police, Washington DC. Not looking forward to the prospect of spending two hours again in explanation to the police, as on the night before, they reported to a uniformed man in the truck, who seemed more than flustered by their appearance. After they both filled in forms, they departed for the hotel where Rick made sure that Sonya was safely ensconced in her room before driving off to AfriBelgo's offices.

'I'm glad you came to see me again,' Marcia said, 'but unfortunately I cannot linger in the office too long this afternoon. Mark Aardt is arriving at Dulles Airport. I have to go out and meet him.'

Rick sneezed, not sure whether he sneezed because of a recurrence of hay fever, or because of the strand of smoke roping through the air towards him from Marcia's thin cigarette. He wondered whether Marcia smoked the long, thin brand because she saw it as symbolic of a diet.

'Do you remember that girl, Sonya, the one who left early when we had dinner the night before last?' Marcia phrased her question in a billowing cloud of smoke. Rick nodded affirmation.

'According to the morning TV, she's missing after an explosion at her apartment,' Marcia resumed. 'I called Louis at the embassy and he said she was alive and safe somewhere.'

Good for Louis, Rick thought. He kept his mouth shut. It would be better if Kraske remained unaware of his proximity to Sonya.

'All this violence gives me the shivers, Rick. Do you know what's happened?'

'They say the man who planted the bomb died with it.'

'Does anyone know who the man was?'

She had a habit of methodically grinding her cigarette butts into an ashtray, Rick noticed.

'Rick, who could have orchestrated this?' she asked again. And then she picked her nose.

'I don't know,' Rick said, taking out the business card Kraske had handed to him at the Embassy reception. 'But, to change the subject, I was handed this card by Peter Kraske at the cocktail party and I would like to know more about him. What can you tell me about him?'

Marcia seemed surprised at Rick's request. She took the business card.

'Peter Kraske? Why would you be interested in him? He's semi-retired. He used to be a top lobbyist with good connections, but these days he handles just a handful of clients. He's more at his house out in the country than in town. Nice man. Always, without fail, sends me flowers on my birthday.'

'Where did his connection with AfriBelgo come from?'

'He was a big enchilada at AfriBelgo right from the word go, as I understand it.'

She picked her nose again. Delicately.

'Oh, right from the start?'

'He's in finances also, things like that. From years ago, they say.'

'Oh yes?'

'I've only been here about seven years,' she seemed to apologise, 'but it's general knowledge that Kraske was the financial guru who set up the international financing package which put AfriBelgo on the road, many years ago.'

'But what exactly did he do for AfriBelgo?'

Marcia did not answer immediately. With almost painstaking precision she slid out another pencil-thin cigarette, lit it and looked Rick straight in the eye, unmistakably formulating her reply.

'A lot of what he did is classified company information,' she said, 'and it's all about how, many years ago, he put together the international consortium of investors that sank capital into AfriBelgo. Late Fifties, early Sixties. The detail is vague but it is said that, when the company took off, he persuaded those investors to sell out to Erick Martens, making Martens what he has become. Kraske made a bundle in fees and shares probably, and Martens built his empire.'

'So Uncle Erick and Kraske made each other,' Rick said under his breath, more to himself than to Marcia.

But Marcia had heard him. 'John used to say they were such great friends that they kept their hands on each other's bladders all the time. Funny thought.' She giggled. 'For some unaccountable reason, John said he always felt uncomfortable with Kraske, but as I told you, I like him. He's a generous man.'

'I understand he's a wealthy man ...'

'Oh, very rich. I've been out to his place in the country. It's unbelievable. Not exactly a pioneer homestead or log cabin. You must see his works of art! He's been collecting these neat paintings and sculptures through the years and he's so knowledgeable! I always feel stupid in his presence. Hey!' she glanced at her watch, 'I can't hang around any longer. Can't have the new head honcho walking out of his plane into a vacuum.'

'I'll leave with you,' Rick said.

'If you want to talk to Peter Kraske, call me Monday and I'll arrange an appointment. He's a real nice guy.'

Outside, the late afternoon was uncomfortably hot and sticky but he felt more than physically uncomfortable. Uneasy rests the mind that argues with itself, he thought.

The Marcia he had first met on his arrival resembled a widow, lost in mourning, lamenting the untimely loss of her love. The Marcia he had just seen had a vibrant zest for life and looked forward to Mark Aardt's arrival. Is it a matter of the king is dead, long live the king? She actually seemed as excited as a lovelorn woman going out with a new date to see Aardt. The Marcia before fully believed in John. The Marcia of the present laughed at John's dislike for Peter Kraske. It could have been his instinct or it could have been her body language but something conveyed a different message. He could not explain it to himself, but her words and gestures had opened a back door to her mind he had not seen before and he could not understand that. On the other hand, he placated himself, he had never fully understood women. How could he fathom the workings of this one?

He stood on the street and looked around him. Although he had spent long periods on his own in the bush with no other soul in sight, he had never felt lonely at those times. Now, he felt alone in the midst of thousands of people around him, talking, walking, standing, laughing, eating behind the windows of fast food restaurants, holding hands, driving cars and riding motorcycles. He had no desire to spend a lonely evening in the friendless house on Lynnwood Hill. He needed to talk to someone.

When he knocked on her door and she opened it, the first thing he did was to sneeze. 'I suppose I am a little like my hay fever, Sonya. Every now and then I come back.'

'Come on in. At least I now have an audience of one to turn to and show off my new clothes,' she said with a laugh and twirled around, mimicking a model on a ramp.

She wore a sleeveless pastel-pink dress and walked around barefoot. Compact though her hotel room was, it was comfortable enough, consisting of two single beds, two armchairs, a coffee table and a television set from which a situation comedy was blaring away with canned audience laughter.

'Lovely dress. It suits you well.' What he really wanted to say was that the dress made her look even more delicious.

'Thank you.' Her smile made his heart jump.

Feeling like a nervous schoolboy, he persuaded her to join him for dinner. She proposed a restaurant serving Maryland crab, a place she said was like Neptune's palace.

Squashed into a small lounge upstairs, elbow to elbow with a noisy crowd at the bar counter, Rick and Sonya each held a glass of Olde Heurich-Maerzen, a dark and rich malt beer brewed in DC.

Every now and then the waiting list grew shorter as a voice came over the intercom, calling out the names of people to go downstairs to the dining area as tables became available. On a Friday night, The Dancing Crab was a bustling spot on a quiet stretch of Wisconsin Avenue. The proximity of her body and her fragrance stirred long-forgotten feelings in him. Downstairs, the dining tables spilled over on to the sidewalk. They had been told they would have to wait at least half an hour for a table.

'That's an interesting ring,' Rick said and took Sonya's hand in his, not only to have a closer look at the gold band on her finger but also just to hold her hand. His fingers tingled.

'It's the only heirloom I possess.' She put down her beer and twist-ed the ring off her finger. 'When I was sixteen, I was given the letter that I told you about from my mother.' She held the ring up. 'The letter was in a box that also contained this ring. It was my mother's and she wanted me to have it on my sixteenth birthday.'

Rick took the ring from her and held it up to the light. 'It looks like Egyptian hieroglyphic figures cut into the gold,' he commented, turning the ring around.

'No, you are looking at the signs of the zodiac. Can you see there? That's Taurus and there's Sagittarius, Virgo, Libra, all of them.'

'Oh yes. Now I see the star signs. Are you into astrology?'

'No. Neither was my mother, I think. In her letter she said the ring had belonged to her mother.'

'So, it's gone from daughter to daughter.'

'Yes. Maybe for a hundred years? I decided, on the day I got the ring, that if I ever have a daughter, I would give the ring to her in turn on her sixteenth birthday.'

'Well,' he said as he handed it back to her, 'a ring is a symbol of love and of life. In this case, it's become part of the circle of life.' Rick brought his glass of beer to his lips and washed away the tightness in his throat.

'Land! Party of two! Land! Party of two!'

They responded to the amplified voice that crackled through the din and descended downstairs.

Seated at a table covered with a sheet of brown paper, they ate Maryland blue crab, fresh from the waters of Chesapeake Bay, and steamed whole in the traditional way with lots of peppery spice. At the end of the meal, the brown paper table cover was strewn with a mishmash of broken crab shells and claws. A waitress approached them, took the corner of the brown cover at the end of the table, expertly rolled up the paper with shells and all, and carried it away.

'I wish life could be like that. I wish we could just take all the refuse of past thoughts, wrap them up in brown paper and throw them away. It's an amazing system.'

'Yes, Rick, but it's also enough to turn anybody towards vegetarianism.'

'I think we humans built our intelligence on being carnivorous,' Rick said.

She lifted her eyebrows.

'Let me put it to you this way,' Rick continued, 'a long time ago, a carnivore hunted down your father. Now more urban carnivores have hunted down John, the old man in New Orleans, Melinda. They are hunting you and me. Whoever those urban carnivores are, they're prepared to break us open like these crabs, to gobble us up and throw away our shells. I notice you have a habit of saying 'point is'. Let me get to the point. Through the years, I have learned from being out in the bush that you have to think like a carnivore to kill a carnivore. If you want to hunt down a lion or a leopard, you have to think like one. You cannot think like a vegetarian. Vegetarians can only hunt for berries.'

'All right,' she cut him short with a wistful smile. 'I see your point about carnivores. As a hunter, how do you suggest we hunt from here?'

'We follow the spoor, the tracks.'

'And, as our expert tracker, what do you see?'

'Two trails. One is an ivory trail, left by a syndicate with gambling links and possibly drug-running connections. Do you think John could have done drugs or sold the stuff?'

'Not the way I summed him up, no.'

'Well, that's the one trail. Now, to me the other trail is becoming more and more clearly defined by the day, and that's the Kraske trail. On that trail I see many coincidences, a man with a vague wartime background who changes colour, like an octopus or a chameleon, and who's around when your father is murdered. I see Kraske's wartime associate, an old invalid, dying under suspicious circumstances before he can talk to you or John about Kraske's past. Kraske's name crops up with Melinda but she dies accidentally in an attempt on my own life. If I had been killed, she would probably also have been killed in the end. I come to DC and a man tries to shoot me on the street. The same man plants a bomb in your apartment ... I think we should spend tomorrow finding out more about Kraske.'

'I'm scared. I haven't wanted to say anything since last night, but I am. I'm terrified. People want to kill us, Rick. I suppose I've lived in a state of fear since I was sixteen, knowing what people are capable of, what happened to my father ... But last night it became that much more real. At any moment, someone could attack us. I've been looking over my shoulder all day. I wish I wasn't like this.'

'Sonya, being afraid is a form of defence. Being cautiously scared is often better than being recklessly fearless.'

Rick suppressed a yawn. He flipped open the leather flap of his watch. It was past eleven and he had not had a good night's rest the previous night on the couch.

She had noticed his stifled yawn and said, 'If you sleep in John's house tonight, I think you will be the reckless one. Why don't you rather take the spare bed in my hotel room? I really won't mind. That way, I won't be afraid for you or for me. And I always trust a good neighbour.'

Her proposal made sense. Particularly because he wanted to be with her.

Just before midnight they were back in her hotel room. She emerged from the bathroom wearing a hotel dressing gown over her pyjamas and sat down on her bed. Even with her make-up scrubbed from her face she remained attractive, he thought.

A night table with a shining lamp separated the two beds.

'I wouldn't trust too many men the way I trust you tonight,' she said and leaned over to switch off the lamp.

'Good night, Sonya. Sleep tight.'

The tingling in his fingers returned again, reminding him to be calm.

'Good night, Rick.'

CHAPTER 16

Truth is in the library of the mind.

–Quin

NATURE HAD BEEN GENEROUS AT Harper's Ferry, giving the ridges, rolling pastures and rich, bottomland valleys a deep coat of green. Shadows of overhanging trees flitted across the Mustang's bonnet as Rick steered them down the country road.

'So this is Harper's Ferry,' she said. 'It says here in this guidebook that Harper's Ferry has remained a small town on a narrow tongue of land between the two rivers, partly lying in the valley along the riverbanks and partly clinging to the steep slopes rising from the water towards the West Virginian sky. There was an ammunitions factory here.'

'We cannot seem to escape violence.'

'It seems that, early in the last century, water power from the Potomac and Shenandoah made the manufacture of rifles and munitions possible with a Federal Arsenal on a site in Harper's Ferry overlooking the Potomac. Have you ever heard the spiritual song about John Brown's body?'

'Mouldering in the grave?' and he hummed the tune.

'Yes, that's the one. John Brown was an abolitionist. The whole of Harper's Ferry has been reconstructed around his memory. In 1859 he and a group of supporters, including his sons, took over the armoury in an attempt to instigate a slave uprising and finally abolish slavery.'

'White guys doing something for black people that long ago?'

'Yep. Unfortunately for them, their attempt failed. They got themselves trapped inside the Armoury engine-house, a stone's throw from the point where the Potomac and the Shenandoah meet.'

'What happened then?' Rick asked.

'They finally surrendered. He was hanged and shortly afterwards, the Civil War broke out.'

As Sonya understood from her call to Louis, Kraske's house was on the Maryland Heights overlooking the town, not far from Kennedy Farm, John Brown's hideout before his raid. Having been to Kraske's house, Louis gave them detailed directions to get there. They followed Sandy Hook Road, a thinly tarred strip that hugged the Potomac along the Baltimore and Ohio Railroad track. The road rose and dipped under two railroad bridges. As they rounded a corner an animal, which Rick took to be a beaver, scuttled across the road almost under their wheels.

'It's so beautiful out here. Why don't we stop and catch our breath for a moment?' Sonya suggested.

Rick found a stopping place at the side of the road. He parked the car in dappled shade. The air was fresh. The town of Harper's Ferry lay directly across the churning river in front of them. Behind them lay a footpath.

She walked in front of him on the footpath, her tight-fitting jeans accentuating the tempting contours of her bottom. From the tarred road they crossed a wooden walkway over stagnant water. A dirt road formed the spine between the serene water surface on one side and the churning river on the other side.

'Is this a canal or just a calm stretch of the river?' Rick asked as he picked up a small stone and threw it into placid water.

'I'm not sure. Maybe he'll know? He looks like a local,' she said, pointing at a lone figure on the riverbank.

They sauntered over to the man who sat on his haunches under an overhanging branch of a tree, peering at the fast-moving water.

'Hi there!' she greeted him.

The old man's weather-beaten lips barely moved when he greeted them. Set in a broad face with the sheen of beaten copper, his beaked nose seemed to have been cut out of stone.

'My friend and I are just stretching our legs. We were wondering what this is.' She pointed at the ditch filled with water between the road and themselves.

'Chesapeake and Ohio Canal.' His voice rasped harshly in contrast with his brown eyes, which seemed to portray an inner tenderness.

'Chesapeake and Ohio?'

He examined her and nodded his head. 'Mm. Comes from a long time ago. It was before the auto. It was the time of the steam trains. Small steam trains. That was when they dug out this canal.'

'To build railways?'

'No, young lady. Dug out to help where trains could not go. Dug out so that barges could move where rivers were too dangerous. Yes it was.'

'I can see why a canal was needed because the river really does flow too fast over there with all those bubbling rapids,' she said.

'Yes,' the old man spoke again. 'This is a place where the Potomac talks so fast it is foaming at the mouth. Too dangerous for travel. But in those days, men could travel on canal water all over this part of America. On that dirt road next to the canal over there,' he raised a firm hand, 'the mules pulled the barges. Long time ago. Yes it was.'

His slightly breathless and grating voice was not in keeping with his physique, which was still strong for an old man. His long, straight hair was the colour of ash and had the brittle dryness of the aged.

'Is the canal still in use?' she asked.

'The canal, young lady, was important in the time of my father and in the time of my father's father. Now it is like me. It is an old man. It has no energy any more.'

Rick could see that Sonya's inquisitive nature had now taken charge.

'Who are you?' she asked, and sat down beside the man.

Rick followed her example and sat down on a piece of dead wood, the other end of which lay in the water.

'Who am I? I'm Quin, that's who.'

'Pleased to meet you, Quin. I'm Sonya and this is Rick.'

'Mm,' he murmured again, almost as if only to himself. 'I once had another name. Long time ago, it was.' Quin spoke in spurts interspersed with pauses. 'When I was a boy I was called 'The Silent One'. That was because I was silent when I was born.'

As if on cue, he fell silent.

'You were named 'The Silent One?'' she prompted him.

'Yes I was. I came out of my mother and I did not want to cry. I did not breathe. Fortunately, our medicine man was there. He was blind, but he could see right inside my breast. So my mother told me. She did. He pinched me here,' the old man pointed at his breastbone, 'and then he took out a turkey bone from inside of me. That turkey bone was obstructing the spirit of my life. It was.'

'A bone from your breast?' She could not hide her scepticism.

Quin stared at the water. 'The medicine man, he took out that bone. He opened up the passage. He made the spirit of my life come out. I started to breathe. Long time ago, it was.'

'So how did your name change from 'The Silent One' to Quin?' she asked.

'Because the world has changed,' he said and sighed in his pause. 'Now everyone calls me Quin because of the language of my ancestors. My people, we were, we are the Algonquian.'

'What kind of language is Algo ...?' Sonya could not repeat the word.

He broke of a small branch and wrote the word down on the soil in front of him.

'Algonquian,' she read it out aloud.

'The language of my people. Very important Indian language all over America, it was. It flows like this river. But it has also grown silent to the world. Very sad, it is. My name is Quin.'

He scratched out his name in the soil.

'It is a beautiful name.'

'Nature is beauty. Name is just air.'

'Do you live here?' she asked, playing with an oak leaf in her hand.

'I have lived here from the day I lost my turkey bone. I am here like my ancestors. White men called this the first frontier of America. For us this is the first land we lost. We did. This was the land of the Tuscarora and the Shawnee. We had many trails through the mountains. You see those mountains?' Quin gazed at the gap in the Blue Ridge Mountains. 'We had trails up there and down here, all along the length of the valleys. Today my people's trails have become your people's highways. Our history has been paved away. Very sad, it is.'

'So you know the area well,' Rick chipped in.

Quin turned his gaze upon Rick. 'The blood of my people runs in this river. The limestone of the rocks runs in my bones, it does.'

Except for the sound of rippling water, there was silence.

'It's so peaceful out here,' Sonya said.

'The river looks peaceful, but it is deceiving, it is.'

'Even between these rapids, the water looks like rippled glass.'

'Here, where the two rivers meet, the water is clear. It is. You want to know why?'

'Please.'

'It is clear because every drop of water once was a teardrop of two young people. They loved each other. They cried because their parents only knew hate.

'Yes, you are here on the edge of a river of teardrops. It is written in the Algonquian library of the mind. In Indian language this river right here, the Potomac, means 'trading place', but the real truth lies in the library of the mind and the core of the heart. This comes from a long, long time ago. It comes from a time of war between our people – a time when two groups of our people would kill each other on sight, they did. For generations hatred ruled them and then a wonderful thing happened. You see, Potomac and Shenandoah fell in love. They did. Potomac? He was the strong son of a chief on the one side. Shenandoah, she was the beautiful daughter of a chief on the other side. The chiefs, the fathers, they hated each other. They did. The children, they loved each other. They did. Shenandoah's name means 'Clear-eyed Daughter of the Stars' because her eyes were like deep pools of clear water. When the two warring chiefs discovered the love that Shenandoah and Potomac had for each other, the hatred in their hearts grew even stronger. It did. They took their children away. They did. They took them up there, high into the mountains. The Clear-eyed Daughter of the Stars and Potomac longed for each other. And they cried for the love they had lost. And their tears started to flow down from those mountains and into the valleys. And the tears flowed to the place where they always met before. They cried so much that their tears formed a lake. That lake formed right here where we are now up against the mountains. And they cried so long that the lake of tears became so large that it burst through the Blue Ridge Mountains, over there. It did.'

He pointed at the gap in the mountain where the Potomac and Shenendoah rivers meet.

'And so, in their tears, the Clear-eyed Daughter of the Stars for ever became part of the man she loved, Potomac. And from that point over there the two of them are one, still today. Here at this gap in the Blue Ridge Mountains they become one. She becomes part of Potomac. One. And from here they go to the sea. They do.'

Quin stopped and started to hum again.

'It's a touching story.' Sonya echoed Rick's feelings.

'Not a story. It is the truth, it is. Here in the library of the mind. Never to be forgotten.'

'So a boy and a girl river meet here,' Sonya said.

'Here where we are, on this side of Harper's Ferry, the Potomac is still a brave fighting man. Can you see how he flexes his muscles? He is pushing himself with the force of youth over the rapids to meet his bride.'

Rick and Sonya looked out over the fast-flowing waters of the Potomac. Yes, it had the vitality of youth.

'Higher up from here,' Quin continued, 'beyond the hill, on the other side of Harper's Ferry, Shenandoah, the Clear-eyed Daughter of the Stars, is at first calm, like the beautiful girl she is. She comes down quietly. She does. She makes her preparations to meet the one she loves. Ah, but the closer she flows to Harper's Ferry, the more impatient she becomes. She dashes and then she jumps with joy, she does. As she approaches her meeting place with Potomac, she becomes noisier over the rapids. She cannot help herself. She stumbles over the boulders in her hurry to keep her appointment with her love. Then, finally, they meet, over there.' Quin pointed at the confluence of the rivers. 'There Potomac and the Clear-eyed Daughter of the Stars marry and they become calm once again. As one they leave through the gap they made in the mountains with their own dammed up tears, they do.'

Rick gazed at the gap forced open by legendary pent-up love.

'It's so sad that the hatred of parents could only be overcome by the tears of their children,' Sonya said.

Her words drew Rick's gaze back to her. Her blue-grey eyes were as wet as the river. Tears glistened on he cheeks.

'Maybe you are crying like Shenandoah because you are also finding too much hatred,' Quin said and stood up. 'Come with me.'

They followed him away from the canal to the edge of the flowing river.

'The world has changed in many ways. I have changed. But the world of love? It always remains the same.'

Quin dipped a hand in the river and scooped up the water, retaining a small pool in the hollow of his hand. He turned around and approached Sonya. 'Your eyes are clear. They are. You have the eyes of the Clear-eyed Daughter of the Stars. I see a river flowing from you, I see it. You need the waters of your loved one so that your rivers can come together. You will merge with Potomac. Your tears must mix with those of the Potomac.'

Quin dipped the fingers of one hand into the water in the hollow of his other hand, lifted a wet index finger to her cheek, and traced the lines of her tears.

'Now your tears are mixing and you will find relief. You will become one.'

He bent over, scooped more water up, turned to Sonya and dabbed at her cheeks.

'Thank you, Quin.' Sonya's wet cheeks sparkled in the sun.

'And you,' Quin said to Rick, 'you must join with the waters of the Clear-eyed Daughter of the Stars.'

Again he ran his fingers down Sonya's cheeks, swivelled around and traced two wet lines on Rick's cheeks.

Rick shut his eyes. The coarse touch of Quin's wet fingers penetrated much further than skin-deep into his being. He felt as though Sonya's tears flowed over his cheeks. He opened his eyes. For a brief moment he was self-conscious, but looking at her he realised she felt as stirred by Quin's action as he was.

For a long time the three of them sat there at the riverside, bonded together. The wind played over their cheeks and through the leaves around them. The water rippled by. Huge shadows drifted across the Blue Ridge as clouds shifted in the sky, throwing dark green shadows in the distance against the green vegetation on the mountains.

Eventually, Quin spoke again. 'Today is a special day for me. I have come here often in the past to this spot at the river but I have never before been able to speak to Shenandoah and to Potomac both. Today I have. You are Shenandoah and you are Potomac,' he said with his eyes closed, 'and I am honoured that you came to an old man like me to let your waters meet. From now on, your lives will never be the same again. You will now flow as one river together. You will. You now have only one decision to make, you have. And that is where you want your river to go from here.'

It was almost as if Quin could read their minds, almost as if he knew that they were searching for answers, almost as if he knew how Rick had begun to feel about Sonya.

After thinking for a moment Rick said, 'We are looking for a man we need to go to.'

Sonya added, 'We need to find a man who lives here, and who, we believe, has brought hatred to our own families.'

'Hatred is sometimes difficult to see. It is like the smell of death, like the smell of decay, it is. You cannot see smell. Bad people hide their hatred in smoke. Who are you looking for?'

'A man called Kraske, Peter Kraske,' Rick said, lifting the flap of his watch. For a while time had stood still at the water's edge but they needed to press on.

'Kraske. I know of him, I do. What did he do to your families?'

Rick and Sonya glanced at each other. Sonya nodded her consent. It would be right for Quin to know. In a few minutes the bond between the three of them had become strong enough.

'We think this man, Kraske, could have been involved in the death of Sonya's father, the death of my brother, and possibly others too.'

Quin looked at Rick and said, 'If that is so, you have to find out the truth and confront it. If he is not guilty you will find peace. If he is guilty, you must avenge his attacks. The guilty can be dangerous. For you to keep your rivers together, you will need me. I will help you.'

It was no offer asking for their acceptance; it was a statement. He would help and that was it.

He produced a grimy pipe from the pocket of his short-sleeved jacket and a small plastic bag, filled with tobacco from another pocket, stuffed the pipe with tobacco and lit the pipe with a plastic lighter.

Sonya and Rick watched Quin as he drew at his pipe with closed eyes, puffed some smoke at the sun and some to the soil under his feet. Then he drew at his pipe again, stood up and puffed smoke at the forest.

'We will go through the forest, we will. I know where he lives. I know because I know people who helped build his house. It was three years ago. He is important. You cannot just walk up to an important man. First you have to watch him. Then you make your plan. Only then can you strike to find the truth. We must move in silence through the forest. We will carry with us the war medicine of my forefathers. We will. Many people do not believe in that power. You must believe. You will now come with me. We must rest until tonight. Then we go, we will.'

Rick and Sonya again exchanged glances. Rick lifted his eyebrows in a questioning manner. She nodded her agreement again. It made sense.

They spent the rest of the day with Quin in and around his prefabricated house on Maryland Heights, a compact dwelling, smelling of herbs and burned food, sufficiently comfortable for an old man in the twilight of his years. His wife, who had grown up in Jamestown, had died many years ago and lay buried there. His two sons had moved away, one to Montreal where he now owned a video store, the other to Houston where he was in the construction business. Quin had not heard from them for years, and it was obvious that he enjoyed the unexpected company of Sonya and Rick. Later they sat on the veranda, like children at the feet of the father neither of them had ever really known.

For a few hours, Sonya and Rick became Quin's children.

Darkness came early in the forest, its arrival heralded by a symphony of insect sounds.

'I'm so glad I opted for jeans and sneakers this morning,' Sonya said. 'Can you imagine what it would be like to walk at night, out there among the trees, with all those insects making a dinner of your bare legs?'

Quin smiled.

'Shenandoah, your legs would have been cut by shrubs, not bitten by insects. There are harmless crickets down here, at the level of your ankles,' Quin pointed at his feet, 'but the insects are mostly up in the trees. Most of the sounds you are hearing now come from the Katydid. Just cup your hands behind your ears, turn your head a little, and you will hear them.'

Rick and Sonya brought their hands to their ears and listened to the surging, pulsating chorus: 'Katy-did, Katy-did'.

'The Katydid,' Quin continued, 'is a clumsy green grasshopper. It looks like a leaf, it does. That's why it's up in the trees. If you look like a leaf a predator cannot see you. Tonight we will also be like the Katydid. We will walk in darkness so that, even if we are heard, nobody will see us.'

In the distance a train rumbled through the valley. Quin lifted himself out of his frayed armchair. Humming the same tune he had been humming earlier that day at the riverside, he walked into his house. The sound of insects continued unabated.

A few minutes later, Quin's humming returned as he walked back onto the porch. He approached Sonya, stood in front of her, lifted a pouch at the end of a leather thong he had hung around his neck, and placed the pouch on her forehead. Speaking in words Rick and Sonya could not understand, he slid the pouch lower and traced the route of her tears earlier that day, first on one cheek, then on the other. Still mumbling unintelligibly, he walked to Rick and repeated the process, passing the mouldy-smelling pouch over Rick's face.

'You are now part of our tradition of bravery, you are. The ghosts of many dead warriors will share in our adventure tonight.'

'Could you please explain that?' Rick could see that Sonya felt uncomfortable with Quin's remark.

'Through all of time my people always knew that, when a strong warrior dies, three parts of him are affected. His body decays, his soul travels to his next life but his ghost remains here with us, near his own dead body. Why? It is so because the spirit wants to share in the excitement of the lives of the living. That is my truth. Tonight, the ghosts of many past warriors will go with us. They will. They have assembled around us. Maybe you cannot see them now but they will protect us. They have courage. They have. They are waiting for us. The spirits can sometimes be impatient.'

CHAPTER 17

Vice thrives and lives by concealment.

—Virgil

IT WAS A MOONLESS NIGHT. They followed on a dirt road leading downhill from the house, with Sonya behind Quin and Rick at the rear. After a few hundred paces Quin turned right and led them away from the starlit road and into the wall of foliage. In the all-embracing darkness the stars barely penetrated. Even when their eyes had adjusted to the forest, they relied totally on Quin's guidance.

Rick found the blister of anti-histamine tablets in his trouser pocket, popped out a double dosage and swallowed it. He would not want his sneezing to break their silence tonight. The bulge of the Smith and Wesson in its holster felt awkward under his arm and he shifted it into a more comfortable position, noting that Quin had an aerosol canister strapped to his belt in a holder that resembled a leather dog-muzzle.

'What's in the can?' Rick whispered from behind.

Quin stopped and turned around. 'Insecticide. Not for Katydids. For dogs.'

'Not exactly a traditional Indian weapon,' Rick said with a smile.

'But very effective, it is. They have vicious dogs. Everybody knows it around here. From now on you have to be like the spirits who are accompanying us. You must keep quiet. It is time for a silent passage through the forest. Come.'

Every now and then their feet sank into the forest floor of waterlogged, decomposed leaves. Images of dark creepers, draped over ghostly branches, loomed around them – frightening forms that could not be reached to push away. In the blink of an eye the images disappeared to be replaced by new ones. Rick suddenly understood what Quin had meant when he had told them of the Indian belief in False Faces, a secret society of horrible faces without bodies which appeared to people in the dark forest and were the origin of Indian masks.

The sound of an owl whooped through the chorus of Katydids, crickets and frogs, adding to the mystery of their dark surroundings. As they followed the slope of the hill, past the trunks of tall trees, and pushed their bodies through the thick undergrowth, it became more slippery. Then the lights of a house filtered through the curtain of vegetation, but they kept to the protection of the forest, wading through the ferns.

Quin stopped. They had arrived at their destination. Waist-deep in ferns at the edge of the wood they surveyed it.

Ahead in the clearing, lights shone in a few windows of a regal-looking manor house. They were standing hidden in the forest directly in front of the house, a few feet from a long, tarred driveway leading up to the front door. Rick counted six tall columns at the front of the red brick mansion. Between the columns and the front door, two cars gleamed in the illuminated circular driveway. Further away he noticed two smaller houses, a barn, and a structure which appeared to be stables.

Quin lifted the binoculars around his neck and brought them up to his eyes. 'There are people in the third window from the left,' he whispered and handed Rick the binoculars.

Rick's vision was blurred. Focusing on the replica gaslight lamp at the front door, he adjusted the left lens until he had clear focus and then shifted his vision to the third window from the left at ground level.

The man sitting with the back of his head to the window was Peter

Kraske but the person sitting opposite Kraske came as a shock – Mark Aardt. Why would John's best friend, the man who had read the eulogy at John's funeral, be here with Kraske? Maybe because he had taken over John's position at AfriBelgo, Rick reasoned. He watched as Aardt gesticulated; Kraske nodded his head in apparent agreement and smoke drifted from an unseen person on the right side of the room.

Rick stifled a sneeze. Just at the moment his hay fever had returned and he closed his eyes to suppress the sneeze, he thought he saw a movement to the right of the window. He popped another antihistamine tablet and swallowed it before training the binoculars on the area that caught his attention. The movement repeated itself and it was immediately recognisable.

He saw two crossed, stumpy female legs, one of which was swinging up and down over the knee of the other, in rhythm with the puffing of her cigarette. Marcia.

He dropped down on his haunches, next to Sonya and Quin, who were both crouching.

'What do you see?' she asked.

'Marcia and Mark Aardt are there with Kraske.'

'I know Marcia but who's Mark Aardt?'

'John's best friend. Also John's successor out here. Arrived yesterday.'

'I don't understand,' Quin said.

'Well, our man Kraske is there in that room with two people who just happen to be the best friend and the secretary of my assassinated brother.'

'Are you surprised, Rick?' Quin asked.

'Slightly.'

Not in his wildest speculation would Rick have entertained the possibility of seeing those three here together.

'Dangerous people are like shit,' Quin crustily summed up his own feelings. 'Sometimes you don't see them but you will smell them. When you finally see them for what they are, you sure as hell know they are shit, you do.'

Rick set his mind on finding out what they were discussing. Was there a way? Possibly. On both sides, knee-high trimmed hedges ran the length of the driveway to the house. Where the brick paving became a circle, two replica gaslights lit the area. The clearing did not afford much cover from the forest to the house, except for a few trees and shrubs against the house and the low hedges. Not much help as cover.

He just had to take the chance. 'Stay here with Quin,' he whispered and started to run.

'No!' he heard Quin as he started off.

Stooped forward, he skipped over the low hedges, ran across the island in the centre of the driveway circle, bypassed the lit area and scurried along the side of the house where it was darker. With a jolt he realised that both Quin and Sonya were running right behind him. They were now all forging ahead, all committed, and there was no time for an argument.

As he ran towards the house he thought of Quin's belief that hordes of spirits of deceased ancestors were running along with them at that moment. He had the strange sensation of feeling the breath of dead warriors in the nape of his neck.

Everything happened so fast there was no time for logic or reasoning. As he ran to the house, Rick was conscious of being chased. The first inkling he had of being hunted was the image of white fangs coming towards him, soundless and frightening, like an Indian False Face. Out of instinct, he brought up his arm in defence and felt wet fangs glancing off his forearm. He stopped to face the attack. For the first time, the Rottweiler made a sound. Growling softly, the huge dog crouched, with glaring eyes and curled lips revealing dagger-like fangs, ready to attack. Quin and Sonya were with him. She was in danger.

He reached for his holster. Knowing it would alert Kraske and the others, he preferred not to have to use the Smith and Wesson but at that moment his instinct for protection counted more. Before Rick could draw the revolver, Quin stepped forward, aerosol canister in hand. The Rottweiler shifted his attention to Quin.

Quin's finger pressed the button at the top of the can and a pungent plume of fine chemicals sprayed from the nozzle into the Rottweiler's muzzle. The dog opened its mouth in what could have been an attempt to bark, but under the millions of lethal droplets, shut its jaws. The dog blinked with a whimper and cringed to the lawn, rattling for breath. For good measure, Quin spurted one more stinging cloud into the Rottweiler's eyes and nostrils. The dog struggled up and slunk away drunkenly, hacking for air.

Rick, followed by Sonya and Quin, ran up to the third window from the left where there were a few shrubs. Crouched behind a shrub, they watched the silent, animated discussion between Kraske, Mark Aardt and Marcia on the other side of the locked window. The three of them sat on white furniture, facing each other in an elegant library with a domed ceiling.

Rick tried to make out what they were saying, but the only sound he heard was two or three dogs whimpering and one Rottweiler still coughing in the distance. The attention of the rest of the dogs was obviously drawn to the sprayed one.

Motioning to Quin and Sonya to remain where they were he edged his way along the house from window to window, searching for a way in until he found an open latch on a darkened window at the end of the building. With a low, scraping sound Rick slid the windowpane upwards until the opening was large enough for him to crawl through.

Finding himself in an unlit bedroom, he put his head back through the window, peered back at Quin and Sonya, and motioned to them again to remain where they were.

The room smelled of polished wood and the dustiness that comes with a lack of daily use. Every step he took sounded like a cannon shot even though he tried his best to tread softly on the hollow-sounding wooden floorboards. With an inward sigh of relief he reached for the doorknob, gingerly turned it, and opened the door slightly. Through the opening he saw a brightly lit corridor.

A murmur of voices floated from the direction of the library. Through the slit between the door and the jamb, he observed that the wide corridor ended at a spiral staircase. He needed to be close enough to listen to them and the area behind the staircase could be a decent hiding place. He just had to try. Unaware he was suddenly breathing heavily, he slipped into the corridor, the pearls of sweat on his forehead cooling under the force of the air-conditioning from above.

A plank creaked under his foot. He stopped before continuing catlike to the staircase at the library door. The sound of conversation grew louder. Taking cover behind the staircase, Rick could hear them now.

'Events are like the tides. They come and they go. Nobody's to blame. He brought it on himself.' Kraske spoke like a priest.

'I know, but if I hadn't made an issue of—' Rick recognised Mark Aardt's voice.

'It was your duty to make an issue of it. It was your responsibility in the business,' Kraske calmed him down.

'But he trusted me.'

'Of course he did.'

'We were friends for so many years. I could have explained it to him.'

'You did the right thing, Mark, and you, Marcia, you also did the right thing.'

'Thank you.' Her voice rang sharply into the corridor.

'We all have to remember that to each and everything there is a purpose,' Kraske said.

'So sad,' Aardt said.

'Indeed. But then, if he had pushed ahead with the Erfdeel thing, it would have been disastrous.'

'I know it's all water under the bridge by now,' Aardt spoke again, 'but couldn't someone have just explained it to him?'

'Mark, he went through the roof with that girl and you know it,'

Marcia said, raising her voice.

'So why could we not rather have gone to the cause of it all, that girl?' Aardt asked.

'How?' Marcia asked.

'Arrange a transfer back home or elsewhere. Maybe allow her to disappear instead of John?'

'Mark, trust me,' Kraske said. 'I've made my living here in DC for many years and I know that cutting off one lock of hair from one diplomat's head is tantamount to inviting the world to tickle your goitre with a razor blade or a noose. Forget about the girl.'

'Yes, but—'

'Mark, believe me, neither you nor us, nor anyone in AfriBelgo killed John. I repeat what I said earlier. It is an unfortunate reality that AfriBelgo has many major international shareholders and some of them are not necessarily public pension funds or tea-time widows.'

'I suppose so.'

'We never invited those guys in as investors but let me tell you, if organised crime syndicates decide that your company is a good investment target to make their dollars respectable, their money in fact becomes respectable. It was the case when Capone ruled his roost and it's still the case in this year of our Good Lord 1994. We are talking of regular investments via regular bank accounts and not shares bought by a guy who opens a car boot and counts dollars from a canvas bag. I've never been one to look a gift horse in the mouth. It is my unfortunate task to keep contact with those people and, as we all agree, there is no way, politically or economically, in which those long-standing links and information could be made public.'

'But—'

'Mark, there was no choice. The warnings we received came from those sources. Those guys were extremely pissed off, to say the least, at possibly being drawn into an international investigation. That's why they decided to get rid of John. His preoccupation with that Erfdeel nonsense pushed them to a point where they could not face the danger of being implicated. You and I know that the Erfdeel thing was, and is, a worthless puff of wind. Why in heaven's name would a company with the stature of AfriBelgo be linked to that? The company was never involved in Erfdeel and never proclaimed, announced, published or delivered any salted sample results. John's Erfdeel gardening in their investment patch led to the decision of our more difficult investors to stop John. He died. We will just have to live with that.'

'Yes, you've got a point, I suppose. Erick's spoken to me in the same terms.'

Rick was surprised at the familiar way in which Mark Aardt referred to the chairman, which was very much out of line with the norm within AfriBelgo. He was also surprised at Kraske positioning himself as part and parcel of AfriBelgo.

'I won't be able to survive on the Hill in DC, if it becomes public that AfriBelgo has shareholders like that. I would be wiped off the political map if people knew that. You and Marcia would also have suffered in your work. After John's murder, they sent a man to me to explain their reasons for the killing. Hell, can you imagine the damage to AfriBelgo's good name if it ever came out that AfriBelgo's own man in DC was investigating certain supposed irregularities, even though they were figments of his own imagination?'

'I still feel terrible about the—'

'For the last time now, Mark,' Kraske said, his voice sage-like, 'you're a sensible young man. You remind me of myself at your age. We all have to accept things in life. You are not a Judas. You didn't betray him. He betrayed himself. Always remember that.'

'I'll try, but it's difficult. He trusted me for so many years. And even though, in the end, I didn't really like his guts, I still feel a little guilty about the whole thing.'

Forced by the discomfort of his crouching position, Rick shifted the weight of his body from his left knee to his right.

'Who said life is easy? More port for you, Marcia? Another one, Mark? All of us are neck-deep in this. No, it's not easy for anyone of us to walk around, knowing that so-and-so had to die. It's not at all easy, particularly seeing that he was a friend and colleague. Not easy at all but we have to be responsible. That's Marcia's strong point. You are so reliable, Marcia.'

'What about a toast?' Marcia proposed with a laugh. No trace of grief there, Rick thought.

'A toast to your drive, Mark, and to your reliability, Marcia.'

Glasses clinked.

'If you move, you're dead!' a voice hissed in Rick's ear.

Rick reached for his holster.

'Don't!' the voice hissed again.

Rick felt cold steel on his right temple.

'Put your hands on the railing in front of you.'

He had no choice but to obey. He reached for the balustrade of the staircase. Where had he heard that voice before? The man slipped his hand over Rick's shoulder and into the holster, taking the Smith and Wesson from him.

'Come on in, Station Two, Station Three,' Rick heard from behind.

'Two here,' a voice crackled over the man's walkie-talkie.

'Hallo there, what's happening?' Kraske asked called out.

'Two, where are you?' the man behind Rick hissed.

'I'm taking a crap here in the quarters.'

'Three? Where are you?'

'Stables.'

'I got us a snooper here,' the voice hissed again. 'Well-known face to you out there. The dipshit carried a piece of hardware but I persuaded him to hand his heat to me. Go for silence now. Cover the area for any back-up snoopers and report to me the moment you see anything. You got it?'

The whispering voice still had a familiar ring to Rick.

'Got it, boss. I'll take south,' one voice replied.

'Yeah? Okay, I'll cut around the opposite side,' another voice sounded.

'For the second time, what are you doing?' Kraske called out again.

'Now, Chuck, slowly get up and walk to the room, but don't go further than the doorway.'

A nudge of steel from behind accompanied the whispered instructions. Again, Rick had no other choice but to walk to the library.

'Mr Kraske, look who I found hanging around.'

Instead of hissing in his ear, the voice behind him spoke aloud and Rick now knew it was the man he had spoken to on Roosevelt Island. There was that unmistakable foreign tinge again.

'What the ...' Mark Aardt's words trailed away. Marcia dropped her cigarette and quickly picked it up. Kraske did not even blink.

Dressed in velvet slippers, dark trousers supported by broad elastic braces over a white shirt, he stood up from his chair, brushed a bony hand over his silver hair, straightened his blue bow tie, his smile not reaching his eyes.

'Mr Rick Land! As they say in kiddieland in Florida, it really is a small world. Please come in. I did not anticipate such a quick second meeting. May I congratulate you? You must surely have amazing powers of deduction to have found your way so soon to my house so far away from town.'

It could have been due to Sonya's story that Kraske had been a Gestapo officer once, but Rick now detected the remaining traces of a European accent.

'I found him at the staircase in the corridor, Mr Kraske,' the man from Roosevelt Island announced. The cold metal of the weapon caressed the nape of his neck.

'Thank you, Jacques,' Kraske said.

So the man on Roosevelt Island was someone called Jacques. Another Jacques.

'Rick, you've certainly met Marcia, but do you know Mark Aardt?'

Rick glared at John's successor, sitting comfortably in a golf shirt, powder-red trousers and white sneakers.

'Of course I know Mark. You can't mistake a son-of-a bitch when you see one. How could you, John's supposed best friend, speak so eloquently at John's funeral, and yet, with your golden words, sit here and talk so smoothly about your knowledge of who killed him?'

Aardt avoided Rick's eyes. The words had hit home.

'Now now, Mister Land.'

'Where's your decency, Aardt?'

'Things are not what they appear to be, Rick,' Aardt countered, almost inaudibly.

'And Marcia, the woman who loved John so dearly,' Rick said.

She shifted her legs, lit another slim cigarette and threw her head back in defiance.

'Marcia!' Rick spat out her name. 'All the time we talked, you knew exactly what had happened to John. How the hell could John have relied upon you? And how could Kraske call you, of all people, reliable? You, who are supposed to have had feelings for John? I don't care what you say, but from what I have just heard, you have prostituted yourself into complicity in a murder.'

His accusation jolted her into looking him straight in the eye.

'I loved John – like a woman loves a man – but he played with me,' she said.

'He played with you? Is that why you are so complacent about his death?'

'John became involved with the wrong people. He was prepared to jeopardise …' She did not finish her sentence but shifted her gaze to Kraske.

'And, Marcia, who were those so-called wrong people?' Rick asked.

'None of your business.'

'I'll tell you. Your view of the 'wrong people' revolves around only one person – another woman.'

'A bitch, if ever there was one,' she said, pushing her lower lip in under her upper lip.

'A bitch? Who is the real bitch?'

She smacked her tongue against her palate and shot back at him, 'Yes, a bitch who poisoned him into becoming irresponsible.'

'I overheard the three of you talking about Erfdeel. Marcia, was that the crux of his irresponsibility?'

'Rick,' Kraske stopped his tirade, 'you will not understand why these things happened. Stay calm. The less said the better. From your remarks I have to accept that you also heard too much. Have a seat. You will of course understand that, under the circumstances, you are an intruder and Jacques will have to keep an eye on you. Please sit over there.' Kraske motioned at a chair between Aardt and Marcia.

He knew that if Quin and Sonya had remained where he had left them, they would now be watching him from outside. He dared not look towards the window for fear of possibly sending a signal to those in the library. Trying to divert his thoughts from Sonya and Quin on the other side of the windowpane, Rick looked at the paintings on the wall.

'Are you interested in art?' Kraske enquired.

'I suppose I am.'

'John also had an interest in art. I actually helped him in acquiring a Pollock.'

Kraske's remark reminded Rick of the painting he had inherited from John – spatterings of colour he had had difficulty understanding but suspected to be valuable. From Kraske's manner of speaking, it obviously was a major work of art.

'You see that one over there,' Kraske continued.

He followed Kraske's eyes to a canvas with abstract cubes brushed in dull colours.

'That's a Braque I picked up many years ago at the Fondation Maeght near St Paul de Vence in the south of France.'

'You obviously love the finer things in life.'

'Indeed. I find it interesting that a wheel does not have to be round in cubism. It's a little like us all. We are not always what we seem to be. Over there is an early Mondrian and behind me a Gauguin. Do you know that this Gauguin once belonged to one of the minor Kennedys? See the black lines? Over there, between the bookshelves,' he pointed to a large oil painting in the classical style, 'that's one of the most representative works of Jakob Jordaens. Bought in Antwerp. Do you know he painted that canvas more than three hundred years ago? Look at it. It's the closest to perfection that you could think of. I always say that the light in a painting should come from within the subject, not from external lighting. Just look at those eyes!'

Kraske's own eyes lit up as he spoke, betraying an over-enthusiasm to Rick that he thought for a moment might border on fanaticism.

'You have quite a collection here.'

'Built it up over many years, Mister Land. My pride. My passion. Never had children. Never married. My artworks have become my relatives and I now have lots of relatives. But, obviously, you didn't come here to appreciate my artworks. So tell me, what prompted you to break into my house? You could have rung the doorbell. Why are you here?'

'Curiosity.'

'You know what happened to the cat?'

Marcia giggled at Kraske's joke.

Rick's eyes shifted to the window. Nobody in the room would be able to see anybody outside because of the reflection of light from the vaulted ceiling against the inside of the windowpanes.

'I couldn't care a shit about your curiosity, Mister Land.' The steel in Kraske's eyes suddenly matched the change in the tone of his voice. 'Just give me a good reason. You might just as well come out with it, because if you don't I'll have to order that Jacques physically pull it out of you before we get the authorities out here.'

'Like you drew information out of innocent people during the war in Paris?'

His remark had touched a nerve because Kraske's head jerked backwards and his eyes narrowed.

After a few moments' silence, Kraske spoke slowly. 'I have spent my life protecting the innocent. Therefore I take exception. I do not understand your remark. You are rude. To me, to Marcia and to Mark. Jacques, please take Mr Land to the games room and keep him occupied until our guests have gone so that he and I can have a decent talk about why he intruded on us. Rick, I will see you in a few minutes.'

'Put your hands on your head. Come along,' Jacques said and pushed the gun painfully hard into the back of his neck.

'I'm so sorry about this, Marcia, Mark,' Rick heard as he left the room.

Jacques shoved Rick out into the corridor, past a door behind which Spanish music and the sound of crockery combined noisily. They descended into a large, windowless basement. In contrast with the rest of the house, which brimmed with Kraske's works of art, this room was bare, save for a billiard table as its centrepiece and an assortment of gymnasium apparatus against the wall.

'Station Two to Station One, come in. Station One, come in.'

Rick heard the crackle behind him.

'Station One, over,' Jacques answered.

'I got me a sighting out here. Two raccoons but they ran into the woods.'

'Two of them? Get the dogs. Go find them.'

The man spoke so close to Rick's neck he could smell bubble-gum on his breath.

'Move!' A barrel in Rick's back guided him towards a weightlifting apparatus in the corner. 'Lie down!'

Until now, Jacques had remained behind Rick's back. As Rick lay down, he had his first glimpse again of the man he had previously met on Roosevelt Island.

'Well, so much for your sob story about how John died because of drugs,' Rick said.

'Shut up!'

'Tell me, Jacques, you heard Kraske say he couldn't care a shit. Do you enjoy carrying Kraske's shit? Do you see yourself as someone in sanitation? Are you his dung beetle? Do you know the African dung beetle? It spends its whole day rolling shit into balls.'

'Shut up!'

Jacques's eyes were now as thinly drawn and immobile as his mouth.

'Put your hands on the bar over your head and keep them there. One move, even a twitch of a finger, and I'll shoot off your balls, Chuck.'

Rick lay down on his back on the upward-sloping exercise bench between two vertical stainless-steel rods. He grasped the barbell-rod resting over his head. Jacques took hold of the skipping-rope hanging over the barbell-rod, looped one handle around Rick's left wrist, slipped the rope over the horizontal bar, and looped the other handle over Rick's right wrist, knotting the ends together. Jacques produced more rope from underneath the exercise bench, picked a large lifting weight, positioned it at the base and tied up Rick's legs to the sides of the dumbbell. Rick's hands were now tied high above his head and his legs spread in a V shape.

Jacques flipped open the leather flap of Rick's watch and clicked it back again. 'I like this watch. I'll take it off when we're done.'

Jacques ran his fingers over the length of Rick's body and then searched his pockets. He found Rick's car keys and put them in his own pocket.

'You can't take those. How am I going to find my way home?'

'I'll keep them in temporary safe custody.'

Jacques also found the blister of anti-histamine tablets.

'Hay fever. Only one tablet left,' Rick said.

'Of course, Chuck. You sneezed all over me on the island. I'm not sure how long you're going to enjoy our hospitality but, while you're here, I would prefer not be sprayed with your spit and snot.' He returned the blister to Rick's pocket, felt the inside of Rick's belt and knocked his knuckles against the heels of Rick's shoes on the side of the lifting weight.

Jacques then disappeared through the doorway. Far away, Rick heard people laugh. The sound of laughter grew fainter and disappeared. In the distance, a car hooter sounded twice. Minutes later, Jacques returned with a fistful of flapping wires.

'What's that?' Rick asked, trying to ignore the pain in his wrists where the rope dug into his skin, and the weight of the dumbbell pulling at his legs.

'An antique talking-machine.'

'To make me talk?'

'Yep. I just plug you into a wall socket and your jaw starts moving.'

Jacques unzipped Rick's pants.

'Don't worry, Chuck, I'm not interested in your genitals. I'm very hetero.'

'That's comforting to hear.'

'I just have to fix you up for Mr Kraske. He's kept his little appliance for special occasions like this for a long time now.'

Rick had to suppress his fear – the only way he knew was to continue talking.

'Do you always prepare his victims?'

'It kind of runs in the family.'

Of course! As Sonya had explained, John had gone down to New Orleans to hear first-hand from the old man Jacques of his wartime activities with Kraske in Paris. This Jacques could be the old man's son.

'Your father worked with Kraske during the war, didn't he? In Paris?'

'Maybe.' Jacques eyed Rick suspiciously.

'Did your father live in New Orleans?'

'He still does.'

'No, he doesn't. He's dead.'

'Then you're not talking of my dad.'

'An old man, living on a bayou? Now, let me see, what's it called again?' Rick pretended to jog his memory. 'Oh, now I remember.

Biarritz Bayou.'

'Yeah, that's it, but he's not dead. Old, yes. Dead? No.'

'Jacques, your father died shortly after my brother was murdered,' Rick said, wondering how Sonya could have known of the death of old man Jacques but not the old man's son.

'Bullshit!'

'I heard he was an invalid. I also heard he died in a strange way because he drowned in the bayou. How does a man drown in a wheelchair?'

'He's alive, alive. It's not true. I would know.'

'It is, unfortunately, true. Dead in the water in his wheelchair without a sign of a struggle to get out of it. Why would nobody tell you?'

Rick saw seeds of doubt in his captor's eyes.

'Do you know that my brother was killed when he was on his way to meet your father? Why do you think John went to New Orleans? Why do you think he was shot down there?'

Rick's words were having an effect. Jacques now sat down on the stool next to him, his head tilted to one side, an even more pronounced grimness in the lines of his lips. Clearly Jacques had never really thought of why John had been killed in New Orleans.

'Why was John not killed here in DC?' Rick tried to reinforce the thought in Jacques's mind. 'After all, this is where he lived.'

Before Jacques could reply they were interrupted.

'Ah good, Jacques,' Rick heard Kraske enter. 'I see you prepared Mister Land well.'

'Yes, Jacques has been telling me about how his father and you worked together in the war,' Rick lied.

'Jacques's dad and I go back a long way. He was a good man.' Kraske fell into Rick's trap.

'Was a good man? Was?' Rick picked up Kraske's words.

'Yes, he was in wartime,' Kraske added almost too hastily, Rick thought. 'A good friend who did me many favours during the war.

That's why I looked after the younger Jacques's education here in later years. He did his schooling right here in DC.'

Jacques stood up and Kraske took his place on the stool, chitchatting in the manner of a friendly dentist, the skin on his forehead creasing and ironing out all the time.

'Could you please pass me my little Florette?' Kraske asked. Jacques handed him the crow's nest of electric cords.

'This,' Kraske dangled the wires over Rick's head, 'is Florette. I named it after an attractive girl during the war. Brown hair, brown eyes, if my memory serves me right. She ran a printing press in, erm, can you believe it, I've forgotten the arrondissement in Paris. Not far from the Bois de Boulogne. She edited her leaflets under the nom de plume, or shall I say nom de guerre, of Florette.'

As he spoke his bony fingers were unravelling the nest of electric cord.

'Ah, Florette. Now there was a flower for the plucking. Her little game could never have lasted. But she was a tough one too and, after we caught her, we had to loosen her up a little. You see these points here?' Kraske held up the ends of the cords. 'You are honoured to be in a position where these points will be administered to your balls because these same points were administered to the vulva of Florette.'

Kraske might as well have been sitting in a meeting with congressmen and senators, drily discussing amendments to appropriations bills. Lying helplessly on his back, with his hands tied, belt loosened, legs slightly splayed and fly unzipped, Rick watched the swaying cords, and he imagined the strength of the electric current that had flowed through the ends and into the body of a long-forgotten girl in a long-forgotten war.

'Of course I had to adapt it to the American current out here. I also changed the cords, but I kept the contact points for 'Auld Lang Syne'.' Kraske flashed a conceited smile. This time it reached his eyes. 'Although it's been modified, it's as good as then. I rarely use it these days but every time I bring it out of retirement it works perfectly. Now you see, just like in the case of Florette, I will be applying this to your private area. I can testify that it has a tremendous effect. Just a moment,' Kraske said, as if speaking to himself, 'I need to use my gloves. Cleanliness is next to godliness, they say.' Kraske wriggled his fingers into two rubber gloves.

Rick closed his eyes. He felt the rubbery fingers taking hold of the top of his underpants, slithering against his skin. With a jerk Kraske pulled down Rick's underpants and he felt a rush of cool air from the air-conditioning on his penis. He closed his eyes. With his naked pelvis under Kraske's beaky gaze, Rick knew he was moments away from excruciating pain. He somehow had to stall Kraske.

'As I said earlier, I knew of your activities, but tell me, Kraske, why did you apply your torture methods to people like this girl?'

'I was an interrogator.'

'Which side?'

'Does it matter?' Kraske flashed an arrogant smile.

'I suppose not but, if you were in Paris, as you said, putting electric currents through the genitals of someone called Florette, I think you were probably in the Gestapo.'

Although Rick could not see clearly from the position in which he found himself, he noticed Kraske's eyes become distant and he realised the man was less preoccupied with the cords and his pelvis for a moment.

'You're quick on the draw, Rick. When you spoke of my time in Paris in front of Mark and Marcia, you proved you know a little too much. Too much knowledge can be dangerous. These days nobody knows of my time in Paris and I'm not sure we should allow that knowledge to spread. Your little remark put a noose around your neck, my friend, or, shall we say, a noose of electric current around your balls. That's why you are here right now.'

'Conversation can be interesting. It isn't every day that my pants are pulled down by an old man with a shocking disregard for my future children, yet I can converse with him.'

'You want to chew the fat for a while?' Kraske laughed. 'Fine by me, my boy.'

'Station One to Station Two, over!' Rick heard Jacques's voice somewhere down the corridor. 'Station One to Station Two. Over!'

'So, you're wondering how I met Florette. Have you ever heard of the Sicherheitsdienst? The Sicherheitsdienst was the jewel of our German security service, much more effective than the Abwehr. Now that you will depart this world in a, let's say, shocking manner, you have my formal confession. Yes, I was in the German forces. I had my own little perch in the Sicherheitsdienst in Paris. Ever been to Paris? Never? Well, I met the girl Florette in the German security headquarters on the Avenue Foch during the war.'

'You were a Nazi.'

Rick tried to shift the weight of his body to rid himself of the pins and needles in his body where his buttocks rested on the plane of the gymnasium apparatus. His hands were also beginning to feel numb from their uncomfortable position over his head and the weight between his shoes pulled ever more at him.

'Call me a Nazi. Call me what you like. It was a world far removed from today,' Kraske said. 'I was in the service, but even then already, I actually worked for me, and only me – Peter Kraske. I rather believed in Heil Me. There was a slight difference in that I had another name – my real name, the name of my father. I was a little like Jacques over here, I suppose.'

From the corner of his eye Rick noticed that the cords were now dangling idly between Kraske's knees.

'So why did you change your name to Peter Kraske?'

'I'll get to that in a moment. It's not often that I get the opportunity to reminisce on those glorious years in the Sicherheitsdienst.'

'Station Two to One. Station Two to One. Over!' Rick heard the sound of the two-way radio in the corridor.

'Station One. Go ahead.'

'I got me a raccoon out here and I'm coming in, over.'

Trying to block from his mind any thought of what was happening outside, Rick forced himself to keep talking. 'What was the Sicherheitsdienst outfit all about?'

'That outfit, as you call it, was the best counter-intelligence unit imaginable. In those years we already had well-equipped mobile direction-finding vans scouring the streets of Paris. Our men cruised the metropolitan area and caught many radio operators in the act of transmission or immediately after transmission. We were the elite! We had our own secret army of French people who helped us build up a good picture of the various resistance groups. The maquis had their secret army but we had our own – right there among them. I handled that part of the action. Ach, what a time!' In that last sentence Kraske slipped a guttural German 'ch'. He raised his face and closed his eyes. His neck sagged in wrinkled folds like powder-dry ostrich skin.

'So how does one start out as a Nazi in Paris and end up as a lobbyist of renown in a place like DC?'

'Ah, good question!' Kraske obviously revelled in opening the door to his past. 'Towards the end of the war I made a point of getting to know a specific operative of the OSS – the American precursor of the CIA. OSS stood for Office of Strategic Services. It was run by a man called Wild Bill Donovan. I have always calculated my odds, and when I saw the writing on the wall towards the end of the war, I decided to cover my bets and to play both sides. I found it easy to manoeuvre myself into the OSS arena. By the end of the war, I was the ideal man to assist the Americans in cleaning up and performing certain back-up services. I became a consultant to the Americans even before the end of the war.'

'You mean you became a traitor to your own country.'

'No, not really. As I said, I always worked for me, myself, and I made the right career move at the right time. I also made my OSS friend look good. It is always a good strategy to improve someone else's standing. He arranged a new life for me in gratitude for my services. That's how I linked up with Erick Martens. Well, kind of ...'

'Oh yes?'

Rick had wanted to come around to the subject of the friendship between Uncle Erick and Kraske. If he was going to die tonight, he wanted to die knowing the whole truth.

'Yes. My new American bosses arranged for me first to go down to South Africa for a drying-out spell, if you could call it that. I arrived in those pre-apartheid days before the election of 1948 but stayed on for many years into the apartheid era. I was given a new name, new life, new career, the whole shebang, as they say here in America. I served my apprenticeship out there and was then brought into the USA under my new identity of Peter Kraske to serve the free world in its battle against communism.'

'I cannot believe the Americans would have looked after you ...'

'Believe what you wish.' Kraske fiddled with his bowtie. 'I'm an old man now and bits and pieces of the Berlin Wall are spread over mantelpieces and showcases in living-rooms all over the world. The battle against communism has been won. I was an unknown soldier in that war. So nobody would even care if I said today that in the early Fifties I cut a lot of cake for America in the East German Ministerium für Staats-Sicherheit – their state security organisation. I had a few friends from the war in that organisation. Often the slices of cake I was able to dish up to this country had rich icing and toppings of cherries that meant a lot to many people on the Hill.'

'And so you became a lobbyist.'

'You're an Einstein, Rick.'

'You're a hypocrite, Kraske.'

'Hypocrisy and deception are the pillars of secrecy. Whatever you think does not matter to anyone. I paid my dues. For many years I was a substantive expert and my adopted country repaid me royally.'

'Mr Kraske?' Jacques spoke from the other side of the doorway.

'Yes?'

Kraske turned around.

'We found his friend outside,' Jacques said and added, 'a girl. The one from the Embassy.'

Rick's heart missed a beat.

'Ah, a diplomatic visit!' Kraske exclaimed. 'Maybe we should give Florette a little breather for now. Let's not upset the lady too soon, Rick. Let us cover up your precious jewels in deference to her and see what transpires. Ah, life is interesting.'

Kraske leaned over, pulled up Rick's underpants and zipped up his pants.

Rick closed his eyes in gratitude for the temporary respite.

'Maybe,' Kraske whispered, taking off his gloves, 'the lady would talk more freely if we start right from the beginning and act a little more civilised.'

Jacques stood alone in the doorway. No sign of Sonya yet. Rick was relieved to see Kraske putting away the wires in their box.

'Well, bring her in, Jacques,' Kraske ordered.

Jacques waved and Sonya entered, her hands clasped on top of her head, another gunman following her. Her eyes betrayed her distress the moment she saw Rick lying tied down on the exercise bench with his legs splayed open. The gunman behind her was the stocky middle-aged angler Rick had spoken to in the parking lot at Roosevelt Island. He felt waves of rage rolling around inside him, bursting to fly out in overwhelming fury at Kraske, building up in crest after crest of hate at the thought of what Kraske might intend to do to her, but he had to control his temper.

'Please have a seat.' Kraske waved her towards a bench against the wall. 'You can put away your pistol now, Winston.'

With a slight flicker of his eyes, Rick tried to ask her about Quin. She gave him just the slightest dip of her head, almost indistinguishable from a lowering of the eyes. And he knew that Quin was still out there, untouched and hopefully raring to go with all the spirits of his ancestors ready to follow him.

'As you arrived, my dear, I was reminiscing with Rick over the past. Those days of youth! A time when you don't know your asshole from your elbow but you go the whole hog. A little like the spirit I see in the two of you. How can people in their right minds expect to trespass on someone else's property and not be punished? What happens to a trespassing diplomat?'

'We just wanted to talk to you,' Sonya answered, sitting stiffly on the bench against the wall.

'By snooping on my property?' Kraske leaned forward. 'You could have called me. I do own a telephone, you know. No, I think there's more to it. A moment ago, when I was under the impression that Rick had come out here on his own, I thought he was merely the impetuous surviving brother acting out his African hunter's fantasy. Incidentally, that was what I was playing at when you walked in – I was just reciprocating by playing my bit of fantasy back on him. I even sold your friend the idea I could have been a German interrogator-type many years ago.'

Kraske smiled a benign smile, completely the opposite of his intense expression only minutes before.

Stunned by Kraske's sudden about-face, Rick tried to reason with himself.

Here he was, lying on his back in a tied-up position. Moments before, Kraske had been sitting there with dangling wires of torture poised over Rick's exposed genitals, reliving the past, relishing in a deathly tale of a girl called Florette. And now Kraske said he had been playing out a fantasy. Fantasy? Why was the man so friendly towards Sonya? And then he remembered. Earlier that night, crouching behind the staircase in the corridor, listening to the conversation in the library, he had heard Kraske saying that if anyone cut even a lock of hair off the head of a diplomat, it would be an invitation to the world to retaliate. That was it! Kraske had suddenly reverted to the two pillars of secrecy he had mentioned: hypocrisy and deception.

'What kind of fantasies are you into if you tie up someone?' Sonya's question proved that she had seen through his game.

'If someone steals into your house illegally and your security people

pick him up, do you offer him a drink or do you handcuff him?'
Kraske flashed her his lobbyist smile.

'Point taken.'

'Good. But it doesn't answer the one burning question I have.'

'Which is?'

'What are a diplomat and a tourist doing prowling around my
property? Why are you here?'

'Why not untie Rick first?'

'No. I need some answers first. Sonya, I know you knew John,'
Kraske revealed. 'It has become common knowledge at AfriBelgo that
you clouded his mind to such an extent that he – what did I say? –
that, in the end, he did not know his ass from his elbow. So I ask you
again, what prompted you to come here tonight?'

She studied Kraske with pursed lips. Rick wanted to scream out to
her not to talk too much.

'Mr Kraske, you talk of reminiscing, even fantasising about the
past. How far back do you want to go? As far back as Barberton in
South Africa? Can you remember Barberton?'

All through his life Rick had always recognised a turning point,
and this was one. His hands hurt where the rope cut into his skin. His
back ached. The nerves in his buttocks were dead from lying uncomfortably still for too long. The damn dumbbell strained at him. If she
wanted to talk, why could she not talk them out of the situation?

'Do I remember Barberton? What do you mean by that?' Kraske
was clearly flustered.

'Well, do you?'

'Of course I do. I was there when it still was a very small town on
the border of the Kingdom of Swaziland. I lived there many years ago
before I came to America. But what skin is it off your nose?'

The skin on Rick's hands burned where the ropes chafed.

'The skin off my nose is my father's skin. He once had a farm out
there in Africa, near Barberton. He lived there and he died there.'

'Oh?' Kraske's eyes narrowed.

'He was a good man—'

'Like most farmers are.'

'But he didn't die like a farmer.'

'Oh yes?'

'No. He died in his bed – with a bullet through his head.'

'I'm sorry, but I don't understand what you mean by all this.'

'My father knew you, Kraske.'

'How?'

'He knew you in life and in death, that's how.'

'Stop your riddles,' he snapped.

'Good. Then I will give you an answer: Mauritz Deine.'

Kraske did not respond immediately but Rick could see the disclosure had caught him off-guard.

With his eyes fixed on his hands, Kraske sat, lost in thought, nodding his head slightly. He breathed in deeply and exhaled with a sigh.

'Deine … your father.' A tinge of red on Kraske's cheeks accentuated his surprise. 'Of course! I knew all along you were Sonya Deine, First Secretary at the Embassy, but I did my homework and found out you were in an orphanage. Mauritz did not have a child. His wife did not seem to be pregnant. There are Deines everywhere and I assumed your interest in Erfdeel could have come from a rumour and misinformation among the wider family of Deines. His wife started talking about that nonsense soon after his death. She moved away and we received word she remarried and had someone's child. It seems she did not remarry then.'

'No. She died and I lived,' Sonya said. 'Well, she lived for a short while afterwards.'

Kraske stared at her.

'She died of cancer when I was still a baby.'

'So?' Kraske drew his skeletal hand over his few silver strands of hair.

'So that's how I ended up in the orphanage. Do you know what it's like never to have truly known your parents, Kraske?'

It was as if Kraske had suddenly drawn an impassive shutter over his face. He looked at her again without a word.

Sonya stood up and put her hands on her hips. 'I'll tell you what it's like. You lie awake at night and you wonder why your mother left you to become a star in the sky. You lean out of a window and you look up at the night sky, and you find the brightest star. And then you talk to that star because you talk to your mother. You tell her you miss her and you ask her why she left you, but she can never talk back. And then one day, on your sixteenth birthday, she talks to you.'

'How could she talk to you if she was dead?' Kraske asked with blank eyes.

'She left a sealed envelope for me to be opened on my sixteenth birthday,' Sonya held up her ring finger, 'and the envelope contained this ring. She also left me a letter in which she told me that you and Erick Martens and my father had been partners.'

'That is true.'

'According to her letter, on the day of his death, my father told her that he wanted to end his association with you and Martens because you were involved in an Erfdeel scam, whatever that meant.'

Rick saw through his dangling arms that Kraske's face had become even more ashen. 'Your dad was a terrible businessman. He could have been a modern Midas, wealthy beyond compare.' Kraske whispered the words, almost as if to himself, still nodding his head.

'My dad was an honest man who died for his honesty.'

'There was nothing dishonest for him to be upset about.'

'Then why did you kill him?'

'I didn't kill Deine,' Kraske responded slowly.

'Shortly after his murder my mother received a threatening letter telling her she would lose her life if she kept on making waves. It was all in the letter to me. She also wrote that you later skipped the country, leaving Erick Martens in charge of everything. At least Martens paid her something for my dad's share, although pitiful, but she lost the farm and had to move to the city. She was so afraid of being hounded to death and of her unborn child dying that, after her move, once it came out that she was pregnant, she dropped the word that she had remarried. Lo and behold, another threatening letter arrived to tell her that, for her unborn child's welfare, she should forget about her late husband. She was convinced about two things, your guilt and that my dad died for a reason related to the Erfdeel scam.'

Silence.

Sonya stood there, fists clenched at her sides. The gunman leaned drowsily with crossed legs against the billiard table. Kraske toyed with the box of electric cords, no doubt reflecting on the past. Jacques yawned in the doorway.

Rick's conclusion was unambiguous: John had been murdered because he had scratched on the surface of some kind of conspiracy. Rick had not even scratched around when an attempt on his own life led to Melinda's death. Yes, tonight he and Sonya were now in the same expendable position as John and they were staring death in the face. He glanced at Sonya. She was just an innocent and defenceless young woman, standing there in a blue blouse, jeans and running shoes.

'Can I come in?' a new voice drifted in.

Rick had to strain to see who was talking to them in the doorway.

'Why didn't you call in on the radio?' Jacques asked.

'But you said we had to be quiet and so I switched off. Anyways, I caught this old guy out at the gazebo,' the new gunman said as he pushed Quin into the room.

Quin's eyes swept the room, resting on Rick's prone body for a moment and ending at Sonya standing with her arms folded now.

'Are you all right?' Quin asked Sonya who nodded.

'Who the hell are you?' Kraske asked.

Quin stared at Kraske.

'We'll have you talking in a while,' Kraske said, glancing at the box containing the cords, and continued, 'Whoever you are, there are three of you now and you all seem to be intent on self-destruction. To return to your father,' he swung around to face Sonya, 'how did you find me?'

'Through someone I found out that one of your ex-colleagues lived in New Orleans. I went there and met an old man – Jacques Daniel.'

'You met my dad?' Jacques blurted out.

'Your dad?' She spun around to face Jacques.

'When I was stationed at the Consulate in New Orleans I met an old man who had lived through the war with Kraske – an old man who had collaborated with the Nazis.'

She turned to Kraske. 'I know more about your sordid life than you think, you bastard! You murdered my father just like you murdered innocent people indiscriminately in the 1940s in Paris. The old man helped you at that time. What thanks did he get?' she asked, spinning around to face Jacques. 'In gratitude he was murdered, dumped into water to be drowned – like so many before him.'

'Mr Kraske, this is the second person to tell me my dad's dead. Do you know about this? Is it true?'

Rick heard the confusion in Jacques's voice.

'Jacques, I'm sorry.'

'What?'

Kraske stood up. 'Yes, he died.'

'When did it happen? Why didn't you tell me?'

'I didn't want to upset you. I was going to tell you.'

'Going to? Going to?'

'He had an accident. He drowned a few days ago,' Kraske stated, embracing Jacques, who crooked a finger and wiped a tear from the corner of an eye.

'How could he have drowned? In a wheelchair?'

'Jacques, you know, as many of us did, that he suffered from a little dementia. Lately he could not think straight. Sometimes he did not even know where he was. In that state of irrationality, you can so easily slip, lose your balance or make the wrong decision. It was an accident. Let it be.'

'He was not himself anymore.'

'He was not. I've arranged for his ashes to be flown up here. With you not being a religious man, I thought it best that way.'

'That's good,' Jacques answered. 'He had a full life. He was ill. Maybe he even welcomed death.'

'I knew you'd understand,' Kraske whispered and added, 'and don't even think of the insinuations you have heard from these people. There's no way in which I would even have touched a lock of hair of a friend for life. Look, why don't you go and find more rope. We are slightly overrun with unwelcome visitors. Winston, go with Jacques.'

The two disappeared through the doorway, leaving Kraske and the third man with Rick, Sonya and Quin.

'Boomerangs always come back,' Kraske broke the silence and sighed. He looked at Sonya. 'Mauritz Deine had to die because of Erfdeel and so did John,' he said and, turning his gaze to Rick. 'John was asking the wrong kind of questions. You, young lady, were poisoning him with Erfdeel nonsense. Bad people knew that and they did not like it.'

'There are times when one can see a smell, you can,' Quin spoke up.

'What do you mean?' Kraske said.

'You murdered her father, you did.'

'No, I didn't, but I know who did.'

Kraske brooded for a few seconds and pointed a finger at Sonya. 'Let me take you out of your misery, young lady. Mauritz Deine was shot by Jacques Daniel.'

Her cheeks seemed to hollow out and her eyes widened. Having searched for an answer for so many years, Sonya had it in her hand. If Kraske told the truth, she had faced her father's killer in New Orleans without realising it.

Kraske glanced at the doorway to see whether the younger Jacques was still out of earshot. 'Jacques was a life-long friend. Such a pity he became senile. When he met you, young lady, he probably never even realised who you were.'

The numbness in Rick's back was becoming serious now and his knees and ankles ached from the pull of the weight on the slope. His hands were beginning to tremble as a result of insufficient circulation.

'Old man Jacques,' Kraske continued, 'came out to Africa with me in those years. He also needed a new life. As things evolved, your father became too inquisitive. He found out about certain things and threatened me with the police. I mentioned my problem to Jacques and he took care of it.'

'You ordered his death.' She said it coldly, without any feeling except for the tears in her eyes and her defiant stare.

'Yes, and now, unfortunately, I will have to order the death of this little trio here. You know too much.' He looked at his wristwatch. 'Damn! I almost forgot. I have to phone Annapolis. Keep a close eye on them,' he instructed the third man, 'and make sure they're tied up securely. Tell the others we'll take our visitors to the mine shaft at Fire Mountain later tonight.'

Kraske left the room.

The man with the gun switched his gaze from Sonya to Quin to Rick and back.

'I suppose y'all know what it means, don't you?'

Rick had difficulty in following the man's Southern drawl.

'Don't you wanna know what this means? No? We're gonna dump y'all down a mine shaft. 'Course y'all will get a nice sleeping tablet beforehand, specially prepared from the best lead in the States and administered from a special syringe.' He waved the nine-millimetre Beretta .92 at them.

Rick noticed the man had a nose like an airport terminal bendy bus.

CHAPTER 18

Where there are secrets there are lies.

RICK'S HANDS HAD GROWN BLUE. The tips of his fingers were cold. His arm and leg muscles pulsated in aching reminders of his discomfort. He had to get rid of the weight below.

Quin broke the silence. 'I'm not with these two. I'm my own man, I am.'

Rick could not believe his ears. He jerked his head, looked at Quin and then at Sonya, whose face conveyed the same measure of shock.

'I don't have no connection with them, I don't. Me? I am confused on what this is all about. I am local Red Indian man. I promise, you let me go, I will keep as quiet as the spirits of the dead, I will. I met them on the road tonight. They stopped. They asked me the way. I was dumb enough to show them, I was. I don't see why you should punish me. I'm just an honest man. I put in my normal, honest day's work every day.'

Sonya looked at Quin with disgust.

'I can even work for you guys. I'm not committed. In fact, I'm looking for a job,' Quin suggested, a ring of hope in his voice.

'Yeah?' The gunman seemed unimpressed.

'I haven't hurt anybody. Why don't you let me go?' Quin pleaded.

Coward! Rick cursed inwardly.

'Yeah, big guy? Local Indian? You will just have to wait for the boss and see what he says. Maybe he'll take you in.' The gunman finished by lighting up a cigarette.

'Thanks,' Quin said, 'but, man, you guys really scared me. I could do with a smoke right now. I can.' Quin pointed at the pack of cigarettes in the gunman's shirt pocket.

The man drew out a cigarette and threw it on the billiard table.

Quin picked it up. 'Could I borrow your lighter?'

The man produced the lighter from his trouser pocket and handed it to Quin.

Rick could not believe what they were witnessing. A few hours before, Quin had spoken to him and Sonya in a manner that had made them feel like his own children. He had been compassionate and wise, not a foolish coward.

Click.

Rick watched the lighter as it flickered into life between Quin's fingers.

Afterwards he knew he had been inattentive, although he had seen that Quin must have adjusted the gas regulator, because the flame from the lighter between Quin's fingers suddenly jumped higher. Quin adjusted the flame lower again. Just as Quin brought the flame towards the cigarette clenched between his teeth, then dropped the lighter to the floor.

'Sorry. I'll pick it up carefully, I will,' Quin said and the man agreed with a bored nod of his head and a wave of his gun.

With his back to the man with the gun, Quin stooped to pick up the lighter. Rick watched Quin's rough fingers gently taking the lighter from the floor. He did not see Quin's thumb again playing with the adjustment knob. He also did not notice how, with his other hand, Quin loosened the aerosol can on his belt.

'Ah, smoking. A nice vice,' Quin said, stood up and brought the lighter closer to the cigarette in his mouth.

The man looked at the lighter flame in front of Quin's mouth. He never saw Quin's left hand reaching for the aerosol can on his belt. Instead of bringing the lighter closer to his lips, Quin whipped the lighter and aerosol can closer to each other.

In an instant, millions of droplets squirted towards the man with the gun, turning into a growing dragon's tongue of flame licking out from Quin's hands.

Quin's flame formed a fiery glove around the hand holding the gun. The man screamed and dropped the gun, lunging instinctively at Quin, who brought the flame up into the gunman's face. Covering his face with his hands and sinking to his knees under the blowtorch, the man uttered a whimper which turned into a soft wail but which did not raise much in volume because Quin cut him off. In the blink of an eye Quin threw the lighter and aerosol can up in the air, extinguishing the flame, while at the same time locking his hands together and bringing them down like a guillotine on the base of the crouching man's head.

Rick knew he heard the breaking of a neck. The man slumped forward on the floor, his hair smouldering, his synthetic shirt shrivelling and melting into his skin.

'Close the door,' Quin ordered Sonya. He rushed over to Rick and produced a knife that had been strapped to his ankle underneath his trousers.

'God, I thought you were turning on us, Quin.'

'I told you I brought all the spirits of my forefathers with me. What would my forefathers think if I turned into a coward?' He smiled with barely concealed boastfulness as he cut loose Rick's hands.

'Quin, you are wonderful,' Sonya said.

For the first time since they had met, Rick noticed that Quin was sweating.

Rick sat upright and massaged his wrists to revive the blood circulation in his deadened hands. Quin cut loose the bonds around Rick's ankles. The dumbbell rolled down onto the floor. 'How d'you feel?' Quin asked as he helped him up.

'Stiff but feeling light without the weight, thanks.'

'Your gun is still there in the corner,' Sonya pointed out.

Rick picked up the Smith and Wesson and put it back in the holster that had not been removed when Jacques had captured him. He also picked up the Beretta which was still lying on the floor next to the gunman, his head now twisted to an unnatural angle. Rick checked the magazine. Enough. Ready for use.

'Here.' He handed Quin the Beretta. 'It's a nine millimetre which can turn these guys into Swiss cheese. Do you know how to use it?' Rick made the movements for loading with his hands. Quin nodded and picked up his aerosol and the lighter.

'Okay. Let's go,' Rick ordered.

'Sonya, stay between Quin and me. And please listen to me this time. Quin, cover our backs as we move through the house.'

'What about a diversion?' Quin asked, holding up the aerosol can in his hand.

'Good idea. Let's go.' Rick opened the door.

Behind him he heard the whoof of a flame as Quin torched something in the room. He thought he could already hear the crackle of fire. He felt good at the prospect that Kraske's cords of torture would now, after almost five decades, maybe melt away.

Leaving the modern-day dungeon, they rushed up the wooden staircase out of the basement. Back in the corridor, he motioned to them to stop. Hearing only the female chatter of Spanish-speaking servants in the kitchen, he waved at Quin and Sonya to follow him.

And then he heard Kraske's distant voice. Kraske was talking on the telephone in the library again. Would he be alone, or would Jacques or the other man be with him? Rick felt Sonya's hand on his arm. Her touch was cold.

'Mm. Yes. That's the way I summed it up,' Kraske said and then fell silent for a long time. 'No, of course not ... mm ... the last leg ... yes, I'll let you know.'

Silence. 'Thanks. Sure. Bye.'

Rick heard the clicking sound of the receiver being returned to its cradle. They waited. The footsteps of only one person on the wooden floor of the library signalled that Kraske was alone. Rick walked into the library with his Smith and Wesson aimed at Kraske's surprised face. Quin and Sonya stood behind him.

'Don't do anything silly. Put your hands on your head.'

Kraske slowly complied.

Through the library window Rick saw that one car, a large Cadillac, was still parked in the driveway. 'Is that your car out there?'

Kraske nodded.

'Where are the keys?'

Kraske lowered one hand, fidgeted in his trouser pocket and handed over the keys.

'Come!' Rick pulled at Kraske's sleeve.

'The three of you are as good as dead.'

Ignoring the threat, Rick guided him out to the driveway. He jerked open the back door and indicated to Quin, who bundled Kraske in. With Sonya in the front seat, and Quin holding the Beretta against Kraske's head on the back seat, they spun off and spurted with screaming tyres along the driveway towards the safety of the dark forest.

Over the noise of the tyres on the tarmac, they did not hear the shots tearing out from the front door of the house, but they saw the effect as the windscreen shattered. A hailstorm of shattered glass flew at them. Sonya and Rick brought up their arms to cover their faces. Rick let go of the steering wheel and Kraske's car started slipping off the road. He grabbed the steering wheel too late to avoid total loss of control. Bucking wildly, they spun full circle and slammed into a tree.

The impact of the collision turned the Cadillac's interior into a dust bowl.

Rick jumped out and fired two shots in quick succession in the direction of the front door, shouting, 'Come on! Get out! Run for the forest!'

Quin had difficulty getting out immediately because the vehicle had folded up against the tree at his side. Rick returned, opened the other door, pulled Kraske out and Quin followed. Dragging Kraske, they stumbled into the forest foliage.

From behind a tupelo tree at the edge of the forest they looked back towards the house. Strangely enough, nobody had followed them. Crumpled up against the tree, Kraske's broken Cadillac still made a singing sound like a kettle.

'You're probably guessing where they are, aren't you?' Kraske muttered between them.

Nobody answered him.

'You're small fry,' Kraske hissed. 'You don't know what you're up against. My men are trained sharpshooters. They're going to come out with night sights. They'll pick you off like plastic ducks at a shooting gallery. You're going to be wiped out with the same gun used on your brother.'

'So you are revealing yourself, Kraske.' At that moment Rick could have crushed the man's head with its thinning strands of uncombed hair into a pulp, but he checked his emotion.

'Aren't you interested to know who shot John?' Kraske asked with a smirk.

'Shut up.' Rick knew Kraske was trying to cloud his mind, break his concentration and influence him into making mistakes. Rick took a deep breath.

'My guy's probably got a sight on you right now, maybe the same sight that was trained on John.'

'Shut up.'

Rick peered back at the house. On the other side of Kraske, Quin had his Beretta trained on Kraske but he was also keeping watch.

'I don't see anyone,' Sonya said. 'Rick?' Her voice had a sudden trace of fear. 'Kraske's got a gun at my throat.'

'Stand back,' Kraske snarled.

Rick and Quin both stepped back and stared at Kraske, who was now gripping Sonya by her hair. In the faint light Rick could see how the barrel of Kraske's pistol formed an indentation against her throat, under her ear. How could they have been so careless? They should have searched the man. Rick cursed himself.

'Lay down your weapons! If you shoot me, you can be sure I'm going to pull the trigger and she'll die.'

As he said it, Kraske pulled at Sonya's hair, eliciting a cry.

Rick sighed and laid down his Smith and Wesson. Quin followed suit with the Beretta. Kraske shuffled closer and drew the two guns towards him with his foot and then kicked them behind him.

'Jacques! Winston! I'm here!' he shouted, facing them with a few yards of shrubbery behind him and then the clearing towards the house. The Smith and Wesson and the Beretta lay between Kraske and the shrubbery behind him.

'If we are going to die, I might as well now know who pulled the trigger on John,' Rick said.

'I don't need to lie. I paid a professional a lot of money for that. So much, in fact, that he donated the gun he used to the man who organised it for me – young Jacques, of course.' Kraske's teeth glinted in the darkness. 'Since you're going to die now, in any case, I might as well also tell you about Winston – the nice young man you met inside tonight. He is the man who went to Johannesburg to get rid of you before you got too wise for comfort. Being a calculated betting man, I planned well in advance. At first we tried to make you think a poaching syndicate was involved. We knew we had to get rid of you.'

'We?'

'Yes, Rick, we.' Kraske smiled smugly, not noticing that Quin had been slowly edging away from them.

Rick realised Quin's strategy. Keeping Kraske's attention trained elsewhere, he moved to the opposite side of Quin and said, 'I still don't understand why all these people had to be killed – Sonya's father, John, Melinda, the old man.'

Rick did his best to stare straight into Kraske's ghostly eyes in the darkness and to divert him from seeing Quin. Quin had retreated to a position where he could, at any moment, disappear into the forest.

'You come around, asking questions about Erfdeel and you don't understand? You dust off the cobwebs from a mechanism that had been lying hidden for decades, and you don't expect to set off a booby trap?'

'No, I didn't …'

Quin disappeared into the darker, deeper side of the forest.

'Erfdeel was a stock exchange share scam,' Rick said. 'AfriBelgo, from what I know, never had share scam difficulties. Why must people die for that?'

'Maybe, Rick, just maybe, Erfdeel could be the booby trap.' Kraske's teeth gleamed in the dark.

Kraske flicked his head around, looking for Quin. Then he smiled. 'Your yellow-bellied friend seems to have taken a gap.' He laughed, keeping the gun at Sonya's neck. 'No big sweat. I'll put Jacques on his tail. Jacques!' he called out again. 'As I said, Erfdeel could be the booby trap. Exercise your mind and allow me to give you something else to think about in these few seconds before you die. Not only did I know your father, young woman, but, Rick, I knew your father as well.'

Rick just stared at him, too shocked to speak.

'An unbelievable coincidence, isn't it? But, to tell you the truth, we never were the best of friends. He was a man who buttered his bread on both sides.'

'What do you mean?'

'Your father was in the Resistance, but he had some good connections which very few people in the Resistance knew about.'

'Nonsense,' Rick said half-heartedly. He had learned in the very recent past that anything was possible.

'Rick, your father was part of the secret army we had in Belgium and he worked for us. For the Germans.'

'You've told us so many lies already, why should I believe that?' Rick tried to sound indignant but pangs of doubt now gnawed at him.

What if Kraske was telling the truth? How could he know what was right or wrong about what he had been told as a child? What if

Albert Land had not been a hero of the Resistance, but merely a German collaborator in disguise?

'My father couldn't have worked for the Germans. He was a Belgian. He was a resistance hero.'

'Sometimes he was a hero and sometimes not.' Kraske smiled and pushed the barrel deeper into Sonya's neck. A soft thud sounded somewhere nearby in the undergrowth, followed by the unmistakable rattling of a rattlesnake.

A rattlesnake?

Very slowly Kraske turned his pistol away from Sonya towards the sound of the serpent. Frozen in silence, they listened to the rattling, which, Rick thought, seemed to fade away.

For the second time that night, a dragon's breath blazed unexpectedly.

This time it was a smaller ball of flame from which a bullet darted out from nowhere towards Kraske's hand holding the pistol. Kraske let go of Sonya's hair as he screamed and the weapon fell from his shattered hand to the ground. Before Rick could react, Quin flew out of the darkness and into Kraske's doubled-up body. A glimmer of steel at the end of Quin's fist shot into Kraske's throat.

The twisting steel made only a little sound in the night. Like an apple being plucked from a tree.

The rattling of the snake had gone and was now replaced with the sound of rattling phlegm. Kraske lay on the ground. Even in the darkness Rick could see blood pouring from his throat.

'I will not ...' he coughed. 'You will never ...'

A convulsion.

Sonya stumbled into Rick's arms. Quin stood over Kraske's prostrate body.

Silence, except for the scraping sounds of Kraske who attempted to move away. He coughed, shuddered a few times and, with one last iguana-like convulsion, he slithered into the arms of death.

Quin wiped the knife dry on the dying man's trousers. 'My forefathers were with us tonight.'

'How did you get a weapon, Quin?'

'Easy, it was. Kraske shoved our guns behind his feet. He was talking much. Too much. So much that I could come back from behind him on my belly, I did. I took the gun inches from his feet. I was as quiet as my forefathers.'

'And the snake?'

'We needed distraction, we did. Rattlers like to be under rocks at night because the rocks stay warm. They sleep there, they do. You lift a rock. You find a snake. Easy if you are Algonquian.'

There were screams in the distance.

From the protection of the forest they now saw Kraske's house ablaze at ground level on the one side. The fire Quin had started in the basement had spread. Two women, probably the kitchen staff, stood in front of the house, etched against the light of the flames, screaming.

'Look!' Sonya pointed at two other figures running towards the forest from the house, each unmistakably bearing a rifle.

'Let's go!' Rick ordered, knowing that if they remained there they would have little chance of survival against the trained assassins coming at them. He picked up his Smith and Wesson. It would not be good to touch Kraske's weapon and leave fingerprints. Quin seemed to think otherwise and picked up Kraske's gun.

Quin led them into the woods. Fronds of maidenhair fern slapped their faces as they ran. Branches of hickory, sourwood, chestnut and oak reached towards them – furtive fingers, grabbing at them on their flight through the forest. All around them, the False Faces of the night screeched in silence. Except for the thumping of their own feet on the ground and the breaking of twigs and branches, the only sound was the incessant song of the Katydids in the leaves overhead.

They traded the damp floor of dead leaves for a slippery uphill route. At the apex of the ridge they stopped. From an opening in the trees they now had a good view of the burning house in a clearing in the forest below. The whole building was on fire now.

'Beautiful in a way,' Rick thought aloud.

An emergency siren wailed.

'Look down there,' Quin said, pointing at the blanket of treetops below, in which a light flickered fitfully through clusters of foliage. 'They're following us. See? There's another flashlight now behind the one in front.'

'What should we do?' Sonya's voice trembled.

Rick took her hand. She gripped his tightly.

'There are two of them,' Quin stated. 'I'm armed and you're armed, Rick. We can either run, wait for them here, or we could split up and take them individually. What do you think?'

Rick weighed up the alternatives. If Quin were to draw one man and he and Sonya the other, they could control the situation better. If something were to go wrong, with only one man in pursuit, Sonya would stand a better chance of survival, he reasoned. 'We split up. I'll take Sonya with me.'

'Okay. I'll go along the ridge to the south, I will.' Quin indicated in the darkness the direction he would follow. 'The two of you must continue downhill in the same direction we've been following so far. You will then come to the Potomac, you will. From there, follow the road to where Potomac and Shenandoah meet. From there take the road that turns left. You will then find my house, you will.'

'I'm sure we will. Good luck,' Rick said.

Quin walked up to them, put one hand on Sonya's shoulder and his other on Rick's, and he hummed the same tune he had hummed when they had met at the water's edge. As suddenly as he had started, he stopped humming.

Author's note: Just as in the case of Erleigh and Milne's Erfdeel, where there is almost no information on search engines today, Peter Kraske has been virtually erased from mining and lobbying history. Like Soviet leaders of the previous era who, when having fallen out of favour, were merely erased from previous official photographs. Politicians and business people have one thing in common: they disassociate themselves from cesspool situations. As they say in my country: Only a grave will cure a hunchback. I am just glad a Kraske neighbour talked freely and that I was able to pick up bits and pieces at the South African Embassy in Washington DC.

CHAPTER 19

The night has a thousand eyes.

–Francis William Bourdillon
(and, much later, put in a song by Benjamin Weisman)

THE NIGHT HAD LEFT ITS marks on him. The skin on his bruised wrists burned, his arm muscles ached, and his hands were swollen and sore. Rick breathed deeply. He had to calm his nerves. Fifteen minutes. They had been waiting for fifteen minutes and still there was no sign of pursuit, no lights following them, no sounds.

Sonya had at first protested, but had finally succumbed to Rick's insistence that she should scramble up a huge oak tree and sit out of harm's way. He knew exactly where she was, twenty yards to his left, so well concealed that not even he could see her in the darkness. The sound of the surging Potomac, a few yards behind, contrasted with the placid Chesapeake and Ohio Canal, a few paces in front of him, where he could see the outline of the only bridge over the canal for a few hundred yards. If they were still being followed, the chances were probably good that the route of pursuit would have to be across this particular bridge.

He had been hiding for the past quarter of an hour in a clump of bushes that had triggered off his hay fever again. He had just taken his last infernal tablet. Every now and then he still had to stifle a sneeze. His eyes were wet with the streaming tears of his allergy.

The canal shimmered in starlight, the bridge clearly perceptible, but the forest around it was enveloped in a blind darkness. A firefly-like light flickered. And then a burst of light shot through the forest. Flashlight.

He anticipated that, once a pursuer arrived at the clearing of the canal and bridge, the flashlight would be switched off in order not to be too vulnerable. In open areas there was sufficient starlight for someone to find his way.

He waited.

He thought he saw a flitting shadow for a moment on the other side of the canal. At first he was not too sure whether it had been an actual movement or whether his allergy had played with his vision but, as a hunter, he knew he had to remain motionless and to concentrate, just to make doubly sure. And not to sneeze.

His patience was rewarded when the phantom appeared again. It drifted down the embankment towards the bridge over the canal. He gripped the Smith and Wesson tighter and glanced towards Sonya's hiding place up in the oak tree.

On the other side of the wooden bridge, the man lingered in a crouching position for a few seconds. In the starlight Rick could still not make out who it was.

Then, with rapidly tapping feet, the spectre came running over the loose boards of the bridge, stooped, with a rifle hanging from his right hand, low and parallel to the ground. Rick wanted to shoot but the trees got in his way and the man entered the darkness of the foliage in front of him, ran towards him but suddenly brushed away so close to Rick that he could smell his body odour. He could have reached out and grabbed him, had he wanted to. It was Winston – the man who, according to Kraske, had planted the bomb in Johannesburg – Melinda's murderer.

About ten yards away from Rick, Winston stopped and squatted on his haunches, his back to Rick. It was time.

'If you move, I will pull the trigger,' Rick said softly.

Winston stiffened instantly, still clutching his rifle with the butt on the ground.

'I have a Smith and Wesson magnum aimed at you, Winston. If you make the slightest wrong movement, a three-fifty-seven bullet will blow a hole through your head. My guess is that the hole will probably be about the size of a tennis ball, so put down your rifle slowly and stand up.'

Winston obliged.

'Now walk a few steps forward and turn around slowly.'

Winston turned around, and Rick came out of the shrubbery.

'Stand where you are. Now turn the palms of your hands to me and keep them open.'

He looked at Winston, standing a few paces from him in the gloom with his feet slightly apart and his hands opened to him – the same hands that had carried death to his doorstep in Linden.

He wanted to twitch his trigger finger and sweep away the despicable figure in front of him. In his mind's eye he again saw a warped, bloodied shoe and a piece of torn, singed flesh. He aimed the Smith and Wesson at Winston's chest. He fought against an almost involuntary muscular contraction in his index finger. One finger spasm on the trigger could arrange a deserved death.

'Rick! Rick!' Sonya shouted, giving away her position in the tree. 'There's another one on the other side of the bridge!'

Rick went down on his haunches. At the same time, even before her words had died down, Winston dived towards his rifle on the ground. Rick reacted immediately; the booming breath of fire from the Smith and Wesson reached out towards Winston. In that deafening instant, Rick dived to his left. He saw the force of his shot sending Winston sprawling back, his head bursting open. Winston's body shuddered and then froze with the rifle on top of him. Winston was dead.

He rolled away into the undergrowth, turning his body in such a way that he could see the bridge again. Lying flat on his stomach, he strained his eyes to find a moving shadow but he found nothing.

Sonya had given her position away to warn him. He needed to move the attention away from Sonya's hiding place. Rick scratched around in the soil around him and found a fist-sized rock. He threw the rock as far as he could in the opposite direction from Sonya's hiding place.

As the rock fell, he saw a burst of flame accompanied by an almost inaudible shot from the other side, a whiffing sound, followed by the crack of the bullet slamming into a tree trunk somewhere in the early morning darkness where the rock had landed. Out there someone – probably Jacques – had a silencer fitted to his weapon.

He could not allow Jacques any opportunity of taking aim at him or Sonya in the dark. He had to be cunning. His mind raced. He could do what poisonous snakes in African would do in such a situation – play dead, wait for the other's curiosity to take over, and then lash out. To do that, he decided, he needed to use Winston's rifle. He slithered over to Winston's dead body, took off the bootlaces on both boots and stuck the laces in his pocket. He undid Winston's trouser-belt, unclipped the flashlight and left it on top of Winston's dead body, and took off the dead man's trousers. He grabbed hold of Winston's rifle and slithered back to his first position with all the items in his hand. He tied the laces, Winston's belt, his own belt and the trousers into one long extension, which he rolled up. He moved in the direction of the spot where the rock had fallen. Winston's rifle, except for the telescope, appeared to be in good working condition. He cocked the rifle, tied the shoelace end of the improvised rope around the trigger, and settled the rifle into a fork in a tree trunk, aiming it in the general direction of the other side of the canal.

Everything now depended on how good a shot Jacques was. Lying six or seven feet away from the rifle, he took hold of one end of the improvised rope, pulled, and rolled away.

The rifle spat a roaring flame.

Jacques responded with an immediate whiff of sound, a flame blinking from the other side of the canal, and a bullet again slammed with a loud crack into a tree trunk, inches away from the rifle.

As the bullet tore into the trunk, Rick imitated a death rattle as best he could, and then stopped.

Silence.

Except for a soft sob from Sonya's direction. She obviously thought he had really been hit. He just hoped she would remain calm and quiet.

Playing dead, he lay flat on his stomach and peered into the threatening darkness trying to identify his hunter.

A minute or so later, he saw the first fleeting movement. For a while, Jacques – he knew it would be him – crouched behind the railing of the wooden bridge on the other side of the canal and Rick waited for him. Finally, just like Winston, he came rattling over the loose boards, running closer and closer to Rick's position in the undergrowth. Rick kept his aim on Jacques all the way. At the end of the bridge, not more than ten paces from him, Jacques fell to his stomach and lay there for a few seconds. Rick held his finger on the trigger.

Jacques got up slowly and made a crouching step to start stalking his prey.

Rick's hand stiffened and the Smith and Wesson spat a bullet into Jacques's chest a few yards away. The force of the shot threw Jacques upwards from his crouching position.

Rick pulled the trigger again, blasting another shot into the man. It was as if two huge fists had punched into Jacques's body. He staggered back a few short paces, dropped his weapon and, clutching at his breast, fell backwards against the end of the bridge railing of the canal.

Rick walked to the edge of the canal. Jacques's foot had become caught in the opening between the bridge and the edge of the canal. His body hung upside-down on its back against the embankment, with one foot wedged into the crevice, one leg hanging limply, his head and shoulders submerged in the dark water.

Rick fell to his knees and ran his hand down Jacques's left leg stuck in the crevice, trying to reach his trouser pocket, hoping that the Mustang's keys would be in that particular pocket. He patted the leg around the pocket area. Nothing. The keys had to be on the other leg. Rick pulled at the body and managed to lift the head and shoulders out of the black canal water. Blood streamed from two gaping holes in his chest over a twisted neck. Rick managed to pull the right leg up, put a hand in that pocket, felt the keys between his fingers and fought to draw them out.

And then the Chesapeake and Ohio Canal won the battle. Jacques's foot popped out from the crevice between the bridge and the edge of the bank, the body performing half a cartwheel. The body with the Mustang's keys in a pocket disappeared into the water below, its ripple turning the reflection of the stars from above into twinkling beauty. All that remained was the shoe left stuck in the crevice. He'd found the gun that had killed his brother. Maybe he'd settled part of the score. He picked it up, and held it in his hands.

He had never seen anything like it before. It was a pistol – in the starlight he guessed it to be a Colt – slid on to a wooden holster that formed the stock, with a silencer on the barrel and a telescope fixed to the grip. The pistol had ingeniously been turned into a short-barrel rifle. With a few short hand movements, the rifle could be broken up again into a pistol that would fit in the wooden holster.

'Sonya!' he shouted towards the oak tree.

'Rick, are you all right?'

He rushed towards her hiding place which was difficult to find coming from the starlight on the bridge to the pitch darkness under the canopy of the forest.

'I think we're all fine now.'

'I thought you were hit.'

He laid the strange weapon on the grass and reached out to her. She put a trembling hand in his and slid down from the lowest branch of the oak tree into his outstretched arms. With his right arm he encircled the softness of her thighs and held her for a moment.

'Oh Rick, I thought you died. I thought you were shot. I heard an awful sound. It sounded like you were dying. I was so worried.'

Clutching her body to his, he realised in that moment that he loved her. Something good had to come out of this, and it had. He had found Sonya.

'Sonya?' There was a catch in his voice.

'Rick.' Her word was a smile.

'I lost my car keys,' he blurted.

'Don't worry. I took Hot-wiring 101 as a special subject at the orphanage. I'll get the car started. Even a brand-new model like this 1994 Mustang.'

'Rick! Sonya!' they heard Quin calling them.

'Quin!' Sonya cried as she ran up to him and flew into his arms.

They stood side by side at the water's edge just before dawn.

'Potomac, you are strong. We offer you more strength,' Quin said, disassembling the Beretta. Then one by one, he threw the parts in various directions into the river.

'The river gave this town a rifle factory. Maybe it is fitting that we give the river these arms and ammunition,' Sonya said.

Rick flung John's Smith and Wesson far out into the Potomac. He then lifted Winston's rifle over his head and hurled it in whirling cartwheels out into the river, followed by Winston's flashlight, belt, trousers and laces. It would not make sense to leave traces behind.

Keeping the custom-made Colt pistol-turned-rifle for last, he cradled it in his hands and closed his eyes.

He could not remember when last he had prayed. Maybe at Lauterbach's dead kudu? But he prayed now and he bowed his head.

'John, may you have joy, wherever you are. I forgive,' he whispered, and then he hurled the Colt in its wooden holster, out against the pre-dawn light.

They watched as, at the apex of its trajectory, the gun and holster parted and the two projectiles plunged into the swirling Potomac to disappear forever from their lives.

Rick reached for Sonya's hand.

The river roared a little louder.

Author's note: Unlike the ammunitions factory in Brussels, the site of Kraske's house did not remain a jumble of ruins but has been rebuilt as a beautiful mansion. The bridge over the canal is still there from where one can almost see the John Brown Museum in Harper's Ferry.

CHAPTER 20

Die duisternis het geen skaduwees nie.
(Darkness has no shadows.)

–C.J. Langenhoven

A BRIGHT RED CARDINAL, THE official bird of Virginia, spluttered in a puddle at the roadside, showering itself with a flurry of feathers. The speeding wheels of the Mustang bit into the hot tar, a few wingspans away, blasting hot air in its wake and prompting the bird to flutter away. The humidity had draped a gauzy veil over Capitol Hill ahead of them.

'It's on the hour. Let's listen to the news,' Sonya said, switching on the radio.

'And so we had that break in bopping to take you shopping. Folks, as they say, every radio station has its rent to pay. You wanna bop? You gotta shop! But now, just before we take you further on today's Bop-a-long Cassidy trail we've got our newsman Mike standing by in our newsroom. Mike?'

'Thank you, Arnie. Yes. Top story of the day remains the mystery surrounding the violent death of Peter Kraske, a respected DC lobbyist. The night before last, a fire razed Kraske's multi-million dollar country mansion to the ground, taking with it his huge collection of priceless works of art. Kraske was found some distance from the house. He had been shot in the hand but authorities say he died from a neck wound.'

'Any motive, Mike?'

'So far no motive has surfaced for the suspected arson and murder of Kraske. The remains have been found of another undisclosed person who died in the fire and, in further developments, early this morning, two more bodies were discovered not very far from the burnt-down mansion.'

'Amazing events, Mike.'

'You can say that again, Arnie. The bodies were of two men who had been shot. One was found in the woods, the other in the Chesapeake and Ohio Canal. Police have not yet made a statement on clues or leads. Tributes are flowing in from both Republicans and Democrats. Kraske was universally regarded as a true broad-gauge political thinker. Well, Arnie, that's the bad news. And now, for the good news. The Baltimore Orioles will go into today's—'

Sonya switched off the radio. 'It'll be the standard urban babble from now on.'

She turned up the air-conditioner.

'We're lucky. Every conceivable clue has either gone up in flames or down in water.'

'Maybe you're right, Rick, but don't you think Marcia or Aardt could try something funny?'

'No,' Rick said as he backed the car into a parking space. 'I doubt Mark or Marcia would want to talk to the law. I've got a feeling they wouldn't want Kraske's death to rattle any skeletons in their own cupboards. And we now know they do have a few skeletons. In any case, neither of them knows you were there. They left Kraske with me. I can always say I also left after them, which is true.'

'I suppose you're right.'

'I know I am right. Otherwise she would have said I should see her at the office, not here,' Rick said, switching off the ignition with the spare key he had found in John's house after their hot-wired return.

The midday humidity was an uncomfortable hurdle to cross and they gratefully walked through the swing door into the cool interior of the huge ultra-modern aviary, dedicated to man-made birds of flight. The only difference was that instead of the chatter of birds, this cavernous place echoed with the chatter of innumerable human voices.

'This is it. Impressive, isn't it?' Sonya lifted her hands in a gesture of presentation and added, 'The National Air and Space Museum.'

It was a stirring sight. High up in the central atrium the fragile wings of the Wright brothers' first successful aeroplane, the Kitty Hawk Flyer of 1903, hovered over the original Apollo 11 command module of Neil Armstrong's flight to the moon. Massive space-age rockets dwarfed the original silver-coloured Spirit of St Louis in which Charles Lindbergh had flown the first solo, non-stop trans-Atlantic flight from New York to Paris in 1927. They passed underneath the long outstretched wings of the first fully human-powered plane, the Gossamer Condor – two wings attached to a bubble containing a mechanism resembling bicycle gear all wrapped in a material resembling thin plastic.

'This is where they say the dream is still alive.' Sonya led him through the crowds towards the right, into a broad mall filled with exhibits, and escalators leading to the upper floors. 'The cafeteria's down here, I think.'

Just past the huge Skylab exhibit, Rick stopped. In front of him were wartime German V1 and V2 rockets. What had Kraske meant about his father? A Resistance fighter who had collaborated with the Nazis? Could it have been possible? Could it not just have been part of Kraske's mental sparring at the time?

'Come,' Sonya said and took him by the arm, 'we're late.'

The aroma of sizzling meat, hickory smoke and fries filled the air where they found her in the smoking section of the cafeteria. She did not smile at them. She merely pushed her lower lip under the upper one, smacked her lips, and drew at her slim cigarette. She nodded a sullen acknowledgement.

'Mind if we have a—'

'You wanted this meeting. Sit down.'

'Good.'

'I agreed to see you, not this bitch.'

'Sonya is with me and you will have to accept that.'

'And you've got to accept that she's still a bitch.'

'No, you will talk to her with respect, Marcia, unless you want me to make a statement to the—'

'Don't go there! I'm busy at the office. I also don't want Mark to know I'm seeing you. Cut the crap and give me the spiel.'

Her lacquered fingers trembled as she brought the cigarette back to her lips.

'We need to talk about Kraske's death. Before John died,' Rick said, 'he suspected his life was in danger. He made a video and he changed his will so that I would be forced to come out to DC and see the video myself. The whole story is there, told by John in person after his death.'

'You're lying,' she said and then touched the inside of her right nostril with a painted nail.

'All right, Marcia. If that's the way you want it, knowing our own lives were in as much danger as John's, we've added our own inserts at the end of John's video,' he lied on the spur of the moment. 'We've arranged for a media briefing at the Embassy at four this afternoon where the video will be shown, whether we're there or not. I just thought you were probably innocently drawn into everything. It seems I've been proven wrong. Marcia, I can see your hands are also dripping with blood. Let's go, Sonya.'

'No, wait!'

Standing at the table, Rick and Sonya glanced at each other and then down to Marcia who now had each of them by the hand. 'Sit down. Give me a chance,' she said, tugging at Rick's sleeve.

'Fine, let's talk, but with respect.'

'All right.'

'No dilly-dallying, Marcia. Ever since I've met you you've been lying. Take an honest line for a change.'

Marcia squashed her cigarette and folded her hands on the table in front of her. 'Peter Kraske was a consultant who often came around. He was always nice to me. A real gentleman. He often brought me thoughtful little gifts. One day, a while ago, he sat in the reception, waiting for John to return to the office. We got talking and one thing led to another. Before I knew it I had told Kraske of all my troubles, about this new girl, you, at the Embassy and that John was driving me mad with vague instructions relating to something called Erfdeel – something which I knew he was following in order to impress you.' She signalled with a dip of her head in Sonya's direction.

'And when you told Kraske about John's instructions on Erfdeel, he became interested,' Rick suggested, after weighing up her information.

'Oh, Kraske was very interested.'

'Why do you think so?'

'I don't know. He just began calling me everyday, told me John was somehow tied up with organised crime in the States and that we had to find out to what extent he had become involved in it. Kraske told me I should not discuss this with anybody except Mark Aardt, who ran the US operation's interests at head office in Johannesburg and who had been informed. Then Kraske had breakfast with John at the Jockey Club. Afterwards Kraske called me. He said John was very deep into organised crime and that we all had to be extremely careful. The word was out that John had upset certain unsavoury characters and that they had a hit man out after him. Kraske said he feared for John's life and that if I did not keep it to myself the risk to John would increase.'

'And you believed it.'

'Of course. John was acting very strangely for quite some time. Secretive is the word I am thinking of. I knew there was something seriously wrong.'

'What kind of crime could he have been involved in?' Sonya said.

'They said it was the smuggling of gold.'

'And what did you do?' Rick asked.

'I gave Kraske and head office confidential daily reports on his movements and work.'

'And so you gave Kraske the flight details of John's trip to New Orleans?'

'Yes.'

'Marcia,' Sonya chipped in. 'Did you not see a link between all these deaths? John, the bomb at Rick's house, Melinda, and the bomb at my apartment? You do know about the bomb at my apartment, don't you?'

Marcia hesitated for a moment.

'Yes. I knew enough to accept, well, believe that you were all somehow connected to John's links with organised crime.'

'When I left Kraske's house,' Rick struggled for a moment to phrase his words correctly, 'as I said, as I left Kraske's house, he was still alive and well.'

So far so good. He was actually telling the truth because Kraske only died once they were out of the house.

'So, Marcia, I'm looking for reasons for a number of things. One aspect that puzzles me is why you visited Kraske at his house the night before?'

'I could ask the same of you.'

'Which means we all would prefer not to get involved in the investigations, I suppose,' Rick said.

'In my case, I picked up Mark at Dulles airport. He told me we needed to go to Kraske for an urgent meeting to discuss John's death, because AfriBelgo couldn't afford the scandal of a link to the underworld in any country. Kraske had a few armed guards out there to protect him and us from further attacks. But,' Marcia looked at Rick with renewed interest, 'Rick, I'd be interested to know why you broke into Kraske's house like a thief.'

'I didn't. I walked in at the front door and Kraske's guard overreacted.' Doing his best to think up another lie, he added, 'I've got my contacts at head office too. Remember, I worked there for a long time. I knew Kraske had been a VIP back in the formative days of the company and I wanted to talk to him.'

'And did you?'

'I sure did,' he said putting on as pious a face as possible. 'Once he understood the over-reaction of his security guard, Kraske and I had a good discussion. He told me very much the same as you did. It seems that many people, including you and Kraske, were drawn innocently into this web. Kraske mentioned Sonya too, a story that reached him via you and which explains why Sonya is here,' he appeased her, ignoring Sonya's stare.

'Why do you think Kraske was killed?' Marcia asked.

'Marcia, just like you, I don't know what happened to Kraske. I suppose he was in the way of certain people for the same reasons John got in the way. I've also had threats against me related to organised crime and the smuggling of ivory. All of this makes sense to me now. I think the best thing is that we all forget about it, write off everything as part of a bad dream and start anew. Don't you agree?'

Marcia nodded.

'What's Mark's view on Kraske's unfortunate death?'

'He's scared witless of any scandal bringing him or AfriBelgo into disrepute. The first thing he told me after we heard of Kraske's death was that under no circumstances should anyone be told that he and I had been there or had seen Kraske that night. First John, then an attack on your home, now Kraske. That's too much for him and AfriBelgo.'

'Well, you can go and tell him that you have spoken to us, that I am not into crime, that I've been living under threat myself. And another thing, I will not disclose to anyone that I saw the two of you there that night. Maybe it would be better if you did not mention Sonya's part of our discussion here, just for you to save face.'

'You don't realise how heavy a weight you have just taken off my shoulders, Rick.'

'There's no sense in chasing up the partridges at AfriBelgo's head office or in its share price. I don't want to hear any stories from my contacts in Johannesburg. Let's all rather bury this and go forward.'

'Thanks.' Marcia sighed and managed a smile. She took out a handkerchief and dabbed at her eyes.

'How honest do you think she was?' Sonya asked as they watched Marcia disappear into the crowd beyond the cafeteria door.

'How honest? Your guess is as good as mine.'

'Just as long as she wasn't as honest as you were now,' Sonya smiled.

'I had no other option but to stretch the truth.'

'It's all over now, isn't it, Rick?'

'Maybe … I would still like to know why Erfdeel was so important that so many had to die for it. I would also like to find out in time how Uncle Erick fits in with everything.'

Sonya reached forward to take his hand. 'At least I now know who murdered my father. And you know that the younger Jacques arranged a hit man for John's murder on Kraske's orders. You now also know that Melinda died on Kraske's orders. All of them who lived by the sword now died by it.'

'That's just it. We've been thrown together by circumstantial coincidence – one of the most wonderful things to have happened in my life, Sonya – and …'

'And I love you,' she interjected softly, raising his hand to her moist lips. She kissed his fingers one by one, and with a smile in her eyes, breathed against them.

It was the most unlikely place for Rick to hear those words, but nothing could have made him happier.

'I love you, too, Sonya, I love you so much.' He grasped her hand tightly, then looked down. He had to finish his train of thought. 'We've been thrown together because people close to us have died. We've eliminated the killers but we still don't know why those people were murdered in the first place.'

'Yes, you are right.'

'I've trusted Uncle Erick my whole life. He brought us out from Belgium; he cared for us after my father's death; he gave John and me our education, and gave us jobs. In short, he's been the father I never knew. Now, it comes out that, in the early days of his business, he was involved with your father and a cold-blooded ex-Nazi killer. Erfdeel meant something to your father and Kraske. The issue I would now like to address is what Erfdeel could mean to Uncle Erick today.'

'Everything will work out, Rick.' Her mouth flowered into a smile. Her blue-grey eyes reminded him of the Shenandoah. Self-consciously she drew her honey-coloured hair back with one hand, tilted her head and whispered, 'What are you staring at?'

'The future.'

RICK KNOCKED ON THE DOOR again but there was no response. He tried the doorknob. The door was shut, as were the windows.

'He's definitely not home,' Sonya said and sighed.

'Maybe we should try the river bank where we met him.'

'Hey you!' The voice came from the road and belonged to a scraggy old man with a scarecrow face but a sunflower grin. 'Yer lookin' fer Quin?'

'Yes,' Rick said.

'Ain't here, that ah kin tell ya.'

'Where is he?' Sonya asked.

The old man scratched his grey beard and grinned from ear to ear. 'He asked me to check on his chickens. Said he needed to go to Jamestown at first to talk with his wife.'

'His wife is dead. He can't talk to her,' Sonya said.

'Yeah? Well, Quin, he kin talk to lotsa dead people. He's always talkin' to his ancestors and they're all stone dead. Yeah. Mebbe he's gettin' a bit old now 'cause he told me he got himself these two new wonderful children and he wanted to go to Jamestown an' tell his old lady. He did that. He went there to tell her about these children.'

'When's he coming back?' Rick asked.

'Nah, he came back this mornin'.'

'Oh, so where is now?' Sonya asked.

'Gone again. He sure came back. Came up to my place an' told me he got down to some serious talkin' with the wife in Jamestown. He's always kinda kooky, speakin' to ghosts an' things, but I believe he kin do that. He told me this very morning he'd spoken to her spirit in the graveyard an' she was glad about the new children. But she also told him to go visit their boys. He's got boys in Montreal an' Houston. He's gone there. Took the Greyhound this morning.'

'When will he be back?' Rick asked.

'I dunno. He dunno. Mebbe a month. Or two. Who knows?' The old man shrugged and turned away, having lost interest in any further discussion, it seemed.

Sonya rummaged in her handbag, tore a page from her diary and started writing. Rick made himself comfortable on the floorboards against the railing and gazed at the hot haze that enshrouded the mountains.

'Here. You could add a few paragraphs, if you wish to, but I think we have to thank him. We could slip this under the door for him.'

She handed Rick the letter.

Dear Quin,

We took the chance of driving out here for the day so that we could see you again. Sadly we missed you. We wanted so much to talk to you again. We wanted to tell you that you changed our lives forever. You brought us together. You protected us when we needed you. You taught us values that will always be part of us from now on. You have become our father – the father we both lost. We want you to know that you will always be important in our lives. We love you as children should love their father. Our rivers will part temporarily, one of us leaving America today, the other following three days from now after which we will become one again. You are the one that made us flow together. We hope to be back with you again one day. May your ancestors help you in the way they helped us but, just in case they also need some help, we will pray to God for your safe return and well-being.

With all our love
Shenandoah and Potomac

Rick had nothing to add. It was perfect. He folded the letter, stood up and slipped it in under the front door. He turned around and took Sonya in his arms.

They stood there for a long time, Sonya burying her head in his shoulder, Rick trying get rid of the lump in his throat.

And the Blue Ridge Mountains suddenly seemed hazier than before.

CHAPTER 21

Everything we see hides another thing.
We always want to see what is hidden by what we see.

–René Magritte

BRUSSELS. SUNDAY MORNING. SHUTTERED, SILENT and cold with the bite of a winter's day in the middle of summer. A city with a grey, curdled sky drawn over a drab skyline.

In streaky, swiping movements, the taxi's windscreen wipers fought against the battering rain.

Dressed too lightly for the weather, Rick shivered on the back seat of the Mercedes, rubbing his bare arms to rid himself of the goose bumps, grateful for the heated air warming his feet even though that warmth below came with a sickly smell of sweet toilet air freshener.

Having kissed Sonya goodbye in Washington the night before, he had landed at Zaventem airport an hour before for his first visit to Belgium since his childhood. Sonya would meet him in the city in three days' time.

His taxi passed a bronze statue of a grim-looking man on horseback, painted to a glossy varnish by the rain. They drove past one dreary building after another, interspersed with blinkered storefronts on desolate sidewalks. The taxi driver, a swarthy Middle Eastern type who barely spoke French and had no command of English or even Flemish, dipped them at high speed through a few tunnels until they finally stopped in front of the Hotel Amigo, just off the Grand-Place.

After checking in and being allocated his room, Rick's body clock was still attuned to the early morning darkness of the American East Coast and he went to sleep. He woke up with no sense of time and glanced at his watch. It was eight in the evening. He had slept the whole day!

Hunger and a need for exercise drove him out on the street where, miraculously, the rain had disappeared and summer seemed to have returned. Hundreds of people thronged the cobble-stoned alleys. In the late evening Belgian sun, he walked across the Grand-Place, one of the great squares of Europe, dominated by an imposing gothic Hôtel de Ville, the town hall, surrounded by sumptuously decorated seventeenth-century guild houses, each with its own emblem – a fox, a wheelbarrow, a mill, a ship.

He stopped for a beer in the rustic atmosphere of the Café de la Grand-Place and sat next to a stuffed horse under several overhanging marionettes and a chandelier made of ballooning pigs' bladders. A waiter in a bow tie, white shirt, black waistcoat and white apron brought him a glass of Jupiler beer, which he sipped, considering his next step.

He had arrived in Brussels without any plan other than to contact people who had known his father during the war. From his mother's photograph album, he vaguely remembered the name of a wartime family friend, Thom Thomas, and of two distant relatives, Harry Ruys and Luc de Smet. Would any of them still be alive now in 1994? If so, where would he find them?

Then he remembered his mother's cousin, Luc de Smet, had worked for the Belgian rail authority. The personnel division of the Belgian railways could be a starting point in the morning. Rick tried to recollect where their apartment had been in Brussels. He knew they had lived in a gloomy building somewhere on the Avenue de Tervuren but he could not remember the number or even its outside appearance.

He finished his beer and went for a walk along the Rue des Bouchers, a cobble-stoned alley, lined with one restaurant after another, set in medieval buildings leaning crookedly against each other like drunken revellers. A constant flow of visitors, with searching eyes and swivelling heads, slow-marched along the length of the alley. The selection of food to still his hunger was varied. Huge, hand-painted menus advertised the dishes on offer. Multi-coloured canvas awnings had been rolled out over tables and chairs set out on the cobble-stored surface. With great ostentation a chef in an open window knifed open fresh oysters. He walked past a waft of fish smells where a medium-sized shark lay on a presentation table, half-buried in white ice in the centre of a variety of other fish and crustaceans.

He took a seat at a wobbly restaurant table on the uneven street surface and ordered a glass of wine and the plat du jour, and then idly watched the passing throng – some of them in flat shoes prowling catlike past him, some in high heels tripping like impalas, some in worn-out boots shuffling along like hippopotamuses and a woman in knee-high boots goose-stepping by like a stately roan antelope.

He wondered how Themba was doing. Most of all, he longed for Sonya's touch and the smell of her hair.

RICK'S EARLY MORNING TELEPHONE CALL to the rail organisation, the Société Nationale des Chemins de Fer Belges, had been productive.

After a search in the SNCB records, someone had called back and given him Luc de Smet's last known address, telling him that De Smet had retired eleven years before. It had been easy to trace De Smet in the Brussels telephone book and to call him.

Rick rang the doorbell of Luc de Smet's house on Pleinlaan in the leafy suburb of Wezembeek Oppem. De Smet lived in a two-storey A-frame villa, set on a small property with a huge old willow tree in the garden.

'Goeiendag,' De Smet greeted Rick in Flemish with a broad smile, lined with stained teeth. He gripped Rick's hand firmly and added, again in Flemish, 'You have grown up to look just like Albert. Come in.'

The interior had an odour of old people, worn shoes and boiled cauliflower.

De Smet was a short, ruddy-faced, friendly man who, despite the smell of liniments when you got close to him, still walked with a spring in his step and spoke like a man who had been in charge of others for a lifetime. His left eye drooped slightly, creating the illusion of a piercing eye.

'I'm very glad to see you again, Rick. The last time I saw you, both you and John were very small. In height, you barely reached my belt and John was very much a baby. Marie was always so proud of you and John. She used to write every now and then, more to my late wife than me, but my wife died two years before your mother and I lost contact. How is John?'

'He died.'

'I'm sorry to hear that. Have a seat.'

Rick told De Smet in broad terms of what had happened in recent years to him and John until John's death, avoiding any references to Kraske, Sonya and AfriBelgo.

'So what brings you to Brussels then?'

'I'm the last remaining member of our family. I had the good fortune to know my mother ...'

'I had too,' De Smet professed with a gentle smile of remembrance.

'Mijnheer De Smet, I knew my mother and John, but I knew very little of my father. That's why I thought that on my way home from the States, it could be worthwhile to look you up and try to learn a little more of my own ancestry.'

'Albert Land.'

Luc de Smet sighed as he stood up from his armchair, stuck his hands in his trouser pockets and stalked up and down the living room, lost in thought. Finally he stopped at the glass sliding door that opened to his back garden and stared through the window for a long time.

'I haven't thought of Albert for a long time,' he said softly.

'Tell me about him.'

'During the war, Albert and I were on the same political wavelength. We became friends as students at ULB, the Free University in Brussels. I remember the first night we met at a ULB clandestine meeting of an anti-German organisation called the Comité de Surveillance de Bruxelles. Albert wanted to follow in the footsteps of his father who had been a teacher in Schaerbeek, the area of Brussels that lies between the city centre and the Royal Park and palace of Laeken. Having been named Albert, and probably also because he grew up in the neighbourhood near the royal palace, your father had a deep respect for King Albert of Belgium, who, during the First World War, had remained on Belgian soil, at the westernmost extremity of our country. Unfortunately, in the Second World War, the new King Leopold III preferred to surrender in 1940. Instead of commanding the Belgian army in the field like King Albert in the First World War, Leopold became a manipulated prisoner-of-war in his palace for many years. He was a German pawn. Being an energetic student, full of nationalist fervour, your father regarded Leopold as a traitor who licked the jackboots of General Von Falkenhausen, the German aristocrat who headed the military government in Brussels.

'I, for one, shared your father's view. We knew we were prime targets for the Gestapo, who were already rounding up young men to be sent to Germany as forced labourers and, when the Germans closed down the university in November of 1941, we drifted into the underground. Early in 1942, we joined a group of partisans and acquired new identities with forged papers to last us through the war. We used to refer to our resistance activities by the ironic code word of 'child welfare'. Looking back on those days, I have to admit that we even shared the communist views of our first group but then many young people did. It was a time of fret and fury. By day we waited on tables at a café on the Porte Louise. By night we worked together on a secret periodical. Do you know what the SS sign looked like, Rick?'

'Two lightning bolts?'

'Precisely. Well, the German word for shit is 'scheisse'. The heading of our underground paper once consisted of the word 'scheisse' with large SS lightning bolts making up the two s's,' De Smet said and chuckled himself even ruddier in the face.

'That really created a lot of shit among the Germans,' he added.

Rick laughed. Looking at the old fighter standing at the sliding door, he wondered what his father would have looked like, if he had still been alive. Would Albert Land have had a similar light of adventure in his eyes and the same strength of character in his voice? Yet Kraske's allegation that Albert Land had been a collaborator had opened cracks in Rick's previously unquestioning hero-worship of his father.

The thought occurred to him that their mother had probably known very little of their father's wartime activities, because even though he and John had always wanted to know more, she had never told them anything of substance other than that Albert Land had been a leading personality in the Resistance. She had always said that, after the war, their father had believed that bygones should be bygones and that he had lost all interest in delving into the past.

'What was my father like, Mijnheer De Smet?'

De Smet walked to his buffet, combed through a drawer and extracted a frayed album. 'Your father? You resemble him a lot,' and he shoved the album on to Rick's lap.

There were three, small faded photographs on the page, two of groups that featured Albert Land. One photograph showed him with four other young men, all with slicked-back hair in the style of the time, seated on open-backed iron and wood chairs around a table, looking into the camera lens with subtle self-consciousness in their conspiratorial smiles.

De Smet explained that the photograph had been taken after a night's labour in the basement of a house in Auderghem where he, Albert and the two others had operated their underground press. De Smet had been an almost unrecognisably thin young man in those years.

De Smet patted his belly and said something about the Belgian national sport of frites and Stella Artois beer which Rick did not hear as he was already engrossed in studying another photograph. This one showed Albert, dressed in a tie and jacket, aiming a rifle from behind a louvered balustrade at a target somewhere to the left of the photographer with De Smet and another young man, also dressed to the nines, seated on the top slat at his side.

'This was almost as funny as the SS in 'scheisse',' De Smet sniggered.

'Why?'

'During the war it was sometimes difficult to arrange for good target practice. We couldn't very well go out and shoot live ammunition, first of all because we had to operate quietly and, secondly, because we had to steal most of our arms and ammunition, which meant it was always in short supply. The Germans kept strict control over the population but for some reason disregarded the light shooting ranges often found at fairground stalls where you could shoot with air guns for prizes. So we used those for target practice,' he said and he laughed. 'Ah yes, fêtes and fairs turned Albert into an excellent marksman.'

'Were you with my father through all the war years?'

'All but the last year or so, when I was forced to move to Antwerp to look after my parents. We met up again after the war.'

'It could have been because I knew so little about my father and nobody could tell me more about him, but I have always had this nightmare that my father could have been in collaboration with the Germans,' Rick carefully posed the question to De Smet.

'That would have been impossible. Albert Land hated the collaborators, particularly the Rexists.'

'Rexists?'

'They were the Flemish Legion of the VNV and DeVlag. Those people recruited young Flemish idiots for the German training camps and the front lines. VNV was the acronym for the Flemish National

League, Vlaams Nationaal Verbond, whose members were rabidly pro-German. DeVlag stood for Vlaams-Duitse Arbeidsgemeenschap, or Flemish-German Working Community, a supposedly academic and cultural organisation created by Jef Vandewiele, a Flemish teacher. DeVlag steered a political course aimed at the integration of Flanders with the Third Reich. I still shudder at the thought of that. Now that I mention DeVlag, I can give you an example of your father's hatred for collaborators. I remember 25 October 1942 for three reasons. One, it was my birthday. Two, it was a Sunday because we refined our part of the plan after mass that morning. And, three, it was the date of the bomb explosion at the Cinema Marivaux on the Boulevard Adolphe Max. In later years the Marivaux sadly declined to exhibiting porno-graphic films, but in those days it was different. Ah, the Cinema Marivaux was stylish and that had prompted DeVlag to organise a film performance which brought many collaborators together under one roof on that day. Albert and I were not directly involved in that explosion. We were part of a back-up group of men, stationed elsewhere in Brussels, to discreetly measure the speed and timing of reaction from various German quarters. Not even the men involved in the actual bombing knew of our monitoring role. I can still remember the glee on Albert's face when it became known that the attack on the Marivaux had been successful. Unfortunately, that event, coupled with the execution of the Rexist mayor of Charleroi, led to ruthless German reprisals. The Oberfeldkommandantur grabbed innocent hostages and publicly executed them. They executed eight at first, then ten, another ten, then twenty more, followed by a further twenty, and so it went. If you had seen the hatred in your father's face each time we heard of those death rolls, you would have known he was a true-blue, dyed-in-the-wool partisan.'

In contrast with the grey gloom of the day before, summer had returned with a blazing sun and blue sky outside. He felt much relieved now. De Smet had been through the war with his father. His descrip-tion of Albert Land's political outlook was first-hand and diametrically opposed to Kraske's accusation. After all, Kraske had instigated John's murder; why should his accusation be taken seriously?

De Smet remarked on the beautiful day, so rare for Brussels, and invited him for a walk in the garden where he proudly pointed out his apple trees, his strawberry patch and a corner where he grew Belgian endives in a tunnel. Standing at the back of the garden, looking back at the house, De Smet spoke of how his garden would change its character in winter and how his grandchildren enjoyed tobogganing on the snow down the slope of the lawn.

'It is strange how lives seem to slip and slide into each other,' De Smet observed, calling up in Rick's mind the image of his growing attachment to Sonya. How he longed for her now. 'You could almost say I was the snow on which your mother and father slipped towards each other,' De Smet said and his lips curled with amusement.

'How did that happen?'

'When I moved to Antwerp at the end of 1943 your father and I lost contact with each other. I later heard from a mutual colleague that Albert had survived a major crackdown which had decimated most of what we called the Mobile Corps. I was told he was still operating under his old nom de guerre of Alain and had become the leader of a reformed group, which included a few people I knew. They operated from the Auderghem area. And then, suddenly, the war ended. I looked him up and we renewed our friendship. By chance, a few weeks after the German retreat, Albert accompanied me to a family wedding in Uccle where I introduced him to your mother. The two of them fell head over heels in love with each other. I could see why. Marie was extremely attractive and ripe for the right man and Albert was a handsome hero of the Resistance – an underground leader who had survived against the odds. So Rick, if it hadn't been for me, you would not be around today.'

De Smet's words had brought back a few niggling doubts in Rick's mind. He needed to speak to someone who had been close to his father during the latter part of the war, when De Smet had lived elsewhere.

'During the time you lived in Antwerp, I suppose Harry Ruys and Thom Thomas were involved with my father,' Rick said, thinking he would have to contact them.

'No, they were not,' De Smet declared bluntly.

'Neither?'

'Not at all,' De Smet said emphatically. 'Harry and I are related. He met Albert after the war for the first time. Thom was a student friend of ours who saw the war through with nondescript apathy. Thom's been dead for many years now and Harry has become so senile his logic is on a par with the apples in my garden.'

Rick cursed inwardly at the thought he had nobody he could tap for more background during that period in the war. 'What about Erick Martens? Was he with my dad during the last year or so?'

'Yes, apparently he was, but I only met him three or four years after the war,' De Smet said. 'From what I gathered once from Albert, Erick Martens worked directly with the Special Operations Executive.'

'What was that?'

'Part of the British Secret Service. The SOE organised sabotage and supported secret armies on the Continent. I'm not too sure how Erick Martens fitted in, except that he was Belgian and had been trained in London just before the outbreak of the war. These days a sneeze in the most remote part of the globe is heard and seen everywhere through television. As they say, the world has become a global village but, in those days, we all lived in ignorant confusion. The less we knew of each other in the Resistance the better. One thing I must admit however is that I would never have gone into business with Erick Martens, like your father did.'

'What kind of business were they doing?' Rick said, trying to hide his surprise.

'I never liked Martens. He had those shifty eyes and that slick tongue. Still, he made his millions. They were involved in a hare-brained scheme to export architectural columns from Belgium to Africa.'

'How?'

'As partners.'

Rick was shocked. The Belgo-Grec business had been a partnership between his father and Uncle Erick! He now had to contend with an additional piece in a myriad of jigsaw puzzle pieces strewn all over the world. And the picture to be assembled was complicated by Uncle Erick's various partnerships with Albert Land, Kraske and Sonya's father.

'How did they conduct the business here in Belgium?' Rick asked.

'How they could have thought to make a profit, I will never know,' De Smet dismissed Belgo-Grec. 'That business was totally non-viable from the start. It was on a small scale. Your father physically poured the columns and shaped them in his own basement with no assistance from anyone. It was a backbreaking job but he would not allow anyone to help him. I think his health was fading because of that and that his rigorous work schedule contributed to his tragic death. He climbed those rocks at Dinant with a tired body. I'm convinced that was why he slipped and fell to his death.'

'Were you there at Dinant that day?'

'No.'

As they strolled past a shrub towards the house De Smet plucked a leaf and rolled it between his fingers.

'Who were there on the day he fell?'

'I'm not too sure, although I know that your mother, Erick Martens, and his girlfriend were there.'

'And who was she?'

'Leah. She was Leah de Loof. I lost contact with her afterwards but she's still around because I saw her on BRT a short while ago.'

'BRT?'

'Belgian Radio and Television. Leah took part in a recent television series on Belgium in the Second World War. She used to be quite a stunner, which stood her in good stead during the war.'

'How?'

'Beautiful girl. She worked for the Resistance by consorting with German officers and extracting whatever information she could get from them. At the time I met her with Martens, they had both just returned from exile in London, where they had worked for the SOE, the Special Operations Executive. Just after the end of the war she had been forced to flee Belgium because many people had seen her being more than friendly with the Germans. They naturally assumed she had been a traitor. There was no way in which she could have explained to irate mobs that she had been quite the opposite and that she spied on them for her country. When I met them, Albert told me Erick Martens had been close to Leah during the war and, for similar reasons, had gone away in exile to allow Belgian memories and tempers to cool down. We all always tacitly agreed not to discuss their past activities. That's why I was so surprised to see her in that television programme and to hear some of the detail of how she had got information from the Gestapo.'

There were so many unexpected lightning bolts now. Uncle Erick and his girlfriend within German ranks in Belgium in a secret war against the Nazis. Uncle Erick in a partnership with Resistance leader Albert Land but in Africa partnering with a ruthless German interrogator called Kraske. If Uncle Erick had worked for the British SOE, how could he have gone into business with Kraske? And his girlfriend had probably slept her way round the German forces. How did that tie in?

The facts clashed with Rick's logic, until it suddenly dawned on him. Uncle Erick had never been directly involved in any of the deaths. All the deaths had occurred around him. He had been present on the day his Belgian partner in Belgo-Grec, Albert Land, had died. Uncle Erick's partner, Kraske, had arranged the deaths of Sonya's father, John, and Melinda, and had been bent on killing him and Sonya. Putting all the deaths in perspective, Rick now realised that they all had a thread – Uncle Erick – and the thread ran from the initial years of the failed Belgo-Grec business right up to the current success of AfriBelgo.

For the first time, Rick wondered whether his father's death had indeed been an accident.

'Where can I get in touch with Leah de Loof?'

'I don't know where she lives but I think there's a way in which we could trace her. The building which used to house the Gestapo headquarters in Brussels is an apartment building nowadays. I remember a retired economist took part with Leah in the BRT programme – a man who lives in that same building on the Avenue Louise and who, as a hobby in his retirement years, has studied the activities around the building in depth. Leah had been drawn into the television programme as a result of his research. I think he will know where we could get hold of her.'

PIGEONS PECKED FOR MORSELS IN the crevices among the cobblestones. A ubiquitous yellow electric tram, like the one he and De Smet had alighted from after a seemingly interminable trip, rattled past.

They were in the vicinity of the old Gestapo headquarters but right now De Smet could not remember the exact location. He only knew the building would be near the forest, which they could already see – the Bois de la Cambre.

They walked along the Avenue Louise, studying the buildings one by one, looking for a narrow one of about ten to twelve floors which De Smet said would also be recognisable by a plaque in commemoration of an air attack.

When they stumbled upon the bronze plaque at number 453, the building's straight, modern, architectural lines surprised Rick. Instead of the more venerable façade he had expected, the building seemed too modern in appearance. Two windows and a double door in width, the narrow old Gestapo headquarters rose twelve floors high over the traffic, like an emaciated Masai warrior accidentally planted in Europe.

De Smet translated the French words on the plaque next to the entrance. 'In broad daylight on 20 January, 1943, this building, occupied by the Gestapo during the 1940-1945 war, sustained the vengeful fire of the guns from the aircraft of Capitaine Baron Jean-Michel de Selys Longchamps of the First Regiment de Guides, Flying Officer in the Royal Air Force.'

As Rick tried to ask him what the plaque meant, De Smet pressed one of the buttons, the one marked 'concierge', and spoke in rapid French to a woman, asking her which of the other buttons was the one for the economist. From her curt reply, Rick deduced they had to ring the button for a Monsieur Vermette.

After another short exchange in incomprehensible French between De Smet and Vermette, a buzz sounded, followed by a clicking noise, and De Smet pushed open the heavy double door of thick glass covered with strong, horizontal steel bars.

They entered an empty round foyer with a floor of black marble that lined the walls up to eye level. The circular wall was broken by two white alcoves, on the left and right. Their footsteps reverberated on the stone floor like macabre boots of wartime aggressors. Transported back in time, Rick wondered how many German soldiers had passed under the concealed lighting of the recessed, white dome. He imagined a sentry standing at each alcove, keeping watch over the front door, the steel bars of which, Rick noticed, were still painted in wartime green. He could almost hear the clicking of heels and bursts of 'Heil Hitler' in the hallway. And he imagined the fearful living that had entered there and left as the dead through some other door, probably in the back.

The out-dated elevator stopped abruptly and its squeaky doors opened to reveal, waiting for them, an amiable small man with finely chiselled features, dressed in an open-necked white shirt. After the customary introductions in French, Yves Vermette invited them into his apartment, which, like all the others in the slim building, covered a full floor.

Vermette told them he had been an economist and director of companies which, Rick concluded, must have shaped his undoubted investment sense and love for art, evident from his furnishings: classical paintings, antique furniture, a Chinese carpet, silverware, crystal chandeliers, a dark sculpture of a morose man, and heavy drapery, which he opened to point out the Abbaye de la Cambre on the other side of the street.

Impressed that De Smet had remembered him from the BRT programme, Vermette spoke about the strong construction of the building, dating to its erection in 1939, which had made it a prime site to be taken over as the Gestapo's war-time interrogation centre in 1941.

Eventually, De Smet managed to ask Vermette the question that had driven them to him: Did Vermette know Leah de Loof's address?

Vermette got up from the table, walked to a wooden filing cabinet and stated that, as an economist still steeped in attention to administrative detail, he carefully kept records of everything. Searching in one of the drawers, he came up with a file, flipped through it, stopped and wrote down Leah de Loof's address.

She lived in Monschau, a small town in Germany, close to the Belgian border. According to Vermette, she had been one of the Belgian civilians who had worked in the Gestapo headquarters during the war – not as a collaborator, but as an undercover member of the Resistance.

Rick's eyes met with De Smet's. No words were necessary between them. He could see De Smet also yearned to meet Leah de Loof.

Author's note: Vermette has now moved from his apartment at 453 Avenue Louise in the old Gestapo headquarters but was still able to give me quite a lot of detail on the war history, as well as on his own interaction with Rick Land.

CHAPTER 22

Der Liebe ist kein Wind zu kalt.
(For love, no wind is too cold.)

–German saying

THEY FOLLOWED A NARROW, WINDING road through two neatly planned hamlets. The German countryside was a summery green eiderdown of gently rolling hills, one folding into another. Under a blue sky, they descended into a verdant valley.

Although having been a wartime frontier town, situated close to the Belgian border, Monschau had miraculously escaped devastation. Half-timbered houses clung to each other in clusters along the banks of the River Rur, their tiled roofs curved in aged gravitational saddles. Flower boxes on wooden windowsills overflowed with colour in a town where time had stood still.

They found Leah de Loof in a quaint house opposite the Hotel Stern. Standing outside and talking to her on the parlophone at the front door proved to be demanding. At first she refused to let them in. De Smet explained that it was him, that he had been unable to make an appointment with her because he had not known her telephone number, and that he and Albert Land's son had driven all the way from Brussels in the hope of seeing her. Finally she relented.

She waited for them at the top of a creaking staircase – a frail old lady in a simple dress, bent double with the spinal decalcifying effects of osteoporosis. Her beauty had waned to the expressionless, dry pallor of flour. The bags under her eyes had long ago caked into wrinkles rippling down her cheeks. She looked at Rick and De Smet through pewter eyes behind bi-focal glasses, eyes which seemed to have seen too much for comfort, and she greeted them through putty lips that had long ago forgotten how to smile with joy.

With an arthritic finger she guided them to two armchairs. Although cramped and saturated with the same acrid smell of mentholated liniments Rick had experienced at De Smet's place, her living quarters were comfortable enough for someone of her age. She vaguely recollected De Smet but regarded him with little interest.

When Rick spoke in his broken Flemish, she appeared to listen more attentively, staring at the floor planks, her fingers pressed against her temples. The skin on her fingers was as dry as her wispy hair.

After having introduced himself at length, Rick phrased a question to draw her into giving him a first-hand account of the events leading to his father's death.

'You have his voice. Your father, Albert, was a patriot and a great Belgian hero,' she wheezed at last in a voice that vibrated like an out-of-tune cello. Her grey eyes glistened at Rick. Rick noticed De Smet nodded in agreement with her.

'Yes,' she continued, 'I was there on the day he died. It was a beautiful day, like today. The sun was shining over Dinant and the Meuse. I felt it was finally shining on me as well. I was back in Belgium and people respected me again. We were so happy then, so young, so carefree. It was a day of celebration. I cannot remember what we celebrated but it had something to do with the business between my friend and Albert. I used to help them with the paperwork for their new business. We were so excited! We had bread, cheese, wine, even a bottle of champagne, and each other.' Leah de Loof fell silent. Bent forward, she stared at her slippered feet.

'Who was there? You? My father, my mother, Erick Martens?' Behind the veneer of ill health, Rick knew there lay a lively brain.

'Ah, Erick,' she said slowly. 'He went under many names but he did the right thing to change his name when the war ended. I should have done that too. You are right, we were all there – Albert, Marie, Erick, as he came to be known, and I, as well as Thom Thomas, his lady friend and another couple. I can only remember the man's first name, Harry.

'We were,' she coughed twice, 'sitting on blankets on the river bank, joking and laughing, drinking champagne and then wine, throwing pebbles into the water, and watching the birds ride the currents up against the cliffs. Maybe we had had too much to drink or maybe the men hankered after the adventure they had tasted during the war, I don't know. I remember they boasted to each other about their fitness until Erick and Albert challenged each other to a race to the top of the cliff. Instead of the main rock face overhanging the church in town, they climbed a cliff to one side of town which was partly covered in vegetation. We watched them as they climbed at arm's length from each other, side-by-side, to reach the top of the first cliff, from where they had to go through steep, dense vegetation to start at a second rock face, which would take them to the very top. It was so sad.' She fell silent.

'Please continue,' Rick whispered.

'Erick told us everything. In that dense vegetation Albert's feet were on slippery soil at the edge. He reached for a rock to pull himself up but the rock broke loose. He slipped and he grabbed a shrub with his other hand but the young twigs were not strong enough to carry his weight. Erick, as you call him, was next to Albert but unable to save him.'

'Did you see him fall?' Rick asked.

'Yes, I saw him. He popped out of the shrubs like a cork from a bottle of the Moët et Chandon we managed to find for our picnic. He fell headfirst. He never had a chance of survival. His body was broken horrendously.' She stared at the floor.

Rick's had to fight against a sudden giddiness. For the first time ever, he had been given a detailed description of his father's death.

Those metallic eyes, set in a face that resembled kneaded dough, had been there on the day of the tragedy. They had witnessed Albert entering the shrubbery side by side with Uncle Erick and bursting out. Like a popped champagne cork.

But something bothered Rick about the graphic detail he had just heard. At first he could not fathom it. Then it occurred to him. Head first? Albert Land's feet had slipped. His hands had grappled with a loose rock and the twigs of a shrub. He would surely have fallen feet or back first. Yet Leah de Loof had seen him falling headfirst. Why?

'Are you sure that he fell headfirst?'

'I told you, he came out like this,' and she indicated with her hands, 'head first, feet in the air.'

It was as if Rick were a small boy again on the gangplank of the ferry, as if an invisible hand had thumped him on his back once more. He had an unexpected piece of information, a new twist that now lay like a coin on his tongue: Uncle Erick could have pushed his father! It was the unthinkable, but he could not discount it.

'Albert was a good climber. I heard that nobody understood his death,' De Smet said.

'Albert was fitter than ... Erick – I still have difficulty with that name – but Albert was quite athletic,' she agreed.

Again the refrain rang in Rick's mind: Uncle Erick could have done it. But why would he have done something like that? 'Mrs De Loof—'

'Miss ... I never married,' she interjected, allowing Rick a few seconds to formulate his next question.

'Miss De Loof, how did Erick Martens react to the death that day?'

'It crushed him. He felt that if he had not challenged Albert to the climb, the disaster would not have occurred. Afterwards he felt so guilt-ridden that, against everyone's protestations, he decided to quit Belgium for Africa.'

'Why Africa?'

'He and Albert had a company called Belgo-Grec and their dream was to export artistic building materials all over the world. Albert was in charge of the production. He manufactured a large stock before he died. Erick, as you call him, travelled the world to find markets and he found good opportunities in Africa. That was why he went there. He promised that, once he was set up, I would follow.'

As she said it, she laid an anaemic hand on Rick's forearm. Her touch was as lifeless as stone.

'What happened to all my father's products?'

She coughed again. 'Ah, mein schatz was very kind.'

'Mein schatz?'

'Erick, as you know him. Very kind. He took over all the stock – the columns, fountain fixtures, benches and lampposts. He managed to borrow money from somewhere and paid out your mother. As I said I had been helping with the administration. Then he left for Africa. My job was to arrange to ship all the columns and other products through Antwerp. The idea was that I would join him later. For a long time he sent me money, and more important than that, he wrote me the most beautiful letters. Wait! Let me show you.' She struggled out of her chair.

Hunched forward, she shuffled out of the room. Rick glanced at De Smet who lifted his eyebrows and shrugged. It had to be the liniment but Rick felt the return of his allergy, and he searched for a handkerchief in his pockets.

'I kept all his letters in here.' She tottered back with a worn-out box file in her hand.

'How did you come to live in Germany?' De Smet wanted to know.

'When Erick, as you call him, became more successful—'

'My apologies, Miss De Loof,' Rick interrupted her, 'but why do you say 'Erick, as I call him'?'

'For me, and in his letters, he will always remain Heinz,' she breathed out his name as if the mere thought of him made her even more breathless.

'Heinz?' Rick had never heard Uncle Erick being referred to by that name.

'Heinz Müller. Mein schatz, Heinz.' She closed her eyes for a moment.

Another bolt. Erick Martens was, or is, Heinz Müller. De Smet looked at Rick again with a raised eyebrow.

'When Heinz became more successful, he took you all out to Africa, bought the small hotel here in Monschau as an investment and asked me to manage it for a year after which it was our plan that I was to leave to join him. I looked forward so much to seeing him again.'

The sadness in her eyes told Rick much more about the depth of the love she had once felt and probably still did. He wondered what could have happened between them that their lives had drifted apart. It dawned upon him that neither she nor Uncle Erick had ever married.

'You were very much in love with him,' Rick stated the obvious.

'I cried for weeks when I received the news of his death.'

'His death?'

'Yes.'

It took Rick a few moments to absorb what she had said. Uncle Erick's death? He deliberately reined in his response, mulling over the implications of her words. She was clearly under the impression that Uncle Erick, Heinz Müller, was dead.

'How did you hear of his death?' Rick spoke slowly.

She now opened the box on her lap, took out the top letter and, still hunched forward, stared at Rick with a lowered head.

'I always keep this letter at the top of the box because it represents the end of my dreams.'

She handed Rick the letter. He took the yellowed page from her. It had been written partly in German in a strong handwriting, slanted to the right with solid downward pen strokes. Unable to read German, Rick glanced lower down on the page where he recognised a signature he had almost forgotten – his mother's!

She had added a postscript in Flemish at the end of the page:

Dear Leah,

Erick's death came as a shock to all of us. I hope you will find the strength to go on and that you will also find someone who will love and care for you as he did.

Deepest sympathy
Marie Land

Rick's mother had taught him and John values that conflicted directly with the incriminating words in his hands. His initial reaction was that she could not have done this but, when he glanced at the signature at the end of the German portion, he could not contain his bewilderment. He could barely believe who had written the German piece. It was signed Peter Kraske! And someone called Franz. How could his mother have been involved in a blatant lie with a murderer like Kraske? Why would she and Kraske have wanted to write the letter?

Rick handed Leah de Loof the letter again. 'What did the German part say?' he asked in a daze. He felt drained.

She drew the letter close to the bridge of her nose and translated it in a whisper. 'Dear Leah, It is my sad duty to inform you that, two weeks ago, Heinz Müller, also known as Eric Martens, drowned on a fishing expedition off the coast of Zululand. His body has not yet been found but the evidence proved his death. My deepest sympathy goes to you. You should know that Heinz has made provision for you and that, pending certain legalities, you should soon receive a lawyer's letter giving you title to the hotel in Monschau. Sincere condolences. Peter Kraske/ Franz.'

For a brief moment, Rick thought he should tell her that Erick Martens was still alive and that he had become a giant among men, but the open sorrow in her eyes for a love she had lost so long ago wrenched him into silence. What would her reaction be if he were to shake her unconcealed belief in the truth about the contents of the letter? She had become a shrunken, old woman, living on memories which would be better to remain as they were. If she were to find out that Erick Martens, alias Heinz Müller, was still alive, she would have to face the reality that her own life had been built on deception.

Glancing across the room, Rick could see that De Smet tacitly agreed there was no need to hurt an old woman at the end of her life.

This poor old lady had taught him one truth today: Uncle Erick was not what he had seemed to be all these years. He now had to use the opportunity to fill in more of the details he needed to know.

'And so, after his death, you owned the hotel here and stayed on.'

'Heinz must have loved me tremendously to bequeath his hotel to me. With such a gift of love, how could I not stay on in Monschau? How could I ever have fallen in love again? That is why I changed the name to the Hotel Heinz Müller.'

Rick was now even more grateful he had left her memories undisturbed.

'I do not understand this issue of name-changing. Why did he change his name from Heinz Müller to Erick Martens?' Rick asked.

'In the Resistance, the men did not use their own names. Your dad was Alain and Heinz was known as Pierre,' she sighed, 'but his real name was Heinz Müller. Let me show you what he looked like. He was a beautiful man.'

She leafed through layers of paper in her box until she found what she was looking for. Her hand trembled as she offered Rick a photograph. He recognised the young man as Uncle Erick. His eyes were possibly even more vibrant and piercing at that time. Already, his thin-lipped smile gave away his strong will power.

Uncle Erick wore a German uniform and cap with skull and crossbones, and lower down the word 'Schutzstaffel' was printed! He turned over the photograph and noted, on the back, the rubber-stamped address of the Atelier De Roover of Brussels.

'Why was he wearing a German uniform?' Rick asked, frowning.

'He was in the German army.'

From the corner of his eye, Rick noticed that De Smet now sat upright.

'I always thought that Erick Martens had worked for the Resistance, not the German army,' Rick countered carefully.

'And so he did,' she said and coughed before continuing. 'He was an amazing man. Erick Martens was born Heinz Müller. His mother was Belgian, his father German. As you probably know, German is the third official language of Belgium. He grew up in the German-speaking part of Belgium, not far from here. I actually also grew up in that part as a German-speaking Belgian, which made it easy for me to work for the Resistance inside the Gestapo. He and I were very similar. Just before the outbreak of the war he was in the Belgian army. He was a very young soldier then, not even twenty, and, because he spoke German, French and Flemish fluently, he was assigned to intelligence work. He underwent secret training in very special courses near Brussels, after which he was sent to England for further training. When Germany invaded Poland, Heinz was in England and ready for fieldwork. British Intelligence gave him a German passport, based on his real name and origin. With his German identity papers, clothing, money and documents which covered a fake career in Germany, he was sent to Germany with orders to join the armed forces, preferably in the area under the control of Heinrich Himmler. In the end, he landed in the Todt, the Wehrmacht's engineering organisation, but managed to arrive in occupied Brussels. I'm not too sure how he managed to change his Brussels posting from the Todt to the Gestapo but he told me once that he had been able to infiltrate the Brussels Gestapo through a young woman in the Resistance who had charmed an Obersturmbannführer into accepting him. After all, Heinz was a German officer who was fluent in French and Flemish – just the type of man needed to assist in the interrogation of Belgians. I was then already working for the Resistance at Gestapo headquarters when he arrived. We never worked together in the same office – we were always on different floors – but we knew of each other through our mutual contacts and struck up a friendship because of that.'

'What did he do at the SS?'

She looked at him with incredulity that he did not understand.

'He was in a very important position for the Resistance,' she began. 'Being fluent in German, French and Flemish, he worked with all the Gestapo's documentation on people who were about to be arrested, or had already been taken into custody. The arrested ones were mainly innocent Jewish people, but most of the people he categorised and documented were political activists and many of them were members of the Resistance. He always knew beforehand who was to be apprehended and where. Of course, he could not save everyone all of the time but he was in a position where he could warn specific members of the Resistance and keep them alive. Within the Resistance Heinz had his own nom de guerre. He was known as Pierre, which means 'rock' in French.' Her eyes lit up when she mentioned the name Pierre.

'Pierre,' Rick repeated the word. Rock. Men climbing the rock face at Dinant.

'I remember the first time he kissed me.' Her lips quivered a little. 'It was in the forest of the Bois de la Cambre on a warm day in July. Whenever I am in Brussels I always visit the spot. It does not look exactly the same nowadays but, when I'm there, I close my eyes and I see everything again as it was then.'

'How did he become Erick Martens?' Rick wanted to know.

'At the end of the war both he and I were forced to leave the country. Too many people had seen us on the Avenue Louise at the Gestapo offices in our daily, supposedly pro-German, situations. Although we were given citations, certificates and support by the British, we ran the risk of being strung up against a tree or a lamppost. Belgian girls who had collaborated with the Germans were publicly disgraced, their clothes ripped from them, their hair shaved off to the skin. They were beaten up in the street. The people on the street would hardly believe that we worked for the Resistance inside the Gestapo. In fact, we had a few close calls, particularly in those first few months after the war when we were recognised on the street. That forced us to leave for a while and to live in England. Anyone with the name Heinz Müller and a personal history as a German lieutenant in a Nazi interrogation centre had no future in post-war Belgium. In England, the name Heinz Müller was too German. So during our stay in Cheltenham he adopted an easier alias and started calling himself Eric Martin – using the English manner of spelling, Martin. By the time we both returned to Belgium, he had succeeded in getting a new Belgian identity from the British and he came back as Erick Martens – spelt in the Belgian manner. Very few people knew his true identity and we kept it that way.'

'And one of the few who knew must have been my father.'

She nodded.

So, both Kraske and Uncle Erick had been German interrogators during the war years. Maybe Leah de Loof could tell him how Kraske fitted in with Uncle Erick.

'The letter you received after Uncle Erick's death was signed by a Kraske. Who was he?'

She coughed and then answered. 'I met him only twice. The first time was on Hitler's birthday in 1944. The second time was after the war when he had also rid himself of being Franz and had become Peter Kraske. I did not like him much and never heard of him again.'

'How did you meet on Hitler's birthday?' Rick asked, surprised by her remark.

She frowned and said, 'I'm still not too sure what happened that night. The German command in Brussels used to celebrate Hitler's birthday each year. That year, the reception was held in a hotel where they had to hire additional staff. The hotel put out a sign at its front door, requesting the services of a number of specialist waiters for a special occasion. As it happened,' she smiled, 'most of the men the hotel took in for the night of the Nazi birthday reception were temporary appointments directly from the Resistance. The leader of that group was your father. He made a mockery of the Germans that night with quite a funny remark, which he got away with. He was so cocky, your father.

'It was so funny,' and she giggled like a young girl again. 'I was at the reception as Heinz's companion in a dress made by a friend in the Resistance. Opposite our table was a table on which all the handguns of the officers were laid. At the end of the evening, our friends from the Resistance had cleaned up that table and had left with several Lugers and Walther PPKs. Heinz, or Erick as you knew him, was a partner in your father's game that night. I watched all of them play with the might of Germany that night and I loved it. What an exciting evening! That's when I met Kraske. Heinz introduced him to me as a Lieutenant Franz Somebody from Paris. At that introduction I did not realise that Kraske, or Franz as he was introduced that evening, had been working hand in glove with our people and that it had also been planned that the Resistance men should steal the briefcase Franz, therefore Kraske, had brought along. It was only a long time afterwards that I found out Kraske and Heinz had been working together jointly with the Resistance. Kraske, or Franz, was a courier from Paris who came to the reception to hand over documents for Gestapo headquarters in Brussels. When he found that the briefcase he had left in safe custody on the table with the handguns had been stolen, he complained bitterly and loudly. I never suspected that he worked with us and Heinz did not mention anything to that effect to me that night. It was only after the war that I realised what had happened.'

Rick had no words anymore. He could not imagine why his father would have joined hands with a blatant killer like Kraske. The briefcase had probably contained military documents. Why would Kraske and Uncle Erick have wanted to arrange for military documents to be stolen by the Resistance and why would his father have obliged?

'Miss De Loof, you say you only found out after the war that Kraske had been on your side that night. Why didn't you know that on the night of the reception, and what was in the briefcase?'

She stroked the box file as she spoke. 'I don't know why Heinz did not tell me beforehand that he and the officer from Paris were like this.' She crossed her left and right index fingers. 'It was known at 453 Avenue Louise that Heinz often spent the night in my apartment in Uccle. Many times that was true but it was also very useful in other ways. Whenever he had to spend a night with the Resistance men, he used me as his alibi. The night of the reception was one of those nights when he took me home, slipped away to join your father and the others, and only returned around daylight. I knew they must have been very active that night because no sooner had he returned that morning than a green Gestapo car arrived to pick him up for an urgent meeting. Later that day I heard that a convoy, carrying an important cargo, had been blown up in the Fôret de Soignes—'

'I apologise. The what?'

'It's the Soignes Forest just out of town. Yes, a convoy had been blown up with no single survivor. I saw Heinz later that day and from his satisfied expression I knew he had to have been involved.'

'And what was the cargo?' Rick asked.

'It was a big secret and, although Heinz confirmed that he had been involved in the attack, he told me to forget about it.'

'So you did not know what the convoy was all about?'

'Not then, but later on I had a good idea of what had transpired that night,' she confided and cleared her throat before continuing. 'Your father was the one who actually gave it away.'

'How?'

'As I told you, when I came back from England, I helped with the administrative paperwork in their business. I remember working on the first planned export consignment of products from Belgo-Grec, just before Albert died. Albert and I were taking stock when we started talking about the events of the night of the reception. I remember the tears of laughter streaming from Albert's eyes as he recalled the audacity of serving drinks to the enemy and stealing their weapons at the same time. When I asked him why they had also taken the briefcase from Paris, he roared with laughter and said something about the goose that had laid the golden egg. At first he did not want to say more, but after I begged him he relented, and told me an amazing story of how they had attacked a convoy transporting gold …'

Gold? A convoy of gold? He vaguely heard Leah de Loof's voice but he barely listened to her. 'I'm sorry, Miss De Loof, my mind drifted for a moment. Could you repeat what you were saying about the convoy, please?'

She regarded Rick with a degree of irritation and then complied. 'Albert told me they had hijacked a gold convoy that night – apparently gold from France on its way to Berlin. They had buried the gold among the ruins of a derelict factory in the Fôret de Soignes where it had remained for a long time before being dug up. I asked what had happened to it and Albert said he had heard that the Resistance had used it in the fight against the Germans. The interesting thing about the abandoned factory was that it had a South African connection. It used to be a factory, set up at the turn of the century by South African Boers who had come to Belgium to produce ammunition for a war against the English. I found it strange that they buried the gold in a South African spot here in Belgium and that my love later died in that very country.'

'So my father, his men, Uncle Erick and Kraske buried a hoard of—'

'No,' she interrupted Rick, 'Kraske wasn't there.'

'Oh, but he was involved, was he not?'

'Your father told me that day, confidentially, that Kraske's briefcase had contained the convoy's routing detail and that the operation to steal the handguns had just been the smokescreen to steal the briefcase. On the French side Kraske had not been supposed to know what he had brought to Brussels, although he knew of course. This meant that the Resistance had received a free hand, with no possible German interference, to execute their raid.'

'And nobody heard of the gold again?' De Smet asked her.

'As I told you, Albert said it had been dug up and used well against the Germans. The Resistance must have gained a lot from that. I rarely talk to anyone about it because everyone who was in the attack on the convoy that night is dead.'

Her statement rang like an alarm bell.

'Are you sure?' Rick asked.

'About what?'

'That all involved with the convoy are dead?'

'All dead, not counting Kraske who did not take part in the fight in the forest.'

Rick knew better. And yet he still refrained from telling her about Uncle Erick.

'How many men took part in that strike?'

'Eight or nine, I think.'

'Then how can you be sure that there are no survivors?'

'Because,' and she swallowed dryly, 'Albert told me on that day we took stock that he and Heinz were the only remaining ones. All the others died afterwards. I vaguely recollect him telling me that Heinz, your late Uncle Erick, vainly tried to save two or three who had been arrested by the Gestapo. One disappeared. I think one of them died in a shooting accident. One even died in those last shots fired on Belgium's liberation day. The last remaining ones were Albert, who died at Dinant, and Heinz, or Erick Martens, who died in South Africa. Kraske was not in the forest and he disappeared since that letter to me. There are no survivors.'

'Do you know anything about something called Erfdeel?' Rick asked.

'No.'

They had been talking for a long time and Rick could see she was exhausted. The pallor of her face seemed whiter and her voice sounded more tired than before. When she offered them coffee, he knew she also needed some respite from his constant questioning. They talked about other things, about the hotel she had sold a few years ago, the climate in Monschau and Africa, and edible mushrooms in the forests around Monschau.

Now and then Rick's thoughts returned to the implications of everything he had heard from her. He now sat with a new set of perspectives.

Uncle Erick used to be an SS officer called Heinz Müller who worked in the Belgian Resistance under the nom de Guerre of Pierre. He was also close to Kraske, Franz Somebody, from the Sicherheitsdienst in Paris and Albert Land, Alain, a Resistance leader. They had been part of a group of men who successfully ambushed a German gold convoy and buried the gold somewhere in the ruins of a forgotten munitions factory with a South African connection. By the end of the war the gold had been used for underground ammunition and everyone involved in the operation, except those three, had died. Uncle Erick, as Heinz Müller, could have been in a position at the Gestapo headquarters to arrange some or all of those deaths. Kraske could have been in a similar position, most probably. The Belgo-Grec business had links with all three survivors until the death of Albert Land in circumstances that, to Rick now, seemed questionable. Uncle Erick had cut his relationship with Leah de Loof by probably arranging for his own death notice through Kraske and Rick's widowed mother. In addition, he had kept Leah de Loof tied to a small town in Germany, away from Brussels. From nothing, Uncle Erick and Kraske had started East Crown Gold Mining in South Africa. Their partner in that venture, Sonya's father, had been murdered.

Now, decades after the war, the word Erfdeel and a thread to a forgotten mining scam led to John's murder. There had to be an association between the wartime gold hoard, the Erfdeel scam and the founding of AfriBelgo.

It was almost like the premonition he sometimes felt in the bush when, for no reason at all, he just knew there was a predator watching him or a trophy animal hiding in the dense foliage. He could not, for the moment, think of how the wartime gold, Erfdeel and AfriBelgo could fit together, but intuitively he knew they did.

When the time came to leave, Leah de Loof struggled with them to the door where she took hold of Rick's hand in a dry, cold and bony touch. She tilted her head to one side. 'Are you married?'

'I had a wife once but she did not love me. Maybe I did not really love her either.'

'Are you in love now?'

'Yes, I am.'

'Then, young man, you and I are probably in the same position. It is sad but also good to have been in love once in your life. I only wish I could have held Heinz once before he went out on the water.'

'I'm sorry, Miss de Loof.'

'At least I have the joy of remembering him as he was. He will always be young for me. Imagine if he were alive today and could see me now for what I am – old and ugly with a spine curved like a safety-pin.'

Rick bowed his head, brought her pale hand to his lips and kissed her cold fingers. 'I am sure that, irrespective of whether he was Heinz, Erick or Pierre, he loved you then as much you loved him. If he were alive today he would also be old. Wherever he is in spirit, I am sure he will always think of you and wait for you to join him one day. You deserve that joy.'

'You not only sound and look like your father. You have his style with the ladies,' she wheezed with a smile as she opened the door.

Rick and De Smet walked back to the car in silence.

He now had to investigate the unthinkable. East Crown Gold and possibly AfriBelgo could easily have profited from a cache of hidden wartime gold.

The questions were how it could have been engineered, and to what extent his own father could have been involved. Did they really use the gold for the Resistance, or part of the gold, or could they have sold some of the gold to start up the ill-fated Belgo-Grec? Could the decision to bury the gold cache in the ruins of a forgotten South African munitions factory have prompted the decision of Uncle Erick and Kraske to move to South Africa? Could East Crown Gold and

AfriBelgo not have taken the gold from Belgium and sold it in some other place, such as Switzerland? Rick knew from his own experience at AfriBelgo that often a large portion of the world trade in commodities was nothing more than book entries. Could Uncle Erick not have started with the gold taken in the Soignes Forest at the edge of Brussels?

They drove up from the Monschau valley to the plateau.

'Do you know your way to the ruins she mentioned?'

'I know the Transvaal area of Auderghem. We could ask around there,' De Smet said, shifting into a lower gear to pass a truck.

A RUDDY-FACED TAVERNER ON THE Boulevard du Souverain had drawn them a rough map on the back of a Stella Artois beer coaster.

'I don't see any walls out it should be here,' De Smet said, inspecting the map again.

'Shall we split up?'

'Yes.'

They parted, each trudging through the bed of leaves on the forest floor. It was exceptionally quiet in the dark shade under the dense tree canopy.

'I've found it!' De Smet called.

Instead of a structure of upright walls and rubble they found ankle-high ruins that showed a floor layout of what used to be thick walls. Rick could imagine that in autumn the ruins would disappear under a blanket of dead leaves.

They stood in the middle of what appeared to have once been a large factory space. Above them, the wind rustled through the dark green treetops. Ahead lay a lake, which, Rick decided, must probably have been the source of water for the production processes almost a century before. A deserted road ran along the edge of the water.

Activities near a munitions factory in Harper's Ferry had led John Brown's body to moulder in a grave. Activities near a munitions factory in Brussels had led many others also to the grave.

Although De Smet was with him, Rick felt lonely.

Many years ago German trucks, their headlights probably switched off, would have rumbled to these ruins along the edge of the water. He could almost sense the ghost of his father between him and De Smet, sharing their view of the floor of the ruins.

Far away he heard the sound of an aircraft. He wondered what Sonya was doing.

And he felt even lonelier.

Author's note: I visited Monschau but it was a dead end for me. Leah de Loof died in her sleep a year after having met Rick Land, still unaware of what had really happened to her love.

CHAPTER 23

Truth, like gold, is to be obtained not by its growth, but by washing away from it all that is not gold.

—Leo Tolstoy

THE INTERIOR OF ROY NEIL'S car bore testimony to a family man right down to sticky window handles and the imprints of children's hands on the windows. It reeked of soiled nappies and traces of leaking petrol fumes wafting in despite air coming in where one door fitted badly, creating an irritating constant wind noise.

They had been travelling for almost five hours from Johannesburg, ensconced in their mobile cocoon, their discomfort heightened by Roy's insistence that all the windows be kept shut to reduce further wind noise so that they could discuss the events around Rick and Sonya's experiences. They were on first name terms now. Rick had called Roy before leaving Brussels, knowing that the only way he was going to get to the truth of everything he had so far uncovered was with help from connected people. People like Roy Neil.

On the narrower roads after the turn-off to Barberton, Roy reduced their speed, which allowed for conversation with open windows, but by now the rush of fresh air had no effect anymore on Rick's fume-induced headache.

On the way Sonya had filled them in with some of the history of Barberton, a small town which had been founded in the hills of the De Kaap Valley where gold had been discovered in 1884. The area bristled with an array of minerals embedded in what was said to be one of the oldest rock formations on Earth. Barberton also still boasted both the oldest and second oldest working gold mines in the world. It was a place of hope, despair and success. During a gold rush before the turn of the century, fortune hunters had used gold pans blackened with smouldering grass in their search for alluvial gold. Now and then gold nuggets had been found in the riverbeds. Later, reef gold was discovered and the implements changed to dollies, hammer mills, sieves, crucibles and furnace ovens.

Roy switched off the ignition.

The engine spluttered into silence and the sound of the ever-present lowveld cicadas filled the journalist's ramshackle Ford. Nobody said a word. They had arrived at the heart of Sonya's origins and the core of Uncle Erick's small beginnings as a mining magnate.

'That's where it stood,' she said, breaking the silence. 'I know it was there when I came out here at the age of nineteen. That's where my parents lived.'

They stared at a power sub-station behind a fence.

'Very disappointing. I came here three years after my mother's letter and the house was locked with nobody home. I couldn't even go inside. Now it's all gone.'

Rick took her hand.

'Well, let's go and look for East Crown Gold,' Sonya said.

They drove off and, after asking around, they found it.

'Not exactly the portals one would expect, considering this used to be the flagship of the company,' Roy echoed Rick's thoughts.

Some time in the distant past a vehicle had probably failed to successfully negotiate the turn-off from the tarred road on to the narrow dirt road and had rammed into the two wooden poles that held up the metal plate. The two termite-ridden posts now leaned like twin Towers of Pisa to one side. At the tops of the posts, the rusty East Crown Gold sign was bullet-ridden, obviously a handy local target for gun-crazy passers-by. The metal of the East Crown Gold signpost had a crooked dent in the middle and rested drunkenly against a Mopani tree.

Rick was relieved to get out of the car. His khaki clothes stank of fumes. The back of his short-sleeved shirt was wet with sweat, his trousers creased and baggy-kneed. He opened the rear door with the childproof interior lock for Sonya.

She took Rick's outstretched hand and got out looking fresh and delightful in her tight jeans, white sneakers and a cotton T-shirt. A golden Alice band pushed into her hair accentuated her open face, adorned by two small golden earrings.

Roy stood on the hot tar, stretched up his arms towards the sky and yawned. It had been a tiring few hours in the cramped confines of the car. He looked the part of a true journalist in his crumpled white shirt, loose nondescript tie with some corporate logo, dark trousers and black shoes.

It was warm for a southern hemisphere winter's day in August. Barberton lay close to the tropical climate of Mozambique. Scattered clouds drifted across a blue sky. In the distance, a thicker bank of clouds had gathered, which was also strange, as it normally does not rain at that time of year. A spicy scent hung in the air. Quite an improvement on the car, Rick thought.

East Crown Gold's origins lay in a bowl of rugged hills covered in thick bush, interspersed with huge granite boulders that stood out like warts. The town of Barberton was hidden behind a ridge clad in aloes. Rick wondered how Uncle Erick, as a recent immigrant from civilised Europe, could have found this god-forsaken spot in the wilds, never mind managing to build a fortune on it.

During their trip from Johannesburg they had discussed all the facts, particularly Rick's discoveries in Belgium and the German town, Monschau. Mulling over the possibilities, they all agreed there had to be a link between the Belgian gold stolen towards the end of the Second World War and the birth of AfriBelgo. They all thought the proceeds of the stolen gold must somehow have been, either partly or fully, invested in the East Crown option.

Roy's opinion was that, most probably, all the money had gone into East Crown.

Sonya thought that, if so much had been available for East Crown, there would not have been a need to murder a relatively poor man like her father. With so much money at hand, they could easily have bought out Mauritz Deine.

Rick still found it hard to accept that the man he had had so much respect for could have been unscrupulous. But in Belgium he had already come to terms with the undeniable probability that Uncle Erick and Kraske had been bladder brothers in the theft of the gold, the killing of Sonya's father and the founding of AfriBelgo.

'They might have invested in a mine, but they sure as hell never invested in a quality signpost,' Roy said.

'Uncle Erick was always cost-conscious, particularly whenever he spent his own money,' Rick tried to come up with an explanation. 'East Crown used to be unproductive. They say he turned this mine around with great management techniques. I suppose that, in a sense, wherever he got his money from in the beginning, he made things work through efficient management. He still has a strong management style today. I would hazard a guess that his sense of efficiency in those days extended to getting the mine to work well, and not spending money on trimmings such as signs. It's not the clothes that maketh the mine.'

'Maybe,' Sonya smiled at Rick's little pun, 'but today you need the eye of an eagle to spot the entrance to the mine from a passing car and, to me, that means that your dear Uncle Erick isn't too interested in preserving any mementoes of his illustrious past management techniques.'

'You're right,' Roy said, 'and you could get a position at our newspaper with that kind of deduction, Sonya. One would've thought that AfriBelgo would operate a museum here today. Jeez, the man isn't too averse to self-glorification.'

Somehow the words hurt Rick and he made an attempt to change the conversation by muttering, 'Helluva drive.'

'I'm stiff,' Roy agreed and, as if to reinforce his words, he broke into a slow jog down the dirt road, lifting his knees high, pounding at the road with his city shoes and swinging his arms elaborately. Rick leaned against the Ford and watched him until he disappeared in the thick bush around the bend in the road.

A yellow hornbill fluttered from a tree and came down to perch on the signboard, gazing sternly at Rick and Sonya, almost as if he could read Rick's mind.

With Roy Neil momentarily out of the way, Rick had a sudden urge to take Sonya in his arms. The hornbill did not waver in its stare. In the distance a dog barked. She smiled at him. He took her hand in his. Her soft eyes were the shade of the Shenandoah. He longed even more to take her in his arms.

Disappointingly, Roy returned too soon. He seemed to be more in a hurry than when he had left. Sonya squeezed Rick's hand.

'I thought East Crown was a disused mine,' Roy said, out of breath, frowning.

'As far as I know, it is,' Rick said.

'Well, I've got news for you. Just around the bend there's a gate.'

'So?' Rick gestured with open palms.

'This place isn't a museum, but it sure as hell resembles a working operation. The gate's set in a very shiny and very high barbed-wire fence running out into the bush and there's an armed guard with an Alsatian dog on the other side. The dog saw me but the guy didn't. This is a place with a dilapidated signpost, no fanfare as a blast from the past, but it has a brand-new barbed-wire fence and an armed guard at a gate. I find it strange, don't you?'

'Roy, I worked at AfriBelgo,' Rick reasoned, more with himself than with the journalist, 'and I know for a fact that this vein was worked out in the late fifties, maybe early sixties. It was a small mining operation, based on a rich surface ore body. Deeper down, the value of the deposit declined and, underground mining being expensive, it became uneconomical to continue here. In any case, by then AfriBelgo had diversified into several other investments. East Crown Gold Mining was definitely closed, lock, stock and bloody barrel. I know from my own experience that AfriBelgo often followed the Elastoplast route of using medical sticking plaster on deteriorating installations to extend their productive lifetimes but, in the case of East Crown, there was no Elastoplast. Everything shut down completely.'

'Why was East Crown the exception to the rule?' Roy asked.

'The equipment was so specialised that none of it could really be used elsewhere.'

'If there's no gold here and no equipment of value, why is there an armed sentry?' Roy countered, shifting his gaze from Rick to Sonya, his eyes twinkling with the unconcealed excitement of a journalist who had just found an interesting lead.

In the distance the dog barked again.

Rick scratched his chin and stared at the rusted sign. 'Roy, you know what? You've got a point. Why would AfriBelgo have an armed guard and new barbed wire around a disused mine?'

'Point is,' Sonya raised her index finger, 'we drove down here to see what it was that Martens and Kraske had invested in. I wanted to find out why they had to kill my father for this place. Before confronting Martens, we wanted to understand the past. Now we've got something of the present that we don't understand. How did I trace Kraske in the States? It was easy.' She smiled. 'I asked AfriBelgo and they told me. How do we find out what East Crown Gold is all about at present? Easy. We just ask this guard.'

The three of them looked at each other. Good idea.

Rick would have preferred to have walked down the dirt road, but Roy ignored Rick's protestations and gestured at them to get into the Ford. Rick licked his lips. He could still taste the traces of spent octane in the interior and his head still felt like a lead ingot.

As they drove up to the gate, a huge Alsatian dog stood up on his hind legs against the criss-crossed wire of the gate, barking raucously, snapping air, his lion-sized paws pounding at the wire, his sharp fangs wet with excitement.

'Wow, I'm glad we're not on foot,' Sonya said.

Rick noticed that the top of the fence was not made of barbed wire, as Roy had said. It was a razor fence with sharp blades. 'Roy, don't you know the difference between barbed wire and razor wire?'

'I'm a city boy,' Roy said as he switched off the ignition.

The dog's barking became wilder as Roy got out and walked towards the guard who leaned against the gate, squeezing the thick, intertwined gate wire with fat fingers, in and out, in and out, his dirty nails groping in the air in imitation of the dog's paws.

In contrast with the alert eyes of the dog, the guard's eyes signalled a boredom created by the tedium of his job and an unmistakable slowness of comprehension.

'Bly stil!' His abrupt command immediately silenced the dog.

Rick was impressed.

'Sit!' The dog obliged. Rick was even more impressed. 'Ja, can I help you?'

The guard spoke stiffly in guttural Afrikaans. Slightly bald for someone not far into his thirties, he wore a short-sleeved khaki shirt with no insignia, khaki shorts, no socks and veldskoen. The grip of a handgun stuck out menacingly from a holster on his belt. A two-way radio handset was slung over his shoulder.

'Is this East Crown Gold?' Roy asked in English.

Rick thought Roy's question was quite valid. The only sign fitted on the mesh wire under the razor top at the gate was one in three languages stating the right to reserve admittance.

'Why are you asking?' the guard asked.

'We are touring the area and thought that, East Crown being such an old mine, there could be a museum or some old equipment to view,' Roy said with a friendly smile.

'There's nothing to see here,' the guard said.

'What about the sign at the roadside? It says the mine's on this road.'

'Ja, that sign doesn't mean anything anymore. There's no mine to see here. Come, Condor,' the guard called at the dog in Afrikaans.

'Excuse me,' Roy snapped back, 'what is here then?'

'None of your blerry business. This is private property,' the guard said, walking away.

'Is this AfriBelgo property?' Roy persisted.

The khaki-clad man stopped and turned to the dog. Rick could not hear but he saw through the insect-spattered windscreen how the guard formed two words in whispered Afrikaans, 'Vat hulle!' Get them.

The Alsatian immediately leapt up against the gate and barked at them. The guard sauntered towards a thatched-roofed guardhouse, glanced back at them with a nasty grin and disappeared inside.

Roy got back, turned the ignition and drove back to the main road where he found a clearing and parked the Ford. Rick opened the glove compartment where he had left his 7.62 mm Unique pistol and ankle holster when they had left home. He clicked the button on the side of the grip and slid out the magazine, rechecked that it was fully loaded, pushed it in again, slipped the pistol into the holster and strapped the holster to his ankle.

'What now?' Roy asked.

'We'll do what any self-respecting leopard would do,' Rick said and stuck a spare box with bullets into his trouser pocket.

Sonya and Roy followed Rick as he led them through the bush along the length of the fence until they could see the gate again. They made themselves as comfortable as possible in the shrubs about fifty paces from the gate and waited. Initially the dog was agitated and barked in their direction until an instruction from the guard silenced him again.

Two hours later they still sat there. Sonya whispered that her knees were aching and Rick contemplated whether they should maybe leave for him to come back later on his own but, before he could suggest that, a vehicle rumbled down the dirt road. The dog barked again, prompting the guard to reappear from the doorway of the thatched hut.

A medium-sized white truck with *Phoenix Flight Bottle Store – Off Sales* painted in blue on the side stopped at the gate. The driver jumped out, approached the gate and thrust a hand with a few sheets of paper at the guard who pulled the documents through the diamond wire. The guard signed, handed back the papers and produced a leash from a trouser pocket. After having minor difficulties in tying the excited dog to the fence, the guard opened the gate and waited as the deliveryman unloaded ten cases marked Lion Lager at the gatepost.

'Either the gatekeeper has bought a year's supply of beer or East Crown Gold is having a party,' Roy whispered. 'What do you think?'

'I think I'd like to join the party now.' Rick exhaled and turned towards Sonya. 'I'm going to find out what's happening on the other side. Wait here with Roy,' he said and opened the leather flap of his watch. 'It's three o'clock now. It should be dark by about half past five. If I'm not back by then I think you should go into town and book into a hotel. There can't be more than two or three in a town of Barberton's size. So it shouldn't be too difficult to trace you.'

'Can't we do anything, Rick?' Roy whispered.

'If I'm not back by the morning, you must use your own judgment.'

Roy's reply was inaudible, but he nodded his head.

'Take care.' Sonya brushed the palm of her hand against his right cheek, leaned over and kissed him. Her lips tasted salty, yet sweet. Her scent aroused him for a moment. He cupped her face in his hands, shifted his eyes towards Roy and said, 'Look after her, won't you?'

'I'm a good student and, professor, you've already taught me in a few days how to look after myself,' Sonya said and hugged Rick. 'Take care, love.'

Rick extricated himself from the warmth of her embrace, turned around and set off into the bush, at first away from the gate and then turning back to the fence. Once again he reverted to being the seasoned hunter.

He followed the length of the fence with rolls of razor fencing fixed at the top. It would be difficult to get over those sharp blades at the top. The fence had been erected high enough that a kudu could not jump over it, but low enough for a small blue monkey to scale. After a few minutes Rick found what he was looking for – a large Marula tree that looked as old as Barberton itself. He strapped his pistol more securely against his leg.

The fence ran within branch length of the enormous Marula. Against the backdrop of the screeching of a go-away bird, Rick scrambled up the tree trunk and followed the thickest branch that stuck out over the fence. As he gingerly edged along the branch over the fence one of the razor blades nicked a trouser leg. He lowered his body, feet first, held on to the branch as long as possible and dropped down on the rock hard ground of the East Crown Gold property.

Knowing he would provoke the Alsatian if he followed the fence back towards the gate, Rick set off in a direction he thought would lead him to the middle of the property. After a few minutes he stumbled on a dirt track and followed that, taking care not to walk on the track itself and leave his footprints in the dust.

He heard the murmur of conversation before he saw anyone. He edged forward until he could see three men dressed in the same khaki uniform as the man at the gate. Seated on fold-up canvas chairs in the shade of the overhanging roof of a large corrugated-iron shack, they formed a strange group.

They appeared to be in their late twenties or early thirties. One was barefoot with his shirt unbuttoned all the way, twiddling his toes and drinking beer from a can he rested between sips on a protruding bare belly. Another had a pipe clenched in his teeth set inside a luxuriant Rasputin-like beard. Blue smoke fumed around his head as he spoke. From his hiding place Rick even smelled the thick pipe aroma and was reminded of Van Hunks. The third man, also bearded, slept in his canvas chair, his head tilted backwards, mouth gaping open, legs spread like a clawed toad.

If it had not been for the semi-automatic rifle, which looked to Rick like a folding stock Galil ARM Israeli assault weapon, propped up against the sleeping man's chair, and the shotgun against the pillar next to the smoker, the group could have been mistaken for three farmers sitting on a veranda discussing the weather – something the smoker and the beer drinker were in fact doing. Rick heard them talking in Afrikaans of the recent lack of rain and the parlous state of the country's dams.

Doing what a leopard does, he settled down, watched them and analysed the situation. Many years before, the shack's exterior walls must have been given a coating of cream paint with a brown depiction of a crown in the centre of one wall. Rick had not seen the depiction of the crown before but assumed it to have been part of the original East Crown Gold emblem. The shack's paint was now peeled down to an aged rippling skin that had cracked open to reveal the underlying galvanised zinc of the walls. He could barely distinguish East Crown's faded emblem but he realised he was looking at what had probably been an office of the mining company. Maybe the original office? Cut into the metal walls, as if with a can opener, were two windows with filthy curtains drawn to ward off the late afternoon sunlight. A red pick-up truck with anti-roll bars was parked in the shade of a tree.

In the clearing around the shack, several bits and pieces of rusted equipment had been strewn haphazardly over the years. Having become obsolete, their only remaining use was that of providing support for climbing weeds. The only other structure near the shack was a dilapidated, corrugated-iron outhouse toilet.

At the opposite end to the veranda where the men sat, a heap of building rubble was partially obscured by the corner of the shack. He moved through the dense bush until he could see the rubble more clearly.

The debris lay strangled with grass, weeds and shrubs, from which broken pieces of Greek columns stuck out like the quills of a porcupine. A cracked fountain rested on its side. An ornate flowerbox lay chipped against a headless cement cherub. A cement bowl topped the heap like a pimple. It was incredible. He knew he was looking at memories of the past.

He had discovered the graveyard of Belgo-Grec. He was looking at the discarded fruits of his father's labour, the bits and pieces that had become Uncle Erick's single business failure. Most of the products his father had produced had been columns. The broken grey columns had been dumped like a pile of gigantic matchsticks as high as the razor-wire fence around the property. It was as if the African law of the wild, where the death of one animal always provides life for another, had applied here because Belgo-Grec had died to be consumed in the belly of East Crown.

He had to suppress an urge to come out of hiding, to reach out and touch a column, to cleanse his own guilt at not having felt any emotion at his father's grave in Belgium. He imagined Leah de Loof watching his father, Albert Land, forming the columns. He imagined Albert's fingers caressing the grooves in a column – hands that must have held himself as a baby.

For a moment Rick's skin went cement cold.

'Ja, bring the bloody bitch,' a sharp command sounded in Afrikaans from the direction of the veranda, followed by another voice complaining from inside the shack, 'I'm fed up with all of this.'

Rick spun around and scrambled, hunched forward, through the undergrowth, snapping dried twigs under-foot and slipping over loose stones, hoping the group would be too preoccupied to hear the noise of his progress.

The 'bitch' turned out to be a barefoot matronly black woman in a crumpled floral dress followed by a guard. The woman and the man walked to the outside toilet where she opened the rickety door and entered. The man waited outside, leaning against the outhouse, a shotgun in his hands. The other three remained on the veranda.

After a while the door squeaked open and the woman came out.

Rick now had a better view of her. He could see that the wrists of her bare arms were linked in front by a pair of handcuffs. Despite her captivity, she walked ramrod straight, her innate pride obviously untouched. As she and the man returned, her face became more distinct and Rick knew he had seen her before. Her eyes flashed with the same strength, her jaw was as determined and her composure as collected as she had appeared on television.

He realised he had found Gertrude Amandla, the abducted wife of the Minister of International Co-operation. He had stumbled upon the lair of the extremist right-wing white group, the White Front.

On the morning before his departure for America he had seen her on the news as the captive of a hooded extremist who had proclaimed she would be killed unless the government stated its willingness to enter into negotiations for the creation of an old-style homeland for whites in South Africa. It had been an amateurish video recording, but the woman in Rick's vision bore the unmistakably strong features he had seen before. The white lunatic fringe had had great difficulty in adapting to the new age of this year 1994 where old-style white politics had ceased to have a meaningful place. In their bitterness, a lost tribe of White diehards still clung to an extinct notion of political blackmail.

Rick understood he had to act, but he also knew that rashness could be dangerous. From a distance, his pistol would undoubtedly be less accurate than the shotgun and Galil rifle on the veranda. The sound of gunfire would also raise the interest of the guard at the gate. He had to assume the possibility that there could be more extremists in the area than these four and the man at the gate. He also decided to avoid creating a situation in which Gertrude Amandla could be shot, either on purpose or by accident.

For a while he toyed with the idea of returning to locate and procure assistance, but his curiosity and hunter's instinct overpowered the alternative. He could not merely stand on the sidelines as a spectator. Passivity had never been one of his traits. A rush of adrenaline in anticipation of out-manoeuvring the four men prompted him to remain seated on his haunches behind a clump of bushes.

Just before sundown the men started a fire in a half-broken braai. The evening was unseasonably warm for a winter's night in August. The four men stood bare-chested and shoeless in a clearing around the waist-high fire, dressed only in shorts. One had taken charge of the meat, turning the portions on the grill every now and then with a sharp two-pronged fork.

Rick lay in wait as dark clouds gathered overhead and brought an early dusk. By the time the flames had turned to embers and they had put meat on the griddle and it was dark. The curling smoke and sweet smell of meat over an open fire reminded Rick he had not eaten for hours.

The men were not very talkative. By the light of a single bulb from the veranda the cook stuck the fork into the meat and cut open a steak with a medium-sized meat knife. He held up the cut edge to the light for approval. The others nodded in agreement. They each loaded a steak on a plate and, leaving both the meat knife and the barbecue fork on the grill, turned around and ascended the four steps to the veranda. A piece of meat still smoked on the grill. They ate in silence.

The cook finished, stood up, walked back to the grill and put the remaining piece of meat on his plate. With a burp he laid the fork and meat knife on the grill. Holding the plate of food in his hand, he returned to the veranda.

The pipe-smoker threw a shirt over his shoulders, put on his boots and said in Afrikaans, 'Kallie, tell the kaffir girl this restaurant serves well-done steaks only.'

The other two laughed as Kallie entered the doorway to take the food to their prisoner.

The pipe-smoker picked up the Galil assault rifle and stood up. 'Piet, are you coming with me?'

'Ja.'

'Kallie, Piet and I are leaving. We'll see you. It's our time at the gate now.'

'Ja, fine,' Rick heard from inside.

The smoker and the other man walked over to the red pick-up truck, got in and left.

As the red taillights of the truck dissolved into darkness in the direction of the gate, the man remaining on the veranda stood up and stretched himself in a yawn. 'Kallie, I'm going up to the shithouse.'

Rick watched the man ambling over the clearing to the outhouse. He knew he now had an improved chance of success, having the opportunity of concentrating on outwitting only two during the changing of the guard. He calculated he would probably have ten to fifteen minutes before the man with the autumn eyes at the gate, and probably the other guy, would appear.

Stooped forward, he raced past the Belgo-Grec dump towards the barbecue grill. He could hear voices inside the building. He kept running. At the grill Rick grabbed the meat knife and ran towards the outhouse. A few paces away from the toilet, he slowed his stride and crept closer until he reached the side. In the darkness of the night, the corrugated-iron walls of the privy still radiated pent-up heat from the day's sun. From inside he heard a heavy sigh. The rickety door was inches away from Rick's nose on his right. The pungent smell of defecation and lime filled Rick's nostrils. He glanced at the veranda. The other man was still inside the building with the prisoner. Time was running out.

Rick sank to his knees. He ran his fingers over the soil until he found a loose rock under his left leg. He stood up. He heard a ruffling sound inside which meant the man was probably getting up from the toilet seat. Gripping the meat knife in his right hand, the greasy blade poised in the air between his nose and the doorway of the outhouse, Rick threw the rock with his left hand on to the ground about three steps away from the outhouse door. The stone thudded. With every muscle in his body strained to the maximum, Rick balanced his weight on his toes against the side of the outhouse, ready for the reaction he expected. The door flung open.

'Wie's daar?'

Rick held his breath.

Like a tortoise-head appearing from a shell, the man stuck his head out first, his close-cropped hair appearing waist-high halfway up the door and within arm's reach in front of Rick around the corner of the outhouse. Rick had to restrain himself from immediately reaching out.

'Wie's daar?' the man repeated as he hobbled forward, still pulling up his shorts with both hands.

In one movement, Rick lunged forward, smothered the man's mouth with his left hand and plunged the meat knife into the man's back with his right. The man's mouth gaped open in a stifled cry, saliva bursting into Rick's hand. Rick pulled out the knife and repeated the stabbing action. Each time he thrust the knife into the man's back he felt the blade slipping between ribs. And Rick had to restrain himself from making a noise too because the man's teeth bit painfully into the hand he held over the victim's mouth.

Afterwards Rick could not remember how many times he had thrust the long blade into the man's back. All he remembered was that the man twitched a few times, slumped forward and died in his arms, still biting his left hand.

He dragged the shirtless body out of view, away from the shack's light, around the back of the outhouse.

'Andries!' The man called Kallie stood in the light of the bare bulb on the veranda, looking out towards the outhouse. He had to outwit Kallie by reassuring him that all was well.

'Ja, Kallie!' Rick called back, cupping his mouth in his hands to create a muffled sound from behind the outhouse.

Hidden from view behind the outhouse, Rick waited a few seconds before he glanced back at the shack. Kallie sat down on a canvas chair at the side of the veranda. Rick jogged away from the light, into the darkness, and circled to approach the veranda from the opposite side. The night was overcast and he could not clearly see where he was going in the dark. Thorn bush scratched his bare forearms. He still gripped the knife in his hand. His fingers felt sticky as if they had been stuck into glue. He had blood on his hands. The blood of someone called Andries.

As he stalked up to the veranda from the back of the building and crept up along the side, he noticed in the light from the shack that his shirt was also covered in blood. Kallie sat whistling on the veranda, his bare back turned to Rick.

Rick gripped the knife tighter. He had no other option but to go all the way. He had done it to wounded animals many times before, particularly around bad marksmen. As a professional hunter, Rick always taught his clients where a hunted animal should be shot to ensure a clean death but many visitors, not used to the African bush, would sometimes miss the vital organs. The more callous clients often preferred to aim at a body area outside of the animal's head and shoulders so that they could have a clean cape and head mounted against a wall. They would prefer to deliberately shoot at an animal's belly or hind legs. In those cases, it became the professional hunter's duty to ensure that immobile animals in pain were put down as quickly as possible. There were two ways of doing it to a buck. You either cut the throat, in which case the animal often still lived for a while and the trophy would be damaged, or you pushed a knife blade in at the point where the animal's head met the first vertebrae of the spine. In that case, you severed the animal immediately from life. Trophy hunters prefer the latter method because it gives them an undamaged trophy to mount on a wall.

The blade of the meat knife in Rick's hand was about twelve inches long and ended in an extremely sharp point. Kallie's head resembled a carrot with its wild tuft of hair at the top. The man sat hunched forward, his back to the edge of the veranda, one leg over the other, clipping his toenails under the meagre electric light. His neck was as broad as that of a warthog. The entry spot between Kallie's cranium and his neck vertebrae loomed in front of Rick as he crept up to the veranda.

'Andries!' Kallie shouted towards the outhouse, startling Rick, who was by now within lunging distance. 'Andries!' Kallie peered in the darkness towards the outhouse and resumed the clipping of his nails, bending his neck forward.

It could have been butter. The blade glided into the back of Kallie's neck. Rick gripped the tuft of hair at the top of the man's head and, in a wrenching action, he slit the main nerve at the base of Kallie's cranium. Kallie never uttered a sound. He merely fell forward and lay flat on the floorboards, a slight trickle of blood oozing from the hole in the back of his neck.

The impact of what he had done suddenly dawned on Rick. In revulsion, he stared at the bloodied knife, protruding from his own bloodied fist and the lifeless body at his feet. He started shivering. The evening was warm but he was cold. The knife fell from his hands. The sound of the knife on the floor brought him back to reality.

'Mrs Amandla?' Rick called, picking up Kallie's shotgun and checking whether it was loaded. It was.

'Yes?'

'Are you all right?'

'Yes, I am. Who are you?'

'A friend. I'm here to help you get …' Rick's words trailed away when he saw her from the doorway.

'Thank God,' she whispered hoarsely.

Gertrude Amandla lay on the wooden floor in a position no wife of any cabinet minister would ever dream of being in, on her side with her hands tied tightly to each other behind her back, locked together in a bracelet of yellow nylon cord. Her feet were bare, her ankles tied to one another with more yellow cord and her legs drawn up uncomfortably because a short hessian rope linked the cord at her ankles to the cord at her wrists.

'I'll cut you loose,' Rick said, turning to fetch the knife on the veranda.

'God has been good to me. Who are you?'

Rick returned with the knife in hand. 'Rick Land,' he said as he cut at the ropes.

'Are you with the security services?'

'No. How many of them are there?'

'Four plus one at the gate. Actually, in the evening two of them stay at the gate. So there should be three here. How did you know I was here?' she asked, rubbing her wrists and ankles.

'I didn't know.'

'Then why are you here?' she said, rearranging her dress.

'It's a long story. We have to get out of here. Quickly.'

Rick took her by both hands and helped her to get up. He looked around them. The room consisted of bare walls and odd pieces of furniture from a bygone era – a small desk, three rundown chairs, a chipped wooden filing cabinet and a pile of box-files in a corner. A two-way radio handset lay on the desk next to an old black telephone. Rick lifted the handset of the telephone and found a ringing tone. A local telephone directory lay on the desk. He flipped through it and found the number of the local police station.

At first, the duty officer was suspicious, thinking he had a prank caller on line but when Rick asked Gertrude Amandla to speak, the policeman's tone of voice changed dramatically and he listened when she handed the phone back so that Rick could explain where they were.

'We are in what appears to be the old headquarters of East Crown Gold outside of town. Do you know the place?'

'Yes, I do.'

'You cannot come alone. You need numbers.'

'We have a prepared procedure for this abduction.'

'Fine. I'm not sure how many members of the White Front are still out there but I do know there are at least three of them and they are armed. It would be dangerous for Mrs Amandla and me to stay inside the building. We must leave. We will wait in the bush outside, but we'll stick close to the shack I am talking of.' He put down the telephone receiver and looked at Gertrude Amandla. She nodded. He felt at his ankle. The pistol was still tightly in place in its ankle holster.

'You are bleeding,' she said.

'It's their blood, not mine. Two gone, three left.'

'Oh.'

'Mrs Amandla, you are barefoot. Do you have shoes here?'

She had.

He grabbed the shotgun and cocked it. Holding the shotgun in one hand, he stretched out his other hand to the woman. 'Shall we?'

Her hand trembled in his but her eyes were steadfast. Her lips parted in a grin. 'It will be much nicer out there than in here,' she said.

She gasped when they stepped over Kallie's prostrate body. Blood still oozed from the hole in the nape of his neck to form a red choker around his throat. Rick hardly noticed her reaction. He listened for the sound of the truck returning from the gate. Except for the sound of their own footsteps as they ran and an owl hooting in the distance, he heard nothing.

Gertrude Amandla was a plump woman, obviously not used to exertion. She breathed as heavily as her footsteps. They sidestepped the rubble of broken columns and fled from the light of the veranda towards the dark obscurity of the bush. The clouds had thinned suddenly to allow the moon to filter through as a dull white disk overhead. They found sanctuary in a clump of Mopani trees and sat down to survey the East Crown Gold building.

The scene was deceptively tranquil. The lighting from inside the shack was the same sepia hue as that of the light bulb on the veranda. The body on the veranda could have been that of a sleeping person. Rick shifted his gaze to the outhouse. The other dead body was out of sight.

'Where are all the White Front men?' she asked.

'You saw the one at your door. One man's dead behind the toilet, two went to the gate, and I suspect the fifth from the gate should arrive soon. That's why I felt we should wait out here.'

They sat in silence for a while.

'What's your name again?'

'Rick. Rick Land.'

'And you said you're not in the police or security?'

'No. I'm just me.'

'Then what do you do for a living, Rick?'

'Professional hunter.'

'Were you hunting here when you found me?'

'No. I'm following up something to do with the history of East Crown Gold.'

'What's East Crown Gold?'

'This property. It's a disused gold mine.'

'I didn't know that. I thought it was a rubbish dump with all the building material. It's maybe because I was kept blindfolded all the way. They only took off the blindfold when I got here.'

'Mrs Amandla, although you were blindfolded you must have heard a lot on your way to this place and then here too. What did they talk about?'

'These people? They don't have all their pigs in one sty,' she said, using a South African idiom for madness. 'These people, they think in circles and ways that people like us will never understand. Many of our leaders were forced to be with President Mandela on Robben Island. These men are on their own island of the mind.

'I heard them talking of how they want a state for whites only, even now after the first democratic election. They want this country to be whiter than white, as if it is like pouring bleaching powder into a washing machine. I understand Afrikaans. I heard them. They want to purify this country, purge it of the unwanted and send black people off again to desolate areas away from the urban centres. They hate Nelson Mandela. They hate the new South Africa of 1994. Last night they sat on the stoep talking of gas chambers and death camps. It was frightening.'

'I can imagine. Were you present whenever they had contact with other people? The outside world?'

'You saw the telephone was in the room. They spoke on that phone,' she said. 'They often called for instructions from someone called The Leader. They called him 'Die Leier' in Afrikaans. They never spoke directly to The Leader. Always to someone they called Earth.'

'Earth?'

'Yes. Earth.'

'That's strange.'

'It was. They spoke in Afrikaans to someone code-named Aarde, which is Afrikaans for Earth.'

'Was it not Aardt?' Rick asked.

'Yes. Mister Aardt. That's what they called him.'

'Mark Aardt?'

'No, just Mister Aardt.'

It was the shock he had anticipated but it still confused him, even though he had by now accepted that Uncle Erick was not what he had purported to be. Mark Aardt linked to the White Front ... What next?

During the course of the late afternoon and evening, he had been so involved in eliminating and evading the kidnappers of Gertrude Amandla he had not afforded himself the luxury of reasoning as to how and why a far-right extremist group could have found a safe haven there. He really should have tried to work out the implications of finding the White Front ensconced in a disused AfriBelgo area next to the cemetery of Belgo-Grec.

'Did anybody else arrive at the building while you were held captive there?'

'No, but,' she pointed at the building, 'the dead man on the porch over there went to a meeting with The Leader. He was away for two days. When he came back I overheard them talking about instructions from The Leader and someone called Solitude or something.'

Rick shivered.

'Was Solitude a person or was it the meeting place, Mrs Amandla?'

'I only heard those two words and I thought they were people, code words or something.'

Bits and pieces of the larger jigsaw fell into place. Uncle Erick, Kraske, John, the Gestapo, the White Front, the kidnapping of Gertrude Amandla, Mark Aardt, financial and physical killings.

Rick thought back on Uncle Erick's words, just before he left for the USA, when the old man had said life was not always perfectly black and white. Did he not say that even racist extremists sometimes had a point and that the worst people in the worst organisations often had positive characteristics? At the time, the remark did not bother Rick. Now it did. Those words were an ominous forewarning.

Rick did not hear the truck until its headlights pierced the darkness at the bend in the dirt road. They watched as the vehicle rumbled up to the shack. Rick brought the shotgun up to his shoulder.

The truck stopped next to the dead man on the veranda. Leaving the engine running, the man with the autumn leaf eyes got out and walked up slowly to the veranda. Rick aimed at the man, who peered at the body, reached out to touch it, suddenly withdrew, retreated a few steps and looked up towards the clouds. The man spun around, jumped into the truck cabin, switched off the lights and sped away down the dirt track in total darkness.

As the sound of the speeding truck subsided, it was overtaken by a distant flip-flopping sound, growing louder by the second. To the sound of a crescendo of rotor blades, a blinding searchlight flitted across the open area, harshly lighting up the Belgo-Grec dump, coming to rest and bathing the East Crown Gold shack in virtual daylight.

The helicopter danced over the trees. The sound waves of the rotor blades and roaring engine pulsated at them. His whole body vibrated. In a hurricane of gusty wind the rotor blades kicked up a huge bowl of dust. They shielded their eyes from the barrage of sand and small stones coming at them. Through his fingers he saw armed soldiers positioned in the open door of the hovering Puma helicopter. Rick dropped the shotgun to avoid being mistaken as one of the captors. He took Gertrude Amandla by the hand. Bent forward, they ran through the dust to the helicopter. Four soldiers in camouflage, carrying R5 rifles, met them halfway and guided them to the door.

The noise was overpowering. Even if he had shouted nobody would have heard him. The soldier pointed to a heap of intertwined ropes on the floor in the back. Gertrude Amandla and Rick seated themselves on the floor. Rick gestured at the man with the headset to hand it to him. A burst of hot air blew through the open doors at them. The helicopter started to ascend. Rick slipped the headset with its microphone over his head.

'Seventy-four degrees and rising,' Rick heard someone in the cockpit crackling in his ears.

'I'm the man who got in with Mrs Amandla a moment ago and I would like to speak to the captain please,' Rick said with the microphone against his lips.

'Go ahead.'

'Two of the men who held Mrs Amandla captive are dead but three are still down there. Two should be at the gate and one in a truck without lights on the property, probably on his way to pick up the others and get the hell out of sight.'

'Thank you. Our instructions are to get the Minister's wife away from further danger. We have ground forces moving in and a back-up chopper arriving in a few minutes. I'll let them know.'

The helicopter banked. Rick listened in as the net closed in on the White Front below. The helicopter sped through the night sky. They touched down in Nelspruit at the airport, where a platoon of uniformed men stood in front of the offices of the Lowveld Forest Fire-Fighters' Association. A woman handed him and Gertrude Amandla sandwiches and steaming cups of coffee. A medical doctor arrived and examined them. Except for chafed wrists and ankles, the Minister's wife was in reasonable health. Someone found a shirt with the Forest Fire-Fighters' logo for Rick, who was grateful to get rid of his own blood-smeared one.

Gertrude Amandla told everyone how Rick had saved her. She

cried when she spoke to her husband on the telephone, then dried her tears and motioned Rick with a smile to the receiver.

'Mr Land, thank you so much. You have saved my wife's life. I will always be indebted to you.'

'Thank you, Minister.'

'I hope to see you soon to thank you personally. Would you like to join her on her trip back right now?'

'Sorry, Minister, but I am here with other people. I need to travel with them.'

'Good. But I insist on thanking you in person. Just confirm to me one thing please.'

'Yes?'

'I understand she was held at a property of the AfriBelgo Group. Is that true?'

'Yes. East Crown Gold.'

'I see. It's late. I will contact you tomorrow, Mr Land. Thank you so much again.'

Outside, a Lear jet taxied up towards the Lowveld Forest Fire-Fighters' Association building. A medalled military man took Mrs Amandla by the elbow and guided her towards the jet. She turned back and walked to Rick.

'Rick, I will always remember you. Thank you very much. I look forward to seeing you soon again.' She drew him close and embraced him. Then she kissed him on both cheeks, turned and walked out to the waiting aircraft.

Rick stood outside on the tarmac and watched the Lear jet lifting off and heading towards Johannesburg. He spent thirty minutes answering questions, deliberately omitting any reference to Mark Aardt or Uncle Erick. To all intents and purposes he had gone up to the East Crown Gold gate, found it strange that there had been such a high degree of security in a disused gold mine, had followed it up on his own and stumbled on Gertrude Amandla.

He wanted to confront Uncle Erick personally.

When the news came in that three more White Front members had been taken into custody, Rick was not sure who were more relieved – he or the interviewing officers. They seemed as tired as he was and it was four in the morning. They offered to take him home.

A few telephone calls located Sonya and Roy Neil in their hotel in Barberton. They were both still up, waiting for word from Rick.

A few minutes later the Puma helicopter was airborne again with Rick as the sole passenger. They landed in the main road in front of the hotel, waking up the whole town.

Sonya ran out to him.

He waved goodbye to the pilot and, in a flurry of noise and wind, the helicopter rose into the dark morning sky.

When the sound subsided, Rick turned to Sonya and Roy.

'We have no time to sleep. Are you okay for five hours of driving right now, Roy?'

'I was naughty. I dozed off during the course of the night waiting for news from you. I'm rested.'

'Good. Let's pay your bill and leave. I'll fill you in on the way.'

Sonya gazed tearfully into his eyes. And he saw Shenandoah again.

Author's note: Roy Neil still owns the car they used and the White Front men at the mine have served their jail sentences.

CHAPTER 24

The truth is lived, not taught.

–Hermann Hesse

ROY STRETCHED OUT HIS RIGHT arm through the open car window and pressed the button under the loudspeaker.

'We're here for Dr Martens,' Roy spoke into the intercom.

'Dr Martens isn't here. He's already left for the office.'

Roy glanced at Rick for assistance. Leaning over Roy, Rick spoke through the window. 'My name is Rick Land. Dr Martens knows me well. We are family friends. I have a lady in the car with me who will shortly celebrate her birthday here. Dr Martens was so kind as to offer to host her party here. He told us we could come in any time to look at the facilities so that we can plan in advance.'

'I am not too sure about this ...'

'Oh, come on,' Rick clicked his tongue against his palate, 'it's all been arranged with Dr Martens. You must know who I am. I'm Rick Land. I have my ID with me. My brother was John Land. He and I practically grew up with Dr Martens. We've arranged with Dr Martens to have the party here and she wants to look at the entertainment area layout. I need to show her where we'll have the party. That's all. You may search the car,' Rick added.

The voice on the intercom did not respond. The only sounds around were those of rustling leaves in the weak early-morning sun and the distant babbling of geese in the direction of the Zoo Lake.

Slowly, Solitude's automatic wooden gate opened. The guard waved them in with a knobkierie in his hand.

They followed the driveway lined with palm trees through a beautifully landscaped garden to the sprawling white Sardinian-style mansion. A Grecian fountain spurted in the centre of an azure swimming pool. Dry leaves swirled around a bare tennis court. They must have driven through a cold front during the night, Rick thought, because it was much colder than the normal temperature in the Johannesburg suburb of Houghton.

Roy rang the front bell. They waited. A lady in a servant's uniform opened the door. 'You look just like your photograph, sir,' she said and smiled at Rick.

'Which photograph?'

She led them through the entrance foyer to the study and pointed at a gallery of photographs on the wall.

'I once asked Dr Martens who the lion man was. He told me all about you.'

In one of about twelve or thirteen framed photographs on the wall Rick sat on a log, his hair matted with sweat, his hands draped over his knees, a dead lion at his feet. He had forgotten about the photograph but he remembered the event well. AfriBelgo had asked him to kill a rogue lion that had been terrorising a village in an AfriBelgo mining area in Botswana. He remembered the two sweltering days he had spent under the African sun before he succeeded.

Next to Rick's photograph hung a studio portrait of John. Next to that was another faded reminder of Rick and John as laughing little boys with their mother standing behind them.

He bent forward and inspected the photograph more closely. They had been photographed in the garden at home on a sunny day. He peered at his mother's smiling face. So benign. Did her laugh lines hide an inner sadness or was it underlying deceit? For the first time ever, he thought of his mother with disappointment. How could the person he had trusted so much have done so wrong? How could she have written that note to Leah de Loof, fabricating a cruel lie, telling the woman that the man she had loved had died?

'The guard called through to say you will be looking at the entertainment area. I knew of you. It's still breakfast time, so can I bring you some coffee?' she offered.

'That would be wonderful,' Sonya said.

'Shall I bring it to the entertainment area?'

'No, thanks. Let's have the coffee here,' Roy said, staring at the books on the shelves.

The maid left the room. Rick looked at Sonya and Roy, both of whom were now immersed in Uncle Erick's collection, searching for clues to links with the White Front. He decided to look around and left the other two in the study.

People have a habit of keeping their innermost secrets for their bedrooms. He could imagine a special safe in that area. Although he had never been in Uncle Erick's bedroom, he knew it was the room with a private balcony at the top in the centre of the house, overlooking the pond. Rick climbed the stairs.

The door to the main bedroom chamber was closed. He turned the handle and entered. He walked into a foyer which contrasted starkly with the rest of the house. It reminded Rick of the entrance area of the old Gestapo building on the Avenue Louise in Brussels. It had similar dimensions, the same subdued lighting from a vaulted ceiling and almost the same marble finishing at the lower part of the encircling wall. Yet it appeared tacky. The upper ring of the wall, painted a gaudy pink, was pockmarked with eight block-mounted posters, three of Marilyn Monroe, five of Marlene Dietrich, pouting in long-legged black-and-white poses. Somehow, the images did not reflect what Rick always considered to be Uncle Erick's dignified manner and taste.

Rick walked through the portal to enter the bedroom, which was a larger version of the round foyer. The curtains were drawn, wrapping the room in an eerie dimness. The focal point was a large round bed with a mound of crumpled bedding rippling untidily on top of it. The ceiling was made of pleated fabric, encircling a round ceiling mirror placed over the bed. The bedroom smelled of musky deodorant.

Rick noticed the framed decorations on the walls – tens of photographs of young men in poses that seemed to mimic those of Marilyn Monroe and Marlene Dietrich, men standing against tree trunks, lying on grass, flexing muscles, brooding at the world with drooped eyelids. 'My God!' He drew in his breath.

All of them had one thing in common – they were as naked as the day they were born. And quite a few were more excitedly forthcoming between their legs. Why had Uncle Erick adorned his inner sanctum with male pornography?

His shock was suddenly compounded when he realised the sound of his voice had created a movement in the mound of bedding. Rick watched, transfixed.

First a shaved leg stuck out, and then another, then the body turned to show a naked backside for a few seconds. In a languid movement of awakening, the body turned around. A swathed hipline of sheets rustled. The person under the bedding yawned aloud.

Rick moved forward. A rush of linen and the man sat upright in bed, bleary-eyed, unshaved, naked and staring at Rick.

It was Mark Aardt.

Rick had often dreamed as a young boy that his mother and Uncle Erick would marry and that they would have a normal family life. The thought had never before occurred to him that Uncle Erick had never showed any physical interest in any woman. Now, here, he had stumbled on an unthinkable truth. Despite his past liaison with Leah de Loof, Uncle Erick was physically attracted to men, not women. The old man was gay. And seemingly active.

This revelation came as a shock but it did not bother Rick. His uncle could sleep with whom he wanted. What really bothered him was that the despicable Mark Aardt was involved. Now he understood how, in conversation with Kraske, Aardt could have referred in such a non-corporate familiar way to the Chairman.

As Aardt raised his hands to wipe the sleep from the corners of his eyes, Rick gripped the man by his wrists. In a swooping movement, he whipped Aardt's arms down and locked them behind his back.

'What the hell are you doing here?' Rick hissed. 'I thought you were in the States.'

The photographs on the walls were mute evidence of Mark Aardt's reason for being in Uncle Erick's bed and Rick, of course, knew it. Aardt did not reply but struggled to loosen Rick's grip.

'What are you doing here, Aardt?' Rick repeated, pushing the naked man's wrists hard against each other.

'It's my business, the company's business, not your business.' Aardt spat out the words through clenched teeth as he tried to wriggle out of Rick's clasp.

'Tell me about your business.'

'You're hurting me. Let go!'

'Tell me. And tell me about you and Uncle Erick.'

'Let go, Rick!'

'I'd like to break every bone in your body, given half a chance.'

'Please! You're hurting me.'

'I want answers.'

'Go to hell.'

For a few moments they were frozen, locked together.

'Aardt—'

'Stick your finger up your arse, Rick!'

Rick wanted to bang his forehead into the back of the man's skull, to hurt him, punish him for eulogising so hypocritically over John. Instead, he strengthened his grip on Aardt's wrists.

'Let me go! I need a ciggie to calm my nerves.'

'You can have a smoke after you've told me the truth.'

'I am and you're humiliating me. I'm naked. I've got to put my clothes on. I have my pride, my preferences in life, and nobody – least of all you – nobody is going to change me now. I've always liked both men and women. It's difficult but that's how God made me. John never knew. He often made coarse jokes about queers which hurt me tremendously but he was my friend and I suffered in silence.'

Rick felt like strangling the man but he kept himself in check. 'You suffered in silence? That's a bit rich. In the end, Mark, your friend suffered death at your hands in silence, didn't he?'

'That's not true, Rick.'

'What is?'

'Please! I need to get dressed. It's embarrassing. Let me light up a cigarette. I need to calm my nerves. I'll talk. I'll tell you anything you want to know. Just let me go!'

'First I want to know why you are in this bed and then why you returned so suddenly from the States. And I sure as bloody hell want to know what the shit all of this means, especially the White Front.'

'I'm not a member of the White Front.'

'I know you are part of them.'

'I don't know what you're talking about.'

'I'm talking of you being the king-pin behind the abduction of Gertrude Amandla, Aardt.'

'You're mad, stark raving crazy!' Aardt screamed, spitting saliva.

'Do you mean to say you don't know Kallie?' Rick whispered at the back of Aardt's head. Aardt's neck muscles stiffened.

'For your guidance, Mister High-Powered Executive, the lady was rescued last night from the East Crown Gold property near Barberton. Her kidnappers were like the Mormon Tabernacle Choir. While she was in their custody they sang your praises as the man they had received instructions from. It's just a matter of time before the police pick you up.'

Aardt's head slumped forward, as if in prayer. 'Oh my God. I was just doing my job,' he muttered.

'Murder? Kidnapping? Is that your job?'

'I never got involved in any murder or foul play,' Aardt said and he started crying.

'What was your job then?'

'I was only helping Erick. It was part of the game. He likes it when I act in a macho manner. Turns him on. Me too, I suppose.'

Rick digested Aardt's words. In all the years he had never suspected Uncle Erick to be anything other than a relatively benign misogynist, a grumpy old man with a slight dislike for women. He would never have suspected him of being a grumpy old man in his eighties with a love for men. But then the same could have been said of Mark Aardt, a strongly built guy with a reputation as a womanising hell raiser. To each his own, Rick thought.

'Mark, I've long ago accepted that love comes in all forms. I have an open mind. Just tell me how long have you been in a relationship with Uncle Erick?'

'Since John introduced us when we were still students. I guess it's always been in my genes.'

'Love is a mystery,' Rick said and he let go of Aardt's wrists

Aardt got out of bed, stood on the carpet without a stitch of clothing, shook his hands to improve his circulation and then strode to a wardrobe. He opened the door, fumbled inside and produced a pair of underpants, which he slipped on. He poked his head into the closet in search of more clothing.

'I knew something serious happened this morning,' he said.

'Why?'

Aardt pulled on a shirt and turned around to face Rick with a pack of cigarettes and a lighter in his hands. He lit up and hurled the pack of cigarettes and lighter towards the bed, adding to the crumpled mound. Rubbing his hands over his wrists in movements that reminded Rick of Pontius Pilate, the cigarette dangling from his lips, he spoke through wisps of smoke.

'Somebody phoned Erick just before daylight and he got up immediately. He asked me to remain here. Said he had to go to the office. I didn't think too much of it. It's the kind of thing that happens often.'

'Why are you here and not in DC? You're supposed to take over from John.'

'When you arrived in Kraske's house the other night, it came as a total surprise to me. What made it worse was that you apparently overheard us that night. But the shit really hit the fan when I heard on the news that Kraske died violently that night and that his house had burned down to the ground.'

'And so?'

'And so I reported everything to Erick who instructed me to come back here immediately for consultation. I was over there and I know I did not raze the house to the ground or kill Kraske. You were there, another link to AfriBelgo, and I could not see you doing that. I was worried. Those AfriBelgo links with Kraske, me and you? Dangerous. Should be handled with kid gloves. We cannot risk discussing those problems over telephone lines without the possibility of the phone being tapped. We knew you had access to facts that could be uncomfortable for AfriBelgo and I was worried about mob investors listening in.'

'You say I had some facts. Well, I have more now,' Rick said slowly. 'I know how John died. You were involved in that, you bastard!' Rick almost lost control over himself again.

'I did not have anything to do with John's death, Rick. Believe me. Absolutely nothing. My regret is that I could have warned him of the danger.' Aardt blew the words at Rick in a cloud of smoke.

'There are still some outstanding questions.'

'Well, don't expect me to answer them for you.'

'You are going to have to answer, not to me but to the police. You're implicated in more than one murder as well as the White Front crap.'

'Bullshit!' Aardt's eyes did not tally with his exclamation.

'You and I both know that you are knee-deep in the brown stuff, Markie. My friends and I merely need to point out a few facts to the police for them to do with you whatever should be done. Of course, if you were to help us in getting just that little closer to the real heart of the matter – clear up a few loose ends – I could conveniently handle things in ways that could suit you.' Rick disliked the duplicity in his statement, but he sorely needed a breakthrough. Aardt was a last straw to cling to. 'Why don't you tell me a little more?'

'I'm not the kind of martyr to allow myself to be sacrificed ...'

'Now you're talking.'

'I suppose so, Rick.'

'Let's sort this out jointly. Firstly, I want to know what Erfdeel was or is all about.'

'Erfdeel?'

'Aardt, John died because of his knowledge of Erfdeel. It's all on a video he left behind for me.'

'A video?'

'Yes. John's video was a kind of last will and testament. He half-expected to be murdered, you see. I know Erfdeel was a share scam many years ago.'

'Don't ask me exactly how it fitted in.' Aardt whispered, leaning back against the closet door, arms folded across his chest. 'I'm not sure. I only know that Erick and Kraske came out to Africa after the war and that they built East Crown Gold on a derivative of the Erfdeel method. What they did exactly remains a mystery. I only know it was some kind of salting scam at the mine. Once I found that out, I was sworn to secrecy by Erick, who told me it had been a minor aberration and that AfriBelgo had followed the straight and narrow afterwards.'

'Weren't you curious?'

'Initially, yes, but there was no obvious documentation and so I lost interest. I'm well paid and one must have some loyalty to the company. I never pursued it further.'

'Did they salt East Crown samples with gold to pull off a share scam?'

'I think it was a little different. When Kraske and Erick came out to Africa they were lovers.'

'Come on!'

'Are you surprised? Well, they were. Their relationship dated back to World War Two. It shows you queers can also be war heroes.' Aardt smiled at Rick as he zipped up his trousers.

'Kraske ... a lover of Uncle Erick,' Rick whispered to himself.

'I always found it difficult to relate to Kraske. He and Erick stopped their physical relationship many years ago but they maintained a strong mental bond through the years. Call it jealousy on my part, call it what you will, but I'm digressing. It was around the time of their arrival in Africa, maybe just before that, that the newspapers were brimming with the story of how two men, Erleigh and Milne, had salted a gold mine and had conned investors into buying shares in their company. Erick and Kraske lived through the events around the Erfdeel affair. From what I gathered, they found a clever way of copying it in such a manner that people invested with them without them ever being found to have committed any fraud. They did it quite some time after the Erfdeel scam and I'm not even sure whether they actually did commit any fraud.'

'Why do you say that?'

'Well, you know the line between fraud and competitive business activities is often thinly drawn,' he said as he turned around to find his socks and shoes.

'Why did John have to die for having found out something relating to Erfdeel, for a fraud that could possibly not even have been committed?'

'I never understood why he was killed, Rick. I knew there was a threat. I thought the best thing to do was to have someone speak calmly and confidentially to him in the way that Erick had explained Erfdeel to me. In the end, it all got totally out of hand. Both Erick and Kraske explained to me that AfriBelgo had – and still has – a large percentage of shares paid for in laundered money from investors involved in organised crime. From them I know that those criminals killed John to avoid the suspicion of irregularities in their investments. Those guys are very much against any detailed analysis of their own share dealings being undertaken by or on behalf of law-enforcement agencies.'

'Bullshit!'

'It's true. John was killed by organised crime.'

'John died on the instruction of Kraske,' Rick said. Mark frowned. 'Do you remember Kraske's security chief, Jacques, the character who accompanied me at Kraske's house the other night?'

'Of course I remember him. He was found dead in the forest the day after the fire.'

'Jacques organised the killing by hiring a hit man on Kraske's instructions. John was murdered on Kraske's orders.'

Aardt stood still, his shoes in his hands. 'Are you sure about that? Kraske ordered his death?'

'As sure as your fairy tale with my dear Uncle Erick.'

'Sarcasm is the refuge of the witless. It doesn't suit you, Rick.'

'The question now is whether Kraske got an instruction from your bed friend Erick?'

'Erick is not only a powerful man, he is a true gentleman and I will not believe anything negative about him.'

'Aardt,' Rick changed course, 'tell me about the White Front.'

'The White Front is Erick's toy. He's still like a naughty boy. He has never lost his playful fondness for adventure and fantasy.'

'Fantasy? That's a strange view. Does he fund the White Front?'

'Yes, and he gave them the East Crown Gold area as a training ground. I don't think he really believes in them or their cause but he likes to play games. At heart he's not a radical right-winger, just a passive sympathiser.'

'It doesn't sound very passive to me if he allows them to use company facilities for right-wing terrorist training and the abduction of important people.'

'You won't find him actively involved in the Front. It's a little like his Nazi game. He's no Nazi, but sometimes, particularly when he's had a touch too much to drink, he likes to dress up in an old German uniform for fun, for a laugh – for the two of us to play with each other, fool around, you know?'

'He's got a German uniform? Where?'

Aardt walked to the wardrobe nearest to the window, opened it and took out a neatly ironed uniform on a hanger. Rick stared at a faded dark-green tunic, frayed at the seam of the left sleeve, graced by an insignia of an eagle with fully spread wings. He took the uniform on its hanger from Aardt and inspected it. A black armband on the lower left sleeve had the word Deutschland on it in old German script. Two badges hung from a pocket, one with a helmet insignia and the other in the form of a cross. A multi-coloured thin ribbon was stuck on the tunic above the left breast pocket. A belt hung like a snake around the black neck epaulets. He fingered the silver buckle.

'Meine Ehre Heisst Treue,' Rick read out the motto on the buckle.

'My honour is loyalty. That's what Erick says it means.'

'Amazing,' Rick said and he put it back in the closet. He looked down. A few items were neatly laid out in a row on the cupboard floor. There were a black and olive-green cap with an eagle insignia and a skull-and-crossbones badge, a black scabbard with a dagger inside, and two shiny black jackboots next to each other.

Rick crouched, picked up the dagger and drew it from the scabbard. The dagger had the same motto of honour and loyalty engraved on it. He slid it back into its sheath and laid it down where he had found it. He leaned over and picked up a boot, heavy in his hand, the leather lined with cracks of age. He noticed the remaining boot propped up a battered leather briefcase against the wall. Rick dropped the boot and picked up the satchel, which had the eagle emblem of the Third Reich embossed on its withered red leather. Rick opened the flap. It was empty.

'Erick always jokes that the case once contained the road-map to his wealth.'

'Why would he say that?'

'I don't know.'

Rick ran his fingers over the embossment. 'I suppose it came with the uniform,' he whispered, again more to himself than to Aardt.

'He told me Peter Kraske had given it to him during the war,'

'Rick!' Sonya's voice rang out from the hallway.

'In here!'

Roy followed hard on her heels as she burst into the bedroom. Rick stretched out his right arm like a traffic policeman towards Aardt and made the introductions. 'Roy, Sonya, my dear Uncle Erick has had many business partners in his life but this is one of his more intimate social partners, Mark Aardt. Mark, this is Roy Neil, a journalist from *The Star*. From certain discussions I remember that, although you had not met Sonya, you knew of her friendship with John.'

Sonya glared at Aardt, who sat down on the bed, covering his mouth with his right hand, his thumb pushing the skin of his cheek into pleats running up to his ear. Rick could read defeat in Aardt's eyes.

'Nice pictures. Who is your interior decorator?' Roy asked. 'So, Rick, this is the man you and Sonya had told me about. Interesting to know that Kraske's platonic friend is Martens's intimate friend. Let's talk a little.' Roy whipped out a notepad and pen.

'I'd like to be in on this too,' Sonya added.

Rick stood up and walked towards the doorway. 'I've had enough. When you two have finished, bring him downstairs. Make sure he does not call anybody. We all need to go together to AfriBelgo's head office to clear up this mess.'

Roy nodded. Sonya sat down beside Aardt. Rick left and went downstairs. In the study he found a clean cup and saucer next to a coffee pot. He poured himself a strong black coffee. Seated on the swivel chair behind the desk, Rick reasoned with himself. He now had a much clearer picture of the puzzle.

Had the reason for bringing Albert Land's widow and sons out from Belgium not also been a smoke screen for something else? Did it not give Erick Martens a link of respectability to heroic war efforts? One way of perpetuating his connection with the heroes of the

Resistance would have been to keep the widow and children of Albert Land under his own wing, where he could control things.

Rick cursed. He had gone through life with blinkers. The obvious had eluded him, possibly because of his inherent trust in the person he had seen all these years as his family's benefactor, but the logical link now dawned upon him. And he shivered at the implications. Uncle Erick had to be confronted.

He decided he needed an element of surprise and, for that, he needed the presence of two people – Major Van Niekerk and Mark Aardt. Van Niekerk would be the right witness and, by keeping a close eye on Aardt, he would ensure the man would not warn Uncle Erick.

In the study Rick paged through the telephone directory, traced the number and placed a call.

'Major Van Niekerk? Rick Land. Yes, I'm back. I need to have you present in plain clothes with me and a few other people in about twenty minutes' time. It's in connection with Melinda's death and the abduction of the Minister of International Co-operation's wife. What's your first name? … Gert, I would like you as a witness at a meeting with a particular man. I will introduce you as my good friend, Gert, not as a policeman. You should be alone. Those are the terms. Could you come with us?'

They agreed to meet at the AfriBelgo's main entrance in twenty minutes' time.

Author's note: After a name-change Solitude became the residence of a currently well-known billionaire who started life in a hut in the Transkei and spent many years in exile in London and Lusaka prior to 1994.

CHAPTER 25

Sometimes the sheep kills the elephant.
(Meaning: Expect the unexpected)

–Themba Twala

A NOISY CONSTRUCTION CREW BLOCKED the entrance to AfriBelgo, laying down granite cobblestone paving on the steps. A foreman watched a stone layer and two men with chisels and five-pound hammers chipping away the edges of fist-sized, rough rectangular blocks to improve their fit.

Major Van Niekerk waited for them in front of a roped-off section that funnelled into an access route of planks laid over the mess of sand and jagged stone.

With a firm grip on Mark Aardt's arm, Rick walked up to the entrance of AfriBelgo House and greeted the police officer whose civilian suit looked a touch too small for him.

At the barrier, Rick hesitated and turned sideways to watch the two men engrossed in chiselling stone.

And, suddenly, he realised he had found what he had been looking for. He had found the meaning of Erfdeel. With a burst of adrenaline it dawned on him that he had been looking at the essence of Erfdeel so often he had not seen it for what it was.

He swung around to face the policeman and said loudly enough for the workmen to stop, 'Major, I don't have time to explain now but we need one of those five-pound hammers.'

Major Van Niekerk nodded, produced his identification from the inside pocket of his tweed jacket and showed it to the foreman. After a short discussion he took possession of one of the hammers.

They formed a motley group: a tall man of the bush, a pale journalist, an attractive woman in jeans, a sullen man dressed in pink golf trousers and a powder-blue silk shirt, and a man in tweed with a pencil moustache and a policeman's haircut who carried a hammer.

'We're expected,' Rick lied as they besieged the security guard.

With an authoritative smile, Rick rushed past the security counter, gripping Mark Aardt tightly by the elbow, followed by Sonya, Roy and Major Gert van Niekerk.

The guard protested, storming after them with the visitors' book and a pen, but they ignored him and walked into the open elevator. Rick pushed the button for the top floor, the thirtieth. The guard protested and tried to enter the elevator but Rick pushed him away as the doors closed.

On the thirtieth floor the Chairman's secretary, ensconced behind her laminated, shatterproof security-glass partition, at first appeared disturbed at the unexpected flood of people, but smiled when she recognised Rick. When he gestured that she should press the button so that the automatic door would swivel open, she leaned sideways to speak into a small microphone.

'Morning, Mr Land, Mr Aardt,' she said in her high-pitched voice that sounded even more nasal through the intercom.

'I'm sorry we've arrived unannounced, but we need to see Dr Martens urgently,' Rick said, smiling back at her.

A buzzer sounded, the door whipped open and they entered. 'Please have a seat while I get hold of—'

Rick led his group past her into the ornate reception area and along the trail of Persian carpets down the corridor towards the Chairman's office. Ignoring her protestations behind them, Rick burst through the open doorway into the large, rectangular office, keeping a tight hold of Mark Aardt, followed closely by the others.

Erick Martens must have heard the commotion. He was standing behind his desk when they entered, bathed in the early morning sunlight that filtered through the ceiling-to-floor window behind him, stooped forward, palms on his desk, a frown on his freckled forehead.

'I expected you, Rikki, but not so soon and not with such a large support group. But then you've been leading quite a busy life these last few days, from what I hear,' he said without the slightest hint of his usual amicability.

'Dr Martens, I'm sorry, but they just came in and—'

'That's all right, Maxie. You may go now. Why don't we all sit down?' Erick Martens said and motioned towards the two antique couches and two armchairs placed around a marble coffee table at one end of his office.

Rick detected that the perplexed look in the Chairman's eyes, eyes that seemed even more sunken against the light, was now directed towards Mark Aardt, who merely shrugged.

They all sat down.

Erick Martens removed his gold, horn-rimmed spectacles and wiped the lenses against his shirt.

'So, Rikki, I'm sure you would want to tell me of all the momentous things you have done since we saw each other just the other day but I have not yet had the pleasure of the acquaintance of your friends. Why don't you introduce them?'

'Uncle Erick, you know Mark, of course.'

The old man ignored the introduction.

'This is Sonya. She is a diplomat in Washington,' Rick carried on.

'Ah, so this is the girl they told me about. I have heard of you, my dear, and I admire your perseverance although I don't understand what drives you.'

'Who told you about me?'

'I can see why they say you're strong-willed.'

Rick took Sonya's hand and their eyes met.

'And this is Roy Neil of *The Star*.'

'Ah, a journalist, a scribe. Are you going to keep the minutes of this meeting, young man?'

The old man placed his glasses back on the bridge of his nose and peered at Roy Neil.

Ignoring the remark, Rick continued, 'And this is Gert van Niekerk, a friend,' pointing at the police officer who had managed to conceal the hammer under his jacket.

'When you go to a party, it's always good to take friends along,' the old man said as he grinned and fiddled with a trembling hand at the hearing aid in his left ear. 'So, Rikki, I'm here and so are all your friends, I see. Could you please tell me what the party is in aid of?'

'The truth.'

'I'm old now. I don't believe in truth fairies anymore,' he said, shifting his gaze from Rick to Mark Aardt.

'Truth is, Uncle Erick, I've learned a lot during the past few days and, to say the least, I'm shocked.'

'Shocked? About what, Rikki?'

'The real Erick Martens. Even the fact that I was named after him.'

'And who is the real one?'

'An officer in the Gestapo headquarters in Brussels during the war and a man who occasionally still likes to dress up in his old uniform.' Rick had spoken slowly to allow the effect of his words to sink in but Erick Martens smiled, unperturbed.

'So what's new? Maybe Mark has become your truth fairy.' He shot Aardt a look. 'It has always been general knowledge, my boy, that I worked for the Resistance as a German officer. I was German-Belgian but a Belgian first. I entered the German army to serve undercover for Belgium. I never boasted about it. I never courted fame. I avoided basking in the glory of having had to put my own life on the line for so many others. You have no idea what it was like. Being there in the interrogation trenches allowed me to warn the Resistance of impending actions against any members so that they could escape being captured. I saved so many lives you have no idea. Because of me the Resistance was always one step ahead of the Gestapo. I was there at the source every day and able to pinpoint targets for attack from time to time. Of course, I could serve only to a limited extent because it would have been counterproductive if the Resistance had lost my services through either their or my own over-eagerness. My position was so sensitive very few people even knew what I was doing. One who did was Albert Land, your father.'

'And a woman.'

'Which woman?'

'Leah de Loof.'

'Leah?'

'She is an old woman now. Do you know the Hotel Heinz Müller in a small town on the German-Belgian border?'

'Rikki, you surprise me. You have done your homework well. It's been so long, I can barely recollect what Leah looked like.'

'It's easy. Just picture a broken old lady. Even in her infirmity she is still in love with a ghost from the past, under the mistaken impression that her loved one died a long time ago.'

'And so he did, Rikki. He died a long time ago for her,' the old man said. 'Leah was good for me at the time. She was my alibi many times. All my colleagues at the Gestapo on the Avenue Louise knew I often spent nights with her. When I had to join my friends of the Resistance on nightly outings, which often occurred, Leah would always make a point of spreading the right kind of information to the right people at headquarters, telling them what a wonderful night we had had. And, indeed, there was a time when we had a relationship. She was young. She was attractive. Very attractive. The war pushed us into each other's arms in a way. She was more conservative than me in her ideals. She wanted married life with a house and children. I was a wild and confused dreamer. It had to end. There was no other way. It was best for both her and me. You have to be cruel to be kind.'

'Cruelty cannot be love.'

'Well, my circumstances changed and I did not need Leah in my life anymore.'

'I met her, Uncle Erick.'

'You are indeed a bundle of surprises,' he said.

'She showed me a letter, signed by Kraske, with a postscript from my mother, telling her you had died. It did not make sense to me. How could my own mother have been involved in a cruel lie like that? How could you have drawn her in?'

'She wasn't.'

'She didn't write the note?'

'She never wrote to Leah. Peter Kraske, bless his departed soul, always had an artistic bent. He forged her handwriting.'

Rick had glanced at the writing and assumed it to be his mother's. This revelation came as a welcome consolation, a reconfirmation of his faith in his mother's strength of character.

'Well then,' Rick persisted, 'why did you want Leah de Loof out of your life, aside from having grown tired of her? You could just as well have ignored her. Instead you came up with an elaborate lie. My understanding is that she did some office work for you and my father in Belgo-Grec as an administrator. I never realised my father was part of Belgo-Grec.'

'Now you know.'

'I think your letter to her was deliberately intended to end the Belgo-Grec saga.'

'Why would I have wanted to do that?' The Chairman laughed.

'Because she was there when it all started. And there when it all ended.'

'I don't understand your confused thinking.'

'Allow me to sketch the scenario.'

'Please enlighten us, Rikki. I'm sure your friends will find this as much off the rails as I do.' But there was concern in the old man's eyes.

'You grew up in the German-speaking part of Belgium, the son of a Belgian mother and a German father. This made you a juicy catch for British counter-intelligence. They trained you in England after which you made your way into the German army where you started off in the Todt, engineering side, and then the Gestapo. You were a very young lower-rank officer.'

'That's all old hat,' Uncle Erick said, ridicule in his grin. 'I went to school in Germany, but I was a Belgian nationalist at heart. The British first trained me secretly near Brussels and later in Britain. They provided me with a new, full-fledged, German identity. They gave me a false passport, identity papers, money, clothing and a cover story with carefully placed references, and packed me off to Germany. My instructions were to infiltrate the Secret State Police. The Wehrmacht swallowed the cover story, which portrayed me as someone with a technical talent, and they placed me in the Todt, the Wehrmacht's engineering arm. I had an aptitude for engineering even then, which later helped me in my mining career. Because of my knowledge of French and Flemish, I was able to apply successfully for a transfer to the Geheime Staatspolizei – the Gestapo.'

'And so you became a leading light in the Gestapo's interrogation activities in Brussels.'

'I became a leading light in the Resistance. I worked for the Allied cause in the Gestapo, not in a trench coat but in my uniformed SS guise. I was in counter-intelligence. I don't see why you're getting so heated up about my good work,' Erick Martens said, throwing his arms up, a twitch in his left eye.

'All right, Uncle Erick, you said something about this being a party. Allow me to take you back to another party in April 1944 when you attended the official celebration of Hitler's birthday in Brussels. Leah was there. So was my father, accompanied by a few others from the underground, acting as waiters? Kraske arrived at the party as a courier from Paris with important documentation in his briefcase. That party ended abruptly.' Rick stood up and walked to the window before he continued.

'The waiters had the time of their lives that night because they were able to steal a pile of weapons from under the noses of the most senior

German officers in Brussels. But they also stole your friend Kraske's briefcase with its documentation – the real reason for staging the heist. A smoke-and-mirrors trick, it was. Instead of the small arms, the group's true mission was to get hold of the briefcase with its documents. Later that same night a German convoy was ambushed outside Brussels and the Resistance took possession of a large consignment of gold. You were part of that ambush that night and it was for your own benefit.'

'It is irresponsible of you to imply such things!'

'Uncle Erick, the original briefcase with an embossed eagle is in your wardrobe at home.'

Erick Martens glared at Mark Aardt.

'For your information, the embossment is of the Reichsadler. That was my own portefeuille during the war,' he said, 'and how did you get into my wardrobe at home?'

'You say so but I believe the opposite. I think you have the original briefcase of that night's birthday party with you at Solitude. But it really does not matter anymore. What we should discuss is what happened that night.'

'And what happened that night, Rikki?'

'You and your friends took hold of a massive amount of gold, maybe worth two hundred and fifty million US dollars in today's value.'

'Did you get that from a James Bond movie?' The old man laughed. 'It is nonsense. A delusion. If you make a wild allegation like that you should base it on evidence and there is no proof of this far-fetched notion.'

'Maybe, but I think I know the truth, Uncle Erick.'

'So what is the truth then?'

'Your group buried the gold in the forest bordering Brussels, by coincidence in a location with a South African connection. Another year or so and the war ended. But then strange things happened. Somehow, everyone in the party that night died by the end of the war, everybody except for you, our friend Kraske, and my own father. I have a feeling those poor guys were all cherry-picked by the Gestapo or the Sicherheitsdienst, the intelligence agency of the SS where your friend Kraske worked. Maybe one or two died in other suspicious circumstances but they all disappeared.'

'Rikki, you are totally mad! I will not stand for it!' The old man stood up.

'I'm giving you a scenario, Uncle Erick. Listen to me. Then tell me I'm wrong. Sit down!' It was the first time he had given Erick Martens an instruction.

The old man walked over to his desk and sat down in his swivel chair. Rick crossed the floor to lean back against the tinted glass window next to him. The others remained seated at the coffee table. Rick noticed Major Van Niekerk was speaking softly on a cellular phone.

'Uncle Erick, let's get back to the end of the war. All those valiant men who had taken part with you in the ambush that night disappeared. The only survivors were you, Kraske and my own father. You guys controlled a massive amount of hidden gold bars. Some of the gold came from central bank reserves, but much of it had been stolen by the Gestapo from so-called sensitive sources. Do you know what I mean by sensitive sources?' Rick aimed the question at Major Van Niekerk and Roy Neil. 'Jews.'

'Nonsense!'

'You had to find a way of turning that gold into usable money. One option would have been to take the gold to Switzerland but it would have been dangerous to move such a large haul because it would have brought too much attention on gold with a sensitive background. Besides, I have a feeling the gold of sensitive origin had been resmelted and restamped as being from The Reichsbank. After the war it would have been difficult to hand over a Reichsbank Nazi-stamped piece of gold to anyone in a sale. You guys were young nobodies from nowhere who could not suddenly appear with millions. Obviously, you were not interested in attracting the suspicions of all those post-war snoopers. No, you needed laundering. Clean laundering. And the three of you were patient.'

'Your story is too far-fetched, Rikki.'

'You and your two friends sat with the gold. South Africa was the world's major gold mining country. That's why the three of you decided to send someone down to South Africa – you – to see how you could launder your treasure in a manner that would not attract unwanted attention.'

'I cannot believe I'm listening to this rubbish from you, of all people.'

'It's not that far-fetched at all, Uncle Erick. Look at Sonya over here.' Rick walked towards her.

The old man stared at the ceiling.

'She grew up in an orphanage. Did you know that?'

The old man shrugged.

'Well, would you like to know why she was an orphan?'

The old man did not react.

'Her father got in your way.'

Suddenly Major Gert van Niekerk's cell rang loudly in his plain-clothes jacket.

'And your phone is in the way!' the Chairman said.

'Sorry. I'll take it outside.' The policeman walked back to the secretary's office.

'Sonya became an orphan because her father was in the way. Your way.'

'Ah please,' and the old man rolled his eyes.

'Her father died, like John and Melinda and so many others. You see, he was your initial South African partner. His name was Mauritz Deine.'

The old man's head whipped around to look at Sonya. 'I should have known that surname, Deine,' he said, 'but Mauritz Deine never had children.'

'I was born after his death,' Sonya said through pursed lips.

'I knew Mauritz's wife died of cancer a few years later but I never knew of a child,' the old man said. A pearl of sweat glided down his forehead. He wiped his brow.

'She died too young and so did my father. I never knew him. He never knew me. But I know that someone came in one night, and shot him in the head in bed.'

'The murder was never solved,' the old man croaked.

'No, it wasn't. The reason for that was that Peter Kraske, who had pulled the trigger, had left the country!' she said and scowled at him.

'Uncle Erick, Kraske personally told us he did it and even how he did it,' Rick interjected.

'Kraske could not have done it. He could not have told you that!' The old man's eyes darted from Sonya to Rick.

'Kraske was on the point of killing us both, Uncle Erick. He had the upper hand at that moment and thought the secret would go with us to our graves. Unfortunately for him, he lost out.'

'No.' The old man shook his head.

At that moment the office door opened and a completely unexpected group walked in from the secretary's office led by the plainclothes policeman.

'What? Vronsky? Robert? Minister? What are you doing here?' Erick Martens asked.

'I am sorry to push in like this, Erick.'

'Robert, even a Cabinet Minister should have the decency to make a formal appointment.'

'You're right,' Robert Amandla said, 'but Mr Vronsky, as the facilitator of the upcoming Saint Petersburg Mining Agreement, has been keeping me up to date on certain developments related to AfriBelgo. You are no doubt aware that certain activities took place in your ambit last night and those events led to Major Van Niekerk here drawing us into this meeting.'

'Major? Is that man a policeman? Rikki, you introduced him as your friend.'

Rick ignored the remark.

'Erick, I am the Minister of International Co-operation and your work falls in my sphere to an extent. It was only a few months ago that we had the first democratic elections in our country with President Mandela elected as our new leader. My job is to ensure the smooth integration of old and new activities. I am here to listen. Accept it.'

'Fine. Sit down.'

The Minister, his bodyguard and Vronsky sat down.

'We interrupted the discussion,' Minister Amandla said.

'I was telling Dr Martens here,' Sonya said, her voice seething, 'that both Rick and I were present when Kraske told us of my father's murder. Martens is implicated.'

'Kraske?' Robert Amandla asked, whereupon Vronsky leaned over to whisper in his ear.

'Listen, young lady, I'm not interested in hearing this nonsense any more. Leave my office. If you think you can order me around, you are wildly mistaken!'

Sonya approached the old man.

'Get out!' he ordered again, pointing at the door with a quivering hand.

'Martens, you are now going to listen to me!' she screamed, pushing her right index finger into the fold under the old man's collarbone. 'The greed of men like you and Kraske made my life a misery. You trampled on my family. You shattered our lives.'

'Get away from me, woman!'

'You created the circumstances in which I was forced to grow up as an orphan. Many children in that orphanage had been discarded by their own parents. They were the children of drug addicts, prostitutes and alcoholics. I had decent parents but I had to share in their broken lives. I had to fight my way to normality. Their parents discarded them but I was discarded because you discarded my parents.'

'I never knew of you,' the Chairman whispered slowly.

'That was your mistake, Martens. If you had known of me, I would probably not have been here anymore. I would be dead. One more detail you never knew was that my mother left me a letter for my sixteenth birthday in which she wrote to me of what you and Kraske had done to us. I've been after your skin ever since my sixteenth birthday. I've made it my life's work to exact revenge.'

'You're mistaken if you're looking for revenge here today, young lady,' Erick Martens managed to wheeze, his cheeks even paler than before.

'Uncle Erick, we know Mauritz Deine died at Kraske's hand because of Erfdeel,' Rick said.

'Rikki. As a mining man I know of Erfdeel, but I don't see how you could connect that nonsense to all the nonsense you and this young lady are spewing here.'

'In a way I'm sorry, Uncle Erick, that I have to tell you all of this in front of the Minister and Mr Vronsky but I believe that, right from the start, there were only two truly loyal partners in your deal: you and Peter Kraske. What was the motto of the SS again? 'My honour is loyalty.' In your case, you had selective loyalty. You used a wider group to assist in the ambush and then you ensured their elimination afterwards. In Europe you relied on an initial third partner, my father. He had to operate the mechanisms you and Kraske masterminded. When his work was done, you eliminated him too.'

'Rikki, you are wrong. Albert died in a climbing accident.'

'Leah de Loof cured me of that mistaken belief.'

'What do you mean?'

'She told me you were the one who insisted on a challenge to climb the cliffs at Dinant that day. She witnessed the fall and, from the way she described it, I am convinced it was no accident. Albert Land was deliberately pushed to death. By you!'

'He slipped,' Erick Martens insisted.

'No, he fell in a way in which he had been pushed but let's get on with the scenario. Albert Land – by the way, Minister, Albert was my father who worked with him in the Resistance in the war – yes, Albert, your third partner in Europe, disappeared into a grave. By then you already had a farmer with land in a known gold mining area, Mauritz Deine, as your new third partner in Africa. You started on his land but he also slipped into death along the short and straight trajectory of a bullet to his head. When John recently started asking unpalatable questions about Erfdeel, the spotlight turned too close for comfort on your involvement with Mauritz Deine, Belgo-Grec and the first stirrings of AfriBelgo. It would have been disastrous if it were to surface that the AfriBelgo Group, one of the major mining groups of the world, had not only been built on stolen Second World War bank reserves, but also on unaccounted gold fillings, gold jewellery and artefacts taken from innocent Jewish victims. John's curiosity about Erfdeel prompted his own death. I believe you agreed to and even sanctioned his killing as well as the attempt on my life, which was rather unfortunate for Melinda. Just like you got rid of Albert Land, you had no compunction in being involved in eliminating his sons, John and me.'

'Rikki, you're totally mad! I lead one of the great corporations of the world. Why would I want to hurt you and John, the sons I never had. You've been my protégés! Mr Neil,' Erick Martens implored Roy, 'you are a newspaper man. You should be able to understand logic, pure and unadulterated logic. I would never hurt a hair on the heads of my godsons and all this rubbish about stolen gold is so far-fetched, it's laughable. Robert, you must also know that.'

'Erick, my wife was rescued at East Crown last night. I am here to listen.'

'It's got nothing to do with me, Robert. Mr Neil, as a journalist you must have logic.'

'Dr Martens, I think one has to investigate the validity of what Rick's been saying,' Roy said.

'What can be valid in all of that?'

'Dr Martens, face the facts. As of late, people have been dying like flies around the AfriBelgo name. Moreover, the wife of the Minister of International Co-operation here, kidnapped by the White Front, was found last night on East Crown Gold property. She was on AfriBelgo related property. Mark Aardt is implicated and so are you.'

'You've obviously heard the news,' Erick Martens said.

'We haven't heard the news. We actually made the news. We were there,' Roy said.

'I'm not involved.'

'According to Mrs Amandla the White Front men spoke of someone called 'The Leader' with Aardt as their contact man. They even spoke of Solitude, your house.'

'I disassociate myself from anything that happened there last night or at any time. If Mark's involved, so be it. I'm not. I'm a respectable businessman.'

'Erick, you can't leave me in the lurch!' Aardt cried out. The old man stared at Aardt. 'Erick, how could you do this to me?'

'Mark, what you do to yourself is none of my business. Robert, Mr Minister, you hear me.'

'Erick, I have been with you for so many years and now you say it's none of your business?' Aardt screamed in rage. 'I share my life with you, my very body, and my soul. I take part in your silly games with silly people who cannot adjust to today's political realities. I run your errands, act macho with those dirty men at East Crown just to impress and humour you and what do you do? You betray me like you betrayed that De Loof woman. Is this also cruelty with kindness for you? Without batting an eyelid, you push the blame on me and sell me out for your own gain. Well, I won't take that lying down! I'm not your floor rag, Erick. I have my own life to live. I don't need you. That's why I asked to be transferred to take over from John in Washington. I wanted to find myself again, find somebody new. I never want to see you again as long—'

'You two can discuss this later,' Rick said. 'We need to finish. AfriBelgo was started at a birthday reception for Adolf Hitler in 1944.

AfriBelgo was built on one of the largest robberies in history. You were Heinz Müller and Kraske was Franz Somebody, and the two of you controlled the gold. You learned from Erfdeel and you executed a similar salting scam at East Crown Gold to monetise your booty.'

'Rikki, you are really insane. You don't understand what a salting scam is. It's to add limited amounts of precious metal to borehole samples or other mining samples so that the seller can fraudulently sell shares at much higher values, or fraudulently sell artificially inflated mining property. Salting is done with a few specks of gold in ore samples, not two hundred and fifty million dollars worth, as you imply. On the question of that high value, think for yourself. If it would have been difficult to move something like that to Switzerland, as you said, how could it be moved across the globe to this corner? How would we have done what you purport to have happened and got away with it? It's nonsense! Worse, you have no proof of anything.'

'Uncle Erick, I looked at the proof so often in the past that I never saw it. It was so obvious to anyone that it became your best disguise.'

'Disguise?'

'The one mistake you made was to dump broken Belgo-Grec columns, supposedly ornamental goods, in one spot at a disused gold mine. I want to prove something.'

Rick crossed over to Major Van Niekerk and held out his hand. 'The hammer please, Gert.'

Gert van Niekerk produced the five-pound hammer from under his jacket.

Rick took it, turned around and eyed the imitation Greek column near the window, with its small, bronze plaque stating: *Last Remaining Import Product of Belgo-Grec.*

He approached the column, ran his left hand over the smooth, cold cement surface. He remembered how he and John had played among the columns as children.

'No! Don't! It's my last memento.'

'Uncle Erick, I've always looked at this column as a symbol of how to overcome defeat. I now think I've been misled.'

He glanced at Dr Erick Martens, slumped behind his desk.

'You always said you made no money from Belgo-Grec. I also believed it had been your one and only failure. Now I have a feeling that Belgo-Grec wasn't a financial disaster at all. I think you made your fortune from it.'

'How can you say that?'

'I noticed that all the broken columns at East Crown Gold had been snapped in exactly the same spot, here in the middle, as if with one blow.' Rick tapped the column with the hammer.

The old man pursed his lips, sighed and closed his eyes.

'Uncle Erick, you made a few mistakes. One was to create a reject-ed child without a parent. The other was to be too perfect. You standardised the method of breaking reject columns.'

He gripped the hammer with both hands, aimed at the spot where he intended to connect. Slowly, he brought the hammer into a backswing and then brought it forward at speed at the centre of the pillar.

A hollow-sounding thud exploded into a crack. The column snapped in two. It toppled from the stand in a cloud of dust. Rick went down on his haunches, the hammer still in his hand.

CHAPTER 26

EVERYONE IN THE OFFICE STARED at the debris on the carpet. Although severed, the two pieces of cement were still held together by thin strands of reinforcement. It was obvious that an object, wrapped up in canvas, had been inserted into the reinforcement wire.

Rick tapped away excess cement around the object, stuck his fingers into the wires and flexed them until the opening was large enough to extract the object. He laid the hammer down, reached inside and withdrew it. Encased in dirty canvas, it lay heavy in his cupped hands. And he knew his gamble had paid off. He had found the answer.

A thin strand of rusty wire had been wound around the canvas. Still on his haunches, he twisted the rusted wire, which broke easily. Using his thumb and forefinger to grip one flap of the canvas, which felt like aged parchment, he unrolled the shroud in a single, flicking movement.

A bright yellow bar of gold tumbled out, glinting in the early morning sunlight that filtered through the tinted glass window. Rick picked up the bar and got up from the floor, cradling it in his hands. He turned it over. It was stamped with the letters RB, two sets of numbers and the date 1938.

'I believe RB stands for Reichsbank,' Rick said and he stared at Erick Martens who remained silent and stony-faced. 'It's dated as pre-war, but I guess the Germans would have resmelted and restamped whatever they took from whomever.'

He handed the bar to Roy who admired it and held it out for Sonya. She took it and gently stroked the smooth surface. Then

Vronsky and the Minister handled the evidence.

'Uncle Erick,' Rick spoke heavily, suddenly overcome with emotion, 'you've asked for proof. This is it. You, with the help of my father, produced this and smuggled the stolen gold to South Africa, stashed away in these columns.'

Erick Martens leaned back in his high-back chair, expressionless now, his head resting on the windowpane behind him.

'You were clever, weren't you?' Rick continued.

The old man merely raised his eyebrows and pursed his thin lips tighter, yet Rick could detect the bitterness in the man's eyes. The plans of a lifetime, so carefully laid out, implemented so well, now lay in fragments.

Rick's mind raced ahead of his own thoughts as he spoke again. 'Mr Minister, smuggling happens from source. One would've expected precious metals to be smuggled from, not into, South Africa. Nobody in his right mind would ever have thought that anybody would want to smuggle gold into South Africa. But that's what Belgo-Grec was – a smuggling ring. It's like smuggling coals to Newcastle, senseless on the surface but, deeper down, it made a hell of a lot of sense, didn't it?'

'Pray tell, my know-it-all godson, how would it have made sense?' the old man whispered.

'You knew exactly how the Erfdeel salting scam had been executed. You knew the mistakes made in that scam. You learned from it and you perfected it.'

'How could I have done that?'

'All you needed was a gold mining area where you could get cheap mining options. Being out of the mainstream of gold production, Barberton suited you well. You found a struggling outfit called East Crown Gold Mining in Barberton. It was a disastrous company with virtually no gold anymore and its owners wanted to dump it. So Erick Martens persuaded them he could manage it, make a profit and buy out the company from profit. They gave you that management option.'

'I turned it around with good management and that was that.'

'Good management? No, it was more like good manipulation. At the same time of your negotiations with the owners of the faltering company, you negotiated with a certain Mauritz Deine, a farmer out there whose land bordered on East Crown Gold. Previous prospecting had probably shown no gold at all on Deine's farm but you convinced him you could find gold where others had not succeeded. It was easy to win him over into signing an option on his land with you, probably for next to nothing. So, lo and behold, you found gold! Naturally, you merely salted mineral samples Erfdeel-style to prove gold on Deine's farm but, on the strength of that sample you, possibly Kraske, raised the money to buy out the company shortly after you had signed the management option with East Crown Gold. In the process you persuaded Deine to become your partner and co-shareholder with Kraske by merging his land with that of East Crown Gold.'

'Preposterous!'

'Not at all. Mauritz Deine must probably have found out very quickly that all was not so kosher among his new-found partners, if kosher is a word one can mention to Nazis.'

'Rubbish!'

'Unfortunately he signed his own death warrant when he questioned your methods. You and Kraske quickly got rid of him. One shot in the head. In his bed. Easy. Probably done to some of the guys who had stolen the stuff originally in Brussels. In the meantime, all the Belgo-Grec columns, each containing a bar of gold, had been prepared by Albert Land and shipped out to South Africa. You did not need poor Albert anymore. He had inserted the gold bars in the columns. His job was done. So, like the Resistance members who disappeared after the heist, you engineered the death of your friend Albert by arranging a climbing accident on your return visit to Belgium. Leah de Loof had done all the paperwork on your products and so you took care of her by farming her out into oblivion, setting her up to believe you died. In a brilliant move, as an insurance policy, you brought Albert's widow and two sons out here where you could control them.

Everybody who had anything to do with the environment around the stolen gold was neutralised or taken care of. You and Kraske now sat with all the gold.

'My guess is that you probably used a stock of regular columns without gold as a smokescreen in regular business for a while. I remember the stockyard of old columns when I was small. One can only assume that certain columns with gold bars inside were carefully marked. Those marked columns were sent up to Barberton where you broke them open and resmelted the bars at East Crown Gold. Your mine suddenly started to produce high-quality gold. The beauty of what you accomplished was that not only did you monetise your stolen hoard, you were able to set up a business empire. Suddenly, Erick Martens was a whiz kid, a Midas with the ability to turn to gold everything he touched. You were praised for your good management techniques in turning around what seemed to be a completely unproductive and unprofitable mine. On the back of that reputation, that you damn well never deserved, you and Kraske attracted investment and built your initial nest egg into a major conglomeration. But you and Kraske made one mistake – you should have killed Mauritz Deine's wife. Maybe you knew she had cancer by then and that she would die in any case. Who knows? In the end she did die, but Sonya lived on to haunt you and to prompt John into opening up the whole can of worms. Sonya's eyes saw through you. For your information Kraske's house was close to the Shenandoah River, which is an Indian word for Clear-eyed Daughter of the Stars. In a way Sonya was the only one with clear eyes who saw the reality all the time. That's the scenario.'

Rick's monologue ended to the sound of slow clapping from Erick Martens, still seated behind his desk, leaning back against the window.

'And now you think you've got a prize trophy in your sights, don't you, Rikki?'

'I don't hunt people. People aren't trophies.'

'Ah, but, Rikki, you will cull for natural survival whereas your lady friend wishes to cull as a reprisal.' Erick Martens shot a bitter glance at Sonya.

'Uncle Erick, that's the other side of the situation. In my own case, you planted ideas of reprisal by ivory syndicates as a reason for John's death, and the attack in which Melinda died. You probably even faked an attack on yourself – you made up that story – to deflect attention and to put me on the wrong track, the wrong spoor. You never changed your spots. I think that in your heart you probably remained a heartless Gestapo type through all the years, to the extent even of supporting rabid extremists like the White Front. I now know that you've been a selfish egoist and, as you said, that your kindness was often tinged with cruelty.'

'Robert,' Erick looked at the Minister, 'I am sorry your wife got caught up. I was playing a little modern day war game. The toy soldiers took it a little too far and too late to suddenly change but she would have been fine in the end. Trust me.'

'Erick, you are a pig. Vronsky was right.'

'Ah, Mr Vronsky. Why are you, of all people, here exactly?'

'I'm just a servant doing my duty.'

'Ah duty. The whip on our backs.'

The old man swivelled his chair to face the window. He sat staring at the distant metropolitan horizon. From the side Rick could see he was smiling. It was as if he had lost interest in the proceedings around him.

For a minute or two, nobody said anything.

'Dr Martens,' Major Van Niekerk finally spoke, 'as a police officer I must inform you now that what I have seen and heard here has been extremely disconcerting.'

The old man swung his chair around to face the policeman, took off his horn-rimmed glasses and put them on the desk in front of him. He bowed his head, put his elbow on the table and propped up his head with a trembling hand draped over his freckled forehead, a few silver strands of hair flopping over his index finger.

'Dr Martens, we need to take you in for further questioning.'

'What purpose will that serve?' he said, fiddling with his hearing aid.

'Dr Martens, Mrs Amandla was rescued from a white terrorist group that operated with your support from your facilities. Minister Amandla is here now. Mr Land came up with an initially outrageous story of theft, fraud, deception and murder, which now does not seem that outrageous anymore with the evidence of this bar of gold. Many things tie up to make an integrated picture. Before jumping to conclusions, however, and in deference to a highly respected man like you, all these issues need to be checked thoroughly, which is why I have to ask you to accompany me from here.'

'Officer,' Erick Martens said, eyeing the policeman who stood holding the bar of gold cupped in his hands. 'You have a bar of gold as evidence. Allow me to show you something else.' He leaned sideways.

From the other side of the desk Rick could see his erstwhile benefactor opening the drawer of this desk. Lightning quick, Erick Martens raised his hands, joined together, with one finger on a trigger, the barrel aimed at Sonya.

'This is a Luger – one with a long line of dead targets behind it. Officer, if you change your grip on the bar of gold you are holding, she dies. And Robert, if your security guard lifts his finger, she's dead,' Erick Martens hissed.

'I have nothing to lose. Young lady, stand as you are. Rikki, if you and your friends don't listen to me, she dies. You and these men, including you, Robert, and Mark my dearest, put your hands on your heads and move backwards to the wall, except for you, constable keystone, you come over and place the bar of gold here in front of me on this desk.'

Major Van Niekerk complied and left the bar on the desk.

'Good, now Major, raise your hands, keep them on your head and move back to the wall with the others.'

Rick looked at the man behind the desk. He saw the eyes of a trapped animal and he blamed himself. He should have known better. The old man had kept his emotions in control, lulling all of them into a sense of false security, thinking that he would meekly accept everything. He had forgotten that Erick Martens was a calculating man, who had had no qualms in getting rid of his opposition in the past.

'Stand still. Do as I say!' the Chairman instructed, still pointing the Luger at Sonya.

'Rick?' Sonya whispered.

He nodded as encouragingly as he could but felt quite helpless.

'Now we will talk,' Erick Martens said.

'Uncle Erick, why don't you just put down the gun and—'

'Rikki, I never thought I'd say this to you, but shut up, you interfering shit.'

'Sonya is an innocent girl. Don't point the gun at her.'

'I should have listened to Kraske. He said a clean break was needed. Officer,' the old man glared at Van Niekerk, 'before you and Minister Robert attempt to take me in, I should tell you that I am almost eighty years of age and have learned a few tricks in those eight decades. I've had good years, all of them. Still today, I hold my ground in all activities, whether in business or in physical enjoyment,' and the old man stopped to smile at Mark. 'I hate with gusto. I love with passion. That's the way God made me. He made me an independent thinker, a leader, a creator. I built this business up from nothing by taking a few scraps of wartime information and transforming them into a master-piece of commercial enterprise.'

'So what Rick told us is true? You used stolen gold to build Af-riBelgo?' Roy asked.

'Yes, scribe, and I'm not ashamed of it. I'm almost an octogenarian now and I couldn't care a shit anymore. Never felt I had a foot in the grave – not even when I had my stroke the year before last – but, Rikki, today you planted both my feet in the grave. Now I don't care anymore. Yes, it was stolen gold. But we didn't steal it. The German army stole it from the central banks of Europe and from individuals involved in anti-German activities.'

'Jews,' Roy stated calmly.

'Some of the gold, yes. The army had stolen it. We just took it back from them in regular wartime efforts.'

'Leah de Loof was right,' Rick said softly.

The old man nodded, still keeping the Luger trained on Sonya. 'Leah was there and so was Albert, your father, and Peter Kraske. We all attended the birthday reception for the Führer. That was a wonderful day in history, a beautiful day of deception. At the end of that night we owned the gold. Not Leah of course. Just the rest of us. Rikk, if you want to complain now about the past, you should be careful, because your father wasn't such a pristine white knight as was made out to you. He and I and Peter planned it all together. It's true that those who joined us in the raid that night all disappeared. Albert agreed with Peter and me that our own security was at stake with so many people in the know and that we had to eliminate the others. It was painful but it needed to be done.'

'And in this painful process your slices of the cake became a little larger.'

'Don't be facetious, my boy. Our reasons for getting the others out of the way had to do with security. Believe me.'

'So, did you kill my father also for security reasons?'

'Albert was a crook. He died as a common crook.'

'So you killed him.'

'He misappropriated a portion of the consignment, which was against the spirit of our partnership. His job was to insert gold in the products. Some of the gold did not find its way into our products because he took it for himself. At least he was clever, compared with that idiot Mauritz Deine with his holier-than-thou attitude that it was not righteous to resmelt war booty. We offered him a good deal, which he refused. That was it.'

'May you rot in hell!' Sonya cried out.

'Young lady, I prefer to retain my composure. If you frighten me again like that, I could very well pull the trigger. I would advise you rather to shut your mouth.'

'Dr Martens,' Roy said, 'how did you turn the gold bars in your columns into East Crown Gold's product?'

'Good question, Mister Journalist. I know I'm nearing the end of the line now. All old men have to die, probably sooner than later. The world might as well know how I did it. I used rough bullion bars from Barberton to channel our gold into fine gold bars in Johannesburg.'

'I don't quite understand what you're—'

'Yes, of course you won't. A gold mine works like this. You take ore from the ground and you crush it to expose the gold-bearing material. When I arrived in this country we still used noisy, belt-driven stamp batteries for the crushing, often crushing a few fingers as well in the process. We had things called amalgamation tables, mercury, heating processes in retort ovens, copper, coal and water to produce a porous spongy material, which we melted in a crucible with flux of sand and borax. From that we got slag. Out of these processes, we produced a hot rough, bullion bar which, when tipped into water and cooled, would allow one to get rid of the slag that rose to the top. Why am I telling you this?'

'I'd love to know how your mind worked because you were obviously very brilliant, Dr Martens,' Roy Neil said.

'Obviously,' Minister Robert Amandla added, hands still on his head.

'Very well then. Environmentally these processes were quite dangerous but the mine would then have a cooled-down bar of reasonably high gold content, which they would weigh and drill for assay samples, usually sent to a bank like Barclays or Standard. The rough bullion bars were then transported by rail in fixed boxes, padlocked and under police escort to the Rand Refinery company near Johannesburg. At Rand Refinery everything was off-loaded, checked and weighed. Rand Refinery would take two to four bars from a lot, depending on the size of the mine, put them in a crucible again and melt them. They would take samples and send the consignment to the refinery area where they would blow chlorine gas through the heated liquid. Silver chloride would form on top and be poured off and the underlying contents would be poured to produce fine gold in, what we call, London Good Delivery Bars.'

'I'm probably too slow, but I still don't understand what you're driving at, Dr Martens,' Roy Neil said.

'Easy. The rough bullion sent from the mine to Rand Refinery is really rough. In those years, if it came from Barberton, it contained ninety-six per cent gold. If it came from a mine on the West Rand, it contained about eighty-seven per cent gold in the fifties. In both cases, once the Rand Refinery had done its work, the rough bullion bar was turned into a fine gold bar containing around ninety-nine point seven per cent gold. That's why I chose Barberton.'

'Why?' Roy asked.

'And you call yourself a journalist? Fine enquiring mind there! All of you just keep your hands on your heads,' Erick Martens said, waving the Luger at Sonya.

'Yes, how do the two types of bullion tie up with Erfdeel?' Rick asked.

'I'll try to explain again, seeing as it seems as if I'm coming to the end of my business career today. All gold mines, even today, send their rough bullion bars to Rand Refinery, which turns it into bars of almost one hundred per cent gold. The gold in those rough bullion bars is mixed with other metals. When we started up in the early fifties, rough bullion from Barberton mines had a purer gold analysis than anywhere else. Instead of the West Rand mines' eighty-seven per cent, Barberton mines' rough bullion was at ninety-six per cent gold content. The rest consisted of about two per cent silver, less than one per cent copper and small traces of iron, lead, zinc and nickel. We made up our own rough bullion. We broke open our Belgo-Grec columns, took our own fine gold of almost one hundred per cent, resmelted it and added the other metals in the required dosages. We had a bit of difficulty adding the iron in those days but we circumvented that. Naturally, we also added a few chemicals to give it a slight slag content.'

'And you were able to do that without raising any suspicion?'

'All that Rand Refinery required was a rough bullion bar with the mine's identification stamped on it and the correct accompanying documentation. The mine's waybill bore the assay and that's all that would be checked really. We chose Barberton because we were able to add relatively less filler metals, four per cent, than elsewhere such as the West Rand where we would have had to add thirteen per cent of filler metals. Barberton was easier and less costly.'

'So Erfdeel led you to set up a bogus mine,' Rick reflected.

'Rikki, we used all the fine gold from those broken columns you say you saw at East Crown Gold to produce our artificial rough bullion. Erfdeel was the inspiration. I created the dream. Naturally, we gave this country a great gift. We brought in a massive value in gold at no cost at all to the country and we turned that into export product, generating very high export revenues.'

'And Kraske drummed up international investment,' Rick said.

'He did it very well. On the strength of the investment money we attracted, we, with me at the helm, were able to move into the mining industry on a much bigger scale and, through good management again, I built up AfriBelgo to what it has become today.'

'Uncle Erick, please put down the gun. Sonya is an innocent girl.'

'Just shut up, you shit.'

'How can I? You talk as if you've contributed positively to society, to the economy, but you killed my father with your own hands. You killed him to set up these mechanisms. You were also instrumental in killing John, your own godson, to protect yourself and your money.'

'That was very, very painful. Not what I wanted. I still have nightmares about it. Things flew out of control in his case. And with you. There was no reason for the havoc at your house.'

'But why?'

'You were right. It was easy for me to organise the removal of the others in our team during the war, until Albert, Peter and I remained. Albert supported the elimination of the others. The remaining three of us had been through the war together and had supported each other without question. Albert operated under the nom-de-guerre of Alain and I was Pierre. Peter worked from the SD in Paris.'

'SD?' Roy asked.

'Sicherheitsdienst. We had a strong bond between us. Unfortunately, after the war things were not the same any more. At first I did not understand what was happening but Albert underwent a change and became unapproachable. That's when I found that he had been stealing from us, diverting some of the gold. He was the greedy one. Being the sole custodian at the European end, he found himself in such a powerful position that he drifted into misusing his power. I could not allow the diversion of some of our assets for his benefit. I will never forget Albert's face. It was difficult for me. It was almost as if I cut off my own arms that day on the cliff. All I can say is that he died cleanly and without lingering pain. I often think of him.'

The old man reclined his chair so that his head touched the glass of the window behind him. For a few moments he sat there in deep contemplation, the Luger still aimed at Sonya.

'Peter Kraske, my friend Franz, went ahead against my wishes, Rikki. I had no control over that. I did not want John's death. Or the attack on you. I was upset with it but I had to accept John's death. I was upset at Kraske trying to get rid of you as well on the day of the funeral. You must remember I brought up both of you. I felt it my duty to look after you.'

'Did you look after us to salve your conscience or to ensure that you could control Albert Land's remaining family?'

'Maybe both. Even with that, I had strong feelings for you and John. You were truly like my own sons. You were a pleasure. Everything's a mess now,' the old man brooded.

How could this man, who had done so much for them, have been so brutal? Rick felt lost in time. He looked out to the city behind the glass. It was as if the room were gliding through the sky like a massive aircraft on its way to nowhere.

Finally the old man stood up from his chair and broke the silence. 'I am old.'

He uttered the words almost inaudibly and then waved the Luger at Sonya for her to retreat towards the others.

'Officer, there is no way in which you can take me in for questioning.'

'We need to talk to you,' Major Van Niekerk said, 'not only in connection with the gold scam but because, for a while now, we have suspected that you were funding the White Front. Mrs Amandla's abduction was—'

'The White Front was my hobby.'

'A dangerous one,' Minister Amandla said.

'My stupidity maybe. You see, I enjoyed the old South Africa. It fitted in with my views on the world. Robert, I find this new country under you and Mandela worrying. I cannot see much good coming from being ruled by a bunch of men who sat behind bars on an island—'

'I spent many years on Robben Island. It was my university of life.'

'You were a bunch of radical terrorists on that island.'

'We were freedom fighters. Robben Island taught us leadership with compassion. It taught us how whites, particularly Afrikaners, think. We learned how to understand those people. Maybe, if you had had more time to think in your life, like us, you would have had compassion and understanding.'

'I understand the ANC. I even donated money to them, for the good of the company of course. Hedge the bets.'

'And yet you support the White Front.'

'It's a game. Life's a game.'

'Are you the secretive 'Leader' of the White Front?'

'Robert, it was my little joke. The Leader. English for Der Führer. I never led them. I just assisted them a little to make life more interesting. Hedge the bets, as I said.'

'Dr Martens, we are going to take you in whether you like it or not,' Major Van Niekerk said.

'No, you will not take me in for questioning. Like all political players in this country the White Front is irrelevant to me. Just a bit of fun. In any case, you already have most of the answers you would be looking for. As I stand here I hate myself for having killed Albert. Bringing Marie, John and Rikki down here to live with me was a genuine effort to correct that wrong I did them as a family, but it wasn't good enough. I have come to the end of my life. There comes a time when wealth has no value anymore. John's death touched me very much. Kraske was out of line. It should never have happened. In the process, although I seem to have everything, I have nothing.'

The old man's eyes now brimmed with tears. Slowly, he laid down the Luger on the desk.

'I have done enough harm. I am no threat to any of you here.'

He picked up the bar of gold, looked at it as if with a renewed interest, crossed back to the window and faced the horizon, his forehead resting against the windowpane.

Rick looked at the frail figure, a shadow of the energetic man who had greeted them on a station platform such a long time ago. The man who had given him a life in Africa, who had been like a father to him, now stood against the pane, a skeletal relic, exposed as an immoral rogue, a murderer. But a murderer with regrets.

Major Van Niekerk paced towards the lone figure at the window.

'Dr Martens ...' the officer started to say.

The old man looked up. His eyes rested on Rick.

'Rikki, everything started with these gold bars.' He raised the bar shoulder-high. 'I think everything should end with them. Forgive me for my sins.'

In a flurry of flailing arms, the old man spun around, hit the windowpane with his bare left fist and followed up with the bar of gold in his right hand. He did it with such surprising speed, agility and strength for a man of his age that Rick had no time to react. Rick saw and heard the pane crack with the first blow as the bar of gold struck the glass.

Screaming, Erick Martens hit the tinted glass with the bar of gold time and again. As Rick lunged forward to restrain him, the gold bar hammered into the window pane one last time. The pane crackled like exploding fireworks and the window shattered with flying shards.

Rick managed to grip the old man by the back of his collar for a split second. He tried to pull him away from the open hole but a huge shard of glass knifed down on the right arm of the old man, sliding on him like a guillotine, drawing him forward violently and out into the morning air.

Glass splinters showered on Rick as well. He felt his fingers opening and he lost control.

And he watched Erick Martens flying out, turning in the air in a slow dance with pieces of glass, going downwards thirty floors above street level.

Erick Martens had become the eagle on a long-forgotten briefcase. He finally wanted to follow the friend who had died on a cliff so many years before. Silently, still clutching his last bar of gold, the love of Leah de Loof and the light of the Land family, swooped through the air.

Fighting a rush of air coming in through the gaping hole, Rick clung to the window's aluminium frame, drew himself forward and stared as the frail figure that had touched his life in so many ways descended like a rag-doll downward along the tapered side of AfriBelgo House into the morning traffic.

For an instant, he was reminded of a man with a pipe falling off Table Mountain.

He saw Erick Martens's life burst to an end thirty floors below as the body hit the canopy of a parked truck, denting the metal and spraying blood in a small radius. The bar of gold flew in a shimmering arc from the truck and landed next to the pile of granite cobblestones at the front door of AfriBelgo House.

A huge shard of glass fell harmlessly on the tar next to the truck, radiating glass from the point of impact like quicksilver. It was as if he had just seen his own father's death, as if the next to follow would be himself, and he shuddered in a sudden feeling of vertigo. He felt Sonya's restraining hand in the crook of his elbow.

A lifetime of questions had been answered in a few seconds. It was as if a light had been switched on in Rick's soul.

Rick stood holding the window frame, staring at the awkwardly broken body below. The wind tugged at him, inviting him to follow the trajectory of death.

But there was also Sonya, tugging at his elbow.

Somewhere in the early morning traffic Rick heard laughter. He listened more intently. It was more than laughter.

He distinctly heard hysterical cackling. And in the early morning air he smelled pungent pipe tobacco.

Sonya drew him away from the open hole. He turned around, walked over to the broken column, picked up the plaque that had broken loose and read the inscription again.

'I'll go down and sort it out,' Rick heard Van Niekerk say.

Minister Amandla spoke on the telephone to someone in rapid Xhosa. On his own cell phone Vronsky spoke to someone in a language Rick could not identify.

'Let's sit down for a moment, Rick,' he heard Sonya's voice. Almost mechanically, he sat down on the broken column and stared at the plaque in his hand.

Sonya sat down next to him. 'Rick?'

He responded by looking at her.

She cupped his face in her hands and kissed him.

With Sonya's warm lips on his he felt at peace. He could shut off now. He had arrived at the end of a journey. Behind him lay a trail of devastation left by Erick Martens, a trail littered with the wasted lives of heroes of the Resistance, including that of his own father. He felt Sonya's hands on his closed eyelids. One last time, he built sandcastles on the seashore with John. His mother's voice mingled with the voice of Leah de Loof, two women who suffered at the hands of a man called Heinz Müller, a man he had not really known. In his mind images were tumbling about – Melinda, Kraske, John, the back of a man's neck on a porch in the Eastern Transvaal and the shaved leg of a man in a circular bed.

'It's all over now, Rick,' he heard Sonya say.

He opened his eyes and felt his soul slipping into her sparkling, blue-grey eyes. He traced her cheeks with his fingers. She smiled.

How he loved her. He wanted to bury himself forever deep inside her, like one river burying itself in another to become a stronger body than ever. Their love had overcome the hate and destruction wreaked by their elders and he knew they would be joined for the rest of their lives.

'Quin was right,' he whispered.

Sonya kissed him again.

Oblivious to the sound of wailing sirens at street level they both knew they had finally found contentment.

MINISTER ROBERT AMANDLA LOCKED THE door and put the key down on the coffee table.

'We need to talk. As a group we need to decide on how we are going to handle this. Shall we sit down?'

Down at street level a siren moved away into the distance.

'I see this as probably the most important meeting of our lives. We need to think about this. Me, my security man here, Mr Vronsky who is also in mining, Rick, you and Sonya, Mr Neil, Mr Aardt and, when he is back from downstairs, Major Van Niekerk. My other security man is with the secretary. No worry there.'

'From our side, Minister, we will work as always very closely with your government.'

'Thank you, Mr Vronsky.'

'What an incredible mess,' Rick said.

'Yes, and now we have to think of how to handle this. As you all know we are barely a hundred days into a new South Africa, removed from race discrimination and hatred. In this new world we all have to work to find reconciliation between old enemies. We have a fragile democracy in which old enemies now have to work together, shoulder to shoulder. White policemen and soldiers who used to shoot blacks are now the colleagues of black people who used to plant bombs and fought whites as soldiers of Umkhonto we Sizwe. The past is gone, the feature lies ahead and it is only through reconciliation that we can build a strong future. Would you agree?'

'Absolutely,' Roy said.

'These events, these issues around AfriBelgo, are very disconcerting for a young democracy like ours. The world is looking at us, marvelling at how we were able to change from enemies to friends, from racial warmongers to peaceful builders of a new future. It is a miracle but it is a very breakable one as well. For the good of all our people and for our image in the world I believe it would be very detrimental to trumpet to the world some of the sins we discovered today—'

'Are you intimating that you would like to gag the media? The newly democratic South Africa stands for press freedom,' Roy said.

'Freedom of the press is essential. Of that there is no doubt. I am talking about voluntary reconciliation.'

'What do you mean by that,' Rick asked.

'Responsibility.'

'To do what?' Roy shot back.

'To have the responsibility to understand the unintended consequences of our own actions.'

'Our actions have nothing to do with this monster,' Roy said.

'They have. We have to tell the world that we were here when Erick Martens died.'

'Of course. I will put that in my newspaper report.'

'Good. If we tell the world we know he committed suicide after having been found out as the sole benefactor on his own of a radical terrorist group? A confused individual?'

'Shock,' Roy Neil said.

'For how long?'

'It would be forgotten quickly.'

'Now, for the purposes of this meeting, if we tell the world that this same man smuggled sensitive Nazi gold into the country and that a large section of South Africa's economy is built on that, what will the world's reaction be?'

'It will set many cats among the pigeons,' Sonya said.

'AfriBelgo shares will plummet,' Mark Aardt contributed.

'There will be a huge ripple effect world-wide. The new South Africa will have been built on stolen Jewish gold,' Vronsky said.

'And the country will once again be the polecat of the world. On top of that, South Africa will probably be the target of restitution claims for decades from governments and individuals,' Rick added.

'My dear friends, exactly.'

'But, Minister, it is my duty as a journalist to report events truthfully as they happen. It is not my duty to protect the image of the country.'

A knock sounded at the door. 'It's me,' Major Gert van Niekerk said. The security man opened the door and Van Niekerk entered carrying the bar of gold from downstairs.

'Mr Neil, I agree it's not your duty to protect the image of your country but you should think of the responsibility on your shoulders today.'

'I have an incredible scoop in the story of the demise of the White Front and Erick Martens.'

'Do you have children, Mr Neil?'

'Yes, Minister.'

'They will forever be proud of you for being the man who broke that story to the world. And so they should. The question is how much pride you will have in yourself one day if you leave them a completely tainted future. Belgo-Grec is a blot on our country. It is best forgotten. We cannot put our new democracy in jeopardy with decades of claims from people whose stolen gold built our country. No way.'

'I would prefer to forget,' Mark said.

'Whether you like it or not, I am going to write about you as Martens's flunky with the White Front,' Roy stated in measured tones.

'I cannot stop you and I understand.'

'Mr Aardt, thank you for being the first to agree to let the Belgo-Grec issue go. For that I will do my best to help you. If we can all agree on my proposal for confidentiality, I would also appreciate your assistance in ensuring that this bar of gold is listed as an asset of AfriBelgo without too much fuss,' the Minister said.

'I have had enough. I do not want a lifetime of living under that cloud,' Sonya said.

'I agree, and it will be better for the country, for all of us,' Rick added.

'Mr Minister, you have my word and the word of those close to me,' Vronsky said.

'Well, Mr Neil, could you voluntarily handle the Belgo-Grec issue quietly to serve your country?'

Roy looked at Rick for a long time and then he spoke.

'Rick and Sonya suffered from the mistakes of the past. For my children I am not going to make a mistake for the future. I will disregard the Belgo-Grec story. Bloody sad. But better.'

'Mr Neil, thank you.'

Author's note: On the day that Erick Martens died history repeated itself when his office held a secret known only to nine people – eight who were present at the death and one other man. Of the eight people present, only one, an accidental historian, knew of the existence of the ninth man who had helped to uncover the background to the secret and afterwards gained full knowledge.

Deception is a tradable commodity.

About the Authors

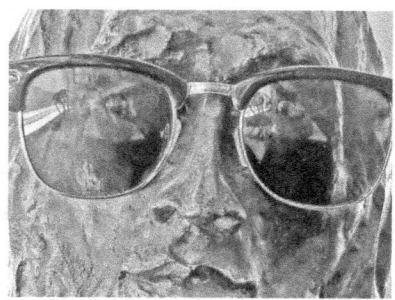

I. Vronsky was born in Kiev and is a former intelligence operative in Europe and Africa.

Now a borderless cyber citizen.

Rhynie Greeff, holds a doctorate in economics but never became an economist. Ex-diplomat, entrepreneur and boardroom brickhead he lived in Britain and became an Afrikaans columnist for eight years with a series entitled Letters from Britain. He now lives near Cape Town. His collaboration with Vronsky is his third book.